Star Bright

Other Novels by Catherine Anderson

"Harrigan Family" Novels

Morning Light

"Coulter Family" Novels

Phantom Waltz
Sweet Nothings
Blue Skies
Bright Eyes
My Sunshine
Summer Breeze
Sun Kissed

The Comanche Series

Comanche Moon

Other Signet Books

Always in My Heart
Only by Your Touch

Catherine Anderson

Star Bright

A SIGNET BOOK

SIGNET
Published by New American Library, a division of
Penguin Group (USA) Inc., 375 Hudson Street,
New York, New York 10014, USA
Penguin Group (Canada), 90 Eglinton Avenue East, Suite 700, Toronto,
Ontario M4P 2Y3, Canada (a division of Pearson Penguin Canada Inc.)
Penguin Books Ltd., 80 Strand, London WC2R 0RL, England
Penguin Ireland, 25 St. Stephen's Green, Dublin 2,
Ireland (a division of Penguin Books Ltd.)
Penguin Group (Australia), 250 Camberwell Road, Camberwell, Victoria 3124,
Australia (a division of Pearson Australia Group Pty. Ltd.)
Penguin Books India Pvt. Ltd., 11 Community Centre, Panchsheel Park,
New Delhi - 110 017, India
Penguin Group (NZ), 67 Apollo Drive, Rosedale, North Shore 0632,
New Zealand (a division of Pearson New Zealand Ltd.)
Penguin Books (South Africa) (Pty.) Ltd., 24 Sturdee Avenue,
Rosebank, Johannesburg 2196, South Africa

Penguin Books Ltd., Registered Offices:
80 Strand, London WC2R 0RL, England

First published by Signet, an imprint of New American Library,
a division of Penguin Group (USA) Inc.

Printed in the United States of America

ISBN 978-1-60751-458-9

In memory of my mother, Nory,
whose light still shines in the hearts
of those who love her.

Francis Wayne Harrigan (1945–)
married
♥1969♥
↓
Emily Sue Phillips (1946–1977)

Second Marriage (March 12, 2007)
Deanna (Dee Dee) Kirkpatrick (1948–)
♥

Clinton Harrigan (1970–) **married** ♥2007♥ ↓ **Loni Kendra MacEwen** (1976–) ♥ *Morning Light,* 2008	**Quincy Harrigan** (1972–) ↓ ♥ **Story Yet to Come!**	**Parker Harrigan** (1973–) **married** ♥2009♥ ↓ **Lorraina Ann Hall** (1983–) ♥ *Star Bright,* 2009	**Zachary Harrigan** (1975–) ↓ ♥ **Story Yet to Come!**	**Samantha Harrigan** (1977–) **married** ♥2007♥ ↓ **Tucker Coulter** (1970–) ↓ ♥ *Sun Kissed,* 2007

Prologue

Rainie Hall Danning paused after exiting the ship elevator onto the third deck. Her whole body trembled with nerves, and she wanted nothing more than to collapse against the wall for a moment to gather her composure. But she didn't dare, not with cameras hidden everywhere. *Just start walking. Act normal. Every move you make may be recorded.* Upstairs inside the posh ladies' lounge, where electronic surveillance was forbidden, she had altered her appearance. Now she wore a stretchy black sheath, an Elvira wig, brown contacts, black cat-eye glasses, and so much makeup that her face felt stiff. *Tasteless but effective.* No one who saw her later on film would recognize her as the wealthy and elegant Lorraina Danning who'd gone to dinner wearing a sequined evening gown and a forty-thousand-dollar diamond necklace.

Yearning to run, Rainie walked slowly along the corridor, shoulders back, chin held high. No ducking her head to hide her face. Her friend Janet had assured her only minutes ago that this disguise was good enough to withstand close scrutiny later. *Oh, God, oh, God.* Was it possible that she and her friend were actually going to pull this off? Rainie stifled a hysterical urge to laugh. Now dressed as Lorraina Danning, Janet was somewhere on an upper deck, moving toward a camera-free area where she could duck into a closet, change clothes, and emerge as herself.

Rainie's heart slammed with every footfall, and cold sweat filmed her body. The ceiling of the hallway, which seemed endlessly long, felt low and oppressive. With every breath she took, she prayed she wouldn't hear the elevator doors slide open behind her. Her husband, Peter, seemed to have a sixth sense where she was concerned, enabling him to guess what her next move was going to be, sometimes even before she knew herself. If he caught her . . . Oh, God, she couldn't let herself think about that. She needed to stay calm, keep a clear head. Just one little mistake could ruin everything.

The numbered plaques beside the cabin doorways swam in Rainie's vision. Where was 3056? Her back tingled, and an awful burning sensation had taken up residence right between her shoulder blades. She glanced back, half expecting to see her husband—tall, elegant, sophisticated Peter, whose kindly demeanor and gentle smile fooled everyone. The hallway behind her was empty. She was still safe, and she would stay that way if she could just find the damned room.

It seemed as if she covered the length of a football field before she reached the right cabin. She fumbled with clammy fingers for the plastic key card that she'd slipped inside the bodice of her dress. *Hurry, hurry.* Glancing up and down the corridor to make sure Peter hadn't suddenly appeared, she shoved the card into the slot. Nothing. She realized the card was upside down and inserted it again. At last the little green light came on. Frantic to vanish, she almost fell into the room. After closing the door, she collapsed against an interior wall, trembling so violently that her knees threatened to buckle.

The housekeeping staff had flipped on the lights and left clever towel sculptures on the turned-down bed. The room was cramped compared to the royal suite on deck ten, where she'd dressed for dinner earlier. There was barely walking room between the queen-size bed and the ocean-view window. Opposite the sitting area, which consisted of only a short couch and a coffee table, the wall was lined with storage cabinetry, a built-in vanity, and a closet. But to Rainie, the accommodations looked wonderful—a small hidey-hole where she would be safe from her husband.

When she recovered enough to move, she hooked the Do Not Disturb sign over the outside door lever. Then she began stripping off the dress as she approached the suitcase on the couch. Though a claustrophobic breathlessness made her lungs hitch, she needed to shower and cover her body with sunless tanning lotion before she went out on the balcony to gulp fresh air. Having dark skin was part of her disguise, and the colorant might take a few hours to work. From this moment forward, Lorraina Ann Danning had ceased to exist, and Anna Pritchard had taken her place.

Rainie's friend Janet, who worked aboard this ship, had kept her promise. The suitcase contained everything Rainie would need to make good her escape—black leather and denim clothing, a silver-studded belt, chunky boots, lots of Goth-style jewelry, oversize sunglasses, fake tattoos, makeup, the tanning lotion, and all the necessary fraudulent identification. Rainie fingered a roll of cash tucked into a storage pocket, stared with burning eyes at a Visa card imprinted with her alias, and sent up a silent prayer of thanksgiving that she'd been blessed with such wonderful friends. All set and ready to go. Now she had only to keep her head down for the next seven days until the ship returned to Seattle.

Rainie stepped into the small bathroom to shower. By the time she'd finished washing off the expensive French perfume that Peter insisted she wear, her skin smarted, yet it seemed to her the scent lingered. *His mark.* Needing to get it off, she scrubbed with soap again, and then again. Finally she came to accept that her compulsive urge to scour until her skin felt raw stemmed more from emotional reasons than her sense of smell. She wanted—no, *needed*—to get everything she associated with Peter Danning out of her life.

After toweling dry, Rainie smoothed the tanning lotion over her body and then scrubbed her hands clean before tugging the Elvira wig back on. Before slipping into a white terry guest robe she'd found in the closet, she reinserted the brown contacts and outlined her mouth with purplish black lipstick. Only then did she feel it was safe to step out onto the balcony to cleanse her lungs with the moist sea air. As she gripped the railing and fixed her gaze on the sinking globe of orange on the western horizon, the night breeze whipped the synthetic strands of pitch-black hair across her face.

Peter would be looking for her by now, going first to the ladies' room and then possibly to their suite. When he failed to find her, how long would he wait before raising an alarm? *My wife is missing.* Her earlier urge to laugh had now been replaced by fear. What if a search of all the cabins was executed? If anyone could make the ship's captain and crew hop to, it was the rich and influential Peter Danning. By morning, law enforcement teams would descend on the vessel to unravel the mystery of Lorraina Danning's disappearance.

Rainie forced herself to think positively. If they came to her quarters, they would find only an awkward, sunbaked young woman with brown eyes, an Elvira hairdo, and weird-looking clothes. No one would suspect anything.

In only moments, darkness would descend. To Rainie, who'd so frequently gone to the theater with her husband over the last two years, the sunset seemed symbolic. The curtain was falling. The nightmare her life had become was over, and the next act was about to begin.

Bright with promise, tomorrow beckoned. Rainie had once endured a horrible beating for dropping one of Peter's precious crystal goblets, so it had seemed almost prophetic to her when she'd found a rural town called Crystal Falls on an Oregon map. It appealed to her sense of irony. *When the crystal falls, Lorraina may die.* So that was her destination, Crystal Falls. She had no idea what difficulties she might face when she got there. She knew only that anything would be better than what she'd just left behind.

Chapter One

The ticking of a teapot clock and the hum of an ancient refrigerator were the only sounds to fill the silence in Rainie's one-story duplex, which she'd rented only a week ago and equipped on the cheap. Mismatched dishes, eating utensils, and cookware graced the freshly scrubbed shelves and drawers of the outdated kitchen. Thrift-shop throw rugs covered worn areas in the speckled linoleum, which she'd scoured and waxed on her hands and knees. In spots, she'd washed the walls with such vigor that she'd removed the paint, but now all the surfaces were clean and each room sported a sparse collection of secondhand furniture.

Since the house and everything in it was old, Rainie had aimed for a 1950s look, purchasing inexpensive wall art, doilies, dresser scarves, decorative pillows, and cozy throws from Goodwill to camouflage nicks, gouges, and holes in the upholstery. The result was comfortable and quaintly attractive, a place that Rainie could call home until her circumstances improved.

Improving her circumstances was the main focus of her attention right now. Long strands of curly brown hair streaked with blond, compliments of a home perm and frost job, fell forward over her face as she perused the Help Wanted section of the Crystal Falls newspaper. The table at which she sat, made of ancient chrome and Formica, with one bent leg and four vinyl-cushioned chairs, wobbled slightly every time she moved. To steady her writing surface, she pressed down with her elbows as she circled each job possibility.

So far, all she'd found of real interest was a bookkeeping position at a ranch. The other opportunities either held little appeal or required training she didn't have. Still, she flagged the dismal maybes. Her funds, loaned to her by friends, would soon run out. Flipping hamburgers might not be very glamorous, but forty hours a week at minimum wage would help pay the rent and some of her utilities.

Dusk was quickly descending beyond the windows, filling the room with the bluish shadows of an early July evening. Though she'd been in central Oregon for a week and a half, Rainie was still amazed at how quickly it grew dark here after the sun dipped behind the Cascade Mountains. Reaching over her shoulder to flip on the overhead light, she resumed her task of job hunting, an endeavor that would have been much easier if she'd owned a computer. *Yeah, right.* Her shoestring budget hadn't allowed for many convenience items. She had splurged on a secondhand television for fifty dollars, but only because it was important that she keep abreast of the latest developments in the ongoing investigation of her mysterious disappearance.

The thought made her smile. In her case, the old adage that every dog had its day was proving to be true. During her marriage, Rainie had sweated bullets whenever Peter was home, never knowing when some little thing might ignite his temper. Now he was the one on pins and needles. When wives vanished without a trace, it was usually the husbands who first came under suspicion. *Too bad, so sad.* Peter's sterling reputation was taking some hard hits. Though members of law enforcement hadn't yet said it aloud, they clearly didn't believe that a healthy, reasonably fit young woman had fallen overboard without a helpful push.

Oh, yes, Peter was now on the hot seat, a turn of events Rainie hadn't anticipated but couldn't regret. *Just deserts.* No matter how much misery the man endured, it would be nothing compared to the horrors he'd inflicted on her and possibly others. Though it wasn't very admirable of her, she found it gratifying to watch her handsome, treacherous husband squirm as he fielded questions from reporters. Some enterprising newsperson had dug up information on Peter's first two marriages, and it was now gossip fodder for the tabloids as well as prime-time news anchors that Peter's former wives had died mysterious deaths and left him huge sums of money. *Put that in your pipe and smoke it, Peter.*

For Rainie, walking away from what remained of her father's estate had been extremely difficult. Her dad had worked his entire life for that money, and Peter Danning didn't deserve a single cent of it. But it had bothered her even more to turn her back on Peter's first two wives. During one of his brutal fits of temper, Peter had once confessed to Rainie that he'd murdered her predecessors because they'd been planning to divorce him. At the time, Rainie had prayed he was lying in an attempt to intimidate her. *I'll never let you leave me. I'll see you dead first.* But old Internet news archives hinted that Peter's incredible confession might be true. His first wife had died of a lingering illness that baffled her doctors. The result of some obscure, undetectable poison, possibly? The second wife had perished in a car wreck when her brakes had failed on a curvy mountain road during a rainstorm. Accident or design? Rainie had very good reason to suspect that her husband had killed both women and walked away with their inheritances. If so, he deserved to squirm. No misfortune that befell him was too severe a punishment if he had ended the lives of two healthy young women.

During those first news broadcasts, Rainie had huddled on the sofa, smiling through tears. Thanks to the help of

Margaret Bresslar and Janet Teague, Rainie had actually pulled it off and given Peter the slip. What had she ever done to deserve such faithful and devoted friends? They'd risked so much for her, so very much. Oh, how she missed e-mailing them or talking with them on the phone. Margaret, the more serious one, had been Rainie's rock during the final days of her marital imprisonment, and Janet, the funny, irreverent one, who'd often been mistaken for Rainie's sister in college because they looked so much alike, had always managed to keep Rainie laughing. *Don't lace the bastard's coffee with rat poison yet,* she'd cautioned. *We're going to get you out of there.*

In the end, Janet had kept that promise, putting her career and her freedom on the line. Wearing an Elvira wig, sunglasses, and punk-rocker clothing, she had boarded the ship as Anna Pritchard, flashed fake identification, deposited the luggage in a cabin where Rainie could later go to hide, and then changed into the stretchy-back sheath that Rainie would later don in the ladies' lounge. For the intervening hours before dinner, Janet had called in sick to delay reporting in for work and browsed in the ship's classy boutiques while wearing the disguise, thus establishing the existence of Anna Pritchard by passing in front of countless cameras. Then, at the beginning of the seven-course meal in the opulent dining room, Janet had excused herself from her table and gone to the lounge only minutes before Rainie had. Once inside, safely hidden from electronic surveillance, Rainie and Janet had switched clothing. Familiar with the ship's surveillance system, Janet had gone to an area where there were no cameras, changed into her work uniform, stashed Rainie's sequined gown, heels, jewelry, and evening bag in her oversize purse, and then resumed her duties as ship operations coordinator.

Just like that, Lorraina Hall Danning had vanished without a trace.

Sometimes Rainie actually picked up the phone and almost dialed Margaret's or Janet's number. But sanity always returned in the nick of time. If Peter suspected that she was still alive, he might sic a private investigator on her friends. Any contact, no matter how brief, might be traced. Rainie couldn't take that chance. Peter would kill her if he found her. There wasn't a doubt in her mind about that. *Don't call us; don't write to us,* Janet had warned. *No news will be good news. We'll know you're out there somewhere, starting a new life. That's all we need to know.*

And so it had to be. If it ever came out that Janet had been aboard the *Ocean Jewel* the night Rainie vanished, someone might start connecting the dots.

With trembling fingertips, Rainie touched the small scar that angled over her cheekbone, a memento of one terrible night when Peter had flown into a rage. In time, the scar might fade, but it would never disappear entirely. Every time Rainie looked in a mirror for the rest of her life, she would be reminded of her past mistakes and all the reasons she'd vowed not to repeat them. She would never again jump into a relationship with blinders on. She would never again give a man control over her life. She would never again trust someone just because he seemed wonderful and kind.

With a mild start, Rainie realized that her mind had wandered from the task at hand, which was to find gainful employment. Bookkeeping. She circled the ranch job again, and then tapped the tip of her pen on the paper. It wouldn't be a very challenging job, but it was better than waiting tables, filling fast-food orders, or working in a motel laundry room. And, hey, the advertisement said "benefits," which led her to think the pay might be halfway decent as well. It was worth making a phone call.

As Rainie pushed up from her chair, a slight rattling sound came at the back door. Her heart skittered and missed a beat. Was someone trying to break in? The old lady next door had assured Rainie that this run-down neighborhood was safe, that she'd lived in the other half of this two-family dwelling for almost twenty years and never had a single problem. The door rattled again, making Rainie jump. *Peter?* The thought was never far from her mind that he might be only one step behind her.

Reacting instinctively, Rainie hit the light switch to plunge the kitchen back into shadow. Then, shivering with trepidation, she moved toward the battered door. The dingy curtain that covered the window prevented her from seeing out onto the porch. She lifted a lank ruffle, leaned cautiously forward to peer out into the semidarkness, and saw . . . a cat, pushing at the barricaded kitty door with a bewhiskered nose.

Over the last week, Rainie had often wondered about the oversize feline who'd needed a Fat Cat door. This furry tom was indeed large, but if he'd ever been rotund, lean times had trimmed him down to little more than skin stretched over bone. Pity tugged at Rainie's heart. She quickly bent to remove the metal panel that prevented the poor animal from entering. With a disgruntled meow, the cat jumped through the opening and immediately began circling Rainie's feet, his meows increasing in volume until she had no doubt that he was hungry and hoping to be fed.

Crouching down, Rainie ran her hand over the gray tabby's arched back. "You poor baby. Did your family move away and leave you?"

The possibility was inconceivable to Rainie. On the other hand, she'd come to understand during her marriage that not everyone lived by her rules. Maybe the cat's former owners had fallen on hard times. People in low-rent districts often led a hand-to-mouth existence, barely managing to care for themselves, let alone a pet. There was also the possibility that the cat had a strong homing instinct and had left his owners to return to familiar turf.

Rainie had always wanted a cat or dog. Unfortunately, her dad had been allergic, and Peter had objected to anything furry, fearing that Rainie might come to love an animal more than she did him. Peter and his insane jealousy no longer ruled her life, though, and she could have a pet now if she wanted. Surely one cat wouldn't cost that much to feed. Lifting the tom into her arms, Rainie couldn't help but notice how gaunt he was. She pushed her nose against his soft fur. He smelled of grass, fresh air, and male-feline musk.

"It's apparent to me that you need a friend almost as much as I do," she said. "And, lucky you, I'm open to having a roommate who can't help pay the rent. I get lonely living by myself."

She turned the cat to study his battle-scarred visage. He blinked his green eyes.

"What do you think about Thomas as a temporary handle? We can change it later if a better idea occurs to me, but for now, it'll give me something to call you besides kitty."

The cat blinked again. Rainie decided to take that as a yes. "Thomas it is, then. It has a nice ring to it, don't you think? I'm Rainie, by the way, aka Anna, but I doubt my alias will matter much to you just so long as I can find something for you to eat."

Thomas made no comment, just looked at her with those huge emerald eyes.

"How does a can of cheap tuna sound?" she asked. "Cats like fish, right?"

As if he understood, Thomas purred and rasped her cheek with a rough tongue, making Rainie laugh. "One can of water-packed tuna, coming up."

She set the animal back on the floor, fetched some tuna from a cupboard, and went to work with a can opener that had cost her twenty-five cents at St. Vincent de Paul. The cat tucked into it as if he were starving. Rainie got him some water to accompany the meal, then stood back to watch him eat. It occurred to her that a lack of cat food was only one of her problems. She had no litter box—or any litter to go in one. Hopefully, the tom was housebroken and would exit via the cat door when he needed to go out.

Rainie's gaze flicked to the opening, guarded now by only the flexible flap. The hole wasn't large enough to accommodate a man, and it was more than an arm's reach from the doorknob. It would be safe enough for her to leave the portal open so Thomas could go in and out. *Good plan.* She didn't want to be accused of cat theft if the tom belonged to a neighbor up the street.

After eating, Thomas seemed in no rush to leave. Instead of going back outdoors, he curled up on the worn sofa in the living room, had a bath, and then drifted off to sleep. Rainie felt mildly disappointed. She'd been hoping for . . . what? An intellectual exchange? He was a cat—hello. Maybe he'd be more sociable once they got acquainted, but for now, it just felt nice not to be completely alone.

Rainie returned to the kitchen, grabbed the advertisement section of the newspaper, and dialed the telephone number listed for the bookkeeping position. As the phone rang, she rinsed out Thomas's empty food dish, refusing to let herself feel nervous. If the job was still open, maybe she could get an interview. If it was already filled . . . oh, well. Keeping books at a ranch wasn't exactly her dream job.

Parker Harrigan had a corn dog stuffed in his mouth when the phone rang. He plucked it back out without taking a bite and wiped his lips with the heel of his hand to remove the ketchup-and-mayonnaise concoction he used as a dip. His luck, it was his brother Quincy calling. If so, Quincy would be sure to ask what Parker was having for dinner. The conversation would go downhill from there, with Parker receiving a long and extremely boring lecture about his bad eating habits. Quincy, the health nut of the family, rarely missed an opportunity to share his dietary wisdom.

It never ceased to amaze Parker that he and Quincy were from the same gene pool. With their pitch-black hair, brown eyes, and compact builds, they looked enough alike to be twins, but the way they thought about things was totally different. Maybe that was why they talked only about food. It was a little hard to get pissed off at each other over the healthful properties of a carrot.

Only it wasn't Quincy calling. Parker didn't recognize the number that flashed. "Yo. This is Parker."

Silence. For a second, Parker thought it might be a computer call. He often got them at this time of evening. He was about to hang up when a feminine voice came over the line.

"Um, hello. I'm responding to your ad in the paper for a bookkeeper?"

Parker had gotten only two responses so far, and neither applicant had been qualified. "You experienced?" He saw no point in wasting his time on another interview that went nowhere. "I'm not offering any on-the-job training."

"Yes, I have some experience."

She sounded halfway smart. A little on the young side, though. In Parker's estimation, women under thirty tended to be flighty. He didn't want to hire someone, go through the process of getting her acclimated, and then have her quit on him. "How old are you?"

"I'm sorry?"

He glanced at the four corn dogs, not wanting them to get cold. He desperately needed a bookkeeper, though. He repeated his question, adding, "No offense, but you sound awfully young. I want someone who'll stay on."

"Have you ever heard of age discrimination?" she asked.

Parker added *sassy* to the counts against her. Not that he had a problem with sassy women. He just wasn't sure he wanted one in the stable office, flipping him shit five days a week. "It's not against the law to ask someone's age when they're applying for a job. I need someone dependable."

"And my being young means I won't be?"

Parker grinned. Definitely sassy. "How young is young?"

"I'm twenty-five years *old*. I have an undergraduate degree in accounting. I interned for a year as a business analyst. I can keep books with my eyes closed, run any software program you throw at me, and I also make a mean cup of coffee. What else would you like to know?"

Beginning to enjoy himself, Parker leaned his hips against the kitchen counter. Maybe he wasn't being entirely fair about the age thing. At twenty-five, he'd been running a ranch, after all. "With all that going for you, why are you interested in a dead-end bookkeeping job?"

"My circumstances changed unexpectedly, and I have bills to pay."

"You're a tad overqualified for the position. What if a better offer comes along? You gonna quit on me first thing out of the bag?"

"I'm willing to sign a contract, agreeing to stay for a specified period of time. Provided, of course, that the wage and benefit package is attractive and the work environment is adequate."

He liked this lady more by the moment. "You got a name?"

"Anna Pritchard. Is Parker your last name, or your first?"

"First. Last name's Harrigan. You like horses, Anna?"

"Is that a job requirement?"

"I raise quarter horses, so, yeah, it'd be a big plus."

"I like all animals. I've never been around horses, so I may find them a bit intimidating at first, but I'm sure I would get used to them quickly enough."

She was honest. He liked that, too. "Well, then." He rubbed his jaw. "If you're interested, I'm open to your comin' out tomorrow to fill out an application."

"What's the address?"

"Out here, it's easy to miss a house number. I'll have to give you directions."

As he did so, she kept halting him to ask questions. What did the hay barn look like? How many roads would she cross after the stop sign? Was a cattle guard one of those grates in the ground, or was he referring to something else? What did he mean by a country mile?

"A country mile," he explained, "is more or less the same as a regular mile, the keywords being 'more or less.'"

"I see. Could you translate that into something more precise so I don't overshoot your driveway and get lost in the middle of nowhere?"

"After you hang a right at the Y in the road, you'll drive about five miles before you see the hay barn. It might be a hair less than five, maybe a hair more. Just watch for the barn."

She said, "Sheesh," her tone disgruntled.

He found himself smiling again. He could definitely tell that she'd lived in the city most of her life. "Just keep my number handy. If you get turned around, give me a call."

"I don't have a cell phone."

That blew Parker's mind. Everyone he knew had a cell phone now, even his dad, who complained ceaselessly about having to carry one. "You *don't*?"

"I'm unemployed, remember. They cost money."

It had been a lot of years since Parker's family had been short on money, but he could still remember how it felt. "Well, if you end up working for me, a cell phone will be a must. I'll have to give you an advance in pay so you can get one. It's not smart to drive these back roads without any way to call for help."

"Why? Are the roads bad or something?"

"Not bad, just remote. You never know when a herd of elk

may run out in front of you—or when you might have car trouble. It's just safer to carry a phone."

"Elk?"

He chuckled. "Yeah, you know, those big, brown creatures that live in the forest?"

"I know what an elk is, Mr. Harrigan. I just didn't realize they were in this area."

"We have a couple of resident herds out this way."

They agreed to meet at one o'clock, when Parker would still be on his lunch break. No point in interrupting his workday for an interview that might be a waste of time.

When Parker hung up the phone, he turned back to his corn dogs, which were now stone-cold. He sighed and stuck them back in the microwave, hoping the extra heating time wouldn't turn them rubbery. A degree in accounting, huh? He wondered what this Anna Pritchard looked like. Probably a bookworm, he decided, with wire-framed glasses, a no-nonsense hairdo, and an aversion to makeup. No matter. He didn't honestly care about her appearance as long as she could bring order to his business. Tax time last year had been a bitch. Receipts and purchase orders seemed to procreate in the file drawer where Parker stuffed them, and he'd somehow lost track of his income, unable to reconcile his bank deposit records with the amount of money he thought he'd made. When it came to stuff like that, the IRS wasn't very understanding.

He plucked the plate out of the microwave, dipped a corn dog into the mayo mixture, and sighed with contentment. Quincy could have his damned tofu.

Smoke spiraled upward from the cigarette Peter Danning held poised between elegant fingers. He had only recently started smoking again and knew the private investigator sitting across the desk didn't appreciate the smell. The man kept pressing a handkerchief to his nose and giving Peter disgruntled looks. *Too bad.* Peter was the one with the money. Therefore he had the power. The skinny little prick could put up with the secondhand smoke or find another client.

"I want her found, Mr. Riker. I was told you're the best, and yet you've done nothing thus far to earn your fees."

"I've done plenty." Riker rocked forward on the chair. "She's dead, Mr. Danning, at the bottom of the sea. I can't locate someone who no longer exists."

Peter stubbed out the cigarette with such force that the filter ruptured. "I refuse to accept that. Before the main course was even served, my wife left the dining room to powder her nose. The ladies' lounge was only a few steps away from our table. Yet I'm supposed to believe that she somehow wandered out onto the deck and fell overboard? No. She staged the whole thing. She's out there somewhere now, laughing her ass off because I've come under suspicion. I want her found. Do the job I hired you to do."

The investigator sighed, his expression impatient. "We've been over this a dozen times. People are checked in every time they board the ship and checked out every time they disembark. Two thousand forty-three people booked passage for that cruise, and two thousand forty-three people boarded prior to departure. When the ship returned to Seattle, only two thousand forty-two people disembarked. One person, your wife, was missing. The vessel stopped at no port of call prior to her disappearance that evening. No late passengers were flown in, enabling her to somehow stow away on a helicopter before it lifted off again. In order for her to be alive, she would have had to jump overboard and swim to shore. Do you realize how cold those waters are?"

Peter lit up another cigarette. Acid indigestion seared the back of his throat as he took a deep drag. He knew that Lorraina had been wanting out of the marriage. Nothing could convince him that she hadn't pulled a fast one. "Think outside the box, Mr. Riker. I don't know how she did it. I only know she did."

"The checkout procedures show that all but one passenger returned to Seattle," Riker repeated. "Passports were required. Are you listening to yourself? In order for what you're saying to be true, your wife would have had to board the ship twice, each time under a different identity. While the ship was still in port, was she at any time out of your sight?"

"No. We were together every second until she excused herself from the table to go to the ladies' lounge." Peter thought for a moment. Then he arched a blond eyebrow at the investigator. "What if she had help?"

"What kind of help?"

Peter clenched his teeth in frustration. Riker was reputed to be one of the best in his business, yet he had to be led by the hand around every corner. "Suppose, just for a moment, that my wife had a female friend who booked passage under a fictitious name, boarded with fake identification, and then left the ship prior to departure. Lorraina could have gone to the empty cabin, donned a disguise, and stayed aboard ship using another identity for the duration of the cruise."

Riker shook his head. "No one can leave the ship after boarding, not without there being a record of it. You went through the security checkpoints. Those guards are vigilant, and no one is allowed to disembark without following procedure. It's extremely important that they be able to account for the whereabouts of every single passenger at all times. The only way a second party could have been involved is if that person were a cruise line employee, someone who could board under a fake name and then vanish into the woodwork."

Peter considered that possibility. "A cruise line employee?" Something tugged at his memory, but he couldn't think what. He wished now that he'd paid more attention to Lorraina's jabbering in the early days of their marriage. Did one of her friends work for a cruise line? He couldn't remember. "Get me a list of names, both passengers and crew. Maybe something will ring a bell."

"A list of names?" Riker huffed under his breath. "That may not be easy."

"If the job were easy, I wouldn't be paying you so much," Peter replied. "Get me that list."

The following day, Rainie stood in front of her cloudy closet mirror, turning first right and then left to study her outfit, a Goodwill purchase that looked as dated as her house. The hemline of the gathered cotton skirt was unfashionably long, the white peasant blouse looked limp and tired, and to top it off, her home permanent was so curly, even with styling gel to tame it down, she looked as if she'd stuck her finger in a light socket.

She discarded that outfit and slipped into a blue suit—a prim jacket and straight skirt, finished off with a pair of matching pumps. *Not.* Parker Harrigan wanted a horsey person, not a Wall Street wannabe. She tossed that ensemble onto the bed and tugged out a knit top and a pair of faded jeans. Too casual. Definitely something she might wear on a boring Tuesday if she got the job, but not appropriate for an interview. Next in line was a basic black dress, sleeveless with a modest scoop neckline, but again, it looked too formal, even with a scarf at her throat. She went through the remainder of her hundred-dollar wardrobe and eventually returned to her first choice, the airy gathered skirt and peasant blouse. It said, "I'm not trying to impress anyone." Unfortunately, it didn't make her look very professional.

Oh, well. If Parker Harrigan didn't hire her because of her appearance, then he wasn't very smart, and she'd be better off working for someone else. She took a final glance at herself in the mirror, thrust her feet into white canvas slip-ons, flicked the skirt with her fingers, and marched from the bedroom.

When she arrived at Parker Harrigan's front gate, she saw an intercom mounted on a concrete post. There was a number pad for people who knew the gate code. Along the fence line, she saw what looked like infrared cameras. Was this a ranch or a high-security compound? She punched the button on the intercom. Some man came on the line who used improper verb tenses and had a thick Southern drawl.

"Who'd you say you was, lady?"

"My name is Rai"—*oops*—"Anna Pritchard. I'm here to apply for the bookkeeping position. Mr. Harrigan is expecting me."

"Well, Rae-Anna, I reckon you can come on in."

The gate swung open. Rainie thumped her hand on the steering wheel of the dilapidated Mazda as she drove through the entrance. "Your name is no longer Rainie, you idiot. You have to remember that."

As the car bumped along the rutted dirt road, she took in the scenery that lay ahead. Separated by a packed gravel parking area peppered with dusty pickups, a huge post-and-timber home, a monstrous metal structure, and a clutch of outbuildings composed the ranch proper. Beyond that, fenced pastureland undulated like a rumpled green carpet. Rainie saw a potbellied man in jeans and a cowboy hat ambling toward the house. *Parker Harrigan, no doubt.* Maybe she should have worn the faded jeans and knit top, after all.

She parked beside a battered red Dodge with huge tires and a jacked-up undercarriage. The vehicle put her in mind of the monster trucks she'd seen on television that competed in mud races. This would be like working in a foreign country—traveling over a tooth-rattling road, parking in the shadow of a monster truck, and trying to communicate with people who spoke a different language.

Unfortunately, beggars couldn't be choosers, and she needed this job.

As Rainie collected her purse, the older man disappeared into the house without a backward glance. That was a bit odd. The polite thing would have been for him to wait on the porch to escort her inside.

As she exited the car, the front door of the house swung open again and a younger man stepped out. She guessed him to be an inch or so shy of six feet tall, but his bearing compensated for the lack of height. Broad shouldered and narrow at the hip, he had an athletic, muscular build. Faded jeans skimmed his powerfully roped thighs, and a wash-worn blue chambray shirt showcased an upper torso well toned from hard work.

"Howdy," he called, flashing white teeth as he grinned. "You must be Anna. Glad to see you made it without any mishaps."

Rainie recognized the voice. *This* was Parker Harrigan? If she hadn't been desperate for work, she would have climbed right back in the car. He was way too *everything*. Way too young. Way too handsome. Way too sexy. Glistening black hair fell over his high forehead in lazy waves. His sun-bronzed face was a study in masculinity. His thick eyebrows arched expressively over twinkling brown eyes and a hawkish beak of a nose. His jawline was as sharply angled as a carpenter's square. Underscored by a strong, cleft chin, his full mouth somehow managed to look both firm and yet silken at once.

Rattled, Rainie shifted her purse from one hand to the other. All her instincts urged her to be smart for once in her life and drive away. This would never work.

"I, um . . ."

Just then the older man emerged from the house. With a tip of his Stetson to Rainie, he descended the steps and struck off across the yard. She followed him with her gaze.

"Come in," Harrigan said, gesturing at the doorway behind him. "I just made a fresh pot of coffee, and my stepmother, Dee Dee, brought over a plate of her famous peanut-butter cookies. You'll love 'em."

Rainie's feet had put down roots. "You, um . . . well, you're not what I was expecting. I really don't think—"

"What were you expectin'?" he asked with another devastating grin.

"Someone older?"

He chuckled and narrowed an eye at her. "You ever heard of age discrimination? That goes two ways, you know."

Fair enough. Rainie felt her feet move, and the next thing she knew, she was mounting the plank steps.

Parker's first thought when he clapped eyes on Anna Pritchard was, *Holy shit.* She was the most gorgeous little bookworm he'd ever seen, fragile of build but delightfully well-rounded in all the right places, with delicately molded features, large hazel eyes, and a mop of brownish blond hair that fell in a cloud of curls to below her narrow shoulders. At the sight of him, she froze like a startled doe. For a second, he thought she might dive back into her rattletrap car.

He was relieved when she didn't. He truly was in dire need of a bookkeeper. He just hoped she was as smart as she was beautiful. He swept his gaze the length of her as she ascended the steps. Her clothing, which looked as if it came from a thrift shop, didn't suit someone with such an elegant bearing. *Strange.* She had "rich girl" written all over her, but she dressed like a pauper.

He directed her through the entry hall into the kitchen and motioned for her to sit at the rectangular oak table, where the plate of cookies and an application form awaited her. She hesitated before taking a seat, her pretty gaze darting around the room as if she expected a bogeyman to leap out at her.

"How do you take your coffee?" he asked.

"Um, black will be fine."

Parker dumped some sugar from the bowl into his own cup and gave the contents a brisk stir. She placed her purse on the floor and then picked it back up as he advanced toward the table. After setting a mug in front of her, he took a seat across from her, rocked back on the chair, and took a swallow of scalding hot liquid.

"So, what did you think of the drive? You gonna be able to handle it in the dead of winter?"

She blinked as if he'd posed the question in Greek.

"It snows here," he explained. "By January, we'll have white stuff hip-deep to a tall Texan. They plow, of course, but the surface conditions can still get nasty. You done much drivin' on ice?"

"No. I grew up in southern California."

"You'll need studded tires," he informed her, "and maybe some drivin' lessons in an empty parking lot come winter so you can learn how to handle a vehicle when it goes into a slide."

"I'm sure I can learn quickly."

She truly was beautiful, Parker thought as he studied her face. "Fast study, are you?"

"Fast enough."

He nodded. "Here's my thought on how we should proceed. I'll take care of some work in my home office while you fill out the application. When you're done, give me a holler, and I'll review the information. If everything looks good to me, we'll talk wages, benefits, hours, and all that kind of stuff. I'll also give you the grand tour so you can decide if the work area is suitable."

She popped open the clasp of her handbag, then pressed it closed. "Okay. That sounds good."

Parker inclined his head at the cookies. "Make free with the goodies. Dee Dee will be offended if you don't."

Chapter Two

As Rainie began filling out the application, her stomach cramped with anxiety. She'd never been a good liar. If she wasn't careful, Parker Harrigan might catch her later in a discrepancy. *Name.* That was simple, only not. Over the intercom earlier, she'd almost blurted out her real one. *Date of birth.* She had to look at her fake driver's license to verify that. When it came to everything else, she decided it would be better to stick as close to the truth as possible. That way, she wouldn't make a stupid mistake six months down the road.

In the end, she lied about only her name, date of birth, and job references. Otherwise, she stuck with the facts. *Pray God he doesn't check me out.* Nothing she wrote down could be verified because he'd be using the wrong name. Lorraina Hall had attended Pepperdine University. Anna Pritchard hadn't. Lorraina Hall had lived in San Diego. Anna Pritchard hadn't. She used her dad's real first name, giving Pritchard as his surname. *Marcus Pritchard?* It sounded totally wrong to her, but maybe it wouldn't to Parker Harrigan.

Her blouse was wet under her arms by the time she finished filling out the application. Harrigan had asked her to holler when she completed the form. She swallowed, feeling as if a gooey clump of cracker had caught in her throat. She took a sip of her coffee, now gone cold. Then her gaze fell on the cookies. She stuffed a handful into her purse so he'd think she'd eaten some.

"I'm done," she called out.

Seconds later, she heard the tap of his boots on the wood floors as he moved toward the kitchen. When he stepped into the doorway, her stomach clenched again. She wasn't sure why she found his physical strength and attractiveness so unsettling. A simple matter of aftershock, maybe. Peter had battered more than just her body. A person didn't survive experiences like that without having to deal with some emotional issues over the months that followed.

Harrigan sat down across from her, flashed a disarming grin as he rocked back on the chair, and then slapped a big hand over her application to pull it toward him. The impact of his palm on the table made her jump so violently that she nearly came to her feet. He gave her a long look. There was a question in his eyes. *What's your problem?* After regarding her for a tension-packed moment, he focused his attention on the form. As he read, he nodded occasionally. What did that mean? The frown that pleated his forehead seemed too intent. He kept backing up to reread things. She half expected him to look up and say, "What a pack of lies." Oh, God, she felt sick. Where was the bathroom? Would he hear her retching through the closed door?

"Looks good," he said with a final nod. Settling a twinkling brown gaze on her, he smiled and said, "The job is yours if you want it."

"It is?" Wincing at the squeak in her voice, Rainie curled her toes inside the canvas slip-ons.

He sat forward, bringing the elevated front legs of the chair down to the floor. The sound seemed to crack in the silence like a rifle shot. Rainie jerked, and bile surged up her throat. Were all ranchers so physically imposing? This man's every movement seemed forceful. Maybe it came from pitting his strength against powerful animals all the time. Did most ranchers become incapable of doing things slowly and gently?

"Of course the job's yours," he confirmed. "There's no question that you're qualified. More than qualified, actually. My only concern will be keepin' you happy so you don't decide to leave. Unfortunately I can't make the work more excitin'. I can make the wage and benefit package appealin', though. How does a startin' wage of sixty a year strike you?"

"Sixty?" Unable to collect her thoughts, Rainie could only gape at him.

"With a full package of benefits, of course," he added quickly. "I provide great medical insurance with dental and optical. There's also prescription coverage on a slidin' scale, dependin' upon the cost of the drug. In other words, if you're willin' to take a generic, the percentage you have to pay is far less. I haven't looked at the policy recently, but I think the copay for office calls is still only twenty-five dollars. The insurance covers the rest."

He was talking too fast. Rainie rubbed her temple, barely able to assimilate one thing before he moved on to the next.

"If you want to start a retirement fund, I'll hook you up with my broker. I don't match funds or anything like that."

"No, of course you don't." In her experience, only major corporations contributed to pension and retirement plans. "I would never expect that."

"I do offer paid vacations, though, two weeks the first year, three the second, and a full month after you've been here five years. You'll work Monday through Friday, eight to five, with an hour and a half off for lunch and breaks. We have an honor system here, so it's entirely up to you how you divvy up that time. Some people take a short lunch to allow for more breaks throughout the day. I don't care as long as I get an honest day's work out of you. Unless there's some kind of emergency, you'll have all weekends off. You can take twelve paid sick days a year—or use them as comp time."

Rainie was still trying to wrap her mind around the fact that he'd offered her so much money. She would have been tickled to get ten dollars an hour plus benefits. "Did you say sixty thousand?"

"After a six-month performance review, I'll give you a raise if you're worth your salt."

Rainie shook her head. "No, no." She held up a hand. "I'm not hoping for more. Just the opposite. It seems like so much."

"You'll work hard for every penny. Trust me on that." His dark eyes shimmered with humor. "My office looks like a tornado struck, and my business records are a complete mess. I want someone who'll keep me organized, file everything, and track my financial transactions on a daily basis. I'll also take you up on that mean cup of coffee occasionally, and sometimes I may ask you to drive into town to run errands. You'll give one hundred percent when you're here. Think you can handle all that?"

Even though Peter had destroyed Rainie's self-esteem on a personal level, she still had faith in her professional abilities. "I think so."

A dimple slashed his darkly tanned cheek when he grinned at her. "Fair warnin', I'm extremely lackadaisical with paperwork. You'll have to keep after me like a drill sergeant, and even then, I'll ignore you. I toss things here and there, and then can't remember where I put them. I forget receipts in my truck. Then in a high wind, they go sailin' away. I need someone who'll go out every day and collect them from the cab, because I'm preoccupied with other things."

Fascinated, Rainie relaxed on the chair. "What other things?"

"My horses." He lifted his broad shoulders in another shrug. "They're my raison d'être."

"You speak French?"

"A little, three years in high school and another two in college. I did go to university, believe it or not."

He didn't look like a college grad, but maybe that was a preconceived notion on her part. "What's your alma mater?"

"I went to Oregon State for my ag degree, then to the University of Idaho to study equine husbandry, animal genetics, and a little endocrinology."

"I never realized it took so much knowledge to raise horses."

"It does if you want to raise truly fine horses, and that's my focus. I'm not in this business to make money. Well," he amended with a laugh, "the money is nice, and I do bring in a substantial annual gross, but that has never been my motivation, maybe because my dad made enough when I was a kid to keep all of us in high cotton until we're pushin' up daisies."

Rainie's father had made a fortune developing computer software, so she understood what he meant. She didn't feel free to share that information with him, though.

"You have a large family?" Rainie had always yearned for brothers and sisters—or even a cousin. But her mother had been an orphan, and her dad had broken ties with his relatives before her birth. She'd grown up as an only child with just one set of grandparents she'd never met.

"I've got three brothers and a baby sister. That's a large family by some people's standards, I guess. I think my mom and dad might have had more kids, but she died in childbirth with Samantha. My father didn't remarry until just recently."

"I'm sorry. About your mother, I mean."

His Adam's apple bobbed. "It happened a long time ago. Sam is a grown woman now and happily married to a great horse vet. Life goes on." He straightened on the chair. "Anyway . . ." He rubbed beside his nose. "When it comes to this ranch, it's all about the horses for me—their physical comfort, improving their bloodlines, trainin' 'em, and makin' sure, before I sell one of 'em, that they go to an excellent home. You wouldn't believe the equine abuse and neglect that goes on across this country. I fly to check out the facilities where my horse will be boarded, talk to neighborin' ranchers, and even interview officers on the local rodeo committee to make sure there have been no complaints against a prospective buyer. Even if he or she checks out with flyin' colors, I still worry before I finalize the sale. Seemingly nice people sometimes beat horses. They put them out into pastures without any shelter in bitter weather. If money gets tight, they buy low-grade hay or none at all. Water lines freeze up and the horse goes thirsty. Placin' my horses with responsible owners is somethin' I take very seriously."

Rainie thought of Thomas, who, she suspected, had been left behind to starve. The poor cat had eaten four cans of tuna since his arrival last night. "Some people have something important missing in their makeup," she said.

"That's a nice way of puttin' it." He pushed at her application, then folded up a corner of the top sheet, worrying the triangular tuft with thick, calloused fingers. "I'd like to lock those people up in a room and give 'em only enough food and water to stay alive. Better yet, put them in a pen and let them try to eat snow and nothin' else. People who neglect animals need to starve and go thirsty themselves. Maybe then they'd have a heart."

"At least animal protection laws are getting stricter."

"Not strict enough."

Rainie agreed. A lot went on in the world that she felt was deplorable.

"Anyway, I didn't mean to get off on a tangent," he apologized. "Back to the original subject, I'm way too busy in the stable to spare much time for paperwork. If I've got a sick horse, I'm not thinkin' about the bill from the vet or the receipts for medication. I'm thinkin' only about the animal and gettin' it well. In short, I'm a great horseman but a lousy businessman."

Searching his gaze, Rainie saw only sincerity, which led her to believe he truly did care for his horses. When it came to men, though, she was a poor judge of character. "So you need someone to balance you out?"

"Exactly. At tax time, I wish I was more organized, but the rest of the year, I seldom even think about it."

Rainie felt more of the tension drain from her limbs. "I *will* think about it," she assured him. "In an office environment, 'meticulous' is my middle name."

"I may drive you nuts, then."

For sixty thousand a year and good benefits, Rainie would happily go a little crazy. "The wage is very generous. I would be happy with two-thirds of that."

He arched a dark eyebrow. "Really? Why sell yourself short?"

Rainie had worked for a major corporation and earned only forty-five thousand a year, and that had been in Seattle, where the cost of living was much higher. She felt like a thief. "How about settling on fifty?"

He shook his head. "My full-time stable hands get forty, and none of them have a college degree." He noticed her incredulous expression and grinned. "There's a method to my madness. I detest rapid turnover, so I pay a livable wage to keep my employees happy. In the end, I come out the winner. I'm not trainin' new people all the time or constantly hasslin' with idiots who don't know what they're doin'. Someone with your education and experience deserves to start near the top of my pay scale. My foreman gets eighty a year, twice what the hired hands get. He's invaluable to me when it comes to daily operations. You'll be invaluable when it comes to the business end of things. I think sixty a year is fair. Over time, with annual raises, you'll make what my foreman does."

Rainie couldn't believe he'd just refused to pay her less. "Is there a money tree in your backyard or something?"

With a chuckle, he pushed to his feet. "Somethin' like that. You ready to take that tour?"

Rainie breathed in the fresh, sun-drenched air as she accompanied Parker Harrigan across the gravel parking area to the big metal building she'd noticed earlier. It was much farther from the house than it had appeared to be from inside her car. The smells out here were different, she realized, some of the scents unidentifiable. A faint pungency underscored the sweet smells of grass, clover, and wildflowers. She thought she detected a piney odor on the breeze as well. Overall, it was a pleasant blend.

As they walked, he gestured around them.

"Those are the outdoor stalls," he informed her, pointing off to their right at a flank of enclosures sheltered by a long, corrugated-metal roof. At the far end, Rainie saw two women giving a reddish brown horse a bath. "We only use them as holdin' pens durin' the day."

Within the structure, three men worked with shovels. One of them, a small, wiry man of about thirty with brown hair and blue eyes, waved at his boss.

"That's Jericho Steelman," Harrigan explained. "Did the rodeo circuit for several years as a clown until he injured his leg. Now he's got a permanent limp and can't do clown work anymore."

"That's too bad." As the young man resumed work, Rainie studied the stalls, which looked perfectly fine to her. "Why do you only use those as holding pens?"

"Unless we're workin' with 'em, I like to keep my horses inside the stable."

"Don't they prefer to be outdoors?"

"They've got paddocks outside their stalls, so they can go out whenever they want durin' the day. And they're exercised regularly."

Some of the larger pieces of gravel poked through the soft soles of Rainie's slip-ons, hurting her feet. She made a mental note to get a sturdy pair of shoes or boots. "I noticed what looked like infrared cameras at the gate."

"And all along the fence line," he informed her. "Good eye. Most people don't know what they are. If you accept the job, I'll give you a sticker for your windshield. There's a camera at the gate that reads the bar code and automatically lets you in."

"Is so much security really necessary way out here?"

He chuckled. "Probably not. But I'd rather be safe than sorry. My sister had some horses poisoned not that long ago."

"Oh, how awful." Rainie shivered and rubbed her arms. "Is her ranch near here?"

He hooked a thumb over his shoulder. With the movement, his blue shirt drew taut over the bunched muscles in his upper arm. "Right over there. See the green metal roofs?"

Rainie squinted against the sunlight. "My goodness, she's close."

"My whole family is close," he explained. "Originally, this was a twelve-hundred-acre ranch. My dad subdivided it into six separate parcels, keepin' one for himself and givin' one to each of us kids when we turned twenty-one. Samantha was the first of us to go with high security. For reasons of his own, my brother Clint came next. Now all of us have protected perimeters."

"Your horses must be very valuable," she observed as they walked along a paddock fence.

"Yes, extremely valuable, but, like I said, it isn't about the money for me. I love 'em." A flush crept up his sun-tanned neck, and he smiled sheepishly. "Not very macho of me to admit, I know, but that's the truth. If someone hurt one of my horses, my good sense would go in my hip pocket, and I'd have murder in my eye."

Rainie hoped she never saw Parker Harrigan in a rage. He wasn't a big man by normal standards, but he had an aura of indomitable strength about him that made men like Peter seem soft and insubstantial.

They circled two pickups that were parked in the shade of the building. Uncomfortable with the silence, she asked, "How do you exercise your horses, by riding them?"

"Whenever possible, yes. When we can't, we put 'em on the walker." He inclined his head at a contraption that reminded Rainie of a huge circular clothesline. "We can exercise four to six animals at a time on that. I prefer ridin' 'em, though. More fun for the horse, and also for me."

He touched a hand to the small of her back as he opened the personnel door of the building and ushered her through the entrance. A gentlemanly gesture, she assured herself, nothing more. There was no reason for her to shrink away.

"Oh, my." Amazed, she took in the well-lit, cavernous interior. A riding area held center stage. The paunchy older man in cowboy garb whom she'd seen earlier worked with a leashed horse, snapping a long whip at the animal's heels to make it run in circles over the packed dirt. Countless stalls lined the exterior walls. At nearly every gate, a horse looked out at them.

"That man won't hit the horse, will he?"

"Over my dead body," Harrigan replied with a laugh. "That's called a lunge whip. We don't use them on the horse, only behind it. The cracking sound encourages the horse to move."

"Just calling its name doesn't work?"

"Not effectively enough to work the horse properly."

"I didn't expect this place to be so big inside."

"In snow country, an indoor arena needs to be big. This is where I work with my horses all winter." Keeping his hand at the small of her back, he guided her safely around horse and man to traverse the length of the riding area. When they reached a long hallway at the rear of the building, he said, "The office is back here."

Rainie could smell hay, grain, and leather. She sent up a silent prayer of thanksgiving that she'd never had allergies like her father. "So I'll work here in the stable?"

"It's the hub of my business."

When he opened the office door, Rainie saw that he hadn't exaggerated about the disorder. The room was large enough to comfortably hold two large desks and several file cabinets, but the piles of paperwork, stacks of books, and general disarray made it seem crowded. Under the clutter, she saw rich cherry wood surfaces that were dulled by layers of dust. That surprised her, because his house had looked spotlessly clean.

"I warned you."

It wasn't often that Rainie laughed nowadays, but the embarrassment in his voice caught her off guard. With a choked giggle, she said, "You did. You're a master at understatement, Mr. Harrigan."

"Parker," he corrected. Then he said, "It's not *that* bad." He stepped over to another door and pushed it open. "I call this the coffee room, even though it's a fully equipped kitchen with a fridge, stove, and microwave. There's an adjoinin' restroom as well. Nothin' fancy."

Rainie liked that she would be able to refrigerate her lunch items and then heat them up when she wanted to eat. Having a restroom handy was another plus.

Turning from the coffee room, he scooped animal husbandry tomes and a jumble of papers from the cushioned seat of a leather chair to her right and then inclined his head at the desk. "This will be your workstation."

Rainie stepped around to check out the computer system, which looked fairly new. "How many gigabytes?"

He dumped the books and papers atop the other desk and rubbed beside his nose. "Damned if I know. I just tell my computer guy what I'll be usin' the system for, and he decides what bells and whistles I need."

"And you just write a check?"

"Hell, no, I give him my credit card number. I don't use checks unless I absolutely have to. I get my check register all screwed up."

Rainie shook her head. "You probably shouldn't give a salesperson free rein. They may overload you with stuff to increase their commissions."

"What I don't know won't hurt me."

"It may do some damage to your bank balance, though."

He nodded in agreement. "That's why I'm hirin' you, to take care of my finances. I just updated both workstations. I haven't used this computer yet, but the guy at the shop assured me that it will do everything you need it to, plus some."

"Software?"

He named some programs she knew well, then an accounting program she'd never used. After confessing that to him, she added, "That isn't really a concern, though. I'll learn the ins and outs quickly enough. Most accounting programs are similar."

He glanced around at the mess, which was considerable. "So, what do you think?"

She found herself smiling again. "I'd be lying if I said it isn't a little daunting." The only window looked out upon the walker and outdoor stalls. In the distance, though, she could see pine-studded hills with the majestic Cascades looming behind them. She'd have a mountain view to enjoy during coffee breaks. "It may take me most of the first week to put everything in order."

He nodded. "I'm sorry it's such a mess in here. But like I said, I'm just not into it."

"If you were, you wouldn't need me." She followed his gaze, thinking of all the sorting and filing she'd have to do. "I'll get it whipped into shape."

"When can you start?"

The question made her laugh again. It felt strange to her, as if the person she'd once been had suddenly reentered her body. "I can start tomorrow if you'd like. My schedule is pretty much open. All I have to keep me at home is Thomas."

"Ah." His dark eyes moved slowly over her face. "It figures that there'd be a man in the picture. You're too lovely to be unattached."

Heat crept up Rainie's neck to pool in her cheeks. "Thomas is a cat."

He arched a jet eyebrow. "A cat," he repeated.

"Yes, you know, one of those small, furry creatures that sleep in windowsills?"

He threw back his dark head and let loose with a laugh, the sound so rich and deep that she felt surrounded by warmth. "We're back to the elk conversation, are we?"

Rainie almost cringed. Getting lippy with her prospective employer wasn't smart. But it had just popped out. "I'm sorry. I didn't mean to sound sarcastic."

The deep dimple slashed his cheek again as he grinned. "No worries. I enjoy someone who gives back as good as she gets."

At one time in her life, Rainie had occasionally enjoyed a bit of verbal sparring herself, but those days were far behind her now.

"It's good to know Thomas is a cat," he said softly. "Can I take that to mean there's no significant other in your life at the moment?"

The gleam of masculine interest in his eyes made Rainie's

heart trip. She clutched her purse close to her waist, her fingers embedded in the leather so rigidly that her knuckles ached. "As it happens, I am unattached at the moment, but for the sake of office harmony, Mr. Harrigan, I think we should keep our relationship purely professional."

"We don't have much harmony around here, only chaos. But I see your point."

Rainie was relieved to hear it. Having an affair with her boss wasn't on her agenda. The very thought made her stomach clench with nausea again. She ran her gaze over the office once more. "Well," she said, hating the tremor she heard in her voice, "I'll see you at eight in the morning, then."

"Hold on. You'll need a sticker." He stepped over to the other desk, opened a drawer, and drew out a small square of paper. "Just affix this to the upper left corner of your windshield. We call it the 'open sesame' sticker. If it doesn't work, back up and come in farther to the left. The camera has to be able to see your windshield."

When he reached to open the door for her and started to follow her out, she held up a staying hand. "No, please, I've interfered with your workday enough as it is. I can see myself out."

"Toby should be finished lunging Monte Carlo by now, so I guess that works." His dark eyes lingered on hers. She got the unnerving feeling that he could see far more in her gaze than she wanted to reveal. "Eight in the morning, then," he agreed. "I'll have the coffee on."

Rainie turned to leave, only to have him stop her with, "Oh, wait a sec." He reached into his hip pocket and drew out a well-worn wallet. "You need to get a cell phone." He handed her three one-hundred-dollar bills. "Consider it an advance on your first paycheck."

"Cash?" Rainie's mouth twisted into a reluctant smile. "There'll be no record of the exchange, Mr. Harrigan."

"Parker, and you can document it tomorrow." He folded

her fingers over the money, the heat of his touch sending jolts of sensation shooting up her arm. "Like I said, I don't worry about stuff like that."

"I can see I'm going to have my hands full."

His gaze trailed slowly over her upturned face. "Yeah, I think you just might."

Chapter Three

En route to the ranch the next morning, Rainie still suffered an upset stomach. Last night, she'd gotten worried that the sudden onslaught of nausea might be an early sign of pregnancy. To her inestimable relief, the home test she'd purchased at a corner drugstore had been negative. She tried not to think about the fact that those tests weren't always conclusive in the early stages of gestation. *Nerves,* she assured herself. She'd always had a sensitive digestive tract. God forbid that she should be pregnant with Peter's child. What on earth would she do? Getting a clinical abortion wasn't an option for her. Somehow, she couldn't see Parker Harrigan being very happy if his new bookkeeper had to take maternity leave in eight months' time.

Her hands tightened convulsively over the steering wheel. She had enough problems without borrowing trouble. Yes, Peter had often gotten so caught up in his own sick sexual pleasure that he'd forgotten to use a condom, and she'd been a virtual prisoner during the last few months of the marriage, not allowed to go grocery shopping unescorted, let alone sneak to a clinic for birth control pills. So there was a possibility that she could be pregnant. But it wasn't likely. During a less volatile stage of their relationship, when she'd still been stupid enough to think they might make it work, she'd wanted a baby more than anything, but her cycles had remained as regular as clockwork. Maybe it had been her failing. Maybe it had been Peter's. She knew only that she hadn't been able to conceive.

At least she had no worries about possibly having an STD. Peter had been perversely monogamous and totally focused on Rainie—possessing her, abusing her, and controlling her being his only passions. There'd been no room in his life for other women, so though it had been a small consolation, Rainie had never been worried about his bringing home diseases. Every dark cloud truly did have a silver lining.

Clinging to that thought, Rainie tried to calm down. Just getting through today would be challenging enough. Most employers checked out an employee's references. Parker Harrigan seemed to be lackadaisical about things like that, but she would be foolish to forget the gleam of intelligence in his eyes. The man was no dummy. He'd invested heaps of money in security systems to keep his horses safe. How likely was it that he would toss her application aside and never look at it again? Surely he would at least want to make sure she had no criminal record.

A background check didn't concern her. The persona of Anna Pritchard would appear to be bona fide. She had a driver's license, passport, and Social Security card that would hold up under close scrutiny. But if Harrigan decided to check out any of her references, her goose would be cooked, pure and simple. So far as she knew, no Anna Pritchard had ever attended Pepperdine University, and all the former employers she'd listed were fictitious. With one phone call, he'd discover, lickety-split, that she was a complete fraud.

Rainie could only pray he was as lazy about stuff like that as he pretended to be. She needed this job desperately. The tires on the Mazda were worn down to nothing. The engine was throwing oil. Now, thanks to Parker Harrigan, she also had a cell phone bill to pay. She needed to start bringing in some cash.

Parker was mixing prenatal vitamins into Monte Carlo's morning grain when Anna arrived for work. After entering via the personnel door, she hesitated for a moment, looking more than a little uncertain. The men who composed this morning's stable crew stopped what they were doing to stare. Parker couldn't blame them. A couple of the gals on Parker's payroll were pretty easy on the eyes, but Anna Pritchard was downright stunning, despite the timeworn cotton skirt and faded knit top that she wore. Her hair fell to below her slender shoulders in a cloud of rebellious, gold-tipped brown curls. Even at a distance, her hazel eyes and delicate features grabbed a man's attention and wouldn't let go. In Parker's estimation, she was a little too thin, but what there was of her packed a wallop.

"Put your eyes back in your heads," he grumbled at his men as he exited the mare's stall. "That's Anna, the new bookkeeper."

"She can fiddle with my books anytime she wants," Gary Morton, a twenty-eight-year-old part-time employee, observed in a low voice.

Parker rounded on the younger man and jabbed a finger at his nose. "There'll be no more talk like that. If any one of you gives her a moment's grief, you'll be pickin' up your final check and hightailin' it out of here. Is that clear?"

"Crystal clear," Gary replied. "Don't get your panties in a twist. I was only saying—"

"I know what you were sayin'," Parker snapped, cutting the hired hand short. "And I'm tellin' you comments like that aren't gonna fly. Let it go at that."

Parker went to greet his new bookkeeper. Her face was pale. As he drew closer, he noticed dark circles under her lovely eyes. Yesterday, she'd seemed inordinately tense during the application and orientation process, but he'd decided maybe that was normal. Lots of people grew rattled while interviewing for a job. The job was hers now, though, and she still looked coiled tighter than an eight-day clock.

"Mornin'," he said, making a point of glancing at his watch. "You're a few minutes early."

She shifted her old purse from under one arm to the other. "I prefer to be a bit early rather than late."

The members of Parker's family jokingly said that he would be late to his own funeral. Parker couldn't argue the point. It was his philosophy that hurrying up to wait was a total waste of his time. "Maybe that'll rub off on me. I never get anywhere early." He stepped in close to grasp her pointy elbow. "Come on. I'll walk you back."

She stiffened under his hand. "I know the way."

He didn't release his hold. "Not sayin' you don't, but this time of mornin' is busy. Until you get used to it here, I'll escort you. If someone brings a horse out of its stall, I don't want you gettin' stepped on." He glanced down, pleased to see that she wore sturdier footwear. "Nice boots." They were Western-style riding boots that looked kind of corny with the ruffled skirt, but he'd seen other young women in similar getups. "At least they'll protect your toes."

"I know I'm not making a fashion statement, but for the moment, these are all I have."

Parker had a hunch she'd stopped off at a thrift store on her way home yesterday and the riding boots had been all that she could find. Telltale scuffs on the toes told him the leather had seen a lot of abuse, and he couldn't believe Anna had been wearing the boots when it occurred. By her own admission, she'd never been around horses until now.

"Nobody here worries much about fashion," he assured her. "Come winter, you may be wearin' moose-hide mukluks lined with sheepskin."

Her soft mouth curved. "Does it get *that* cold?"

"There are times when my breath freezes in the air and causes a small hailstorm as it hits the ground."

"Are you given to telling tall tales, Mr. Harrigan?"

He grinned and ignored the question. "You get a cell phone?"

"Yes."

"Good. There are a couple of dead zones between here and town, but mostly the reception is dependable. I'll worry a lot less about your makin' the drive if you can call for help." Drawing her along with him, he cut a wide berth around an open stall gate. All of his horses were gentle and well mannered, but Parker had learned long ago never to let down his guard around such large animals. "I made a pot of coffee," he told her. "Don't know if it'll measure up to your high standards, but it's hot and wet."

When they reached the hallway, he released her arm and stood back, lifting a hand in farewell. "I'll check in with you later. If you need anything or have any questions, just holler."

She paused in the corridor to glance back at him over her shoulder. "I won't need you. Thanks for making coffee."

"You bet."

Once Rainie settled in to work, she found it difficult to concentrate. She kept expecting her boss to storm into the office to confront her about all the lies she'd told on her application. What would she say to him? *I'm sorry I fibbed?* It wasn't in Rainie's nature to deceive people, so she had no experience in how to handle it when the truth came out. Parker Harrigan struck her as being a direct, honest man. He wouldn't be happy if he discovered that she'd played him for a chump.

An hour into sorting through the office rubble, Rainie froze in motion when he suddenly burst into the room. Oh, God, he'd found her out. A scowl drew his black eyebrows together over his prominent nose. His firm mouth had thinned into a grim line. When he settled those intense brown eyes on her, Rainie's skin felt the burn.

"Have you seen my checkbook?"

Rainie struggled to regain her composure. "I, um, didn't think you used one much."

"I don't." He advanced toward his desk to paw through the clutter. "Damn it. I've got a new guy deliverin' hay. He won't bill it to my account. Says he was told to collect payment on delivery at all his drops, and his boss isn't answerin' the phone."

Rainie opened a drawer and tugged out a large dark blue binder notebook. "Is this it?"

"You're my guardian angel."

He opened the book and bent to fill out a draft. When he failed to document the amount in the register, Rainie did it for him.

"Thanks," he said as he exited the room, banging the door closed behind him.

Rainie was trembling. After closing the checkbook, she hugged her waist and shut her eyes, so shaken that she almost wished she hadn't taken this job. Her nerve endings were raw with tension. Her mind kept circling the fact that he was bound to check up on her sooner or later. At this point, she hoped it would be sooner. She didn't know how much longer she could stand this waiting.

What had she been thinking yesterday to interview for a high-paying, permanent position? People like her took jobs at fast-food joints to avoid any questions. They didn't set themselves up for detection by accepting sixty thousand a year in wages, plus benefits. Employers who offered that kind of package were successful business owners who hadn't gotten where they were by being naive.

*   *   *

Sweat beaded on Parker's face as he swung another hay bale off the stack and carried it into the storage shed. Normally, he used the forklift, but right now he needed the physical exertion. It was a habit he'd developed over his lifetime. When confronted with a problem, he worked while he sorted his way through it.

Anna Pritchard was definitely a puzzle he needed to figure out.

Parker had visited the office precisely four times over the course of the morning, and the lady had nearly jumped out of her skin each time. At first, he'd chalked it up to nervousness because it was her first day on the job, but then he'd noticed the fear in her eyes. Unless he was misreading her, she was terrified of him. How the hell did that make sense?

Parker had never spent much time analyzing how he might be perceived by others, so he didn't go around guarding his every word or gesture. People either accepted him or they didn't. He supposed it was fair to say that his manner could be a little gruff sometimes, and he'd be the first to admit he completely lacked the sophisticated polish a lot of guys had. But never, to his knowledge, had he terrified anyone.

Something about her wasn't right. It reminded him of a slightly crooked picture on a wall. He always noticed immediately, and it bugged the hell out of him until he straightened it. It was that way with Anna. Something about her just didn't line up. He wasn't a boisterous man. He didn't lose his temper at the drop of a hat and punch holes in the walls. He seldom raised his voice in anger. So what was it about him that frightened her?

Parker couldn't say. He knew only that Anna trembled in her secondhand boots whenever he entered the office. *Weird.* He didn't know what her deal was, but he hoped she got it ironed out. He didn't relish the thought of working with a woman who jumped a foot every time he so much as looked at her.

For the rest of the afternoon, Parker did his best to put Anna at ease, but by the end of the day, he'd decided that nothing short of a Valium chased by two fingers of whiskey would do the trick. He gazed thoughtfully after her rattletrap Mazda as she drove away. The lady was a puzzle, no question about it. She'd done a great job of straightening his office. It wasn't organized to her satisfaction yet, but he felt sure it soon would be. She'd also made fast work of logging today's expenditures, not only the hay delivery, but also several nickel-and-dime purchases, one from a traveling salesman who peddled Parker's favorite brand of equine supplements. Normally payouts like that never got recorded because Parker forgot to do it.

All in all, he was happy with her performance so far. But her odd behavior disturbed him. Glancing at his watch, he saw that it was too late to do anything about it today, but first thing tomorrow morning, he needed to check out her references.

When Anna got home, she kicked off the boots, sank onto a kitchen chair, and lay forward over the table, resting her head on her folded arms. Nervous tension had drained her empty. Her limbs felt as if they weighed a thousand pounds each, and she had a painful crick in her neck she couldn't massage away. At least Parker Harrigan hadn't made any phone calls today, she reminded herself. Instead he seemed willing to accept her at face value. As crazy as it was, that only made her feel guiltier for lying to him.

Thomas leaped up onto the tabletop to nuzzle Rainie's hair. She smiled wearily and sat back to scratch the cat behind his ears. "Hi, there, skinny boy. Did you miss me, or are you just hungry?"

He started to purr, the sound a deep rumble in his chest. Rainie continued petting him for a moment and then pushed up from the chair to feed him. She'd purchased some cat food yesterday, but the tom seemed to prefer the kibble mixed with tuna.

As she opened a can, she said, "I guess I can afford a can of tuna per day now that I'm making good money and have health insurance."

The cat rubbed against her bare calves while she prepared his meal. After setting the bowl down, Rainie returned to the table to watch him eat.

"Let's just hope I can keep the job," she added. "If he finds out I lied to get it, he may fire me on the spot. Then I'll be lucky to get work at Burger King."

No reply from the cat. Rainie sighed. Bottom line was, she missed her friends. Oh, how she wished she could unload on Margaret right now or hear Janet crack one of her silly jokes. Smiling slightly, Rainie tried to imagine what her irreverent friend might say. *A cowboy? They're all dumber than boxes of rocks. That's why they engrave their names on their belts, so they know who they are when they put their pants on in the morning.* Still grinning, Rainie rested her chin on the heel of her hand, gazing thoughtfully at Thomas. Maybe, just maybe, Parker Harrigan wouldn't check out her references. He hadn't bothered to record a single check that he'd written today, and he'd tossed the receipts at his desk, not even looking to see where they landed. Being so meticulous by nature, she found that inconceivable, but it took all different types to make the world go around.

Feeling slightly better, Rainie got up to fix herself something to eat. Her habitual comfort foods, tomato soup and a grilled cheese sandwich, sounded good. When her meal was ready, she sat on the living room sofa. Thomas joined her on the cushion to beg for morsels of cheese. Rainie shared her food with him, then settled back to watch the news. For about ten minutes, the commentator focused on world affairs. Then Rainie saw her own face flash onto the screen.

She'd grown accustomed to that over the last few weeks, but it still never failed to startle her.

"What really happened to Lorraina Danning?" the news anchor asked the audience. "Did she accidentally fall overboard, or was she pushed? It's a mystery that the police have been unable to solve." Rainie's picture vanished from the screen, and the camera zoomed in on a live news conference. Detective Raymond Lord, with the King County police, stood at a podium. Expression solemn, blue eyes piercing, he announced that the FBI was officially taking over the investigation. The King County task force would, however, continue to lend support, assisting FBI agents in whatever way it could. Rainie's face came back on the screen as the commentator resumed her narrative. No body, no clues. Lorraina Danning had disappeared without a trace.

Staring at her own likeness, Rainie touched her cheek with a trembling fingertip. The picture had been taken before she'd gotten the scar, and she'd lost some weight as well. The sleek brown hair that had once been her trademark was now a wildly curly mane, as blond as it was brown. She no longer wore expensive clothing, either. Overall, she looked completely different. Or so she hoped. But what if Parker Harrigan was watching this newscast and recognized her?

Composure shattered, Rainie went to the kitchen to open a bottle of merlot. It was becoming a habit, she realized. Her nerves were shot, and she was self-medicating. Not a good thing. Problem was, she couldn't afford to go another night without sleep, and the wine would make her drowsy.

The following day, Parker got busy in the morning and couldn't find time to check out Anna's references. When things slowed down shortly after lunch, he decided to do his detective work at the house. After seeing Anna several more times, he felt a little foolish for his suspicions. No one with big, guileless eyes like hers could be a practiced liar. That said, her behavior continued to raise warning flags in his mind. She was still as nervous as a long-tailed cat in a roomful of rocking chairs whenever he entered the office.

Parker's first call was to Pepperdine University. He was transferred from the main offices to those of Seaver College, a subsidiary school under the Pepperdine umbrella that apparently offered on-campus undergraduate degrees in accounting. A woman named Anna Pritchard had indeed taken that coursework and received her degree from Seaver in 1981. Wrong person. The Anna working in his stable office was only twenty-five. Parker asked the woman on the phone to please check her records for another Anna Pritchard who'd probably gotten her accounting degree in 2004 or 2005. Dead end. No one named Anna Pritchard had earned an accounting degree at Seaver College since 1981.

As Parker ended the call, his blood began to heat with anger. Next he called one of Anna's former employers. Some little old lady in Orange County answered the phone. She'd never heard of the company Parker named. He got off the phone and turned to his computer. A Google search for the company brought up no matches. Parker double-checked the name of the place and typed it in again. Still nothing. If the company existed, it wasn't listed in this search engine.

Before jumping to conclusions, Parker grimly placed several more phone calls. Once, he got a small child on the phone. The next time, he got a grease monkey at some gas station in Chico. At least the lady seemed to know her California area codes. So, what did that tell him, other than that she'd probably once lived in that state? It sure as hell told him nothing more—except that Anna Pritchard had lied on her application.

Parker was pissed. He seldom lied to anyone, and he expected the same courtesy in return. He tried to calm down as he headed for the stable, but it was an effort in futility. He'd trusted her. When he remembered their conversation the day before yesterday, humiliation seared his cheeks. She'd made him look stupid. Correction, he'd made himself look stupid by allowing himself to be taken in by those innocent hazel eyes.

Anna was standing at a file cabinet, hands full of papers, when he burst into the office. He made a conscious effort not to slam the door closed behind him.

"We need to talk," he bit out.

Her face drained of color. "About?"

"Sit down."

She put the papers on top of the cabinet and went to sit in her chair. Today she wore a fake suede skirt that had seen better times and a sleeveless blouse with one button that didn't quite match the rest. As Parker advanced on her, he noticed that her face grew paler by the second and that the cherry surface of her work area gleamed with fresh polish.

"I don't appreciate being lied to," he said evenly.

Agitated and needing something to do with his hands, he reached for the granite paperweight on the blotter. At his movement, she flinched and jerked up her right arm to shield her face, clearly convinced he meant to strike her. *Whoa.* Parker was angry. He'd be the first to admit that. But he'd never hit a woman in his life, not even his little sister when they'd fought as kids.

Fingertips still resting on the paperweight, Parker studied his frightened bookkeeper with mounting bewilderment. She had a small scar on her left cheek. It still bore the pinkness of a recent wound. Now that he examined it more closely, a very unpleasant possibility sprang to his mind.

In his younger years, he had occasionally gotten into honky-tonk brawls, and he'd seen his share of cheeks laid open by the force of a man's fist. Had some jerk struck her? The question had no sooner entered Parker's mind than he knew the answer. Everything about her suddenly added up—her fear of him, the countless lies on her job application, the way she shrank from his most casual touch. She had recently been involved in an abusive relationship. He saw it in her eyes—a trapped, wary look that made his heart catch. Now she was on the run, trying to stay one step ahead of the bastard who'd roughed her up. If he was wrong, he'd eat his hat for supper and his boots for dessert.

This added a totally new wrinkle. He couldn't very well blame a woman for lying to him about her references if she was trying to escape an abusive bully.

The anger that had made him see red a moment ago eased from Parker's body. Turning, he rested his hips against the edge of his desk and blocked her escape with his outstretched legs, angling them across the center aisle between the two workstations. He folded his arms loosely over his chest, hoping his relaxed posture might reassure her a little.

"You never attended Pepperdine University or Seaver College," he said without preamble. "The places of employment you listed don't even exist."

She pushed up from the chair. Parker was surprised that she could stand. Her legs were shaking like aspen leaves in a brisk breeze. She went to the file cabinet to collect her purse and then turned toward him, holding the bag to her midriff as if it were a shield. Without a word, she tried to step over his crossed boots. No way was Parker going to let her leave, not until he had some answers. He thrust out a hand to grasp her arm.

"Oh, no, you don't. I hired you in good faith. I offered you an extremely attractive employment package. The very least you owe me is some sort of explanation."

He could feel her arm muscles quivering under the press of his fingertips. He knew she was terrified. Yet still she said nothing.

"Well," he said softly, "if you've got no explanations to

offer, let me venture a couple of guesses. I think some asshole beat the ever-lovin' hell out of you, and not that long ago, judgin' by that scar on your cheek." Her body jerked as if he'd slapped her. "My second guess is that your name isn't really Anna Pritchard. How am I doin' so far?"

Chapter Four

Rainie felt as if she might faint. This couldn't be happening. She had anticipated that Harrigan might check her references, but she'd never in her wildest dreams thought he might look beyond the lies and come up with a hypothesis so close to the truth. She remembered the time he'd gazed into her eyes and given her the uncomfortable feeling that he could read far more than she wanted to reveal. Now she realized that it had been more than just a feeling.

He knew the truth—or a very close facsimile thereof. After all she'd been through to get safely away from Peter, she couldn't allow her cover to be blown her second day on the job. Other people had stuck their necks out on her behalf, not only Margaret and Janet, but also Stan, a computer guru they'd chummed around with in college. Though Stan had been paid to get Rainie a fake birth certificate and passport, he hadn't provided his services solely for the money. The penalties for breaching government firewalls and altering records were stiff. Stan could have robbed a bank for a much larger take and probably received about the same punishment if he were caught. No, he had helped Rainie out of friendship, a princely gesture that had momentarily restored her faith in the opposite sex.

Now, cornered in the office by Parker Harrigan, Rainie had no well of faith left to tap, not when it came to men.

There was no question in her mind that he would turn her in, and when he did, she and her friends would be in big trouble. The search for Lorraina Danning had cost a fortune in taxpayers' money. The authorities would not be happy if they discovered that her disappearance had been staged.

Digging deep for composure, Rainie looked directly into Harrigan's eyes. "What on earth makes you think I lied about my name?" She asked the question with an incredulous laugh that she hoped was convincing. "I have a birth certificate, passport, and driver's license to prove who I am."

"Identification can be faked."

"Not anymore," she countered. "All government records are computerized and protected by impenetrable firewalls."

"Difficult to breach, perhaps, but not impossible." He smiled slightly. "Nothin' is impossible for a talented hacker. For a price, fake identification can still be acquired."

"I—" She gulped to steady her voice. "Can I just go, please?"

"Somehow that doesn't strike me as bein' equitable." His lips shimmered in the overhead fluorescent lights as he spoke. "You come into my world, you make me feel like an idiot for trustin' you, and now you wanna waltz away without one word of explanation?"

That was precisely what she wanted. Why couldn't he just let it go at that?

Only the grip of his fingers on her arm told her that he had no such intention. He wasn't hurting her—yet. But she could feel the suppressed strength that he might unleash on her at any moment.

"What do you want from me?" she asked shakily.

"The truth."

That was the one thing Rainie couldn't give him. Too many people, including herself, would be hurt.

* * *

The tremors Parker felt coursing through Anna Pritchard's body made him feel ashamed of himself. He'd wrestled with foals bigger than she was. A physical confrontation between them could have only one possible conclusion. But did that give him the right to push her around? He had a very bad feeling that she'd already been intimidated enough times in her young life.

When she tried to jerk free of his grasp again, he didn't have the heart to hold on. What kind of a man bullied someone her size? Even worse, what kind of a man had struck her with enough force to lay open her cheek? She looked so scared that he doubted she could spit if he yelled, "Fire."

After releasing her, Parker stepped over to the closed door and leaned his shoulder against the wood, still effectively barring her escape, only now without touching her. He needed to reassure her somehow. Problem was, he had no idea where to start.

"You know, Anna, I'm kind of peculiar in some ways."

Her eyes went wide. He went back over what he'd said and wished he could recall the statement. The word *peculiar* was clearly equivalent to *crazy* in her mind.

"What I mean is, I don't always march to the same drumbeat as everyone else," he amended.

That didn't work, either.

"All right, scratch all that." *Damn it.* Just like his brothers Clint and Zach, he'd inherited his father's amazing talent for always saying the wrong thing. "What I'm tryin' to say is . . ." What the hell *was* he trying to say? He'd never been good at beating around the bush. He was a direct man who shot from the hip. Whenever he tried to soften his delivery, he screwed it up. "Let me just say it without frills. Okay? If you lied because you're tryin' to escape an abusive relationship, I won't hold it against you. A lot of employers might, but I won't."

Taking measure of his audience, Parker decided that she still looked like a rabbit searching for a bolt-hole.

"In fact," he went on, "I admire your courage if that's the case. A lot of women don't have the guts to leave. It's a pretty scary proposition to turn your back on everything familiar. No friends, no job, no home. That takes a lot of backbone."

His mouth had gone as dry as stale bread. His little sister, Sam, had gotten the hell beaten out of her a few times, and she'd been afraid to tell Parker for fear he'd end up in jail for killing her first husband. Major possibility. But how could he impart his feelings about abusive men to this frightened girl?

Yes, in many ways she was only a girl, twenty-five and full-grown, but still far from being worldly. He could see the shattered innocence and pain of betrayal in her eyes. For a few hours, he'd talked himself into thinking her innocence was all an act, but no man with good sense could look at her and hold to that judgment. She was everything he'd perceived her to be during the job interview—young, uncertain, and more than a little skittish. She put him in mind of a pretty little filly he'd once purchased at auction that had been mistreated so badly it had taken her weeks to accept his touch. Befriending her had required more patience than Parker had known he had.

"I have no respect for men who beat women," he continued. "Or animals, for that matter. My father raised me better. If you're runnin' from someone like that, I don't care what your real name is. I don't care where you're from. I don't care if you really have an undergraduate degree in accountin'. I'll keep you on the payroll, trustin' in your ability to do the job. All I'll ask of you is an honest day's work for an honest day's pay."

She still stood there as if her boots had been glued to the floor.

Parker had only one more bullet to fire. "I won't rat you out, if that's your worry. I swear it."

Still trembling from head to toe, she struggled to speak, her slender throat working as if she were trying to swallow a golf ball. "I'm sorry about the falsehoods on my application. I don't usually lie. Maybe that's why I'm not very good at it. But now I just need to go."

Parker didn't have it in him to block her way any longer. Intimidating women wasn't high on his list of favorite things to do. As he stepped aside to let her pass, he pitched his voice low and said, "I don't know where you've been in your life, Anna. I don't know what's happened to you. But I can guarantee you one thing: You can trust me. The job will be waitin' for you if you change your mind. The next employer who checks out your references may not be as understandin'. You need to think about that."

She flashed him a look that nearly broke his heart, one filled with a hopeless yearning to trust that had been battered so badly it had lost its power to sway her. "Thanks."

It was all she said before she grabbed the doorknob, gave it a frantic twist, and rushed from the office. Parker didn't go after her. He had already frightened her enough.

Silence filled the room after she left. He recalled his entrance a few minutes earlier. He'd been mad enough to chew nails and spit out screws. Was it any wonder she'd been afraid he meant to strike her when he reached for the paperweight? *Damn it.* He wished he could give himself a swift kick in the ass.

She'd sought sanctuary here, and he'd driven her away with his penchant for the truth and only the truth. Sometimes people had no choice but to lie.

Parker stepped over to the window to watch her race to her rusted-out excuse for an automobile. When he glanced beneath the undercarriage, he saw a dark splotch, undeniable evidence that the Mazda was leaking oil. *Shit.* He felt like such a jerk. The three hundred bucks that he had advanced her yesterday would be gone in a blink if that car broke down.

Almost as if he'd spoken the thought out loud, she stopped before getting into the vehicle. After hesitating for a moment, she set her purse on the hood, fished deep, and came up with her wallet. *No, damn it, no.* But sure as rain was wet, she retraced her steps to the personnel door.

When Parker lost sight of her again, he pressed the heels of his hands against his eyes. He hadn't felt this ashamed of himself in years. When she knocked lightly, he swallowed hard, turned, and said, "Come in."

The door eased open. She stood on the threshold, looking like an impoverished waif in the grab-bag clothing and battered riding boots. She held a wad of money in one fist, her wallet in the other. "I forgot," she pushed out. "I can't accept an advance on wages that I won't ever earn."

Parker's eyes burned as he stared at her. "Just keep it," he whispered.

"No." She stepped over to his desk. "I may be a liar, Mr. Harrigan, but I'm not a thief."

After dropping the money on the blotter, she left again. Parker stared at the closed door, unable to move. He felt awful. He went to the window to watch her leave. He expected her to speed away. Instead, she folded her slender arms over the steering wheel and rested her head on the backs of her hands.

When several minutes passed and she still hadn't left, Parker got a lump in his throat that he couldn't swallow away. No question about it, he needed a serious attitude adjustment. Who'd elected him to be her judge and jury? He'd had it easy all his life—a great father, a tight-knit family, and unfailing support. The only time he'd ever gotten the snot beat out of him had been at a honky-tonk, when he'd had too much to drink and been pushed into a fight. He had no idea how it felt to be helpless and afraid, day in and day out, or how frightening it was to be on the run. He'd also never needed a job so desperately that he would have lied to get one.

Rainie couldn't drive. She was shaking too badly. Instead of keying the ignition to make her getaway, she just sat there, trembling and battling tears. She was inexpressibly grateful that Parker Harrigan had let her go, but she couldn't erase one of his warnings from her mind: Her next employer might not be as understanding when her references didn't check out. At least Parker had promised not to expose her. The thing was, could she trust him?

Rainie found it difficult, if not impossible, to trust another man. When she remembered how easily Peter had duped her, she felt like an imbecile. Oh, how excited she'd been when he first called, asking if she would accept an internship at Barrestol International. Barrestol, a Seattle-based company, had been at the top of Rainie's dream list of fabulous places to work when she finally got her degree. During her last quarter of studies before graduation, she had interviewed with one of the company's scouts, but despite her high GPA, she hadn't expected a job offer. Having someone from Barrestol offer her an internship had seemed too good to be true. *Hello.* When things seemed too good to be true, they usually were.

Parker Harrigan fell into that category. *I won't rat you out.* What was in it for him? That was the question. Recalling the speculative look in his eyes when he'd studied her the day before yesterday, Rainie had to wonder if his motives were honorable. As much as she needed a job, she wouldn't participate in any workplace hanky-panky to keep it.

Rainie's heart leaped when the passenger door of the Mazda suddenly opened and Parker swung onto the seat beside her. To her frightened eyes, he looked a yard wide at the shoulders. In the faded Wranglers and wash-worn work shirt, he also looked lean and muscular in a way that city-dwelling males usually didn't. He flashed one of those charming grins that never failed to jangle her nerves.

"Hi," was all he said.

"What do you want?" she asked.

"Nothin'." He winked at her and extended a hand. A small silver flask rested on his broad palm. "I've been watchin' you through the window, and I decided you might need a drink to settle your nerves."

"No, thanks."

"Whiskey," he informed her, "is a great sedative."

"I still have to drive home. The last thing I need is a DUI."

"A couple of belts won't raise your blood-alcohol level enough to get you in any trouble." He pushed the flask at her again. "Loosen up a little, Anna. You're runnin' on raw nerves. If there's anything I've learned in life, it's that I can never make smart decisions when I'm upset."

"I've already made my decision."

"To leave, you mean?" He uncapped the flask and took a gulp of the whiskey. As he swallowed, he rubbed the mouth of the container clean with the sleeve of his shirt. "That is an option, I reckon, but to be honest, I don't think it's the smartest choice you can make."

He offered the flask again, and this time Rainie accepted it. She took only a small sip of the liquor, but he was right: It warmed the cold places within her and made her feel calmer. She followed the first sip with a second and then returned the flask to him.

As the whiskey did its work, he began talking softly. "Judgin' by the condition of your car, I think you're in sore need of a regular paycheck." He angled a questioning look at her. "That isn't to say you can't find another job, but in my experience, it's always better to bank on a sure thing. I'm a sure thing."

"Are you?" The instant she posed the question, Rainie wondered if the liquor had loosened her tongue. "I know nothing about you, Mr. Harrigan."

"True, so let me tell you a few things about myself. First off, like I said earlier, if you're on the run from some bastard with a penchant for punchin' women, I'll support you in any way I can. I gave you my word that I won't rat you out, and my word is my honor." His mouth twisted into a self-deprecating smile. "I know it's a corny old sayin', and most people don't really mean it. But I'm a Harrigan."

"A Harrigan," she echoed. "Does that make you special somehow?"

"Not special, exactly. It's just that my dad is an old-fashioned man, and he's drilled the importance of honesty into me all my life. In his opinion, a man who doesn't stand behind his word isn't worth the powder it'd take to blow him to hell. That's one reason I kind of lost it for a few minutes when I discovered you'd lied on your application. In my family, lyin' isn't okay."

"So why are you so willing to forgive me for it?"

His gaze held hers for a long moment. "Because I think you're in a world of trouble and need a friend," he said quietly. "As much stock as I put in honesty and integrity, Anna, I'm not so sanctimonious that I blame someone for doin' what they must to survive. Sometimes that means lyin' on a job application so you can put food on the table."

"And that's it? You just want to help me out, no strings attached?"

His gaze went dark with emotions she couldn't name. He stared at her for so long that her skin started to prickle. "You've been to hell and back. Haven't you?"

Hell didn't describe where she'd been, but she resisted the urge to tell him that.

"You can count on me," he assured her. "Take all the time you need to think it over. Just know that the job is still yours if you want it. All I'll ask is that you give me a name to call you that you'll actually answer to."

Rainie couldn't remember not responding to the name Anna, but she supposed it was possible. It wasn't her real name, after all.

She didn't know what possessed her, but she heard herself say, "In my other life, my name was Rainie."

"Rainie." He said it slowly. Then he nodded. "It suits you. You don't look like an Anna."

He opened the car door and got out of the vehicle. Before walking away, he leaned down to say, "I hope you'll show up for work in the mornin'. Good bookkeepers don't grow on trees, and I'm in sore need of one."

Rainie tossed her purse down on the table and went immediately to pick up Thomas, who'd taken to staying in the house most of the time. He still felt painfully thin when she ran her hands over his body, but she was heartened by the sheen already returning to his fur.

"If I keep that job, I'll be able to buy you gourmet cat food," she whispered to him, "and all the expensive tuna you can eat."

Thomas meowed and licked her cheek with his rough tongue.

"I don't know what to do, little friend. I wish you could give me some advice."

But Thomas put forth no pearls of wisdom. Rainie carried him to the living room for a snuggle on the sofa. She didn't know why holding him lent her comfort. Maybe it was simply feeling his warmth against her.

"I should probably just pack up and leave town," she mused aloud. "But if I do that, I'll have no guarantee that he won't eventually recognize me on television and turn me in.

That means I'll need to change my name again, and a new name means a whole new set of identification. That will cost a bundle, and it'll take time. Stan would have to get me another birth certificate and passport. That could take weeks."

Thomas burrowed close and started to purr.

"On top of that, moving again will be expensive. Even in a low-rent district, the first and last months' rent and deposits add up. I'm already low on funds. I'm not sure how far the Mazda will make it without breaking down. How in the world can I afford to relocate?"

As though he sensed her distress, Thomas meowed softly.

"I could call Margaret or Janet for another loan, I suppose. But what if Peter has their phones tapped? If he suspects that I'm not dead, he'll be watching them, hoping I'll make contact."

After waffling back and forth between staying and running, Rainie finally decided to take a huge chance on Parker Harrigan. If he turned out to be a jerk, she'd be in no more trouble than she already was. If, by some miracle, he was actually all that he claimed to be, then she and Thomas could remain in Crystal Falls until she got back on her feet financially.

The following morning when Rainie showed up for work, the indoor arena was a hive of activity. Two men lunged horses in the riding area, and five other people, two males and three females, worked busily in the stalls, forking hay, shoveling manure into wheelbarrows, and rinsing out what looked like water troughs. Just as Rainie started to cross the arena, Parker emerged from a stall. He grinned, waved, and then held up a hand, signaling her to stay put. As he strode toward her, she couldn't help but notice how devastatingly attractive he was in his Wrangler jeans and Stetson. He walked with a lazy grace, his strides long, his lean hips moving with well-oiled precision. Even at a distance, his twinkling brown eyes and white-toothed grin had an impact on her. He was the kind of man who could make women lose their heads. Determined not to join their ranks, Rainie reminded herself that denim and chambray weren't her thing, no matter how handsome the man wearing them was.

"Mornin'," he said as he closed the distance between them. "I need to install a rear personnel door so you don't have to walk through this three-ring circus every mornin'."

"I'll learn the ins and outs."

He grasped her elbow to guide her around the horses. "Main thing is to remember that horses can spook if you walk up behind them without givin' 'em a heads-up. Also remember that they're big animals with four feet. You ever been dancin' and gotten your toes stomped on?"

Rainie suppressed a smile at the question. Was he real, this man? He acted as if the events of yesterday had never happened. The knot of tension in the pit of her stomach loosened slightly. "A couple of times."

"Well, it hurts a lot worse when it's a horse doin' the stompin'." He steered her clear of a yellow-brown horse with a black mane and tail that was trotting in circles. "So it's best to cut a wide circle around a prancin' equine until you know the animal."

"And once I know the animal?" She glanced up to see the glint of humor in his eyes. "How will that save my feet?"

"Because you'll recognize which horses are clumsy and which ones aren't. It takes a certain amount of agility to know where all four of your feet are at all times."

Rainie had never thought of it that way. "I suppose it must. I have enough trouble controlling only two."

He drew her to an abrupt stop to avoid a collision, then urged her forward at a faster clip to vacate the area. "Not to say that many of my horses are clumsy. I'd trust most of 'em to tap dance around a baby without touchin' a hair on its head. But I've got a couple with four left hooves."

"Which ones are they?"

He chuckled. "For now, consider all of them to be clumsy. I don't want you gettin' hurt."

"I'll avoid them. You really don't need to put in a rear door."

They reached the hallway that led to the office, and he released his hold on her arm and thrust out a hand. "Before you go, can I have your car keys, please?"

The knot in Rainie's stomach instantly returned. She searched his gaze, wondering if he'd seen her face on the news and wanted her keys so she'd be unable to escape before the police could arrive. "What do you want them for?"

"That Mazda is throwin' enough oil to settle the dust on a two-mile stretch of dirt road. You can't depend on a car without doin' some maintenance on it now and again."

"I can't afford to do any repairs on it right now."

The dimple in his lean cheek deepened to a long crease. "I had that figured."

"So the oil problem will have to wait."

He rubbed beside his nose and shifted his weight from one leg to the other. "Well, now, that's up for debate."

"It is?"

"Yes, ma'am. Here's my thinkin' on the subject. If you keep drivin' that Mazda in the shape it's in, you're gonna break down on your way to work, sure as rain is wet. When that happens, who you gonna call?" He thumbed his chest. "Yours truly, that's who. And chances are it'll be early in the mornin' when I'm back at the house, fixin' my breakfast. Not that I'd hold it against you. Don't think that. But I gotta tell you two things, the first bein' that I don't like missin' a meal, the second bein' that I'm a piss-poor mechanic. Not quite as bad at mechanics as I am at bookwork, but it's a close call. You know what that means?"

Rainie found herself struggling not to smile again. "No, but I'm sure you're going to tell me."

He nodded. "It means that I'll raise the hood, stare at the engine, kick dirt, and cuss a blue streak before I finally have the good sense to tow you to the ranch. By that time, we'll both have lost a good hour of work, and I'll be in a foul mood till lunch. I hate when a vehicle breaks down and I can't fix it. It's just not manly, you know? Any rancher worth his salt ought to be able to fix most anything." He paused to arch an inquiring eyebrow. "You with me so far?"

Rainie couldn't help it. She smiled. What was it about this man that made her want to laugh so often? "I think so."

"Good, because accordin' to my brother Clint, I'm almost as bad at towin' as I am at gettin' cars to start. He's got a harebrained idea that I should warn him before I stop." Devilment danced in his brown eyes. "I keep tellin' him that's what brake lights are for, but he insists that the length of a tow chain gives the person I'm towin' no time to react."

"I see."

"Yeah, me, too. But every time I tow somebody, I forget." He paused to smile at her again. She was beginning to suspect that he practiced that sheepish grin in front of a mirror. "Bottom line is, you don't want me towin' you to the ranch. It could get ugly."

"Where are you going with this, Mr. Harrigan?"

"Parker," he corrected, "and I'm gettin' to it. There's also the thing about your tires. All four of 'em are balder than onions. You noticed that?"

"I have, yes, but tires are expensive."

"Not around here, they aren't. I've got enough old tires in the shed to build a pyramid to rival Tutankhamen's."

"Why on earth do you keep old tires?"

"Well, for one thing, they aren't biodegradable. You can't dump 'em just any old place. For another, we always change our tires *before* they go totally bald, and I hate throwin' 'em away when they still have some tread on 'em. Seems wasteful, and I always think they may come in handy sometime in an emergency."

"And I'm an emergency?" she ventured.

"Not yet. That's my whole point, that you're gonna be one unless you give me your keys so the ranch mechanic can give your car a good goin'-over." He held up a hand to stop her from speaking. "Mac is on the payroll. He gets paid the same each month whether he works or not. Some days I keep him plenty busy, but the shop's slower than a whorehouse on Sunday right now. He's probably swillin' coffee and playin' solitaire on my dime. The way I see it, he'll be happier with somethin' to do, I'll be happier knowin' that your car's safe for you to drive, and you'll be happier, too."

"I will?"

"Yes, ma'am. Your car won't be throwin' oil, and you'll be able to put off buyin' tires for a few more months."

"I feel funny about taking a free set of tires."

"Why? They'll just sit out there and rot over time. Somebody may as well be gettin' some use out of 'em."

Rainie couldn't argue the point. She fished her keys from her purse and handed them over. He smiled and held her gaze for a moment. "Thank you."

The way Rainie saw it, she was the one who should be grateful. "For what?"

He winked at her. "For workin' up the courage to trust me just a little. You looked more than a little alarmed when I asked for your keys."

Rainie could think of no response to that. In truth, she had been alarmed.

"Mac will have your car ready to roll before your shift ends." He tossed the keys into the air and caught them with a swing of his hand. "He's good. He'll have that Mazda purrin' like a kitten."

"Can I at least pay for the oil and any parts he has to buy?"

"Sure. We'll work somethin' out."

As he walked away, Rainie made a mental note to find out how much the car repairs cost and deduct the total from her first paycheck. She refused to become any more indebted to Parker Harrigan than she already was.

Chapter Five

Twenty minutes later, Rainie was at Parker's desk, sorting through mounds of paperwork that had obviously been there for weeks, or possibly even months, judging by the layer of dust on some of the pages. She began the daunting task of bringing order to chaos by creating small piles, attempting to put the documents in alphabetical categories. But she soon had so many stacks that she ran out of space and couldn't remember which pile was for which letter. She needed a better system.

After thinking about it, she pulled all the file cabinets over to stand in a semicircle around his workstation. When she opened the top drawer of the first cabinet, she nearly groaned. He'd dumped even more loose papers inside it—hundreds of them. How on earth did the man do business like this? The next drawer down was in just as big a mess. How long had he been throwing receipts and purchase orders into these cabinets? For years, she guessed.

And he expected her to sort through all of it.

Rainie reminded herself that he was paying her handsomely for her trouble. What she needed was a box. Strike that. She needed at least three. Then she could empty the file cabinets and start over. In the bottom pullout of one cabinet she found unopened containers of hanging files and folders, which nearly made her laugh. Parker had had good intentions at some point.

Out in the hallway, Rainie had glimpsed several closed doors. Venturing forth, she opened three of them to investigate, discovering grain, tack, and medicine rooms. On the fourth try, she found what she sought: a storage area filled with boxes. She found three empty containers that were large enough to suit the purpose. Armed for battle, she returned to the office to make war on Parker's paperwork. The first skirmish was to remove everything from the file drawers so she could use the vacated space to categorize his records. Later, when she had accomplished some semblance of order, she would file the receipts and invoices under company headings, putting everything at her fingertips.

Within minutes, she grew so absorbed in her task that she lost track of time. She'd filed one-third of the loose papers that she'd dumped into one of the boxes when a thump came at the door. When she went to investigate, Parker pushed into the room, his arms laden with take-out cartons.

"Lunchtime," he informed her.

"Oh!" Rainie brushed her palms clean on her skirt. Though she'd had the office to herself for only a few hours, his sudden presence felt intrusive. She wished he'd just go away and leave her alone. "I brought a sack lunch. Normally I eat while I work."

"Not around here, you won't. You have an hour and a half designated for breaks each day, and I expect you to use every second. You can eat, take a walk, or play games on the computer. I don't care how you spend your free time, but I'm a firm believer in takin' breaks. You can keep your sack lunch in the fridge and have it for dinner." He sauntered toward her desk. "You like Chinese, don't you?"

For two years, Rainie had barely been able to breathe without asking Peter's permission, so now she resented anyone who tried to boss her around. It seemed to her that she should be able to spend her breaks working if she wished. Unfortunately, she hadn't yet recovered enough from the brutality of her marriage to argue the point. "I, um . . . Chinese is all right, I guess."

"All *right*?" He posed the question with feigned amazement as he set the cartons on her desk blotter. "Darlin', that's damned near a sacrilege. I've got pork and chicken chow mein, Szechuan beef, Mandarin beef, chicken fried rice, beef and broccoli, and snow peas with water chestnuts. Surely, with a selection like that, there's somethin' in there that you think is better than just all right."

Rainie hadn't really looked at the cartons until now. He'd ordered enough to feed an entire army. "Who all's coming?"

"You, me, and two forks." He started toward the coffee room but stopped dead when he came to the boxes, now filled with the contents of his file cabinets. "Holy hell, how will I ever find anything?" When he saw the look on her face, he chuckled. "Just kiddin'. You've taken on quite a chore."

In Rainie's opinion, that was putting it mildly, but she refrained from saying so. Speaking her mind was yet another freedom she'd been denied during her time with Peter.

Boots thumping on the hardwood floor, Parker returned a moment later with a roll of paper towels, two plates, and a fork for each of them. It still amazed her how he seemed to dominate a room. Hooking a toe under the pedestal of his chair, he rolled it to her desk.

"Don't be shy," he urged as he arranged the plates. "I order takeout for lunch a lot, and I'll feel uncomfortable eatin' if you don't join me."

Rainie reluctantly sat down across from him. He tore off two sections of paper towel and thrust one at her. She placed it on her lap as she watched him pile food on his plate. When he realized she was staring, he paused with his fork poked into a carton to give her a questioning look.

"I'm sorry," she said. "It's just . . . well, such a lot of food."

He went back to serving himself. "I work hard. It takes a lot of calories to keep my weight up. I start my day with a half pound of bacon, three eggs, a small bag of hash browns, and three pieces of toast with butter and jelly. For morning break, I have two peanut-butter-and-jelly sandwiches. By noon, I'm starving."

"You're not serious."

"I burn it off." He pushed a couple of the cartons toward her. "You'd better dish up before it's all gone."

Rainie giggled, an involuntary sound that burst forth and became a muffled snort when she tried to stifle it.

Parker glanced up at her again. "You got a problem with how I eat?"

"No!" she rushed to assure him. "No, no, not at all. I just can't believe you can consume so much and not gain weight. I'd be as big as a house."

He gave her a measuring look. "No offense intended, but you could stand to put on a couple of pounds."

"I've lost some weight recently." Rainie realized what she'd just said and wanted to call back the words. Issuing him an engraved invitation to ask questions about her personal life was not in her game plan.

Instead of pressing her for more information, he surprised her by crossing himself and silently blessing his meal. Then, between bites of food, he asked, "So how's it goin' in here? You wantin' to quit yet?"

He was paying her too well for her to consider quitting, but that seemed an inappropriate thing to say. "I've made some headway." She glanced at the mess she had unearthed. "It's going to take me a while to get things organized, though."

"No worries. Rome wasn't built in a day. I wish I could tell you that I'll clean up my act, but chances are, I won't. I keep a tidy underwear drawer, I never leave dishes in the sink, and I can't stand a messy house. That's about as good as it gets."

Rainie had no desire to hear about his underwear drawer. Striving to keep him focused on the business at hand, she replied, "My initial plan is to get all the paperwork in alphabetical order. When that's done, I'll create company folders so everything will be at my fingertips when you need it. But it is going to be time-consuming."

"I'm not settin' any deadlines." He tucked back into his meal with unabashed enthusiasm. The muscles along his jaw bunched each time he chewed. "On a ranch, you learn that deadlines only frustrate you. Just when you think you have everything planned out for the day, God, the weather, or Murphy's Law blows your schedule all to hell."

A brief silence fell, and Rainie dreaded what might come next. This morning when she'd arrived, he had acted as if nothing untoward had occurred yesterday, but she would be foolish to believe that he intended to let it go at that. He was surely curious about her past, and sooner or later, he'd start pressing her for answers. She braced herself for a probing question, or another of those penetrating looks that made her feel as easy to read as large print.

But once again, Parker Harrigan surprised her. Gesturing with his fork, he said, "A rancher's philosophy is, 'What doesn't get done today will wait till tomorrow.' " His dimple flashed in a slow grin that tipped up one corner of his firm lips. "You'll hear different versions of it, of course. My foreman, Toby, will say, 'Ain't a lick of work I ever seen that'll take off runnin' if I don't find time to git to it.' My dad is fond of sayin' that a chore is like a faithful woman: She'll always wait for you." After taking another bite of Mandarin beef and pausing to chew and swallow, he added, "I'm not a procrastinator, don't get me wrong, and I don't suffer laziness in any of my employees. But by the same token, I've also learned to be laid-back. If I weren't, I'd go nuts. Every blessed mornin', I plan the day and hold a crew meetin' to get everybody lined out. Some days, the chores get done like clockwork. Other days, shit happens, and nothin' on the work roster gets finished. Say a horse gets sick. Everything else takes a second seat. Everything but the other horses, that is. You learn, in short order, to get the urgent stuff done and do the rest as time allows."

"Being an office employee, I'm sure that philosophy will never apply to me," she inserted.

"Maybe not," he agreed, "but then again, maybe so. If I have an emergency out there"—he inclined his head to indicate the arena area—"I may interrupt your workday by sendin' you to town for horse medicine or some kind of paraphernalia I need to treat an animal. On a ranch, you never know from one minute to the next what might happen. About a month ago, Montana, one of my prize studs, got a hornet up his nose and went berserk. The walls of those stalls are reinforced nine ways to hell, but he managed to put a rear hoof through the wall anyway, and got his leg stuck up to the hock. Talk about a mess; that was it. I damned near lost a fine animal in that go-'round. By the time I got his leg free, he'd cut himself and was bleedin' bad. My vet—he's also my brother-in-law—was out in the field and took forty-five minutes to get here. Trust me when I say everybody within a mile was at a dead run, doin' whatever needed doin' to save my horse." He forked some more food into his mouth and made short work of swallowing it. "Like I said when I hired you, the horses come first. The paperwork won't up and die on us if you don't tend to it for a day. An injured stud or a foal with pneumonia won't be so patient."

Rainie had never considered all the mishaps that could befall horses. Now it was easier for her to understand why this man's office was in such turmoil.

"It sounds like a demanding line of work. Were you and your siblings born into the business?"

"We teethed on saddle leather." He poked a big piece of broccoli in his mouth. "Not really, of course. It's only a sayin'. But if any kids ever came close to teethin' on leather, we did. Right after Clint was born, our mom insisted that Dad put new flooring and walls in one of the stalls to create a playpen."

"A *what*?" Rainie had forgotten all about her earlier tension. "She put her baby in a horse stall?"

"By the time Dad got done with it, it was a pretty fancy horse stall. I know it sounds strange, but it wasn't really. They converted a birthin' stall, and they're quite large. Mom liked to work in the stable with my father, and back then, they couldn't afford a babysitter, so a confinin' area for us kids was the only solution. Less than two years after Clint was born, Quincy came along. I came a year later, Zachary two years after me. Life can't end for a woman just because she has four little boys. It was kind of cool, actually. We had a big space to play in, and she kept tons of toys in there to keep us entertained. When one of us cried, no tellin' who'd come, sometimes my mom, sometimes Dad, and sometimes one of the hired hands. Hooter—he's Clint's foreman now—used to take his breaks in there with us. He got me hooked on chocolate Hostess Cup Cakes—those ones with the cream centers? I still love 'em to this day. And Jerome—he's Samantha's foreman now—got me hooked on his Blue Buzzard Ranch Chili. Do you think he'll give me the recipe, though? Hell, no. He's gonna take that recipe with him to the grave."

Rainie was quickly coming to realize that Parker loved to talk. He also had a tendency to flit from one subject to another. But she was so fascinated by his stories that she didn't mind. Her initial uneasiness began to dissipate. If he intended to grill her about her past, he was taking his own sweet time in getting around to it.

"You gonna eat?" he suddenly asked. "The food will get cold."

"Oh." Rainie dished herself up a small portion of the chicken fried rice and a few snow peas. "Mmm," she murmured appreciatively after taking a bite. "So, Hooter and Jerome have been with your family for a long time?"

"Long before Clint was a twinkle in my father's eye. In fact, all of my dad's original crew is still with us, some still workin' at his place, some workin' for us kids. When each of us branched out on our own, we inherited one of his most trusted hired hands as a foreman. He wanted us to stand on our own two feet, but he didn't want us to be without an adviser. I got Toby, one of the best horsemen you'll ever encounter. He's the fellow you saw that first day, comin' up to the house to tell me you had arrived."

Rainie recalled the paunchy, slow-moving man she'd seen. She took a bite of chicken fried rice. "He's still able to work with horses?"

"Don't let his looks deceive you. The old codger can move like greased lightnin' when the notion strikes him. He's like a second father to me." He flashed her one of those heart-stopping grins. "That's fittin', I guess. He's my godfather. When I was a kid, he made me recite my catechism while we did stable chores together. I learned the Apostles' Creed at the business end of a pitchfork."

"It must be nice to have so many people in your life that you've known since childhood."

"It is nice," he agreed. "I sort of take it for granted, though. It's how I grew up. My dad started out poorer than a church mouse, with only this spread as an asset. He was dumber than a rope about quarter horses and had to count on the knowledge of others to get his start. Later, when he became successful, he never forgot the people who'd helped him get there. He treats 'em like family, and in turn, they're as loyal as family. If this place went tits-up tomorrow, Toby would stand by me to the end."

Having experience with only the corporate world, Rainie was more accustomed to a dog-eat-dog mentality. "I can't imagine."

"Around here, it's the norm," he said with a laugh. "Not to say I don't have new employees who'd leave in a blink. But mostly I try to hire people I think will stay on, and then it becomes my aim to make it so good for them here that they'll never consider quittin'."

Rainie remembered his refusal to pay her less than what he felt was fair.

"Bein' a good boss is one of the things that my dad drilled into all of us. 'When the clover's high, share the pink,' he says. And he's not just blowin' smoke. Right after I got off on my own, I felt rich, havin' the workin' capital he gave me in my bank account. And trust me when I say spendin' it wisely didn't come naturally to me. That was somethin' I had to learn. First crack out of the bag, I bought myself a brand-new Ford pickup, tricked out like you wouldn't believe. I was so damned proud of that truck. When my dad saw it, the first thing he asked me was, 'When did you last give your hired hands a raise?' Truth was, I hadn't given anyone a raise yet, not even Toby. Dad let me know in no uncertain terms that takin' care of my employees came first. New rigs and luxuries for me always had to come second. I felt guilty every time I looked at that damned truck until I was able to give Toby and all the others an increase in wages."

"You're very fond of him, aren't you? Your father, I mean."

Cheek bulging, he nodded. "More than fond of him. My dad is—" He broke off and wiped his mouth with the paper towel. "Well, he's indescribable, one of the best men I've ever known." Sighing with satisfaction, he tossed the napkin on his plate and rocked back on the chair. "Enough about me. I've talked your ear off. What's your father like?"

Here they came, the personal questions she'd been dreading. Only he'd caught her off guard, and Rainie couldn't think how to dodge the query. She decided that giving him tidbits of information would do no real harm. "My father passed away when I was seventeen."

His expression went suddenly solemn. "Ouch. That's mighty young to be losin' your dad. It must have been really hard on your mom."

"She was no longer with us when he died. We lost her to ovarian cancer when I was twelve."

"So you were left all alone at seventeen?" His dark eyes filled with appalled incredulity. "Shit. That must have been rough."

Most people tried to console Rainie with platitudes when they heard about her parents' deaths, but Parker said nothing more. Instead he stared at the desktop as if he couldn't conceive what it must have been like for her. His silence touched Rainie in a way that artfully phrased condolences never had.

"It was lonely," she heard herself say. "It still is. After my mom died, my father became my whole world. Though he loved me and tried to go on because of me, I don't think he ever got over losing her. They were—" She broke off. Her parents' relationship was difficult to describe. "I don't know. What they had was special."

"In other words, they were truly in love," he supplied softly.

Rainie gave him a questioning look. It struck her as an odd thing for a rough and rugged man like Parker Harrigan to say.

"It was the same for my folks," he explained with a smile. "Nowadays, a lot of people think all that crap is only for storybooks, but even though I was young, I can still remember how it felt in a room when my mom and dad were together. It took him years to get over her death."

"Daddy never got over losing my mother. I can't remember now when he started drinking, only that one day I realized he was drinking way too much. The alcohol eventually destroyed his health. The last thing he said to me as he lay dying was that he was sorry." It occurred to Rainie that she was sharing more than tidbits of information with Parker Harrigan, but somehow she couldn't stop the words from coming. "He was in such pain that I was relieved when it was over, but at the same time, I wished he wouldn't leave me."

He nodded. "When we lose a loved one, our feelin's can get as tangled as line wire. Who'd you live with after he died?"

"I was in my senior year of high school, and he had enough left in the bank to arrange for the housekeeper to stay with me until I graduated and the house could be sold. The proceeds from the sale went into a trust fund to cover my college education, and I began my freshman year the following September." Rainie fiddled nervously with a button on her blouse. "I actually do have an undergraduate degree in accounting. That much wasn't a lie."

"As long as you can do the work, I don't give a rat's ass about the degree. Why couldn't you live with someone in the family after he died? Surely you had an aunt or uncle or grandparents."

"My mom was an orphan and grew up in foster homes. My father cut ties with all of his relatives before I was born. I don't know for sure, but I think his family disapproved of my mother. Daddy would never talk about them. He just looked angry when I asked questions. So after he died, I had nobody."

Rainie's throat went tight with the admission. She pretended interest in her meal, but her appetite had vanished. Looking back on those years immediately following her father's death, she wondered if she ever would have fallen for Peter if she hadn't felt so horribly alone.

"It's hard for me to imagine havin' no one," Parker observed. "I don't know my mom's side of the family very well, but my dad's side makes up for the lack. I've got uncles and cousins out the yang."

"I tried to find my grandparents after Daddy passed away, but none of my letters of inquiry were ever answered. I can only assume they're dead—or maybe they just don't care to meet me."

"They might be dead, I reckon." He pushed erect and collected his eating utensils. As he strode back to the coffee room, he said over his shoulder, "Seems more likely to me that they never got your letters, though. You're only twenty-five. They're probably not that old."

Rainie listened as he rinsed his plate and fork. When he returned, he paused by the desk to gaze down at her for a moment. "You should try to find them again."

The time for that was past. Rainie couldn't even telephone her best friends, let alone risk trying to contact long-lost relatives. Lorraina Hall Danning was dead.

And she had to remain dead.

As Rainie settled into a work routine at the ranch, lunch hours with Parker became commonplace. One day it would be hot pizza, the next take-out Italian or Texas barbecue. Parker paid extra for the food to be delivered because the ranch was so far from town. He always ordered enough for Rainie to join him. At first, she protested. Then she offered to pay for her share. His response was that she could make it up to him with overtime. Only whenever he caught her in the office after hours, he reminded her of the rancher's philosophy: What didn't get done today would wait until tomorrow.

Rainie was guarded during their mealtime conversations. Parker, on the other hand, seemed to say whatever crossed his mind. He talked almost nonstop, skipping from one subject to another, and though she said very little, silences were rare. Once, when he realized he had been droning on and on without pause for several minutes, he laughed and said, "Sorry. It can go two ways with ranchers who spend most of their time with animals. We're either the silent type, or our tongues are tied in the middle and loose at both ends. I love my horses. Don't get me wrong. I never feel lonesome when I'm with them. But when a human ear is available, I'm a motormouth."

Rainie didn't mind. At home, she had only Thomas for company, and the cat wasn't a great conversationalist. Listening to Parker's ramblings every day at noon was something she began to enjoy. When he wasn't in the office, which was most of the time, she played music on her computer while she worked, but the moment he showed up, she muted the speakers so she could enjoy his stories, which ranged from tales of his childhood to present-day information about his family members, whom she hadn't yet met.

"You never say much," he noted one afternoon. "Is that because I bore you, or are you just shy about speakin' your mind?"

"You don't bore me," Rainie replied. "I'm just not much of a talker, I guess."

He seemed satisfied with her answer, and Rainie thought that was the end of it.

Only for Parker, that wasn't the end of it. It seemed to him that she often bit her tongue to keep from contradicting him. That bothered him. It bothered him immensely. He came from a boisterous, brutally honest, and fun-loving family that enjoyed a good argument. Sometimes someone would say something inflammatory just to stir the shit and get a heated debate started. Parker had a tendency to do the same when he was trying to make up his mind about his stance on an issue. To his way of thinking, there was no better way to sort his thoughts on a subject than to hear someone else's opinion, and the easiest way to get diverse feedback was to get people riled up. His little sister, Samantha, never hesitated to state her opinions. If Parker said something to irk her, she thought nothing of standing toe-to-toe with him and yelling to get her point across. It was the Harrigan way. Maybe his family was dysfunctional, but Parker didn't think so. He always came away from family get-togethers feeling good, and people in dysfunctional relationships usually didn't.

Parker worried about Rainie. It couldn't be healthy for her, emotionally or physically, to hold everything in all the time. It also troubled him to think that her reticence might be due to fear of him. Each day after lunch, he pondered the expressions that he'd seen flicker across her pretty face during the meal. At times, when he brought up a controversial subject, her cheeks went pink with what he felt certain might be anger, but she'd never once challenged him. What was she afraid of, anyway, that he'd cloud up and rain all over her for thinking differently than he did?

One day at lunch, Parker deliberately brought up a subject that he thought would piss her off. He knew it was perverse of him, but he had to see what her reaction would be. "So how do you feel about women who dress provocatively and then scream to high heaven when they get raped?"

She froze at the question with a French fry caught between her front teeth. Damn, she had beautiful eyes. Sometimes when Parker looked into those hazel depths, he found it difficult to look away.

"Way I see it," he went on, "if you walk around in public

half-dressed, you have to know some nutcase might go for the bait."

Her eyes went sparkly with anger. Color rushed to her cheeks. But instead of saying anything, she plucked the French fry from her mouth and pushed the end of it around in the ketchup on her plate. If Parker's sister had been present, the air would have been turning blue. Samantha got bent out of shape fast when this particular subject came up. She maintained that women had an inalienable right to dress however they pleased. Men went bare chested in public, and no one criticized them or felt they were asking for trouble. *Double standard,* she'd be saying, and in truth, Parker agreed. The sex offenders out there would continue to prey upon women no matter how they dressed.

All he wanted from Rainie was some sort of reaction. He didn't get one—unless he counted the fact that she stopped eating and went to the coffee room to wash her plate and fork. He stared at his own unfinished meal and realized that his appetite was ruined, too. Even worse, he had a sick feeling in the pit of his stomach. She was afraid of him. He could circle it however he wanted, trying to come up with another explanation, but he kept returning to those dark shadows in her eyes. She had plenty to say, but she hid behind silence because that felt safe.

He remembered how he'd once drawn similarities between Rainie and the mistreated little filly he'd purchased at auction a few years ago. Parker had overcome the filly's fear of him by confining her in a small pen and constantly pushing her into a corner where she couldn't escape his touch. Eventually she'd come to understand that he wouldn't hurt her, no matter what. Sadly, Rainie's concerns about Parker couldn't be so easily addressed. By remaining silent, she could avoid having words with him, and as long as she continued to do that, she would never come to understand that he wouldn't jump all over her for disagreeing with him.

The only solution Parker could think of was to goad her until she got so pissed off that she forgot to keep her mouth shut. He had a feeling it would take a lot of goading.

Rainie wasn't sure when it happened—or why—but she began to notice a change in Parker's manner during lunch hour. Instead of telling her stories about his family, childhood, horses, or employees, he had developed a penchant for ranting about politics or religion. Some of his opinions were so outrageous and, in Rainie's opinion, stupid that it was all she could do not to speak her mind. But each time she almost worked up the nerve to contradict him, caution prevailed. Arguing with Peter had been a surefire way to get her mouth slapped—or worse. Though Rainie no longer felt quite as wary around Parker as she had at first, she still wasn't relaxed enough with him to push her luck.

Unfortunately, her reticence only seemed to encourage him. About a month after she'd gone to work for him, he entered the office at lunchtime in a huff. Rainie knew before he opened his mouth that he was in rant mode again. In the beginning, she'd found herself liking the man, but now he was fast losing ground in her estimation.

After tossing a pizza box onto her desk and sending his Stetson sailing to land with a plop on the file cabinet behind her, he scooped a hand through his black hair, shot her a quarrelsome look, and said, "I'm so sick to death of politicians who vote for tax hikes that I could spit!"

Rainie sat back and clasped her hands on her lap. "Has there been a tax increase?"

"Not yet, but mark my words, if those damned bleedin'-heart politicians get their way, there soon will be." He jerked open the pizza box, helped himself to a wedge, and sat down across from her, twirling his finger in a string of melted cheese that dangled from the crust. "I'm tired of workin' my ass off, only to fork over half of my gross. And for what? So some lazy, good-for-nothin' bum can draw welfare while he lounges in a recliner to watch sports on a big-screen television and swill a six-pack of beer every night? I say cut all the stupid gimme programs and put the bastards back to work."

Rainie's stomach knotted. She didn't believe in giving the able-bodied a free ride, either, and she knew that a lot of welfare recipients abused the system, but she also felt very strongly that a lot of people truly needed the assistance.

"Last week at the supermarket, I got in line behind this pregnant woman who was about ready to pop. She already had three little kids, the oldest one about five. You could tell by lookin' at her that she'd never done an honest day's work in her entire life, and guess what?"

"What?" Rainie asked.

"She got all the food for free!" He thumped his chest with a rigid forefinger. "I'm payin' for that bull hockey to happen. Reality check: If you already have three kids and then get knocked up with a fourth, you'd better be willin' to support 'em. Instead, I'm payin' the tab. And even worse, they'd like to raise my taxes even more. I'm fed up, I'm tellin' you. Let her do it the hard way. That's what the rest of us do."

Rainie clenched her teeth and fixed her gaze on the pizza box. The red lettering blurred and swam.

"I say we should force her to get her tubes tied. That'd fix her wagon. No more poppin' out babies to stay on the dole. Next time she goes lookin' for a handout, have 'em tell her to get a job."

"What about the children?" Rainie couldn't resist asking.

"What about 'em? I didn't take 'em on to raise. They're her problem."

This time, his views were so contrary to Rainie's own that she couldn't keep her mouth shut. "How can you sit there, stuffing your face with pizza, and say such a thing?"

He flashed her a startled look.

"You know nothing about that woman. Maybe she was married to a jerk, and she finally worked up the courage to kick him out. What would you have her do, stay in the relationship, allowing him to beat on her and the kids? And how's she supposed to work if she's in her final month of pregnancy? If she has no education, it's not as if she can get a desk job. More than likely, she'd end up on her feet ten hours a day, and then have to go home to take care of her children. I'd like to see you try to do that at eight months along."

He pocketed a bite of food in his cheek. "I'll be damned. You *do* have an opinion or two floatin' around up there."

Rainie was suddenly so angry she was shaking. "I have more than a couple of opinions, Mr. Harrigan, and at the moment, one of them isn't very flattering to you."

He rocked back on the chair, swallowed his food, and grinned. "Really?"

"Really," she affirmed. "There's only one right way to think: the Parker Harrigan way. You're opinionated and narrow-minded. If you had your way, the rich would just get richer while the sick, helpless, and disadvantaged starved in the streets."

"Finally the lady speaks. Go on, darlin'. Sounds to me like you're on a roll. Let me have it with both barrels."

It was Rainie's turn to be startled. He'd pushed her into a quarrel, and now he looked as satisfied as a fat cat with a bowl of cream. It took a moment, but eventually it sank in that she'd been had. He'd deliberately prodded her into an outburst.

"You've been baiting me," she said, the accusation laced with both incredulity and certainty.

"I wouldn't put it that way, exactly."

"How would you put it?" Her voice had gone shrill. Rainie struggled to control her temper, but that smirk on his face made her want to hit him. "Answer me. How, exactly, would you put it?"

"It was more a case of pushin' your buttons. And I have to tell you, I was beginnin' to think I'd never push the right one. It's not good to hold everything in the way you do, honey. You're gonna get an ulcer."

"Was that tube-tying comment only a jab, then?"

"That was a good one, wasn't it?"

Rainie stood up so fast she got dizzy. Once her head cleared, she couldn't recall what she'd intended to do.

"I'd say I'm sorry, but it'd be a lie," he told her. His grin slipped away to be replaced by a solemn, thoughtful expression. "I don't know what that bastard did to you, honey, but you can't let him control you for the rest of your life. The first time I ever spoke to you on the phone, you were so sassy I almost cut the conversation short. I was afraid you'd be the type to snipe at me over every little thing."

"So why didn't you hang up?"

"Because I liked your spunk and decided to at least meet with you. Was I ever in for a surprise. I expected a sassy feminist, and instead Minnie Mouse with a nervous disorder showed up on my doorstep."

Rainie felt as if he'd slugged her. A burning sensation washed over her eyes. "Are you finished?"

"Not quite." He pushed erect to stand facing her. "You can be mad at me if you want. But I think the *real* Rainie is the one who talked to me on the phone. She felt safe when it wasn't face-to-face. She sounded smart, confident, and more than capable of standin' up for herself. She's the lady I want workin' for me."

Rainie spun on her heel to collect her purse. "If you want smart, confident, and sassy, Mr. Harrigan, hire someone else."

"I don't want someone else. I want you. The real you, that is."

He said it so softly that she turned to look at him. When their gazes met, he didn't try to charm her out of her anger with one of his grins. He just looked deeply into her eyes.

"I'm sorry for pushin' your buttons. I just . . ." He smoothed a hand over his hair. "I could tell you got upset over things I said sometimes, but you never popped back at me. I don't want it to be that way. I'd much rather have you set me straight when you think I'm wrong."

"That isn't my job," she replied.

"No," he agreed, "but it *is* your right."

Chapter Six

That evening, Rainie repeatedly went over her lunchtime conversation with Parker. He felt it was her *right* to set him straight when she felt he was wrong? She couldn't believe he'd been baiting her for days, attempting to get a rise out of her. He *wanted* her to argue with him? That was so contradictory to everything she'd come to accept during her marriage that it blew her mind. What kind of boss invited one of his employees to be insubordinate? For that matter, what kind of a man preferred sassiness in a woman to submissiveness?

Rainie was so disturbed by this revelation that she went on a kitchen cleaning spree, even though nothing was really dirty. The physical exertion made her feel no better. As she polished the toaster and saw her distorted image in the spotless chrome, she shoved the appliance away and covered her eyes with the heels of her hands. A burning ache took up residence in her chest. When it grew in intensity, she realized the pain stemmed from a suppressed need to cry. Only she didn't know *why* she wanted to cry, and she wasn't about to sit around bawling for no good reason.

Thoughts of her father kept popping into her mind. After she finished cleaning the stove and started on an upper cupboard, a specific memory flashed into her mind. Shortly before his death, her dad had been sitting at the kitchen table, and she'd slapped down a computer printout in front of him.

"See, Daddy," she'd said triumphantly. "You're *wrong*. The self-service gasoline law was never passed in Oregon. It was on the ballot but it was defeated. You still can't pump your own fuel there."

Her father had put on his glasses to read the information and then looked up at her. He'd been sick even then, but Rainie had blamed his pallor on the drinking, never dreaming that he might be gravely ill or that their time together was almost over.

"I'll be darned," he'd said softly.

She'd laughed at his amazed expression. "Even Marcus Hall, software genius of the twentieth century, can be mistaken occasionally." Licking an index finger, she'd made an imaginary mark in the air. "I am now the trivia expert of the family."

"You're a sassy little whippersnapper. That's what you are," he'd told her with an affectionate smile. Then his expression had turned suddenly somber. "Don't ever lose that trait. Promise me that you won't. I need to know you'll be okay when I'm no longer around."

Suddenly afraid, Rainie had whispered, "Daddy, don't talk that way. You're going to be around for a long, long time."

Looking at her sadly, he'd almost said something, but then seemed to think better of it. "Just promise me, okay? If something happens to me, I need to know you'll roll with the punches and come out swinging."

With a forced laugh, Rainie had bounced around the kitchen, pretending to box with an invisible opponent. "Like that?"

Her dad had chuckled, dispelling the fear that he'd sent spiraling through her only moments earlier. "Exactly like that." Still grinning, he'd turned in the chair, caught her wrist, and pulled her toward him. "Come sit on my knee a minute." As she complied, he wrapped his arms around her waist. "My goodness, my little girl is all grown-up. You weigh a ton."

"*Daddy!* You aren't supposed to tell girls that they weigh too much."

"I don't think you weigh too much. You're perfect in every way." He tightened his arms around her. "Beautiful, smart, and assertive, a fabulous combination. You'll never encounter the glass ceiling, sweetheart. You'll wow them with your looks, think circles around them, and have their jobs before they know what hit them."

Rainie knew she was smart. It had always been easy for her to excel in her studies. But she was a little worried about the competition she might encounter in a university environment where all the best students came together and set a higher standard. "I'm not *that* smart, Daddy."

"You certainly are," he retorted. "But what matters more is that you're gutsy. You'll never be intimidated by a two-thousand-dollar suit."

"Of course not. The suit doesn't make the man."

"Exactly right, and there's nothing wrong with a woman having some starch in her spine. It'll serve you well in both your personal and professional lives." He'd reached up to tousle her hair. "I'm so proud of you, honey. You remember that. Okay? You're becoming everything I ever dreamed you'd be."

As the scene faded from her mind, Rainie realized that she stood frozen on the step stool, her tear-filled gaze fixed on the little Umbrella Girl skipping in the rain on a container of Morton salt. A sob built in her chest and suddenly erupted from her throat. Body convulsing with the violence of her grief, she barely managed to climb down off the stool without falling. She dropped the salt container, and granules spewed from the partially opened spout in a fan of white over the worn linoleum. On legs that had gone rubbery, she went to the table, sank onto a chair, and buried her face in her folded arms.

"Oh, Daddy," she cried brokenly. "You wouldn't be proud of me now. I didn't roll with the punches and come out swinging. I broke my promise to you."

Rainie wept until her chest felt hollow and she had no more tears to shed. When she finally lifted her head, the silence in her small house seemed to shout at her. Her gaze jerked to the toaster, which had become the bane of her existence, because she couldn't bear to see her distorted reflection in the chrome. She looked at the new dead bolt that she'd installed on her back door. She glanced at Thomas's cat door, which she always left open for him, but not without some trepidation when she retired at night. Then her thoughts trailed to her bedtime rituals: Before she could shower, she had to wedge a chair under the doorknob. Before she could sleep, she had to make sure the window was locked. And when she finally drifted off, she slept restively, listening for strange noises even in her dreams.

Parker was right. On the telephone with him, she'd felt brave, but when she'd stood face-to-face with him, she'd lost her courage and behaved like a mouse. She resented the fact that he'd played head games with her. In fact, it made her so angry that she trembled. But it had also forced her to see herself clearly. What had happened to the girl who'd made her father so proud? When had she become a frightened mouse instead of a young lioness, eager to take on the world?

Peter. It always came back to him. Trusting in him had been the worst mistake of her life, and marrying him had been sheer insanity. It had taken him a year and a half to beat her down, but in the end, he had achieved his goal. When she'd finally found a way to get away from him, she'd been a shivery mass of raw nerves, so terrified he might catch her that she could scarcely breathe.

Looking back, Rainie couldn't pinpoint the moment when he'd finally broken her. Had it been the night she'd wrinkled her nose at the tartness of his prize merlot? Or had it been the time she'd gotten her days mixed up and served him cordon bleu for dinner instead of his customary Thursday-night filet mignon? Rainie couldn't recall the details of that beating. Peter had flown into so many rages that many of the events had all blurred together.

Only two facts were clear in her mind: She had emerged from the relationship a changed person, and she didn't like what she had become. Sadly, she didn't know how to fix herself. She had escaped from Peter physically, but emotionally, she was still his prisoner.

Somehow she had to rectify that. Otherwise, no matter how long or how far she ran, Peter would still control her life.

After a great deal of soul-searching, Parker decided that he was definitely his father's son. If the old man had hired someone like Rainie Pritchard, her uneasiness would have bothered him like a sore tooth, and he would have been unable to leave it alone. Parker admired his dad and wanted to be exactly like him in many ways, but—and it was a big *but*—he wasn't completely blind to the fact that Frank Harrigan had faults. One of the most glaring was his inability to back off when his friendly, straightforward personality overwhelmed another person. With someone shy and timid like Rainie, Frank would have kept pushing to gain her trust, and that was precisely what Parker had done. *Push, push, push.* He wished now that he'd had the good sense to let it ride. If she wanted to bottle up her emotions, that was her choice. He didn't think it was healthy, but what he thought didn't matter.

Always up at five and in the stable by a quarter of six, Parker had a well-rehearsed apology memorized by the time Rainie showed up for work at eight. After escorting her to the office, he stepped inside and closed the door to afford them some privacy. At this time of morning, the hallway got heavy traffic, and he didn't want another employee to overhear what he was about to say.

"Rainie," he began, "I had a lot of time to think last night, and I want to apologize for baitin' you with all the political and religious nonsense. I shouldn't have—"

"Don't." She slapped her purse down on her desk and whirled to face him, her cheeks high with color, her hazel eyes sparkling, with anger or tears, he wasn't certain. "You were right. I do act like a mouse."

Parker's heart twisted at the hurt in her expression. "That's just an old sayin', Rainie. I didn't mean it literally."

"I realize it's an old saying. Do you know why some sayings have been passed down through so many generations, Mr. Harrigan?"

"Parker," he corrected.

She thrust up a hand. "When and if I feel comfortable using your first name, I'll do so. Until then, stop haranguing me about it."

Well, Parker thought, *I did tell her to speak her mind.* He leaned against the closed door. Though he tried to suppress it, a grin touched his mouth.

"What's so funny?" she demanded.

"Nothin'. Call me whatever suits you, I guess. I answer to almost anything."

The pink in her cheeks deepened, and her gaze flicked to a spot on the wall beside him. "Returning to the subject, the reason some sayings survive the passage of time is because they're so apt. I have become mouselike in certain situations."

Parker wished that she would elaborate on what kind of

situations made her uneasy, but he believed he already knew. Rainie Pritchard—or whatever the hell her real last name might be—was afraid of men. *All* men. He wished she could tell him what had happened to her. But, there again, it didn't take a genius to figure that out. Anger roiled within him when he thought about it. He would have traded his favorite pair of boots for ten minutes alone with the son of a bitch who'd done this to her.

"I never should've said that to you," he told her.

"Yes." Her tear-bright gaze jerked back to his. "I'm glad you said it. I admit I was angry with you yesterday and well into last night. But I've done some soul-searching, too, and the truth is you did me a favor. What you said to me yesterday made me realize how much I've changed and that I don't like what I've become."

She lifted her hands in a gesture of helpless bewilderment. "I don't know how I got like this, and I'm not sure how to change back to the person I used to be. Does that make any sense?"

"Perfect sense." Folding his arms, Parker crossed his ankles and stared solemnly at the toe of his upturned boot. After a long moment of silence, he looked back up at her. "It wasn't my aim to make you feel bad, honey. I only wanted you to relax around me and feel free to speak your mind."

"I'll work on it. Just let me do it on my own time schedule. Okay? Pushing me only makes things worse."

"Worse?"

"How can I relax around someone who rants and raves about politics and religion for an hour every day? I was starting to think you had a screw loose."

Caught off guard, Parker almost choked on a startled laugh. "Only *one*?"

She smiled slightly and wiped the shine of tears from her cheeks. "Maybe today over lunch, you can tell me what you *really* think. If I still believe you're a lunatic, I'll let you know."

"Deal."

Parker searched her pinched face, which bore unmistakable evidence of a poor night's sleep. As the angry splotches of red faded from her cheeks, a chalky pallor returned. Dark circles underscored her expressive eyes. As crazy as he knew the notion was, he wanted to cuddle her up and promise her that nobody would ever hurt her again. Sadly, he wasn't with her twenty-four/seven, and that was a promise he might not be able to keep.

"Can I ask you just one question?" he ventured. "If you don't want to answer, you can tell me to go stick my head in a horse trough."

She lifted a slender shoulder in a noncommittal shrug. "Sure, ask away."

He maintained his relaxed position. "Is there any chance that he may find you?"

Her already bloodless face went even paler. "I don't know what you're talking about."

Parker almost told her that she was a piss-poor liar, but for once in his life, he decided to err on the side of caution. "I'm not askin' for details, honey. I'm just lookin' for a simple yes or no. If there's a chance that the asshole may find you, I'd like a heads-up."

"I don't know what you're talking about," she repeated.

Parker decided that was a polite way of telling him to go stick his head in a horse trough, so he let it go at that.

That night while Rainie was eating vegetarian stir-fry for dinner on her living room sofa, a special news alert flashed on the television screen. According to the female news anchor, there was a new development in the Lorraina Danning investigation. An article of clothing had washed ashore somewhere in the Strait of Juan de Fuca, and the authorities believed the garment might belong to the missing Seattle socialite. The discovery rekindled public interest in the story, and Rainie saw her face intermittently flash on the screen. Though she knew the clothing didn't belong to her and would provide the authorities with no clues as to her whereabouts, she was still alarmed. What if Parker was watching television tonight? Rainie didn't socialize with his employees, so she felt fairly confident that her changed appearance could withstand their casual scrutiny. But she and Parker ate together every day, giving him ample opportunity to memorize her features. What if he saw her face on the screen and recognized her?

The thought tied her stomach into knots, and she gravitated to the kitchen for a glass of wine from her discount box of sweet Berry Splash. Now that she was making decent money, she could afford better wine, but she still hadn't worked her way through the cheap stuff. Besides, it gave her a sense of revenge. Peter would have a coronary. She lifted her goblet in a mock toast to his memory. *Take that,* she thought as she gulped down the wine, eager for its numbing effect to calm her nerves. When the glass was drained and she pushed the box nozzle to refill it, she hesitated, remembering her father's alcoholism. Was she following in his footsteps, using booze to dull her senses? She allowed herself only two glasses of wine per night, but what if two glasses became three over time, and she ended up hooked? Toward the end of her father's illness, one drink had been too many for him and a dozen hadn't been enough.

Rainie dumped the wine down the sink, but even as she watched the pink liquid disappear, she yearned for its numbing properties. That frightened her. Was she becoming a problem drinker? She decided that it couldn't become a problem unless she allowed it to be, and took herself off to bed. Thomas scurried ahead of her into the bedroom. He'd taken to sleeping with her, and he wasn't happy when he got left behind in the main part of the house.

"You won't be able to go outside to potty," Rainie warned him. "Once I'm locked in, I'm not opening up until daylight."

His answer was to curl up on her bed and start grooming himself. Rainie wedged the chair under the doorknob, checked to make sure the window was locked, and went into the adjoining bathroom to begin her own nightly grooming ritual. A few minutes later, when she slipped under the bedcovers, Thomas settled on the extra pillow. Usually his loud purring soothed her, but tonight nothing could. It was hot in there without central air-conditioning. Her body felt electrified, and her thoughts raced. What if Parker had seen her face on television tonight? If he recognized her, would he break his word and turn her in?

The worst part was, Rainie knew she wouldn't blame him if he did. Peter Danning was being raked over the coals. He was the prime suspect in a murder case. It had come to light that his first two wives had died mysteriously and left him large sums of money. The only reason he hadn't been arrested and charged with Rainie's murder was because there was insufficient evidence to convict him. In short, his life was being destroyed. Rainie knew he had it coming. Even if he hadn't caused the deaths of the other two women, he'd made Rainie's life a living hell, and she felt certain that he would have killed her during that cruise if she hadn't escaped when she had. She refused to feel guilty for causing him trouble.

But Parker might not see it that way. *Innocent until proven guilty.* A man was being accused of murdering his wife, and that wife was still very much alive. Parker's unshakable sense of right and wrong might lead him to call the police. Rainie stared blindly toward the ceiling, the rush of her blood sounding in her ears. It was terrifying to think that her freedom could be snatched away at any moment.

Even more frightening was the thought of Peter finding out that she was still alive. Even if they arrested her and put her in jail, she wouldn't feel safe from him. Peter was intelligent and treacherous. His wealth and powerful connections also gave him a long reach. *You're mine,* he'd often whispered as he exercised his conjugal rights. *Do you hear me, Lorraina? You're mine. I'll see you dead before I'll ever let you leave me.*

The memories made Rainie shudder. She turned on her side and drew up her knees to huddle under the covers. In the darkness, it was all too easy to imagine that he was there in the room with her. Her skin shriveled and got goose bumps. Bile burned in her throat. Rationally she knew he wasn't there. She'd checked the closet and looked under the bed. He couldn't be in the room. But still she shrank from the darkness, half expecting his hand to clamp onto her shoulder. *Get up,* he'd say. And when she did, he'd flip on the lights, drag her over to the full-length dressing mirror, and make her kneel in front of him.

Rainie squeezed her eyes closed so tightly that her lids ached, but still the images haunted her. He'd treated her like an object, not a person, and she had allowed it. Why hadn't she fought back? How could she have done such demeaning things just to avoid a beating? She'd read about people who'd gone through repeated tortures and never broken. But she had. Toward the end, she'd been like a robot, doing whatever Peter demanded, always careful not to let her revulsion show on her face, because that would have made him angry. Anything Peter wanted, he got. She'd had no pride by the time she left him, none at all. When she remembered the things she'd done to survive, she felt a shame that ran so deep it made her bones feel cold.

During lunch hour the following day, Rainie tried to feel Parker out to see if he'd watched the Lorraina Danning news broadcasts the night before. "I really enjoyed that documentary last night on tigers," she tried. "Did you happen to watch it?"

He had just taken a bite of submarine sandwich and took a moment to reply. "No. I read for a while and then hit the sack."

"Oh." Rainie puzzled over his answer. Now that she came to think of it, she'd never heard him mention anything that he'd watched on television. Mostly he talked only about things he'd heard on the radio. "Don't you like television?"

His black hair glistened in the sunlight that poured through the window behind her. His clean-shaven jaw gleamed like seasoned oak rubbed to a high sheen. "I rent a movie now and then, but mostly I don't watch regular programming. After a hard day, it puts me right to sleep."

"You don't even watch the news?"

"Sometimes, but not very often. I catch the news on the radio every day. That's good enough for me. Why, are you a boob-tube enthusiast?"

Relieved that he hadn't seen her face on the newscasts, Rainie laughed even though the question wasn't really funny. "Not really, no. I do watch the news every evening, though."

"I'd rather read. It keeps my brain workin'." He grinned at her around another bite of sandwich. "Did you know that you burn only thirteen calories an hour while you're watchin' television?"

"You're kidding."

"Don't quote me on it, but it's something like that. My brother Quincy could tell you exactly. He's the health fanatic in the family."

"How did he end up a health fanatic?"

"Beats the sand out of me," he replied before taking a sip of Coke. "All the rest of us are normal."

Rainie smiled. "Being health conscious is abnormal?"

"In my family, it is." Parker winked at her. "Quincy eats like a rabbit. I'm surprised he doesn't have buckteeth. He thinks it's a mortal sin to eat anything that's fried. Dessert, in his book, is a piece of fruit. The only good thing about his diet is that it keeps family dinners interestin'. You can always count on at least one heated discussion about food."

Now that she felt assured Parker had not seen her face on television last night, Rainie was able to relax enough to settle back on her chair and take a bite of her own sandwich. "It must be nice to have your family so close."

He nodded. "Mostly. Sometimes I think how it'd be if I lived across town—or across the state, but that's only when I'm aggravated with one of them. The rest of the time, I like havin' 'em around."

Silence. Moments of quiet were so rare with Parker that Rainie studied him expectantly, wondering what he'd think of to talk about next. While waiting, she wiped a bit of mayonnaise from the corner of her mouth. When he just continued eating and said nothing, she felt compelled to keep the conversation going.

"I'd love having a large family."

Cheek bulging, he corrected her. "My family's not large, not by Roman Catholic standards, anyway. You don't see it so much in the new generation, but when I was a kid, lots of my Catholic friends had eight or nine siblings."

That many children in one household seemed foreign to Rainie. "Yes, well, when I was little, I begged my mom for just *one* baby sister or brother. I was too young to understand that she was sick and couldn't have another child. A friend of mine—a girl who lived not far from me—came from a brood of six and didn't have a bedroom of her own. I loved staying all night at her house. To me, it was the neatest thing in the world to go to sleep in a bunk bed with other girls in the room."

"My sister, Sam, was the only one in our family to have her own room. I had to bunk with Zach. He was such a little brat."

Rainie had known her boss long enough now to know when he was warming to a subject. She waited to hear the rest of the story.

"Back then, I never knew what I'd find in my bed at night," he went on. "It's a wonder Zach lived to turn twenty-one. One time he put a garter snake under my pillow. Hello? Snakes don't stay put. Along about four in the morning, my father went to cussin' a blue streak. When he started to put on his boots, he found a snake curled up in one of 'em."

Rainie chortled with laughter, which made him pause to look at her oddly.

"What?" she asked self-consciously.

"Nothin'. You just have a nice laugh."

Rainie's cheeks went hot. She bent her head to hide the flush. To her relief, he resumed talking.

"Anyhow, the snake got loose in the house, and Dee Dee, my dad's wife—she was just our housekeeper back then—is terrified of the things. Didn't matter to her that it was only a harmless garter snake. She was fit to be tied. Before school, all of us kids had to go on a snake hunt. Only we didn't find it before the bus came. When we got home that afternoon, Dee Dee was sittin' in the middle of the kitchen table. The snake had slithered across the floor shortly after lunch, and she took to the table, scared out of her wits. Didn't get a lick of work done that day. When Dad came in from the stable for dinner, the only thing on the table was his housekeeper. We had peanut-butter-and-jelly sandwiches for supper, and Zach had to stay up that night until he found the snake."

"No one helped him?"

"Not until bedtime. Then the rest of us started lookin'. It was a good excuse to stay up late."

Rainie smiled. "Nothing so exciting ever happened at my

house. My dad worked a lot in the evening. I read or watched television to entertain myself."

"What did he do for a living?"

Rainie started to answer and then bit off the response.

"Come on," he coaxed. "What harm can it do to tell me that much?"

She thought about it for a moment and decided he was right. "He developed computer software."

"Ah." He wadded the sandwich wrapper in his fist and tossed it on the desk. "A computer wizard." His dark gaze settled on her face. "That fits. You take after him in some ways."

"Is that a polite way of saying I'm a nerd?"

He grinned. "I don't have a polite bone in my whole body, and you know it. The art of subtlety was all taken before I reached the front of the line."

It was true. He wasn't a very tactful man. But now that she knew his ranting and raving at lunchtime had all been a ploy, she couldn't honestly say she disliked that about him. At least with Parker, there were no guessing games. He said what was on his mind.

"Do you really believe that a woman who dresses provocatively is asking to be attacked?" The question was out before Rainie could stop herself from asking it. Ever since he'd made that statement, it had been troubling her. "I mean . . . well, what you think or don't think isn't really any of my business. I'm just curious."

"Don't apologize. It's a fair question. And my answer is that I think women should be able to dress however they please. I've never studied the statistics, but I'd bet my Stetson that most victims of rape are dressed conservatively when the attacks occur. I don't think it has anything to do with how a woman presents herself in public. Guys who do things like that are sick individuals, and they're opportunists. They either follow a woman to learn her routine and make their move when they know she's most vulnerable, or they lurk in places where they know they're likely to catch someone with her guard down. A woman could be wearin' knee-high boots with a long winter coat and still become a target. Rape is an act of violence. It's not about sexual desire, not in the way most of us understand it, anyway." He fell silent for a second. "I'm sorry I threw that at you. It happens to be one of my sister's pet peeves, and I was hopin' you wouldn't be able to let it pass."

Rainie studied him thoughtfully. "Why was it so important to you that I argue the point?"

His mouth tipped into one of those devastating grins. He was so handsome when he smiled that Rainie felt an odd flutter deep in her belly.

"I come from a family that argues about the food we're havin' for dinner. We Harrigans love nothin' better than a good debate. It wasn't my place to needle you into speakin' up, and I wish now that I hadn't. But the truth is, I felt that you *wanted* to say your piece and were just afraid of how I might react if you dared."

He'd hit the nail so squarely on the head that Rainie couldn't think what to say.

"I don't know what that son of a bitch did to you," he said huskily, "but I can tell you this: He'd better not show his face around here."

The flutter in her stomach increased, and delicious warmth spread through her torso. In some inexplicable way, seeing that spark of fury in his dark eyes aroused feelings within her that she'd thought never to feel again. "Where were you when I needed you?" she asked with a nervous laugh, hoping to lighten the mood.

"I'm here now," he replied.

That was all he said, only three short words, but they spoke volumes. Rainie didn't think for an instant that Peter would ever be stupid enough to show up at the ranch. He was far too conniving to make that mistake. No, if he found out she was alive, he'd track her down and bide his time until he could catch her alone. But it did comfort her to know that Parker would fight for her if the situation ever presented itself.

After lunch was over, Rainie tried to focus on her job, but that fluttery feeling way deep within her refused to abate. *I can't do this,* she told herself. So what if Parker Harrigan was attractive? That meant nothing. So what if he seemed nice? Had her experience with Peter taught her nothing? She couldn't develop feelings for the first handsome man she met. It was insane. She needed to get her hormones under control.

Only somehow all of Rainie's rationalizations led her full circle back to the undeniable fact that everything about Parker Harrigan struck a chord within her. She liked the way he threw back his dark head and barked with laughter. She enjoyed listening to him talk. She appreciated his down-home manner. Unlike Peter, Parker Harrigan sought to impress no one. He had an impressive amount of schooling under his belt, but nobody who met him would immediately guess him to be educated.

Why did she find that facet of Parker's personality so appealing? After thinking about it, Rainie decided that it might be because her boss was the very antithesis of Peter, who'd placed too much importance on the opinion of others. Before being seen in public, he'd preened in front of a mirror, turning this way and that to inspect every aspect of his appearance, and he'd been equally particular about how Rainie looked, examining her as if she were a mannequin in a display window before granting his approval. By contrast, Parker was almost too relaxed. He often came to the office with sweat on his brow, and when he plucked off his hat, a quick brush of his hand sufficed to tidy his tousled black hair. Over time, Rainie had determined that his stint at university had given him an impressive vocabulary, but he rarely used it. Instead, he talked like an ordinary Joe, dropping most of his Gs and dumbing down. One had to know Parker well to realize just how intelligent and well-read he actually was. A stranger who met him on the street might take him for a poorly paid wrangler or a mechanic dressed like a cowboy.

Rainie came from an entirely different background. Her father had been both a computer genius and an intellectual who prided himself on being well educated. When Rainie had been in grade school, he'd given her a new word each day, and at dinner, she'd been required to know its spelling, meaning, and proper usage in a sentence. As she grew older, she'd delighted in discovering a word that her father didn't know. Over evening meals, they'd often challenged each other with absurdly long or seldom heard words. Rainie had loved those times, and in college, she'd used her word power constantly to impress her professors or fellow students.

So why did she find a man who talked like an uneducated farmer so potently appealing?

Over the next few days, that became a question always in the back of Rainie's mind. It was also a question that she couldn't easily answer. She knew only that her mounting attraction to Parker Harrigan alarmed her. Was there a pattern emerging here? Though Parker was far younger than Peter, he was still older than her by about ten years. What was it about handsome older men that made her go brain-dead? Was she harboring a deep need for a father figure in her life? Was it their wealth and power that she liked? Parker moved in an entirely different social circle than Peter, but he was no less empowered by status and money. The longer Rainie worked at the ranch, the more aware she became that the Harrigan name was well recognized in Crystal Falls. The family was considered to be a pillar of the community.

Rainie didn't view herself as a gold digger. In fact, she had never been happier since her father's death than she was now, living in a run-down duplex, driving a rattletrap car, and wearing clothing from Goodwill. Being liberated from her marriage was a heady experience. But she couldn't ignore the correlations between her husband and her employer. Good grief, both of them even had names that started with a P. How weird was that?

Rainie had fallen quickly and wildly in love with Peter. Now she felt strongly drawn to Parker. Only a fool would repeat the same disastrous mistake. She could *not* allow her feelings to overrule her common sense this time. Ever since staging her accidental death, she'd vowed *never* to leap into a relationship again. At times, she'd even promised herself that she would never have anything to do with another man. She was clearly a poor judge of character, and she also had a propensity to trust too easily and blindly. She couldn't let down her guard merely because a man seemed nice.

And, oh, Parker did seem nice. She seldom lingered in the stable area, but she often saw him working with his horses as she walked the length of the arena. What always impressed her most was his kindness and gentleness with the huge animals, and there was no mistaking the love that shone in his eyes when he spoke of them. He was also proving to be a patient and generous boss. Rainie hadn't yet been introduced to anyone in his family, but she suspected that she would like all of them immensely if they were anything at all like Parker.

All too often, Rainie caught herself pondering her growing attraction to him and forgetting about her work goals for the day. Instead she considered how her heart rate always accelerated whenever he flashed one of those devastating grins at her, how engaging he was in conversation, and how singularly loyal and devoted he seemed to be to his family.

All in all, Rainie couldn't find anything wrong with the man, and the realization scared her half to death. She'd been able to see nothing wrong with Peter, either, and, oh, what a bad call that had been.

Chapter Seven

As the late-summer sun set behind the mountains that evening, Parker flipped on a table lamp to chase away the shadows, then kicked back in his recliner with a cold beer and a mystery novel. The book had a predictable plot. When he felt certain he'd figured out who the killer was a third of the way through, he snapped the cover closed and finished his microbrew in the soft glow of light. Beyond the halo of illumination, the living room lay in darkness. The only sound that drifted to his ears was the hum of the refrigerator in the kitchen. A lonely, empty feeling came over him. Despite all the stories he'd told Rainie about his family and their chaotic gatherings, he most often spent his evenings in solitude. Normally he didn't think much about it, but tonight, the emptiness of the house made him feel blue and restless.

Early in his twenties, he'd expected to be married and settled down by now. When his thirtieth birthday rolled around with him still single, he'd begun to realize life wasn't quite that simple. Before a man could get married, he had to find a lady special enough to make him want to make a lifelong commitment to her. Parker had dated a lot of women—short ones and tall ones, skinny ones and plump ones, quiet ones and gregarious ones—but not a single one of them had ever rocked his world.

Now Rainie had entered his life, and the more he was around her, the more she filled his thoughts. She was like a piece of cheatgrass that had worked its way under his skin, burrowing deeper and deeper until he had a devil of a time plucking it out. Sometimes when he least expected it, she fastened those expressive hazel eyes on his, and he could swear he felt the earth shift treacherously beneath him. When he drew close to her, he smelled no perfume, only the faint scents of vanilla, apples, and cinnamon, which always made him think of apple pie. Yet the essence of her made his senses spin. His urge to hug her and chase the wariness from her eyes remained strong as well. When he said something to make her smile slightly, he felt as if he'd just hung the moon. And, God help him, when he was away from her, he found it difficult to keep his mind on his horses, thinking instead about ways he might encourage her to trust him.

Why that mattered so much to him, he wasn't sure. Normally, he would not be interested in someone like Rainie. For starters, the lady obviously had a past—and more secrets than an hourglass had sand granules. What if she had been married to the bastard who roughed her up? That could mean she was still the jerk's wife. Parker wasn't an overly pious individual, but he did hold dear the tenets of his Catholic faith. Messing around with a married woman was *not* okay in his book.

Problem was, he felt like a man in a rowboat on stormy seas, with the waves and current carrying him inexorably toward a dangerous outcropping of rocks. He could paddle in reverse all he liked, but he kept drifting closer. Even worse, his common sense seemed to have gone on hiatus. He could easily take his noontime meals at the house or with his other employees. It wasn't written in stone that he had to dine with Rainie, and he'd begun more days than he cared to count determined not to spend any more lunch hours with her. But along about eleven, he lost his resolve and found himself ordering take-out delivery for two. Just recently, he'd also caught himself planning ahead so he would have an entertaining story to tell her while they ate.

How crazy was that? He knew next to nothing about the lady. Hell, he didn't even know her real last name. Practically everything she'd told him about herself might be a fabrication. He had no way of knowing where the truth ended and the lies began, and he found that alarming. Parker wasn't a gambler by nature, especially not when his heart was involved, and he had a very bad feeling that his heart would be part of the ante if he took this any further.

Only how could a man turn off his feelings? Everything about Rainie touched him—way down deep where reason held no sway. That hesitant smile of hers always made his heart catch, and if that didn't do it, the loneliness he saw in her eyes hit him like a fist to the solar plexus. What must it be like to lead such a solitary existence? The only living creature he'd ever heard her mention was Thomas, the stray tomcat. Even more telling, her cell phone had never once rung during their lunches together. She either turned the damned thing off or no one ever called her.

Parker couldn't imagine that. Here he sat, feeling blue because his home felt empty. Earlier in the evening, both his cell phone and landline had rung off the hook. His father had called just to say hello. Quincy had rung twice, once to invite Parker over for dinner, then again to ask if he'd like to go for a workout at the gym. Clint had called about a fence-post order that they'd gone in on together. And that was only tonight. Earlier in the afternoon, Samantha had called twice to ask him questions about one of her horses, and his sister-in-law, Loni, had phoned once to see if Parker had seen Clint. That wasn't counting all the miscellaneous ring-ups that Parker had gotten over the course of his day. It made him sad to think that Rainie lived in virtual isolation without friends or family ever calling to check on her.

He wished he could think of a way to make her feel less alone. Maybe then he would be able to stop thinking about her constantly.

First thing the next morning, Parker rode his Yamaha four-wheeler over to Samantha's place to help her wrap and plaster the leg of a lame horse. Tucker had early calls that morning and couldn't be there to do it. After learning that Samantha hadn't yet made an appearance at the stable, Parker strode over to the house, worried that she might be sick. It wasn't like Sam to lollygag and show up at the stable late.

Opening the door without knocking, he stepped into the entry and hollered, "Yo! Is anybody home?"

"In here!" Samantha called from the kitchen, and then Parker could have sworn he heard her curse.

That was *definitely* an anomaly. Sam abhorred bad language and never missed an opportunity to scold her brothers when they transgressed. Parker shuffled his boots back and forth on the rug before stepping onto the gleaming hardwood floor. As he hung a right through the kitchen archway, he burst out laughing. The entire floor of the room was crawling with black, waddling fur balls.

"Hey, sis, how's married life treatin' you?" he couldn't resist asking.

"Oh, shut up," she retorted, grabbing for a puppy and missing her mark.

Growing up, Samantha had never been much of a dog person. That had all changed when she met her husband, Tucker, and his sidekick, Max, a male rottweiler that had stolen her heart. Now, a year and a half into the marriage, she'd also become the proud owner of Roxie, a female rottweiler Tucker had rescued from euthanasia when the dog's owners had been moving to the city. Problem: Tucker had overlooked one minor detail when he initially examined

Roxie. The dog, bred to another pedigreed rottweiler by her owners, had been in the early stages of gestation. Parker still grinned when he recalled the family dinner debate that had taken place when Roxie's condition became apparent. The final vote had been five to four in favor of spaying the dog and ending the pregnancy. In the end, however, Tucker's vote had carried the day because he would be wielding the scalpel, and he held to the unpopular professional opinion that spaying and neutering were detrimental to canine health. He also maintained that aborting a pregnancy could cause a female rottweiler to develop uterine problems that could be deadly.

Five weeks later, Roxie had proudly presented her new owners with eight bundles of joy. At first, it hadn't been that big a deal, but now the bundles had developed functional legs and were escaping from the plastic kiddie pool that had served as their holding area since birth.

"Damn, Sam." Parker rested a shoulder against the frame of the archway. "This is so entertainin', I could sell tickets."

"I do *not* need to hear any smart-ass comments right at the moment!" Samantha continued collecting puppies and returning them to the pool, but the moment she turned her back, they tumbled out again. "If you were any kind of brother, you'd help me."

"To what end? They just keep gettin' loose."

Bent at the waist, Samantha glanced up, her brown eyes snapping. After puffing at a wayward strand of curly black hair that dangled over her pretty face, she stuck her tongue out at him. "And your point is?"

"That it's an effort in futility. You need higher walls to keep 'em in." Parker glanced into the enclosure where Roxie and Max, surrogate father to the brood, snoozed obliviously. Raising octuplets was clearly an exhausting endeavor. "You need a bigger pool, too. As the puppies grow, it's gonna get crowded in there."

Max stirred awake and emitted a sleepy woof at Parker. A good watchdog had a duty to perform, and the male rottweiler apparently didn't want to be caught sleeping on the job.

"Don't bark at me, you good-for-nothin' mongrel," Parker said as he waded into the fray to help his sister. "You know very well who I am." To Samantha, he said, "Seems odd to me that the scalpel man is conveniently absent when all hell is breakin' loose."

"I told you he had early calls. He's a vet, remember."

"You'd defend him no matter what." In truth, Parker liked his brother-in-law and was tickled pink to see his sister so happy. He just couldn't resist teasing Sam about loving the guy so much.

"Of course I'd defend him. He's my husband."

Samantha had not held her first husband in such high regard, but that was a closed chapter of her life and best not mentioned. Parker still saw red when he thought about her ex, and he probably always would.

She straightened with three squirming puppies in her arms. "And this wasn't happening before he left. It only started about thirty minutes ago. One puppy accidentally rolled over the edge, and then, in a blink, they were all going for it." She glanced at her spotless floor. "What'll I do? They'll poop and pee everywhere."

"That's the name of the game with a litter of puppies. Why don't you move 'em to an outbuildin'?"

"I can't do *that.* Roxie is part of our family now. It'd hurt her feelings."

"She's only a dog, Sam. They don't internalize stuff the same way we do."

"I'll remind you of that the next time one of your mares drops a foal."

She had him there. After one of Parker's mares had a foal, he slept in the birthing stall, sometimes two nights running.

"Horses are different," he said, even though he didn't truly believe that. "They're smarter."

"That is *so* not true, and you know it."

Parker returned two escapees to their bed. "How about buildin' a barricade to corral 'em?"

"With what?"

He surveyed the room. "I could find two wide boards to block both archways. We can cover the floor with newspapers. One nice thing about tile is that it's washable. Won't be the end of the world if puppy piss leaks through."

Samantha nodded. Then she smiled. "Offer accepted."

Parker was about to leave to find some boards when he heard a fierce little growl and felt a tug on his jeans. He glanced down to see a stout little bugger attacking his pant leg. He reached down to pick up the transgressor. "Damn," he muttered. "The little shit won't turn loose."

"He's only a baby, Parker. Just work his teeth free."

Parker tried, but the puppy's needlelike incisors were embedded in the denim. He was afraid to jerk for fear he'd hurt the little guy. "He's got more moxie than he's got good sense." Parker had never owned a dog, but he'd long since determined that if he ever got one, it would be an Australian shepherd. Quincy had two Aussies, Bubba and Billy Bob, and they were fabulous around horses. Not that Max wasn't. The rottweiler had been raised by an equine specialist and had spent a good deal of his life at a horse clinic. "Hey, blockhead," he said to the puppy. "You got any brains between those floppy little ears of yours? In case you haven't noticed, I'm bigger than you are."

"He's got plenty of brains between his ears." Samantha gently deposited the three puppies in the pool. They immediately started trying to jump back out. "Rotts are extremely intelligent dogs. Point in fact, that one is only six weeks old, and he knows you're an interloper. He's protecting his home."

"I'm not an interloper."

"You haven't been here for three weeks. Do you expect a tiny baby to remember you? To him, you're a stranger, and strangers pose a threat."

"You think?" Parker moved his foot to see if the puppy would hang on. Sure enough, he did. "He's just playin', Sam."

"Practicing," she corrected. "Someday, he'll protect his loved ones to the death. They're smart dogs, I'm telling you. If *you* had any sense, you'd take one home with you. Pick of the litter. I'll let it go for free."

"What a deal."

Parker was still trying to extricate his pant leg from the pup's mouth. Definitely a boy, he decided. A girl wouldn't be so ferocious. The little fart had braced all four legs on the floor to snarl and shake. Parker was impressed. If there was anything he admired, it was courage, and this puppy seemed to have it in spades. It reminded him of David going up against Goliath.

By pressing on the puppy's jaw joints, Parker was finally able to free his pant leg. He grabbed his attacker by the scruff of his neck and picked him up. "Ah, he's a tough little nut. Doesn't yelp."

"Of course he doesn't. That's how his mother picks him up."

Parker angled his wrist to get a frontal view and found himself looking at the cutest canine countenance he could recall ever having seen. "He's got wrinkles on his nose."

Samantha stepped closer to look and smiled. "Isn't he darling? All of them are precious, of course, but those nose wrinkles are definitely adorable. He's got a perpetual frown, too."

Something happened as Parker gazed into those almond-shaped, milky brown eyes. He wasn't sure what, exactly, but the feeling that moved through him made him think of

Rainie. From that instant forward, maybe instinct took over, but he suddenly knew he'd just found a cure for her loneliness. "You serious about lettin' him go for free? He's got papers, doesn't he?"

"Yes, but I would never charge family." Samantha gave him a bewildered look. "You're not seriously thinking about adopting him? Puppies are a lot of work, Parker."

"Do I look lazy to you?"

"No, of course not, but raising a rottweiler takes more dedication than it does with most puppies. What'll you do if he eats your sofa?"

"Buy a new one." Parker couldn't stop grinning. There was something about the puppy's face that just got to him. "What do you know about his papa?"

"Not much except that he's a purebred and hip certified. You do understand that Tucker will have a fit if you get him neutered. He's convinced it's bad for dogs, especially rottweilers, because they have sensitive immune systems."

Parker shuddered at the thought of having his best buddy's balls cut off. What was life all about if a guy couldn't have sex? "That's fine." He tucked the puppy into the crook of his arm. "I'm not keen on neutering."

"Intact males can pose more problems. He'll be more inclined to fight with other dogs."

Parker had no objection to an occasional fracas, either. In his younger years, he'd been a scrapper himself. "No worries."

Samantha nibbled her bottom lip. "When Roxie comes in heat, you'll have to make sure he stays home. We can't have Roxie breeding with her own offspring."

Parker figured he could handle that, too. "What's the deal, here, Sam? You offered me a dog. Now you're puttin' on the brakes."

She ran to catch two fleeing puppies. After returning them to their pen, she said, "I'm just afraid you may be biting off more than you can chew. You can't take him, let him develop an attachment to you, and then suddenly decide you don't want him."

Parker nudged his hat up to give his sister a wondering look. "When have you ever known me to be inconstant?"

"Never, but that's largely because you never commit to anyone or anything."

"That's not true. I commit to my horses."

"Doesn't count. Name me one time you've committed to anything else that lives and breathes."

Parker thought for a moment. "I'm committed to my family. You can't say I'm not."

"That doesn't count, either. Any man with half a heart is committed to his family."

"What are you sayin', that I'm not fit to have a dog?"

Samantha folded her arms, a dimple showing in her cheek as she smiled. "Until death do you part. Say it, or you can't have him."

Parker almost put the puppy back down. He didn't like ultimatums. But the little bugger attacked his shirt pocket just then, and the tug-of-war began again. "I think he likes me."

"Birds of a feather flock together."

"What's that mean?"

"You're stubborn, irascible, snarly, and recalcitrant. As I recall, I've called you a blockhead more than once. The two of you suit each other."

"That's not very nice."

"You're also loyal and lovable," she added.

"You forgot handsome."

"With that nose?"

"You looked in the mirror lately?" he countered.

"The Harrigan schnozzle looks better on me than it does on you."

"Who says?"

Her dimple deepened. "Tucker. He *adores* my nose."

"Yeah, well, he's addled." The puppy let loose with a deep growl that sounded amazingly ferocious coming from such a tiny attacker. Parker chuckled. "He's awesome, Sam. I think I've found a soul mate." He glanced back at her. "I'll keep him. You have my word."

After erecting the promised puppy barriers, Parker collected his dog and started to leave.

Sam searched his gaze. "Who would have thunk it? My brother, smitten with a puppy."

"He's no ordinary puppy. He's got mojo."

The office door swung open with such force that it whacked the interior wall, making Rainie jump. Then a huge blue thing appeared in the doorway. Judging by all the grunting and muffled cursing, Parker was somewhere behind it.

"What on earth?" She jumped up from the desk. "Do you need help?"

His dark head appeared. In the light coming through the window behind her, his freshly shaved jaw gleamed, his skin the color of caramel. The blue collar of his shirt framed the thick, corded column of his sun-burnished neck. The weathered toughness around his mouth and eyes was purely masculine, an attribute that she should have found repugnant, but instead it sent her senses spinning, making her feel like a schoolgirl in the throes of her first crush. *Not good.* Developing feelings for this man was not part of her game plan.

"It's not heavy, just cumbersome," he assured her.

Rainie doubted that he considered much of anything to be heavy. She didn't dally in the stable area often, but in passing, she'd seen him bucking bales of hay as if they weighed barely anything. He had a naturally trim and athletic build that had been padded with steely muscle by a lifetime of hard work.

"What in heaven's name is this thing?" she asked, grabbing hold of one end to help work it through the doorway.

"A wadin' pool. You in the mood for a dip?"

The question was so silly it didn't deserve an answer. "What's it for?"

"Mojo."

"Mojo?"

"Yeah, I got myself a dog. Normally, I'm not much for dogs, but he's a charmer. That's how come I'm namin' him Mojo."

Rainie backed up to make room for the pool, which was about five feet in diameter. "Where is he?"

"On the floorboard of my truck, goin' one-on-one with the gearshift boot."

Rainie had no idea what a gearshift boot was. The pool took up most of the walking space after they plopped it on the floor. Bewildered, Rainie said, "One-on-one? I'm sorry. I don't understand."

"He's a puppy with an attitude. He attacks everything." Standing at the opposite side of the pool, Parker winked at her. A lazy smile flirted at the corners of his mouth. "I sure hope you don't mind helpin' me watch him durin' the day. He's a tad too young yet to be around the horses. He might get stepped on."

Because of her dad's allergies Rainie had never had a puppy, but she figured she could do almost anything for sixty grand a year. "Of course." She glanced at the pool again. "I'll help however I can. But what is this for?"

"Playpen. This way when he piddles, he won't do it on the floor. I got the idea from my sister, Sam." He plucked a thick stack of newspapers from under his arm. "I picked these up to use as liners. When he makes a mess, all we'll have to do is pull the soiled sheet and put in another one."

"That sounds simple enough."

He nodded, gave her meal instructions, and said, "I'll go get him and the food, then. You sure you won't mind if I leave him in the office with you when I'm workin'?"

"Not at all."

Thirty minutes later, Rainie had come to regret those words. The moment Parker left the office, Mojo tumbled over the edge of the wading pool and squatted to pee.

"No!" Rainie cried, racing to save the plank floor. Unfortunately, Mojo was a quick whizzer. He had finished and waddled under the desk before she could reach him. "Now look what you've done."

Rainie went to the coffee room for some paper towels and disinfectant. While she cleaned up the mess, the puppy discovered a pile of invoices that she'd set on the floor by her desk chair. Before she'd finished mopping up, he was attacking the papers like a miniature shredding machine.

"Stop it! Bad, *bad* puppy!" Rainie cried, but Mojo apparently had a hearing problem.

She scurried over to rescue the documents. As she bent to gather them up, her calf-length skirt grazed the floor, and the tiny rottweiler latched onto the hem. His little jaws were like metal clamps. She couldn't pry them apart. As she tried, he let loose with a ferocious growl and went into reverse, tugging on the cloth with all his strength.

Rainie burst out laughing. "I don't have time to play," she protested. "I'm supposed to be working."

But, once again, Mojo wasn't listening. Finally Rainie surrendered and sat cross-legged on the floor to engage in a gentle game of tug-of-war. The skirt was ancient, anyway. If Mojo ripped it to shreds, she'd be out only two dollars. He was so *sweet*. As she ran her hands over his warm, plump body, her heart melted.

* * *

When Parker returned to the office with lunch, Rainie stood at the file cabinet with the puppy dangling from the hem of her skirt. In order to hold on and follow when Rainie moved, Mojo stood upright on his tiny back legs. Parker noticed that Rainie took baby steps to accommodate the short stride of her new fashion accessory.

"How's it goin'?" he asked.

Parker wasn't sure what her response might be. He was half-afraid she might hand him a letter of resignation. Instead she laughed, a sweet, airy sound that could easily become addictive.

"*Slowly.* The pool doesn't work as a playpen. Over the course of the last two hours, I've gotten almost nothing done. He's piddled three times and gone poo once, all on the floor. When he's not busy making messes, he's tugging on my skirt, chewing on my boots, or gnawing on the desks."

Parker carried the pizza box over and set it down. "I could lock him in one of the sheds while I'm workin', I guess."

Her eyes widened with dismay. "That would be cruel. He's just a baby. He needs company."

"He oughta sleep some of the time. Have you fed him?" As per Samantha's instructions, Parker had gotten a bunch of pureed meat, a box of infant rice cereal, and canned milk. According to his sister, a soft, runny mixture of those three ingredients, heavy on the meat, was more nutritious than dry kibble for a rottweiler puppy Mojo's age. "Most babies get drowsy with their bellies full."

"I fed him."

Rainie bent to pick up the puppy. As she worked Mojo's teeth loose from the hem of her skirt, Parker got a mind-boggling glimpse of gorgeous legs. Her skin was the color of saddle soap, milky and sort of translucent-looking. He would have bet his Stetson that it felt just as silky, too. One of his favorite things was to open a brand-new tin of saddle soap. He liked how it went warm and slick onto his fingertips—like certain places on the body of a well-loved woman.

What the *hell* was he thinking? Parker jerked himself up short. He was losing his mind. That had to be it. He never looked at one of his female employees and entertained lascivious thoughts. Well, hardly ever, anyway. And when a thought like that did flit through his mind, he never let it remain there long enough to give him a hard-on. *Shit.* What if Rainie noticed? She was just now coming to trust him a little. *Perfect, Parker. Why don't you drool while you're at it?*

He swung away to hang his hat on one of the pegs by the door. *Down, boy.* Unfortunately, that particular part of his anatomy had a mind of its own. "Excuse me a second," he said over his shoulder. "I just remembered somethin' I need to go do."

"Don't be so long you let the pizza get cold."

Right at the moment, Parker doubted he would notice if the cheese had ice crystals on it. He stepped out into the hallway and closed the door. *Damn.* He went to the tack room to lounge against a saddle bar until his jeans fit right again. Only pictures of those legs kept flashing in his mind, and the fly of his pants continued to protrude. He tried to focus his thoughts on something else—the lousy book he'd been reading, world affairs, the state of the national economy. Nothing worked. Finally, in desperation, he began thinking of his horses. Montana, the champion buckskin stud that had put his rear leg through a stall wall, had been limping slightly again. That was a worry weighty enough to dampen Parker's physical urges.

He sighed with relief. It wasn't like him to get turned on so easily by a woman, especially not a woman who might be married. During lunches, he'd studied Rainie's left hand to see if he could detect a telltale depression on her ring finger where a band had once been. No such luck. In weak moments, he reminded himself that lots of people lived together without benefit of marriage nowadays. Maybe Rainie had only been living with the guy when the relationship turned ugly.

Yeah, right. Somehow, she didn't strike him as being the type to shack up with someone. He had her pegged as a forever kind of lady who would expect a ring, promises, and avowals of undying devotion before she hooked up with a man. That being the case, she'd more than likely been married to the creep and probably still was. Where did that leave Parker? It left him lusting after a married woman, that was where, and that didn't sit well with him. He shouldn't allow his feelings for her to deepen any more than they already had.

And wasn't that a hell of a note? He was thirty-five years old and had spent most of his adult life searching for someone like her, and now that he'd found her, she was off-limits. His feet felt heavy as he retraced his steps along the hallway. He hesitated outside the door, his mood gloomy. It hardly seemed fair. Rainie *needed* someone. That was obvious. And, damn it, he wanted to be that someone. What was so wrong with that?

Making a fast U-turn, Parker went back to the tack room, tugged his cell phone from his belt, and dialed his father's number. Frank answered on the fourth ring.

"Hey, Dad. Parker here. I got a question for you."

The *clink-clink* of a spoon stirring coffee came over the line. "Shoot. If I don't have the answer, I'll ask Dee Dee. She knows everything."

Parker heard his plump, redheaded stepmother protest with a good-natured laugh. He smiled slightly, glad that his father had found happiness in the autumn of his life with someone so wonderful, yet feeling sad for himself. It wasn't often that a woman appealed to Parker like Rainie did. What if he passed on this opportunity and no one special ever came along again?

His throat went dry as he started to speak. "I'm fallin' hard for a woman who might be married," he blurted.

"Damn, son. That ain't a question. It's a bomb to be dropped on enemy lines."

"Sorry. I had to come right out with it, or I wouldn't have got it said."

Frank cleared his throat. The clinking of the spoon resumed, only louder now, an indication of the older man's agitation. "Can you pull hard on your Jake Brake, Parker? A married woman is bad news. You don't want to be a home wrecker."

"There's no home to wreck." Parker quickly related his suspicions about the relationship. "I think she's on the run, Dad. Pritchard probably isn't even her real last name."

"You seen any evidence of physical abuse?"

Parker thought of the pink scar that ran along Rainie's fragile cheekbone and related that information to his father. "So, yes. I'm pretty sure the bastard beat the ever-lovin' hell out of her on a regular basis. She's hand-shy and as skittish as a quirt-whipped filly."

"Well, that puts a different spin on things," Frank said. "That's not a marriage. It's an affront to the word. There's nothin' holy about a union like that."

Those had been Parker's thoughts as well, but it helped somehow to hear his father say them aloud.

"When a man pulls that kind of shit, he ain't no kind of husband," Frank continued. "I believe in the sanctity of marriage. You know that. But when Sammy finally told me what her ex had been doin' to her behind closed doors, the first words out of my mouth were, 'Divorce him.' And I supported her every inch of the way. That marriage was an abomination. And I don't believe for one second that God expected her to stay in it."

"No, of course not." Parker's voice drifted away into taut silence. "I've just never been here before. You know? Messin' with a married woman isn't my style."

"Then walk away."

Parker rubbed between his eyebrows. "I can't. I've tried keepin' my distance, but first thing I know, I'm makin' excuses to be with her again."

"Well, then?"

"Technically, won't I be committin' adultery?"

Frank took a moment to answer. "You worried about burnin' in hell over a technicality? I'm sorry, son, but I don't think heaven's judicial system works that way."

Parker had to smile. This was why he'd called his dad—because he could always count on him to talk good, old-fashioned common sense. Frank had a way of breaking things down so the complicated suddenly seemed simple.

"How many times have you told me not to justify a wrong?" Parker asked.

"A number of times."

"So, what if I'm justifyin' and makin' excuses so I won't feel guilty about steppin' over the line?"

"If the girl's got marks on her face from a man's fists, there's no line to step over. My advice is that you stop thinkin' it to death and just follow your heart. You've got a good one."

Parker closed his eyes. "Right now, my heart's tellin' me to jump in with both feet."

"Then jump."

"You won't disapprove if it turns out that she's married?"

"Not for a minute. The marriage ended the first time he hit her. I'd encourage her to get a divorce as soon as possible, of course. But that's a legality, not an immediate necessity."

"Convincin' her to file for divorce could be tricky. She might be afraid her old man will find out where she is."

There was a smile in Frank's voice when he replied, "Send the bastard an engraved invitation to lunch."

Parker had heard that one so many times that he knew what came next. "And serve him a fist sandwich when he dares to show up?"

"I'm thinkin' more along the line of a fist banquet. If you're not feelin' froggy, call Clint. He'll show the bastard how the cow ate the cabbage. Nothin' gets him riled faster than a man roughin' up a woman."

"Clint can take a number and stand in line. This fellow's mine. I got a Tony Lama boot that's just itchin' to kick some ass."

Frank chuckled. "That's my boy. Teach him how it feels to be on the receivin' end. Might make him think twice the next time he gets an urge to beat on a woman."

When Parker opened the office door a few minutes later, he was smiling. Talking with his father had helped him sort his thoughts and get his head on straight. Married or not, Rainie was fair game. Parker wasn't about to let some misguided sense of morality stand in his way.

Rainie sat on the floor playing with Mojo. She was giggling so loudly that she apparently didn't hear him enter behind her. Watching her with the puppy did his heart good. Adopting Mojo had been a stroke of genius. It was hard to be solemn, sad, or frightened with a mischievous, toothy, snarly puppy to break down all your defenses.

"I figured you'd be eatin' pizza like there's no tomorrow by now," he said. "Instead you're playin' with that goofy dog."

She angled a startled glance over her shoulder. "He won't stay in the pool. It's a little hard to ignore him."

Parker dropped his gaze to the kiddie pool. He'd known when he bought it that Mojo would climb out of it in two seconds flat. It had served as a great smoke screen, though.

Rainie would never suspect that he'd adopted the puppy as much for her as he had for himself.

He heard her giggle again and glanced up to see Mojo suckling on her earlobe. In that moment, Parker would have traded places with the pup in a heartbeat. Her hair smelled like apple pie. Strange, that. He'd never been a huge fan of apple pie—until now.

"You reckon he's hungry again?" he asked.

"Maybe."

She started to get up. Parker stopped her with a raised hand. "He's my dog. I'll mix up his grub."

Moments later, when he returned to the main part of the office, Rainie had Mojo cradled in her arms like a baby, his fat little belly shining pink at the ceiling. "Uh-oh. You hornin' in on my turf, tryin' to steal my dog?"

She smiled up at him. Parker decided he'd not only hung the moon, but the stars as well. "He's too sweet to resist," she informed him.

That had been Parker's hope. He put the food bowl down on the floor, and Mojo started squirming to escape. Rainie set him gently on his feet and beamed with pleasure as she watched him waddle over to the meal. "He has a great appetite."

"That's a good thing. He'll grow big and strong. Sammy says he'll be very protective of his loved ones when he gets older, that all his growlin' and tuggin' right now is only for practice."

She pushed to her feet, treating him to another fetching glimpse of shapely leg. "I don't know very much about rottweilers—or any kind of dog, for that matter. My dad had allergies, so I could never have a pet."

Parker filed that bit of information away, pleased that she'd shared it with him. "That sucks. I never had a dog as a kid, but I didn't notice the lack because I had horses. They were my pets. Still are." He sat at the desk and opened the pizza box, motioning for her to join him. "Don't know what possessed me to get a dog, but I'm glad I did."

She sank onto her castered chair. "It was his *mojo*," she said, her cheek dimpling in a teasing grin. "It's hard to look at him without being charmed."

"I was taken with him, that's for sure," Parker confessed. "He grabbed hold of my jeans and wouldn't let go. He's got brass. I like that."

She plucked a piece of pizza from the box, stringing mozzarella to the pink tip of her outthrust tongue. Watching her, Parker felt his jeans grow snug again. But the feeling was quickly replaced by sheer enjoyment at seeing her so relaxed. Mojo had definitely worked some magic.

"He needs some teething toys," she informed him. "You thought of everything but that."

"Hmm." Parker took a bite of pizza, studying her as he chewed. After swallowing, he said, "Would you go with me to a pet store to pick some out?"

He half expected her to refuse, but she surprised him with, "That would be fun."

"Tomorrow? We could drive in together and do lunch before we go shoppin'."

"Lunch?"

"It'll be a nice change from takeout. You like authentic Italian?"

"I love Italian."

"I know a great little mom-and-pop. Red-checkered tablecloths, bread made fresh every mornin'. The food is awesome. They make all the pasta and sauces themselves. I don't go to eat there as often as I'd like."

"What'll we do with Mojo while we're gone?"

"I'll find a box, and we'll take him. The pet store I'm thinkin' of welcomes pets. We'll let him pick out some of his own toys."

* * *

Sunlight slanted through the windshield into Rainie's eyes as she drove home that evening. *Lunch.* Why had she said yes? It felt too much like a date. Every time she thought about it, she got butterflies in the pit of her stomach. *Stupid, stupid.* He was ten years older than she was. His family was rich. His first name began with a P. She felt as if her life had become a television rerun, and she knew exactly what would happen next. People were supposed to learn from their mistakes. Right? Yet here she was, developing a huge crush on another older man.

Parker was nothing like Peter, she reminded herself. It was silly of her to draw comparisons. But how could she not? Peter had been her boss. Parker was her boss. Peter had been opinionated. Parker was opinionated. She'd trusted Peter when she shouldn't have. Now she was starting to trust Parker.

Was she weak-minded or something?

The moment Rainie got home, she picked up the phone. Dates could be canceled. Self-destructive behaviors could be changed. She wasn't doomed to repeat the same old mistakes unless she allowed herself to repeat them.

Parker had just stuffed a large bite of pastrami sandwich into his mouth when his cell phone rang. He immediately recognized the number, not because Rainie contacted him very often, but because he'd been tempted to call her so many times that he had memorized the digits. He made quick work of swallowing the food, hit the talk button, and said, "Hey. You aren't stranded somewhere with car trouble, I hope."

"No. The car is running perfectly now that your mechanic worked on it." Silence. "I, um, just called about tomorrow."

Tremulous and soft, her voice wrapped around him like tendrils of silk. He knew by her tone that something was up. "What about tomorrow?" he asked.

"The lunch thing. I've decided to cancel."

Parker settled his hips against the granite counter and crossed his ankles. It was her prerogative to cancel, and normally he would have let it go at that. Only with Rainie, this went much deeper than a simple change of heart. He felt certain of it.

"Why are you cancelin'?" he asked, wondering even as he formed the question if she would answer candidly.

"I, um . . ." He heard her take a shaky breath. "It just feels too much like a date. And I'm not ready for that. I may never be ready for that."

He had to give her high marks for honesty. By making the confession, she was admitting that she was as attracted to him as he was to her. Otherwise she would have gone with him to town and never given it a second thought. He decided to take a huge chance by responding with honesty himself.

"It can be rough when you're tryin' to recover from a bad relationship."

"Yes," she agreed, her voice pitched barely above a whisper. "I, um . . . I don't want to repeat the same mistakes."

"I don't blame you there."

"You don't?"

The incredulity in her voice made him smile sadly. She'd clearly been expecting an argument. "Not a bit. I've made a few mistakes in my lifetime." And blowing this chance with her wouldn't be added to the list. "Repeatin' 'em would be pretty damned dumb on my part."

He heard her sigh. "Thank you for not being mad at me."

"Mad at you? For cancelin' a silly lunch date? Nah."

"That's just it, don't you see—that it's only a silly lunch date. I don't know why I'm in such a dither about it. Have you ever felt like your life was becoming a rerun?"

"Like on television, you mean?"

"Yes, only a really *bad* rerun, the kind you never want to watch a second time. It's like getting stuck on a monorail track. I want to go a different direction this time, only no matter how hard I try, I can't. I'm doing the same things all over again. Having the same feelings. It makes me panicky."

The frantic edge in her voice told Parker that she truly did feel panicky, and she'd done such an excellent job of describing her sense of helplessness with the monorail analogy that he could almost feel it himself. Mojo waddled over to attack Parker's pant leg, but Parker was so focused on his conversation with Rainie that he barely felt the tugs. This was a turning point in their relationship, he realized, a hugely important turning point. Never before had she opened up to him like this. How he responded would determine where they went from here.

His first impulse was to promise that her relationship with him would be nothing like the one she'd just escaped, but if he did that, they would both have to acknowledge the possibility that they would someday have a relationship beyond that of boss and employee. He didn't think she was ready to contemplate that yet.

"In my opinion," he said cautiously, "a little panic can be a healthy thing."

"Healthy? It feels crazy to me."

"What would happen to all of us if we felt no fear after gettin' seriously hurt? It's called survival instinct, darlin'. You've been through a really rough time. If you felt no panic, that'd be crazy. Bein' afraid is completely normal."

"I'm *so* afraid, though. And I no longer trust my judgment. I was so *wrong* about him. I thought he was wonderful, and he . . . wasn't."

It was the closest that she'd ever come to acknowledging the abuse she had endured. Part of Parker wanted to press her to share more, but another part of him knew it would be smarter to back off. "Everyone makes a bad judgment call now and then. Makin' mistakes and learnin' from them is how we become better people."

"I'm not sure I learned from mine, though, and not everyone makes such a stupid mistake. He set me up, Parker. He knew I had an inheritance, and he pretended to be everything I needed him to be until he got his hands on it. I never even *suspected.* How stupid is that?"

Parker wiggled his boot to entertain the puppy while he collected his thoughts. Normally he never aired any of his family's dirty laundry. It was personal and nobody else's business. But he sensed there was one story that Rainie desperately needed to hear.

"Sweetheart, you need to stop beatin' up on yourself. My little sister, Sam, is one of the smartest, most astute ladies you'll ever meet." His voice had gone husky with sincerity. "And the exact same thing happened to her."

"It did?"

"Oh, yeah. A smooth-talkin', manipulative, money-grabbin' bastard lined her up in his sights, and despite all the warnin's she got from us to the contrary, she went ahead and married him. Correct me if I'm wrong, but I'm bettin' that you didn't have four brothers and a carin' father to warn you that you were makin' a mistake."

"No, I had no one."

"There, you see? At least Sam got some advice, whether she wanted to hear it or not. She was all caught up in the romantic aspect of it. And she believed in all his lies. That didn't make her dumb. It only meant she was young and naive. As it turned out, he was a drunk, a philanderer, and a woman beater who knew just where to aim his blows so the bruises were hidden by her clothing. Sam didn't come to me or any of my brothers for help, because she was afraid we'd kill him, and she was right. If I had known what the bastard was doin' to her, I might have ended up in prison for life. There's a hard-and-fast rule in the Harrigan family, one that my father drilled into all of us boys at a very young age: No man worth his salt ever hits a woman, and he doesn't stand aside while some other man transgresses, either. It's a code that my brothers and I take seriously."

Parker let that hang there for a moment. "My sister is *not* stupid, and neither are you. She made a stupid mistake, no argument there, and she'll be the first person to admit it. But that doesn't mean *she's* stupid. For a good long while after the marriage ended, she questioned her judgment, too, but over time, she healed. What you have to realize, honey, is that there are evil people in this world who don't reveal their true colors. You got suckered in. That isn't a reflection on your intelligence or your ability to judge someone's character. It's a reflection on him. He's a rotten bastard without a heart. That's *his* failin', not yours."

"How did your sister get out of the marriage without any help?" she asked shakily.

A cold feeling moved through Parker's chest. "The man had a bad habit of goin' out, gettin' liquored up, and then comin' home to whale the tar out of her. One night, he got her by the throat, and she thought he was gonna kill her. She took him down with a kitchen chair. Luckily for her, our dad taught her how to fight, and that included fightin' dirty. Sam doesn't talk about it much. I don't think she counts it as one of her finer moments. But I suspect that she kept hittin' him after he went down. When he was unconscious, she dragged him outside to either die or come around. I don't think she cared which. Shortly after that, she told our dad what had been goin' on, and the jerk never dared show his face around here again in the light of day. After the divorce, he caused her some grief, and now he's doin' time, but that's a whole other story."

"He's doing time, as in prison time?"

There was a hopeful thread in her voice that Parker couldn't miss. "Every dog has its day," he said, wishing that Rainie could soon have hers. "What you need to stay focused on is that you're perfectly normal. Your life isn't a rerun, honey. It only feels that way right now because everything is still so fresh in your mind and you're scared. Don't get it in your head that you're stupid. I can't count the times I've waded into a situation and didn't realize the danger until it was too late. Once that happens, all you can do is deal with the mess. You've done that. Right? Now it's time for you to move on."

"I wish it were that easy."

Parker decided to pretend he hadn't heard that. "I'm glad we've talked about this. It drives home to me that you're not ready for anything more than a friendship. What do you say to that idea?"

"Friendship?" She said the word as if it were a foreign concept.

He could almost see the wary look in her wide eyes, and that made him smile again. "You got so many friends that you can't use another one?" he asked.

She laughed, the sound thin and nervous. "No, of course not. I left all my friends behind when I—" She broke off. The ensuing silence seemed charged with electricity, and Parker knew she'd almost blurted out information that she was afraid to share. Someday, hopefully soon, she would come to trust him with all those secrets she guarded so carefully. "I, um, can't keep in touch with them now."

"Why not?" he asked, even though he figured he already knew the answer. "You afraid they might tell Mr. Not-So-Wonderful where you are?"

When she didn't immediately reply, Parker feared he had pushed her too far. But once again, she surprised him. "No, they're the best friends anyone ever had. They'd never do that. But letters and phone calls can be traced."

"You think he's that keen on findin' you?"

"Oh, yes," she whispered.

It was the first time they'd actually spoken of the man in

any concrete way. Parker burned to pelt her with questions. Where was he? Who was he? If only he had a name.

"You're afraid of him."

It wasn't a question, and Parker didn't pose it as one. But she answered anyway, breathing out the word: "Yes."

The pain he heard in her voice made his heart hurt for her. He wished he could offer her protection twenty-four/seven, but in order to do that, he'd have to bring her to the ranch. He didn't think she'd ever agree to that. "Is there any room in your house where you can barricade yourself in if he shows up?"

"I hook a chair under the bedroom doorknob, and I always make sure the windows are locked."

A window could be broken in two seconds flat, Parker thought, and a chair wedged under a doorknob wouldn't slow the bastard down for very long, either. He tried to imagine what it must be like for her to go to bed every night feeling frightened. It was a difficult concept to wrap his mind around. He wasn't afraid of that many things. Snakes made his skin crawl, but he wasn't really fearful of them.

"It sounds to me like I need to come over and do some work at your place."

"What kind of work?"

"Bars on all the windows that open into your bedroom, for starters, and maybe some bars to reinforce the bedroom door, too. You need a safe room, someplace where he can't get to you until help arrives. I've got a portable welder. I can pick up some steel and get it done in an afternoon. What d'ya say?"

"You'd do that?"

"Hey, what are friends for?" As Parker said those words, he instinctively knew he was taking the right tack. She needed a friend right now a whole lot more than a lover. "I could use a friend myself, you know."

"You?" she said dubiously.

"Yeah, me. I'm lonesome."

"With all your family living so close, you're lonesome."

"I can't spend all my time with family. We have three newlywed couples in the clan. I don't like to horn in on their together time too much. And Zach and Quincy have their own things going on."

"What kind of things?"

Parker almost said, *Redheads, blondes, and brunettes,* but he didn't want to give her the wrong impression. "Zach's young, so he's still doin' the honky-tonk-and-buckle-bunny thing."

"Honky-tonk, meaning bars?"

"Bars with live music and a dance floor, yeah."

"And buckle bunnies?"

"Women, usually young, who dress like cowgirls and like to hang out with rodeo champs. When you win a rodeo competition, you usually get a special belt buckle to commemorate the victory, and those young ladies cluster up around any man wearin' one."

"Zach has a championship buckle, I take it."

The statement drove home to Parker how little she knew about his family. "Darlin', Zach has enough championship buckles to wear a different one every day of the month. He's won rodeo competitions all across the nation. The Harrigans raise some of the finest ropin' horses in the world."

"So you've won a rodeo championship, too?"

"Nah, but my horses have won more than a few. All I do is sit in the saddle and look handsome while they do all the work."

He heard a smile in her voice when she said, "No conceit in your family, because you have it all?"

Parker grinned. "Here I am, bein' humble and givin' all the credit to my horses, and you accuse me of bein' conceited? This friendship of ours is gettin' off to a rough start."

"So what does your other brother do in the evening? Does he go with Zach to the honky-tonks to impress girls with his fancy belt buckles?"

"Nah, Quincy is more into spinach shakes and women with striated abs."

She giggled. "Spinach shakes?"

"With raw eggs and seaweed and all manner of other nauseous ingredients tossed in. The man is over the edge. He invited me for dinner last night. I was afraid he might feed me somethin' that'd make me turn green, so I stayed home and stared at the wall." In an attempt to steer her back to the original topic of conversation, he added, "So, you see, I really am lonely. I'm not pullin' your leg when I say I need a friend."

She grew quiet.

"I actually would like to do that work at your house," he quickly tacked on. "Just as a safety precaution. How's about if I do it tomorrow after we visit the pet store? I'll toss the welder in the back of my truck before we leave for town."

She laughed again. "You're forgetting that I originally called to cancel on that."

He grinned. "And you're forgettin' that good friends never let each other make the same mistakes twice. You're safe with me, Rainie. Give me a chance to prove it."

He concentrated on his breathing while he waited for her to answer. Finally, she said, "Only friendship, and nothing more? No strings, no expectations, no sneak kisses when I've let my guard down?"

Parker raised an eyebrow. He hadn't sneaked a kiss in over twenty years. "You have my word. That way, you can relax. Right? And I'll have a best buddy to hang out with who doesn't drink green stuff."

She giggled again. Oh, how he loved that sound. "Okay, we can give it a try, I guess. Just know, right up front, that anything more than friendship is totally out of the question for me."

Parker was fine with that. The only lasting romantic relationships that he'd ever seen had been built on a solid foundation of friendship. The other stuff came later—and he was a patient man.

Chapter Eight

Rainie had never fretted and fussed so much over what to wear out to lunch with a friend. She'd put most of her first paycheck in the bank, saving to buy a new set of snow tires before winter, so her wardrobe was still pathetic. She discarded three outfits before settling on a gauzy floral-print skirt and a pale pink V-necked sweater with three-quarter-length sleeves and small, pearlescent buttons down the front. For her feet, she chose the white canvas slip-ons. The ensemble set a casual mood yet looked dressy enough for eating out.

After pushing up the sweater sleeves, she gave herself a critical study. It never ceased to amaze her how different she looked since moving here. The sun-tipped, curly hair. The airy clothing. It was almost as if she'd subconsciously mimicked a certain style, only when she tried to think where she'd seen it, she came up blank. *No matter.* She'd succeeded in drastically changing her appearance. That was all that counted. The old Rainie no longer existed.

Before leaving the house, she crouched down to give Thomas a good-bye scratch behind his ears. "You're going to meet a new friend this afternoon," she told the cat. "His name is Mojo, and he's only a tiny baby. I'm counting on you not to scratch him. Okay?"

Thomas purred happily and rubbed himself against her

knees. Rainie brushed the fur from her skirt before grabbing her purse and cell phone. Then she raced to the car.

The morning was gorgeous, sunlight pooling like melted butter in the emerald green fields that lined the winding road to the ranch. Soft, cottony clouds streaked the azure sky. She rolled down her window to enjoy the breeze, rife with the scents of pine, freshly cut alfalfa, and stagnant water in irrigation ponds. Or was that cow manure? *Hmm.* She preferred to think it was water. Her hair whipped in first one direction and then another. Fortunately she carried a clip in her purse and could pull her hair back when she got to work.

Parker. Rainie still wasn't sure how he'd talked her out of canceling their lunch date. Looking back on the conversation, she could scarcely believe it had even taken place. She'd told him way too much. Only, somehow, it had seemed right. Her heart felt lighter today, her mood buoyant. Granted, she'd been cautious about what she said, but, oh, how nice it had been to let her guard down for a few minutes.

Sometimes she felt like a tightly sealed vial with the contents under pressure. She talked to Thomas a lot, but it wasn't the same as talking to a person who actually answered back. Last night as she lay in bed, listening to the house creak, she'd thought about all the things Parker had told her. He truly understood how a person could get sucked in, how she could think she was in control of a situation until it was way too late. It had been like that for her with Peter—like stepping off into shallow quicksand that didn't suck at her feet until she'd waded in too deep.

The memories made Rainie feel as if a vise were tightening around her chest. She flipped on the radio, found a station, and sang along with Mariah until her heart-attack moment had passed. She was okay. Peter was only an eight-hour drive away, but he'd never think to look for her in a midsize central Oregon community where high-end, resort-style living meshed almost seamlessly with ranch-focused enterprises and small-scale farms. She was a city girl—a high-minded city girl who'd once dreamed of breaking the glass ceiling of the corporate world.

"I'm okay," she assured herself.

She would soon have bars installed over her bedroom windows and a reinforced bedroom door. Her landlord might have a fit, but she would placate him with promises that she'd remove all the ironwork, putty the holes, and repaint when she moved. Now that she was making sixty grand a year, she could actually afford to paint, after all. If the old man complained too loudly, she could even upgrade to a better neighborhood. No matter what, she would have the bars. It had been so long since she'd slept soundly that she sometimes wondered if the dark shadows under her eyes were permanent. *Sleep.* Even during her marriage, she hadn't been able to rest well. She'd never known when Peter's biting fingers might curl over her shoulder.

Rainie's eyes filled with tears when she remembered those times. She brushed angrily at her cheeks. Parker would understand. He'd talk about survival instinct and how everyone made mistakes. She had an overabundance of survival instinct. She'd learned that the hard way, with Peter as her teacher.

Parker was putting the welding equipment into the back of his truck when Rainie pulled her Mazda into the ranch parking area. Looking too handsome to be legal in a fresh pair of Wrangler jeans and a blue chambray work shirt, he turned to wave at her. She waved back, then knotted her hand into a fist on her lap. Was she out of her mind to be going to lunch with him? No matter what he said, she *wasn't* safe with him. No woman was.

"Mornin'!" he called as he strode toward her car in that loose-hipped, lazy way of his. He gave the impression that nothing short of a bomb going off could make him move quickly, and yet she'd seen his lightning-fast reaction time while working with his horses. His unhurried, relaxed manner was deceiving. "Gorgeous day, isn't it?"

It truly was a gorgeous day, and his smile—a devastating tilt of firm lips that displayed incredibly white teeth—made the sun seem to shine even brighter. He drew off his brown Stetson to blot beads of perspiration from his brow with a rolled-back sleeve. His wavy hair glistened like polished jet in the morning light.

"Gettin' warm already."

Determined not to panic at the burn of feelings he kindled within her, Rainie got out of the car and reached back in for her purse. "How'd it go with Mojo last night?"

"We got off to a rough start. I made him a bed in the laundry room, and he didn't care for the accommodations."

"Uh-oh. Did he cry?"

"Did he *cry*? The caterwaulin' carried to every room of my house, so loud I couldn't even think about sleepin'." His smile widened. "I got out the book I bought on puppies. It said he'd calm down if I wrapped a tickin' clock up in a towel and put it in bed with him. It took me almost an hour to find one."

"Practically everything's digital nowadays."

"Exactly. Fortunately I have a little windup I take on trips. In the book, they claim the tickin' sound mimics the mother dog's heartbeat and soothes the puppy."

"Did it work?"

"Hell, no."

Rainie couldn't smother a laugh. "What did you do?"

"Well, at first, I lectured him about knowin' his place and not gettin' any highfalutin ideas about sleepin' with me. *That* wasn't gonna happen. I don't mind him bein' an inside dog, but a man's got to draw the line somewhere. Right?"

"Right. So where did you draw yours?"

"Right down the middle."

"Right down the middle of what?"

He gave her a slow, conspiratorial wink. "Of my king-size bed."

She laughed again. Parker had that effect on her. That was one of the reasons he made her so nervous: because she found him so disarming.

"Only he doesn't understand boundary lines," he continued. "I fell asleep with him suckin' on my armpit hair."

That did it. Rainie collapsed against the fender of her car, so overcome by laughter that her knees would barely hold her up. He watched her with a bemused grin.

"You think that's funny, do you?"

She nodded as she wiped tears of mirth from her cheeks. He sighed and plopped the hat back on his dark head. "Yeah, well, I have to admit I found it a little humorous myself. I got a dog that'll grow up to be more stubborn than I am. I never thought I'd see the day when I'd sleep with a critter that's got a perpetual leak. Got up this mornin' and had to change my sheets."

"He'll get over missing his mother soon," she assured him.

"Maybe. But what if he switches his devotion to me and wants to sleep with me when he weighs a hundred and fifty pounds?"

"At least you've got a roomy bed."

His lips twitched. "You're a huge help."

Rainie spent the morning trying to work. Unfortunately Mojo wanted to play, and he refused to take no for an answer. The wading pool was absolutely worthless as a holding pen and took up so much of the walking room that she finally wrestled it out to the hallway and left it leaning against the wall. Then she covered the floor with newspaper, which Mojo thought was immense fun. She would just get the sheets neatly arranged when he would attack them. By the time Parker showed up for their trip to town, the office looked as if the ceiling had rained confetti.

"Dear God. Is this my *office*? Maybe I should buy him a cage."

"You can't leave an active baby in a cage all day."

He conceded the point with a pensive nod. "It doesn't look like you got much work done."

"That depends on how you define work. I've kept busy, just not doing anything productive. I need to log some entries from yesterday. Maybe we can start watching him in shifts."

Parker leaned down to scoop up the puppy. Mojo immediately attacked his shirt collar. "I found a deep box and put a saddle blanket in there for him. You reckon we should take along some food and water, too?"

"I reckon," she echoed, trying to suppress a grin.

While Rainie went to the coffee room to mix Mojo some meals, which she stored in empty baby-food jars, Parker collected the puppy's dishes and filled a sports bottle with water.

"This is as bad as havin' a baby," he complained. "All we're lackin' is diapers."

"He'll grow up soon and it won't be so much trouble to take him places."

He put everything into a plastic shopping bag, collected the puppy, and said, "Well, I think we're all set."

Rainie thought that might be an overly optimistic statement, and she was right. Mojo immediately began yelping when Parker put him inside the box. They drove only about half a mile before Parker pulled over to the side of the road. "Would you mind holdin' him?"

Rainie held out her arms. Mojo whimpered and cuddled close in her embrace. "He's so relieved. I think the box scared him."

Parker pulled back out into the lane. "He's gonna get

another fright, then. They won't allow him in the restaurant. It's against health regulations. I can't leave him loose in the truck. He'll poop and pee everywhere."

"We could just do fast food."

"No way. You're fixed up too pretty. I promised you a real lunch, and you're gettin' a real lunch."

Rainie would have been just as happy with a hamburger. It bothered her to think that Mojo would cry the entire time they were gone. When they got to the restaurant, a little hole-in-the-wall place on Main, she cast a gloomy glance at the window, where the name ROMANO'S was painted on the glass in red shadow block. Parker plucked the puppy from her arms and gently returned him to the box on the backseat. Mojo instantly started to yelp and whimper. The sound tore at her heart.

Parker gave her a long look. "I could order takeout and we could eat out here."

A smile swelled in Rainie's chest. No wonder Parker Harrigan was so hard for her to resist. "That'd be fun. Or we could go to the park."

"Mojo can't go to places like parks until he's fully immunized. Tucker says he could catch parvo or distemper."

"Is the pet store safe? Other dogs go in there, too."

"Tucker says that's safe because they disinfect the floors every night." He nudged his hat back to grin at her. "Let me go in and order. Rosa will fix us right up. She's a sweetheart."

Expecting Parker to be gone for quite a while, Rainie took Mojo out of the box and held him in her arms. To her surprise, though, Parker returned in only seconds to tap on the glass. She lowered the window. "They don't do takeout?"

"They do, but they want us to bring him in. Rosa invited us to eat in back at their kitchen table. She says the health regulations don't extend to their private living area and the inspector won't care."

"But Mojo may make a mess on her floor."

"She's got newspapers." He grinned and shrugged. "Like I said, she's a sweetheart."

Rosa Romano was a short, plump Italian woman who wore her graying black hair in a coiled braid at the crown of her head. A flour-streaked red apron protected her clothing, a grandmotherly ensemble of polyester stretch pants and a diagonal-print blouse. The moment Rainie stepped inside the restaurant, Rosa began talking and gesturing, her friendliness and warmth so contagious that Rainie instantly relaxed.

"So this is Mojo!" the woman cried, taking the puppy from Rainie's arms. "Papa, you gotta come see. He's a little pistol!"

Mr. Romano was as thin as Rosa was plump and only marginally taller. His shiny bald pate, rimmed by a band of short gray hair clipped high over his ears, shone like a polished globe in the fluorescent light as he crossed the empty dining area. A broad grin creased his wrinkled visage when he saw the puppy. "Oho, he'll grow to be a monster, Parker. Just look at those paws. It is good you come early!" He motioned for them to follow him into the back rooms. "Rosa and I have no customers yet. It doesn't get busy until twelve thirty. Then we barely get a break until closing."

They passed through a commercial kitchen area that was so aromatic Rainie's mouth started to water. Homemade bread, marinara sauce, oregano and basil—the air smelled good enough to eat. The apartment in back was small and cluttered but spotless. Rosa seated them at a small oak table with a centerpiece bowl of colorful dried peppers and gourds.

"Finally," she said to her husband, who was filling water glasses, "our Parker has found himself a nice girl! No goop on her face, no claws for fingernails." She beamed at Rainie. "It is good to know he has some good sense somewhere under that hat he has glued on his head."

Parker waggled his eyebrows lecherously at Rainie, then removed the Stetson and hooked it over the back of a chair beside him. "Sorry, Rosa, I was raised in a barn. Well, a stable, actually, but the point is the same. I forget my manners."

The older woman laughed and rumpled his black hair. "You are like my Michael when he comes home. No worries about manners in his mama's kitchen. It is where he can forget being a fancy businessman."

"What kind of business is he in?" Rainie asked.

"Our Michael is a bank president," Rosa said proudly. Rubbing her fingertips together, she laughed and added, "He makes big money."

With an expertise born of long practice, Rosa put place mats in front of them and quickly arranged their place settings, complete with artfully folded bright red napkins. Then she handed them each a menu. Rainie felt strange sitting in someone's kitchen to order a meal. But at least Mojo was happy. Mr. Romano tossed down newspapers on the kitchen floor, which the puppy promptly attacked and started to shake. The couple laughed in delight at the puppy's ferocious growls.

Parker highly recommended that Rainie try the spaghetti and meatballs or the lasagna. In the end, she ordered one, and he ordered the other. Rosa gave them each an extra plate so they could share. Then she and her husband, who Rainie learned was called Pete, joined them at the table to grab some lunch themselves. At their insistence, Rainie was soon forking up ravioli from their bowls to taste the different fillings. Pete's were made with a variety of fine cheeses, Rosa's with chicken and beef. It was impossible for Rainie to remain tense with such warm, relaxed people. She was soon laughing and talking with them as if she'd known them all her life.

"Yum, this food is indescribable," she said in all sincerity. She glanced over to see Parker break off a large chunk of crusty, piping-hot Italian bread. "Thank you for bringing me."

"Don't thank me," he said. "I'm doin' my own belly a favor—to heck with yours."

Rainie so enjoyed the meal that she hated to see it end, but all too soon the food was gone, and the Romanos were drawn from the table by the customer bell chiming out front.

"Just leave the dishes," Rosa said with a wave of her plump hand. "They must be washed in the commercial machine."

"You haven't billed me," Parker protested.

Rosa flapped her hand again as she vanished from the room. "You are like family. Do you think I bill our Michael when he comes home for lunch?"

After Rosa departed, Parker looked at Rainie. "Can you remember how much the lasagna was? I can't eat their food and not pay for it."

Rainie agreed and fished through her purse for a pen and paper to add up their bill. Then she insisted on paying for her half. Parker rolled his eyes but finally accepted her money. "You're a stubborn woman, Rainie Pritchard."

"We're just friends, remember, and friends go dutch."

After picking up all the newspapers, they exited through the front part of the restaurant with Mojo hidden under Parker's shirt. Well, sort of hidden. It looked as if he had a lumpy bosom that jiggled when he walked, which set Rainie to laughing. Her face was hot with suppressed mirth by the time they got back in the truck.

"I haven't had this much fun in I can't remember when," she confessed, her mouth still curved in a smile.

"Stick with me, darlin'. I'm more fun than a barrelful of monkeys." He handed her the puppy and started the truck engine. "Next up, the pet store," he said. "I don't have a collar or leash, so we'll have to carry him while we shop."

That sounded like a workable plan to Rainie—until

Parker made the mistake of putting Mojo down for just a moment to help her find a purple Tasmanian Devil in a display basket. The moment the puppy's feet touched the pet-store floor, he was off and running.

"Shit!" Parker said under his breath.

And the chase was on. Rainie nearly had a heart attack when she saw Mojo heading straight for a huge male Great Dane. She felt sure the puppy would be killed on the spot. But instead the adult dog suffered the puppy's tumbling assault with gentle forbearance. The Great Dane's owner, a slender, middle-aged woman with blond hair, laughed at Mojo's enthusiastic attempts to make friends.

Before Parker could catch Mojo, the little rascal was off, and Parker was soon cursing under his breath again. Rainie clapped a hand over her mouth when she saw the problem. About ten feet ahead of them, Mojo had squatted to pee. By the time they reached him, a puddle glistened on the tile floor. Parker scooped up the runaway puppy, winked at Rainie, and started humming the Marine Corps anthem as he shuffled his boot in the wetness to spread it thin.

"What are you *doing*?" Rainie whispered.

"They'll never know," he assured her with a grin.

"That isn't *nice*," she said. "Shouldn't we clean it up?"

"They'll mop after closin'. Relax."

When they checked out, Rainie's arms were filled with puppy and Parker's were filled with several toys, a tiny studded collar and leash, spill-proof dishes, and a fake-fur dog bed. The tab was almost two hundred dollars.

"I had no idea puppies could be so expensive," Rainie observed as they returned to the truck.

"I had no idea they could be so much work. I'm flat tuckered."

Rainie grinned. "I wish I'd had my phone with me to take a video of you, chasing Mojo up and down the aisles. And the look on your face when he attacked the Great Dane was *priceless*."

"I figured he was about to be lunch." He chucked Mojo under the chin. "He's not afraid of anything. Is he?"

As Rainie cuddled the puppy close to her chest, she found herself wishing she could be as fearless. Everything was an exciting adventure to Mojo.

"I'm glad you talked me into coming," she confessed.

As dark as burnt umber, Parker's eyes twinkled over at her. "I'm glad I did, too. It's been fun." His mouth twitched at one corner. "But, hey, the day's not over yet. Next stop is the buildin'-supply place for some steel."

"You're tired. You can do that some other day."

"A cup of your coffee will revive me." He shifted the truck into reverse to back out of the parking spot. "I'll sleep better tonight knowin' you're safe."

Seeing where Rainie lived filled Parker with sadness. Though she'd tried to give the place warmth and had done a marvelous job of decorating on what had clearly been a shoestring budget, every room reflected how empty her life was. He saw no photographs of family or friends, no souvenirs from trips that she'd taken, and no keepsakes or heirlooms. It was weird—kind of like a movie set. She'd set a beautiful stage, but there was nothing real about any of it. Until now, Parker hadn't fully comprehended what it must be like to leave one's life behind and try to create a new one from scratch. Even his sparsely decorated home had mementos in it to remind him of all the people he loved. He had wedding pictures in almost every room, and candid shots of his family members, their faces aglow with happiness. In his bedroom, he had framed photographs of his mom and dad when they were young, plus images of his siblings at different ages, one of Sammy with a gap-toothed smile being one of his favorites.

Everything in Rainie's house was secondhand. Her kitchen towels were faded and limp. The throw pillows in the living room were as worn as the threadbare sofa they adorned. He'd known Rainie was in dire financial straits when he met her, but he'd led such an advantaged lifestyle for so many years that the nuts and bolts of poverty were no longer real to him. It bothered him to think that this lady had to scrub her beautiful face with a hand-me-down washcloth and that even her bedsheets had probably been used by someone else.

"It isn't much," she said, nervously fingering the tiny buttons on her sweater. "I, um, didn't have much money to spend."

"It's nice." Parker stopped at a bookcase to touch a gold picture frame that still held a stock photo of a blond little girl in a pink outfit. The picture said it all, namely that this woman was absolutely alone in the world. "Cute kid."

Her hazel eyes darted to the picture, and two bright spots of color flagged her cheeks. "I don't have any pictures of my own, and I just needed the feeling of that. I left sort of suddenly."

"Maybe someday you can go back and get your stuff."

The pink drained from her cheeks, and her lips went white. "No, that will never be possible."

Parker wanted to tell her she wouldn't have to go alone, that he'd be there to protect her, but he decided it would be best to let it go. Instead he went to have a look at her bedroom. Again, he was struck by the stage-set feeling that seemed to bounce off the walls of the colorfully embellished room. Someone else's handmade quilt served as a bedspread; someone else's crocheted doilies and dresser scarves camouflaged the nicks and gouges on the rickety dresser and bedside tables. Even the clothes hanging in the closet weren't her own.

Mojo scampered ahead of Parker to attack the dust ruffle

on the bed. Then the puppy turned on the throw rug. Rainie laughed. "I'm glad I don't have carpets. At least everything on my floors is washable."

Parker went to examine her windows. They were old, aluminum-framed, with ineffective latch locks. Seeing them made him cringe. Before he left, he intended to make sure she would at least be safe while she slept.

He set up shop on Rainie's back stoop, which earned him several suspicious looks from her elderly neighbor. Parker just smiled and inclined his head when he saw the lace curtains twitching next door. In only minutes, he'd cut and welded bars to fit over the inside frame of one window and was starting on another set.

"You're good at this," Rainie said when she brought him a cup of coffee.

"Lots of practice." Parker flipped up his welding goggles to take a sip from the earthenware mug she'd handed him. "I did all the upper bars on my stall gates. It's really pretty simple stuff." He angled a warning look at her. "Be sure you don't watch when the flame is on. Okay? It can damage your eyes without protective lenses."

"I won't," she assured him. "I was thinking that I might cook dinner. Do you like meat loaf?"

"I love meat loaf."

"Then you'll stay?"

He nodded, set the coffee aside, and resumed his task, which sent her scurrying back indoors. When he had the window bars ready to install and reentered the house, the kitchen smelled fabulous. "You never mentioned that you can cook."

"Oh, yes. Peter expected gourmet—" She broke off and sent him a startled look.

"It's okay, Rainie. I've always known the man must have a name."

She quickly averted her face, hiding her worried expression behind the curtain of her curly hair. "I hope you like chocolate cake."

"What's not to like about chocolate cake? Just don't go to a lot of trouble, okay? Unlike good old Peter, I don't expect gourmet."

While he installed the bars over her windows, Rainie came in to perch on the edge of the bed. "Thomas must be afraid of men. He's usually here when I get home."

"Thomas, the tomcat?" Parker sent her an amused grin. "Maybe he knows Mojo is here. Cats and dogs don't always get along."

She bent to pick up the puppy, who had sunk his teeth into the hem of her skirt. "That could be, I suppose. How long do puppies do this chewy thing?"

"I have no idea. I'm a novice, remember. I imagine it gets better once they're finished teethin'." Parker braced his feet to put some muscle into tightening a bolt. "There you are, Rainie mine," he said as he stepped back to survey his handiwork. "You've got bars on your windows."

She set the puppy aside to come and look. With slender fingertips, she tested the steel. "Oh, Parker, these are fabulous."

"Well, fabulous is overkill. They need some paint. Will you do them in black or some other color?"

She frowned thoughtfully. "Probably ecru, like the walls, so they won't be so noticeable."

"Good plan." He collected his tools. "Now to reinforce the door."

Before the sun set that evening, Parker had finished with her bedroom, and Rainie had supper on the table. She felt oddly nervous as he sat down across from her.

"It isn't exactly Romano's," she told him.

"It looks awesome!" He started to reach for the meat loaf, then remembered his hat and cast her a sheepish look.

"Sorry." He removed the Stetson and set it on a chair beside him. Then, as he leaned forward to lift the platter, the table wobbled, slopping wine over the edge of her goblet onto the embroidered tablecloth. "Uh-oh. Damn, honey. I'm sorry."

"It's fine. I'm an expert at removing wine stains."

He glimpsed a haunted darkness in her eyes just before she glanced away to blot up the spill of crimson. She was such a mystery, this lady. He had understood her sudden pallor when he'd mentioned the possibility of her going back home someday to retrieve her things. But why had she gotten so upset about revealing Peter's name? And now she was in a dither over a wine spill? Parker suspected it all would make sense once he learned more about her, but for now, he was left trying to connect the dots and couldn't see a picture forming.

"I'm sorry about the table," she said. "One leg is bent. The wobble can be bothersome."

He leaned down to examine the leg. "When supper's over, I'll have a look. Maybe I can shore it up on that side with a wedge of steel."

"That would be great."

Rainie had shared enough meals with Parker by now to know that he would pray before he started to eat. She waited with her hands folded in her lap, giving thanks for the food in her own way while he crossed himself and murmured his blessing. Afterward, he helped himself to a large serving of meat loaf before passing her the platter. He was so relaxed that Rainie felt the tension easing from her shoulders.

"Oh, man, this is good," he said, cheek bulging with meat, a fork heaped with mashed potatoes hovering at his lips. "I hired you for the wrong job."

Rainie laughed, pleased that he was enjoying the meal. "I learned everything from books. This is a pretty simple meal, actually. Sometime I'll fix you my Tuesday-night special, chicken cordon bleu."

Parker stopped chewing. "Did you make it for Peter?"

Rainie dropped her gaze to her plate. "I'd really appreciate it if you'd forget his name and never say it again."

"You didn't answer my question."

She glanced back up. "Yes, I fixed it for him. Why do you ask?"

"Because your eyes looked sad when you said it was your Tuesday-night special." He took a sip of wine. "I don't think I want you to make it for me, not if it brings back bad memories. Come up with a new special that you never fixed for . . ." He set the goblet back down. "What did you say his name was, again?"

Rainie laughed. She couldn't help it. "I can't remember."

He winked at her. "Let's keep it that way."

For the remainder of the meal, he talked about his childhood, telling her funny stories about the mischief he and his brothers had perpetrated. The silliness helped Rainie to separate herself from the memories of Peter's rage when she'd gotten her days mixed up and served him chicken cordon bleu on the wrong night. It also distanced her from the time when he'd rubbed her face in the spilled wine. With Parker sitting across from her, those moments seemed to have happened a lifetime ago.

While Rainie was serving dessert, Thomas came home. Mojo, who'd been napping at Parker's feet, was awakened by the sound of the rubber flap of the pet door opening and closing. The puppy yipped with excitement and made a beeline for the cat. Thomas bristled and arched his back, clearly ready for battle, but before Mojo could reach him, he avoided the altercation by leaping onto the table. Rainie held her breath, afraid Parker might grow angry. A lot of people didn't like it when cats jumped up on kitchen surfaces.

But Parker only grinned, reaching out to pet the cat while steadying his wineglass. "So this is Thomas."

The tomcat was soon curled up on Parker's lap, purring to beat the band.

"He likes you," Rainie observed.

"I'm an animal person. He probably senses that." He glanced down at Mojo. "Doesn't seem to like dogs much, though. Maybe, over time, they'll become friends."

Rainie took Parker a piece of cake. To her surprise, he allowed Thomas to remain on his lap while he ate the dessert.

When the meal was over, he insisted on helping her with the dishes and going around the house to do puppy cleanup. When everything was tidy, he collected his equipment and tools, took them out to his truck, and then returned to get Mojo and tell her good night.

Standing at the door with the puppy tucked under one arm, he said, "Supper was awesome, Rainie. I really enjoyed it. Thanks for invitin' me."

Rainie's cheeks went warm. "It was the least I could do. Thank *you* for all your hard work. I'll sleep like a baby tonight."

He opened the door to leave, then turned back. Before she could guess what he meant to do, he bent and placed a quick kiss on her forehead. "Good night. Sleep tight."

And with that, he was gone. Rainie rubbed the spot where his lips had set her skin to tingling. Then she hurriedly engaged the dead bolts on her front door. Outside she heard his truck engine roar to life. A moment later, she caught the sound of the knobby tires grabbing asphalt as he drove away.

She had just released a dreamy sigh when her cell phone rang, making her jump with a start. No one ever called her anymore. She ran into the kitchen to pluck the device from her purse.

"Hello?"

Parker's voice came over the line, as deep and rich as if he were still in the room. "Just for the record, that wasn't a sneak kiss. You saw it comin'."

Rainie grinned in spite of herself.

"It was also only a kiss between friends, so don't start readin' any hidden agenda into it. All right?"

She cradled the phone to her cheek as she sank onto a chair. The table wobbled under the press of her elbow.

"Rainie, are you there?"

"I'm here. You forgot to fix my table."

"Uh-oh." She heard the deep rumble of his laugh. The sound sent waves of warmth through her. "What do you say to us workin' out a deal? I'll fix the table in exchange for another home-cooked meal."

Rainie hadn't anticipated having Parker as a dinner guest again. But then, she was quickly coming to realize that Parker Harrigan was full of surprises. That brotherly kiss on her forehead had not been what she would have expected from him. It had touched her, actually. He'd kept his word, treating her like a friend. For some reason, the realization made her eyes burn.

"That sounds like a deal to me," she managed to say without a wobble in her voice. "I forgot to pay you for the steel. It totally slipped my mind."

"You're in charge of the ranch checkbook these days." His truck engine rumbled in the background. "Deduct it from next month's wages. I'll leave the receipt on your desk."

"I'll do that."

"Grab a pencil and paper, would you? I need you to write somethin' down."

Rainie hurried over to the counter where she kept her phone book and shopping list. "Okay, I'm ready."

He recited his phone numbers to her, saying each digit slowly. Then he asked her to repeat them back to him. When he was satisfied that she had them right, he said, "Enter them into speed dial on all your phones, including the cell. If anything happens when you're there alone, call me before you dial the cops."

Rainie squeezed her eyes closed, surprised and touched yet again. "You live so far out."

"I can be there in ten minutes."

"What?" Rainie had made the drive many times and doubted that was possible. "That's crazy, Parker. It's a thirty-minute trip."

"You haven't seen me open this baby up. Just trust me on it. Okay? If anything happens, I'll get there before the police do, guaranteed."

Rainie nodded, then realized he couldn't see her. "All right. Consider yourself entered in my speed dial."

"Thanks. I'll rest better knowin' you can hot-dial me. Just don't panic and forget to do it. No need to stay on the line. If I get a hang-up call from you, I'll know you're in trouble and be there before shit becomes shat."

Rainie had never heard that expression. "Thank you, Parker. No matter what, I'll remember to call you. I promise."

She was smiling as she broke the connection. Then she immediately did as he had asked, entering his numbers into her phones. It comforted her to know he was only the push of a button away. The realization troubled her. Parker Harrigan was worming his way straight into her heart, and she couldn't seem to stop it from happening. He made her *want*. Not in a sexual way. Peter had cured her of those yearnings. No, Parker made her want other things—to feel his big hand holding hers, to feel his strong arms around her, to hear the steady thump of his heart when she pressed her cheek to his solid chest. She wasn't sure when it had happened, but being near Parker made her feel safe, and to her, feeling safe was complete bliss.

A few minutes later, as she prepared for bed, she felt Parker's presence everywhere in her bedroom. He was in her phones. He was in the bars over her windows and door. For the first time since she'd moved in, she didn't bother to lock the bathroom door while she showered. Not even Peter could pass through steel. In order to get to her, he'd need a hacksaw, and even then, it would take him several minutes to cut his way through the heavy metal.

After turning out the lights, Rainie snuggled under the covers with Thomas. She didn't shiver with dread as the shadows closed in around her. Peter no longer lurked in the darkness.

Parker Harrigan did.

Chapter Nine

Mojo loved his new toys. The Tasmanian Devil squeaked, and the puppy seemed to find that highly entertaining, which allowed Rainie some uninterrupted time to work. Or so she thought. She'd just settled at her desk with a mug of coffee and a pile of invoices that needed to be logged into the computer when a rap came at the office door. She glanced up in bewilderment because Parker never knocked and his employees rarely visited the office.

"Come in," she called out.

The door swung open to reveal an older version of Parker standing at the threshold. He wore the usual ranch-issue clothing, a faded blue chambray shirt, and equally faded Wrangler jeans. His dark brown Stetson sat at a jaunty angle on his salt-and-pepper head. At his narrow waist, he sported a hand-tooled leather belt with a fancy silver-and-gold buckle. His dusty, nicked riding boots looked almost as old as he was, which Rainie guessed to be about sixty, although he had the physique of a much younger man.

"Hi," she said, determining immediately that he must be Frank Harrigan, the family patriarch.

He gave her a long study that made her feel like a bug specimen in a bottle. Then his brown eyes warmed on hers and began to twinkle. He inclined his head in a brief nod. "Howdy. I'm Parker's dad, Frank."

As he stepped into the room, he moved with the same easy grace as his son, the contours of his well-muscled body impressive for a man his age. The powerful set of his shoulders drew the cloth of his shirt taut over his upper arms, and the denim of his jeans showcased strong, roped thighs.

Rainie pushed up from her chair and stepped around the desk to offer him her hand. “I’m the bookkeeper, Anna Pritchard.”

As his leathery fingers closed around hers, he said, “I thought Parker said your name was Rainie.”

“Oh. That’s my nickname.”

“You cry a lot as a kid or somethin’?”

She laughed nervously. “No, not really. It’s just what my dad called me.”

“That’s what I’ll call you then.” He released her hand to nudge up his hat. After watching Mojo for a moment, he grinned and shook his head, his resemblance to Parker so marked that Rainie couldn’t stop staring. “This place looks like a tornado struck.”

“The tornado’s name is Mojo. He likes to rip up the newspapers.”

“I can see that.” Frank crouched beside the puppy and grabbed the toy. Mojo braced his stout little legs, let out a ferocious growl, and began tugging in the other direction. Frank laughed. “He’s got spunk. I’ll say that for him.”

“Can I get you a cup of coffee?” Rainie offered. “I just made a fresh pot.”

“I’d love one,” he replied. “A dollop of cream and one sugar, please.”

Rainie went to the coffee room. When she returned a moment later, Frank Harrigan had settled his narrow hips against the edge of Parker’s desk. He accepted the coffee with a nod of thanks, took a cautious sip, and then said, “I meant to come over and meet you sooner, but Dee Dee has had me busy with honey-dos. Got it into her head that the house needed fixin' up—new drapes, new furniture, and all manner of other changes." He shrugged. "Looked fine the way it was to me, but Dee Dee wasn't in a frame of mind to ask my opinion."

Rainie smiled. "Maybe she just needed to put her own stamp on things."

He nodded. "Could be, I reckon. When we got married, she sold her place. Maybe this is her way of makin' a new nest."

Rainie settled back down at her desk, wondering about the purpose of his visit. "Parker is in the arena, I think."

"He is. I saw him on my way in." He flashed a grin at her. "I'm not here to see Parker. I'm here to see you."

"Oh." Rainie waited for him to say more, but no explanation was forthcoming. "What are you here to see me about?" she finally asked.

"Nothin' in particular. Just wanted to meet you and say welcome." He took another swallow of coffee. "Parker says you're a damn fine bookkeeper."

"He does?"

Frank chuckled. "You seem surprised. Don't you agree with that estimation?"

Rainie picked up her mug and cradled it between her hands. "I suppose I do, yes, although I must say that bookkeeping isn't my specialty."

"What is your specialty?"

"Business analysis, only in a very personal, hands-on way. I worked with entrepreneurs, helping them to redesign the workplace, develop employee incentive programs, and streamline expenses, allowing for higher pay structures and increased profits."

His grizzled eyebrows arched. "You can do all that?"

"I was learning. Things happened, and I never finished my internship."

"Ah." He mulled that over for a moment. "Life got in the way, huh?"

Rainie found herself starting to relax. He had kind eyes and an irresistible smile that made her feel as if she'd known him for years. "That's a good way of putting it," she agreed. "Life does get in the way sometimes."

"Are you sorry? About havin' to quit your internship, I mean."

It had been a long time since Rainie had allowed herself to think about her destroyed dreams. It came as something of a surprise to realize that she no longer mourned their loss. "Not really, no. I'm happy here." She took a sip of her coffee, marveling at the truth of that statement. She *was* happy here—absolutely and completely happy. "The work isn't too demanding, Parker pays me well, and"—she glanced at Mojo, who was still chewing on his toy—"things never get dull."

Frank laughed. "Hold your hat, darlin'. Things will only get livelier. Come next spring, you'll be bottle-feedin' and imprintin' foals."

"Oh, no." She shook her head. "I didn't sign on to work with the horses."

He grinned mischievously. "And you think that'll make you exempt? Think again. Things get crazy around here when the mares start droppin' foals, and Parker's not shy about enlistin' volunteers."

In Rainie's experience, Parker wasn't shy about much of anything. "What, exactly, is imprinting?"

"That's how those horses out there got so gentle, from bein' imprinted. You essentially desensitize the foal to all manner of things that will frighten him when he grows older. Parker starts 'em off right after they're born. He'll have you out there helpin' him, mark my words. Durin' foalin' season, he gets stretched mighty thin, and imprintin' is the single most important thing he does durin' that time."

A month ago, the mere thought of being recruited to work with the horses would have alarmed Rainie, but now she no longer felt quite so intimidated by the huge creatures. Montana had come to expect treats from her when she entered the stable each morning, and soon all of the other horses had started expecting them as well. She'd been nervous at first, but the animals were so careful not to bite her as they took a carrot or apple slice that she soon stopped being afraid.

"I love babies. Working with the foals might be fun."

"They are cute," he agreed. "And earnin' their trust is rewardin', with the double benefit that you know you're savin' 'em a lot of heartache on down the road."

"How is that?"

"An imprinted horse is easy to work with and seldom requires a twitch or rough handlin' to control 'em. They're as gentle as lapdogs, and not much of anything spooks 'em."

"What's a twitch?" she couldn't resist asking.

"There are several different kinds. One is a stick with a rope or chain loop on the end. You fit the loop over the horse's nose and twist the stick until it grows uncomfortably tight. Another kind is a clamp that's inserted in the horse's nostrils. Supposedly the horse is so focused on the discomfort of the twitch that it barely notices what you're doin'. The truth, in my opinion, is that it hurts so bad, the horse is afraid to move."

"That's terrible."

He inclined his head in agreement. "That's why we Harrigans imprint all our horses. We don't like havin' to restrain our animals. It's much better for us, not to mention the horse, if they're imprinted."

"Now I know where Parker got his love of equines."

"From me, no doubt about it. Horses are my passion." His eyes lit with amusement. "And Dee Dee, too, of course." He finished off his coffee and took the cup to the other room.

When he returned, he tipped his hat to her in farewell. "You'll do, Rainie. You'll do nicely."

Rainie stared at the closed door for several seconds after he left. She would do? She felt as if she'd just passed some kind of test.

During lunch, Parker invited Rainie to go horseback riding with him that afternoon. She glanced down at her skirt. "I can't go riding in this."

"You're wearin' boots, and I took the liberty of borrowin' a pair of Sam's jeans and a hat for you to wear."

Rainie hadn't yet met Samantha. "What if they don't fit?"

"They'll fit." He gave her a measuring look. "I've got an expert eye. You're about her height and the same width in the beam."

Rainie realized that he'd been looking at her posterior. Heat rushed to her cheeks. "I've never ridden a horse."

"I got a sweetheart picked out for ya. Come on. Say yes. I promise you'll have fun."

Rainie unwrapped her hamburger and took a bite. "I'm not so sure about that."

"Trust me."

In that moment when Rainie met his gaze, she had a feeling that he was asking for far more from her than was apparent on the surface. A taut silence fell between them. *Trust.* To him, it was such a simple thing.

"I'm not a very trusting soul," she quipped, trying to keep the mood light.

"I know," he said, his voice suddenly gravelly and low-pitched. "Trust me, honey. I swear you'll never have reason to regret it."

The bite of hamburger in Rainie's mouth went dry and sticky. She struggled to swallow and nearly choked. Grabbing for her soft drink, she finally managed to wash it down. "Are we just talking about a horseback ride?" she asked.

"For now," he replied softly.

"For now? I don't understand."

" 'Life's a dance. You learn as you go.' " His mouth tipped into a winsome grin. "You ever hear that song?"

Rainie shook her head.

"It's one of my favorites. Life truly is like a dance, you know. Sometimes you get to lead, and sometimes you have to follow. We're all just learnin' as we go. And you know what else? You have to show up for the dance in order to hear the music."

Rainie felt as if she'd just waded out into deep water with stones in her pockets.

"Dance with me?" he invited softly. "Just turn loose, Rainie mine, and go with the music."

Rainie could see no correlation between horseback riding and dancing, but she ended up accepting the invitation, anyway. She found it nearly impossible to tell Parker Harrigan no.

The horse he'd chosen for her was named Barcelona, after the famous city in Spain. While helping Rainie to mount up, Parker explained that he called the mare Lona, for short.

"Lona," Rainie repeated, softly stroking the mare's chestnut mane. "She's beautiful, Parker." Oddly, Rainie didn't feel afraid to be so far off the ground. "I think she likes me."

"What's not to like?"

"Lots of things."

"Name me one."

"I'm cranky in the morning until I've had my coffee."

He grinned up at her. "I'll remember that." He stroked the mare's nose. "Lona here is surefooted, steadfast, and almost impossible to spook. Came up on a rattlesnake when I was ridin' her once, and she never even flinched."

"Really?" Rainie ran her hand along the mare's silky neck. "How did you teach her not to be afraid?"

"I crinkled cellophane around her all the time when she was a baby. It mimics the sound of a rattler, so the noise doesn't worry her. She stood rock still, allowin' me to shoot the dad-blamed thing from the saddle."

Until that moment, Rainie hadn't noticed the holster that rode Parker's hip. "You're carrying a gun?"

"I never go into the woods without one. Don't usually need it, but it's best to be prepared."

"We're going into the woods?" Rainie had grown up in densely populated California and had been raised by a computer nerd who'd considered a visit to the Los Angeles Zoo to be a wilderness experience. "I thought we'd be riding around here."

"Nope. There's a great ridin' trail just across the road." He glanced up at her, a question mirrored in his dark eyes. "You nervous about goin' into the woods?"

"I haven't ever been."

"You haven't ever been where?"

"In the woods."

He stared at her as if she'd just grown an extra head. "You're jokin'."

"No, I'm not. I grew up in California—in the city. My dad wasn't into camping or hiking."

His lean, sun-burnished cheek creased in a slow smile. "Come dance with me."

Rainie rolled her eyes. "If a big animal eats me, it'll be your fault."

He patted the gun at his hip. "I'm packin'. If any big animals come around, I'll scare 'em away."

Twenty minutes later, Rainie was deep in a forest for the first time in her life, and she absolutely loved it. Parker was right: If you listened, there truly was music. The wind whispered in the tall pines like the mournful voices of lost souls.

Birdsong drifted on the air. On both sides of the trail, insects whirred in the grass. In the distance, she heard water rushing. And, oh, how she enjoyed the smells—pine, the musk of decomposing needles, the scent of summer grass, and the perfume of wildflowers. She felt as if she'd stepped through a hidden portal into a whole new world. The steady clop of the horses' hooves lulled her senses. The constant motion massaged the tension from her shoulders. In all her life, she'd never experienced the simple pleasure of being alive in quite this way.

After about an hour, Parker stopped at the edge of a grassy meadow, unstrapped a blanket from the back of his saddle, and came to help her dismount.

"Why are we stopping?" she asked.

"For one, I don't want you gettin' saddle sore," he explained. "And for two, no horseback ride is complete without some cloud watchin'."

He left the horses' reins dangling, which he explained was called ground tying. The equines began grazing even before he spread the blanket. Rainie watched as he stretched out on his back, his Stetson resting on his chest. He gazed solemnly at the sky for a long moment and then patted the empty place on the blanket beside him.

"Come on, darlin', you're missin' it."

"Missing what?"

"All kinds of things."

Rainie was suspicious of his motives. What if he made a move on her? But when she lay down beside him, he didn't even look at her. Instead he directed her gaze to a cloud that was drifting by. "See the old man?"

She stared hard at the cloud formation for a moment, and then she finally saw him—a godlike figure in flowing robes with long hair and a curly beard. She laughed in delight. Next he pointed out a misty lake surrounded by forested mountains.

"I've never done this," she confessed.

"What did you do for fun?" he asked.

"Lots of things, but never this. I mean, well, everyone looks at the sky sometimes. I used to sunbathe by the pool, and I must have then. But I never looked for shapes in the clouds."

"See the horse?"

Rainie frowned in concentration. "No."

"Look harder. It's there."

She continued to stare but saw nothing. "I can't see him."

"Blank out."

"What?"

"Sometimes if you look too hard, you can't see things. Kind of like in real life when you can't come up with a solution to a problem until you stop worryin' about it. Just let your mind go. Maybe then you'll see it."

Rainie did as he said, and then she saw the horse, a beautiful stallion, rearing up on his hind legs. "See the lamb?" she asked, excited to have found a shape before he did.

"Where?"

"There." She pointed, and now it was his turn to frown. Finally his mouth tipped into a grin. "Ah, there it is." He chuckled. "Even has a tail."

They fell silent for several minutes, both of them watching the sky. Rainie was so relaxed she began to feel sleepy. "This is awesome, Parker. Thank you so much for bringing me."

"I'm glad you're enjoyin' yourself. The last woman I took cloud watchin' bitched the whole time about bugs."

"Bugs?"

"Ants. I never saw 'em, but she swore they were crawlin' all over her."

An odd, clutching sensation filled Rainie's chest. She wanted this to be something special that he'd never shared with anyone else. *Stupid, stupid.* He was thirty-five years old. There were undoubtedly very few things that he hadn't done with other women. And what on earth had come over her that she would feel such a crazy yearning? She was coming to value Parker as a friend, but anything more than that was out of the question for her.

"What?" he asked softly, as if he sensed her change of mood.

"Nothing." She tried for a light note in her voice. "I was just thinking."

"About what?"

"Nothing," she said again.

He fell quiet, and she thought he meant to let it drop. But then he surprised her by saying, "She was nobody special, Rainie. There's never been anyone special for me."

Rainie considered bluffing her way past the moment by pretending she couldn't care less if there had ever been someone special in his life, but the truth was, she did care. As alarming as that realization was to her, she couldn't resist turning her head to meet his steady gaze. "Never?"

"Never once." Turning slightly onto his side, he lifted a hand to brush the hair back from her face, his thumb lightly tracing the curve of her cheekbone. "Until now."

She thought he might say something more, but he seemed to think better of it. That was as frustrating for her as reaching the end of a book to find the last page missing.

"There's never been anyone special for me, either," she heard herself say, wondering even as she uttered the words if she'd lost her mind.

"Not even What's-his-name?"

She smiled. She'd asked him not to say Peter's name, and he was honoring the request. "Especially not What's-his-name."

He resumed his former position to stare at the sky. Her heart was thumping wildly, and it was suddenly difficult for her to breathe. As insane as she knew it was, she didn't want him to resume cloud watching. She yearned for him to say something more, only she couldn't think what.

"I got stew in the Crock-Pot," he said softly. "I'm not much of a cook, but I can make halfway decent stew." He angled a questioning glance at her. "If I say pretty please, will you stay for supper?"

A thick, choking sensation filled Rainie's throat. "Where are we going with this, Parker?"

He arched a jet eyebrow, his eyes alight with teasing mischief. "Damned if I know. I figure it's your turn to lead."

"From the first, I made it clear that our relationship must remain purely professional."

He chuckled. "Fine. Will you stay over to be my professional stew taster?"

Rainie knew she should say no. It was the only smart choice to make. She was still married to Peter. She had no business starting to feel this way about another man. And yet she did. Somehow the emotions had just sneaked up on her. "No funny business?"

His chuckle became a deep, rich laugh. He held up his hands in a gesture of innocence. "No funny business. We're only friends. Remember?"

Rainie got that sinking sensation again, but somehow she couldn't stop herself from wading in deeper. "All right. I'd love to stay for supper."

He smiled smugly. Seeing that, she almost changed her mind, but he distracted her by pointing out another cloud shape.

Rainie had seen only Parker's kitchen, so it was with some curiosity that she accepted his offer of a house tour. Leaving Mojo to his nap in the kitchen on the oversize dog bed, which would soon be too small, Parker assumed the manner of an official guide as he led her from room to room. He soon had her smiling.

"This," he said as he patted the television, "is my only antique. No flat screen for me."

"Why not? I thought all men wanted a huge flat-screen TV these days."

"Remember, I don't watch television very much. Mostly only a movie now and again."

"Don't you miss keeping up on world events?"

He shrugged. "I catch the news on the radio." He led her to a display of photographs on the adjacent wall. "Here we have the family portrait gallery." He inclined his head at the framed image of a handsome couple, a smiling man who looked enough like him to be his twin and a small brunette with lovely blue eyes. "My brother Clint, and his wife, Loni." Then he pointed to a picture of a little boy holding a chubby baby girl in his arms. "That's Trevor, Clint's son, with his little sister, Aliza. Loni's been feelin' queasy of a mornin', so there may be another picture on my wall soon."

Rainie studied the little boy's face. "He looks so much like you."

"Looks like all of us," he said with a grin. "It's the Harrigan curse. We all take after the old man, big nose and all."

"Your nose isn't big."

"I love you. Will you marry me?"

Rainie laughed. "It truly isn't that big."

"Ah, now the truth starts comin' out. It goes from not big at all to not that big."

She found it difficult to believe that he was seriously self-conscious about his nose. He was one of the handsomest men she'd ever known, his skin burnished dark by the sun, his jet-black hair falling in lazy waves over his high forehead, his body honed to perfection by years of physical labor.

He went on to show her pictures of the rest of his family, his voice deepening with affection as he pointed at the images and recited names. Rainie didn't even have a snapshot of her father, a loss that made her ache with regret.

"I always wished for brothers and sisters," she confessed. "Even a few cousins would have been nice, but I was never so fortunate."

He chuckled. "Be careful what you wish for. Comin' from a big family has its perks, but there are times, even now, when I could use some breathin' room. Quincy's always after me about how I eat. Zach is always razzin' me about one thing or another and has an uncanny knack for sayin' inappropriate things at the most inopportune moments. Clint sets an example that only a canonized saint could follow. His wife unnerves me with information about my past that feels like an invasion of my privacy, whether she can help it or not. Sammy criticizes my lifestyle, my workaholic schedule, my bad language, my speech patterns, and my dating habits. Then there's my dad, who watches over all of us and can't stop bein' protective." He sighed. "I actually turn off my phones sometimes to get some peace and quiet."

"Your phones haven't rung all afternoon."

He chuckled. "That's because I've got them set to screen all my calls. Nobody can get through."

"What if there's an emergency?"

He sighed and hooked a thumb toward a window. "They'll throw a rock at my house to let me know."

After showing her the formal dining room, which sported a huge, ox-yoke trestle table and ten rustic chairs, he led her toward his office. Before opening the door, he held up a staying hand. "Not one word about the clutter on my desk."

Rainie bit back a grin as she leaned in the doorway to survey the room, which was richly appointed with cherry furniture that brought out the rust accents in the cream-colored imperial plaster. "Nice," she said, then couldn't resist adding, "Except for the mess on the desk, of course."

"I *knew* you wouldn't be able to resist."

"Never. Office tidiness is almost a religion to me."

As he closed the door, he jabbed a finger toward the vaulted open-beam ceiling. "Upstairs are the bedrooms, five of 'em, no less, just in case I ever get married and have kids. I'll strike those from the tour. I don't want to be accused of any funny business."

Smiling to herself, she followed him back to the kitchen, her gaze fixed on the rich outline of his strong shoulders beneath his blue shirt and then on the easy shift of his narrow hips as he walked. He exuded strength, this man, and yet, somehow, she didn't find it intimidating anymore.

The wonderful aroma of stew greeted her as she moved into the room behind him. "Your Crock-Pot creation smells divine."

"Good. But I'll put off servin' you for a while, all the same. I learned the hard way that starvin' my supper guests makes them more appreciative of my less-than-stellar culinary skills."

"I'm not that picky."

He arched an eyebrow. "Excuse me, but I've tasted your cookin'. You're used to better vittles than I can serve up."

"Not really. I usually have soup and a sandwich. It's not much fun to cook for myself."

"Was it fun when you cooked for What's-his-name?"

Memories of Peter's rages when a meal hadn't measured up to his standards flashed through Rainie's mind.

"I'm sorry," he said. "I shouldn't have asked."

"No, no, it's fine." She shrugged. "In answer to your question, no, it wasn't fun to cook for him. He had very exacting tastes and wasn't easy to please."

He gave her a long, unnerving study. Then he stepped over to a built-in wine cooler.

She sat at the oak table, watching as he expertly uncorked a bottle. As he filled two crystal glasses with the pale pink liquid, he talked more about his house, telling her that he'd designed it himself.

"Really?" She cast an admiring glance at the cabinetry. "Everything, you mean?"

"Every last nook and cranny. I'm not very imaginative, so I went for practicality and convenience—lots of room for large family gatherings, heaps of storage, big bedrooms. I chose post and beam because of the settlin' problems with whole-log construction."

"It's a beautiful house," she said, meaning it sincerely. The home's rustic simplicity mirrored his character. If he'd opted for fancy and splendorous, the surroundings wouldn't have suited him nearly as well. "I'd love to have my own place someday."

"Then I'm sure you will. You don't strike me as the type to give up on a dream."

Rainie's smile faded, for she had given up on all her dreams after marrying Peter. "You give me too much credit."

He led the way outside to sit on the porch swing to watch the sun set. After Rainie had perched on the swaying seat, he handed her one of the wineglasses. "Do you realize how critical you are of yourself?" he asked. "It's one thing to give up on a dream and quite another to have it stolen from you."

She gave him a sharp glance, wondering how he'd developed the ability to read so much between the lines with such amazing accuracy.

When she took a sip of the wine, she sighed at the taste. "This is lovely. I've never tasted this kind."

"It's white zinfandel, mildly fruity. I like a good merlot occasionally, but I'm not into the dry, bitter stuff."

She took another sip. "Neither am I. Peter was a wine snob. His idea of good wine made my tongue shrivel." She held up her glass. "Something like this never would have been allowed in the house."

He sat back, relaxing his broad shoulders against the

wooden slats. "A wine snob, huh?" He pretended to shudder. "No wonder you left him."

Rainie relaxed beside him, acutely conscious of the warmth of his thigh against hers, even through two layers of denim. The evening breeze was soft on her face, and she breathed deeply of the now familiar scents: grass, alfalfa, grain, pine, and field clover. For the second time that day, she experienced the incredible sensation of simply being. Perhaps it was the surroundings—or some kind of magic that the man beside her emanated—but she felt content and at peace in a way that had eluded her for far too long.

"You are so lucky," she said softly.

He gazed off across the fields at the gorgeous Cascade Mountains in the distance. "I really am," he agreed without hesitation. "God has blessed me with almost everything a man could want."

"Almost?" She sent him a curious look. "It appears to me that you're a man who has it all."

"Nope." He gestured at the ranch. "I have so much, but no one to share it with. It's kind of like cookin' is for you: not much fun when there's only one person to enjoy it."

Rainie understood precisely what he meant. Her life was lonely, too, the only difference being that she didn't yearn to rectify that anymore. She'd done the marriage thing and learned the hard way that giving a man dominance over her life was a mistake she never wanted to repeat.

They fell into a companionable silence, yet another thing about Parker that she appreciated. Though he loved to talk and normally entertained her with almost nonstop conversation, he was content with occasional lulls of quietness as well. She felt no need to think of something to say.

Suddenly her stomach rumbled. He turned his head to look at her. Then he grinned. "Well, I reckon you're finally hungry enough to endure my cookin'. You about ready to eat?"

Rainie followed him back into the house and helped to set the table. He had gorgeous earthenware dishes in bright mix-and-match tones of red, yellow, green, and brown. She had to smile over his flatware, which was heavy and bulky stuff well suited to his big, work-roughened hands.

"I'm not into dinnertime folderol," he told her as he set the Crock-Pot on the table and stuck a ladle into the stew. "I hope you don't mind paper towels as napkins."

"Not at all."

They settled down to eat their stew with a sleeve of saltine crackers lying between them. Normally, he said his meal blessing in silence, but tonight he crossed himself, took hold of her hand, and said it aloud. She enjoyed finally getting to hear the words. It was a simple prayer and over with quickly. She liked the fact that he didn't drag it out as some people did, which in her opinion was more about impressing others with one's piety than to express gratitude to God for providing daily nourishment.

When he released her hand, he said, "Now for my dad's version. Three beans for four of us; thank God there ain't no more of us. Lay back your ears and dig in."

Grinning at his foolishness, Rainie ladled some stew into her bowl. "You don't have to tell me twice." After taking a bite, she made an appreciative sound. "This is wonderful. The meat almost melts in your mouth."

"Like I said, I can make a halfway decent stew. I fail miserably at everything else, except for steak and baked potatoes. I drive Quincy nuts."

"The spinach-shake fellow?"

"You've got his number. Spinach, kelp, raw eggs—if it's weird and raw, he eats it. I keep tellin' him he's gonna drop dead from food poisoning, but he says the most deadly of food poisoning comes from consumin' the crap I do."

"Are your eating habits that bad?"

He grinned at her. "Probably. I love canned chili, which

he says is full of fat and hell on my cholesterol levels. I love chips, fried food, frozen dinners." He shrugged as he shoveled in another spoonful of stew. "Hell, I eat like a bachelor. It's not my fault I can't find a woman who wants me, and even if I did, she might be a career woman with eatin' habits as bad as mine."

Gazing over at him, Rainie marveled that he had escaped marriage for so long. She had a sneaking hunch that the true problem for Parker was that he'd never found a woman who measured up to his standards, not the other way around.

They finished the meal in silence. Rainie burst out laughing when he offered her a Twinkie for dessert. She accepted and sank her teeth into its creamy center. "Yum. I haven't had one of these in years!"

"They don't measure up to your homemade chocolate cake, but they'll do in a pinch."

Smiling, he reached over to flick a bit of white from the corner of her mouth. His touch made her skin tingle, and her heart started to race. *Not good.* She was falling for this man. Falling hard. And all indications were that he was developing feelings for her as well. His eyes had gone cloudy with affection and tenderness. His usually firm mouth had softened to a shimmering temptation in the light from the canned ceiling fixtures.

Panic welled within her. "Peter was older than me, a lot older," she blurted.

"He was?"

"Yes, and so are you. Peter was wealthy, and so are you. He was influential in the community, and so are you. He was physically fit, and so are you. He was opinionated, and so are you. Remember when I told you my life is starting to feel like a bad rerun on television?"

He sighed and sat back suddenly in his chair, reminiscent of that first afternoon when he'd startled her so badly by striking the chair legs sharply onto the tile. When had she lost that edge of nervousness around him? When had she grown accustomed to his raw masculinity and supercharged vitality?

"What are you sayin', Rainie, that I'm Peter all over again?"

"There are similarities," she said tautly. "Similarities I can't ignore." Her eyes stung with tears she refused to shed. "Being with him was the worst mistake of my life, and yet in the heat of things, I thought it was true love and incredibly right."

He searched her gaze, his expression solemn and thoughtful. "And now it's happenin' again?"

"I didn't say that," she replied, her panic increasing.

"You don't have to. This is the second time you've told me that your life is startin' to feel like a rerun. That says it all. Well, let me put your mind at rest. I'm nothin' like Peter. I don't know the man, but I do know you, and when you first came here, you were obviously a dyed-in-the-wool city girl, so it'd take a long stretch for me to imagine that good old Peter was a rancher raised with the down-to-earth and sterling values that my father taught me. I'm also guessin' that he was older than you by more than ten years. I'm also guessin' that he was a mean, ruthless son of a bitch. I'm not."

Rainie stared at him through a misty blur, knowing that was true. She'd seen his patience with his horses, and more recently with Mojo. A cruel man didn't allow a puppy to nurse on his armpit hair as it fell asleep because it missed its mother. A cruel man didn't walk through piles of shredded newspaper and pretend they weren't there. A cruel man didn't shrug when that same puppy peed and pooped on his beautiful plank flooring.

"I'm sorry," she whispered shakily. "I never meant to imply—"

"Don't say you're sorry. I'm not offended."

She could still see the tenderness in his gaze and knew he spoke the truth. He really wasn't offended.

"There's no sin in feelin' afraid, honey. If you're feelin' like I'm feelin', it's pretty scary shit. And I haven't been through what you have."

So, there, it was out. He *was* developing feelings for her. "What about our being only friends?" she asked, her voice gone thin with anxiety.

"Aren't we? Friends, I mean? I haven't kissed you. I haven't made any physical advances. For right now, all I want is to be friends. That wasn't a lie." He pushed at his empty bowl, fiddled with his spoon. "Let's address each point. I'm only ten years older than you are. I know lots of people, both men and women, who have much younger spouses, and their marriages are great. In a successful relationship, it isn't about age. It's about understandin' each other and enjoyin' each other, and I enjoy bein' around you. I really do."

Rainie enjoyed being with him, too. For the first time in far too long, she'd felt at peace today and in touch with herself. Something about Parker enabled her to let go of all of it and just *be*.

"As for me bein' rich, that was an accident of birth. I'm the son of a very smart, ambitious, hardworkin' man who was generous enough with his kids to share his wealth *before* he died. It sure as hell isn't my fault I've got money."

Rainie couldn't help it. She snorted, trying to smother unexpected laughter. And in that moment, she realized a truly terrifying thing: She'd already fallen in love with this man. An indefinable something drew her to him like a hapless moth to a bug zapper. The relationship could never be. She was a married woman who couldn't file for a divorce for fear Peter might find her, and Parker was a devout Catholic who wouldn't even eat without praying over the meal first. Hello? Catholics didn't believe in divorce, let alone committing bigamy. In short, any relationship between her and Parker was doomed. She could never undo the mistake of her disastrous marriage, and he couldn't be with her until she did.

And why was she even thinking about that? Marriage wasn't for her. She'd tried it and hated it. In a very real way, it had nearly been the death of her. The very fact that the thought of marrying Parker had entered her mind should have paralyzed her with fright.

"I can't do this." She said it without thought, which was an effect of Parker's charm. In the beginning, she'd guarded every word she said to him, afraid of his reaction or of telling him too much, but somehow, over time, he'd assuaged her fears and lulled her into thinking it was okay to speak her mind. "I just can't."

"I know."

That was all he said, two simple words, and yet they meant the world to her. *He knew.* She couldn't do this, and he accepted that. With Peter, that had never been the way of it. When he'd asked her to marry him and she'd expressed her concerns about her internship and her dreams, he'd grown furious and accused her of placing more importance on her career aspirations than her relationship with him.

"I'm sorry," she whispered.

"Don't be. Tomorrow is another day, darlin'. Right now, you feel overwhelmed. I understand that. You're fearful about trustin' again, and I understand that. No pressure. I'll never ask you to go where you don't feel comfortable goin', physically or emotionally. You've got my word on that."

And when he said it, she believed him.

Then he startled her into tearful laughter by asking, "Am I really that opinionated?"

The answer was, "Yes," only in an inoffensive way. Parker Harrigan had standards and morals and expectations of himself and others. Rainie couldn't fault him for any of those traits.

"No," she finally replied. "You do have very cemented ideas about things, but I don't really have a quarrel with any of them."

"Not even when it comes to spinach shakes?"

What was it about this man that always urged her to smile, even when her heart hurt? "Not even then."

He nodded. "So what's the problem, here, that I'm older than Methuselah, or that I'm just an all-around bastard, like good old What's-his-name?"

"I can only say there are problems, insurmountable ones."

He took that in, thought about it for a moment, and nodded. But then he looked her directly in the eye and said, "Nothin' is insurmountable, honey. Until I can convince you of that, can't we keep things as they are, with us just bein' good friends?"

Rainie almost said no, but the thought of doing so made her feel bereft. He *was* her friend, and her world was far less lonely now that he was in it.

"If you promise me that you'll never try to take it to another level, yes, we can continue as we are, just being friends."

Mellow light spilled over Peter Danning's desk as he perused the printout that Riker had just delivered. The list of single female passengers who'd been aboard the *Ocean Jewel* the night of Lorraina's disappearance was unimpressive. He glanced up at the private investigator.

"It took you this long to come up with a list this short?"

Riker's lips thinned. "Getting my hands on a passenger log was no simple matter, Mr. Danning. Determining which female passengers traveled alone was even harder. These things don't happen overnight."

"How about a list of the crew members?" Peter asked.

"I'm still working on that. The cruise line is stingy with information." When Danning looked sharply at him, Riker quickly added, "I'll get a list of names. It will just take a few more days."

Peter resumed studying the list of female passengers who'd traveled without a companion. His gaze snagged on one name, Anna Pritchard. He whispered it aloud. "My wife's middle name is Ann." He glanced up. "How long will it take you to check this Pritchard woman out?"

Riker shrugged. "Probably not long. Why, do you think there's a connection?"

"The similarity of names may be a complete coincidence," Danning replied. "But then again, maybe not. If Lorraina created an alias, she might have chosen something similar to her middle name to make it easy to remember."

Riker held his own copy of the passenger list. He underlined the name in question. "If she's got a driver's license and uses a credit card, I should be able to locate her in only a few days." He gave his employer a questioning look. "What if it's her? Your wife, I mean?"

Peter's jaw muscle ticked with suppressed rage. "Then your job will be finished, and mine will begin."

Chapter Ten

The next morning, Rainie was ankle-deep in shredded newspapers and puppy toys, with Mojo hanging tenaciously from the hem of her skirt, when another knock came on the office door. For an instant, she thought it might be Frank, dropping by again for coffee, but this was a decidedly feminine tap. Rainie managed to pry Mojo's teeth from her skirt and gather him into her arms before calling, "Come in." She didn't want the puppy to trash someone's panty hose or slacks.

When the door opened, she instantly recognized the woman from a photograph she'd seen on Parker's wall last night. This was the lovely, blue-eyed Loni, Clint Harrigan's wife.

"Hello," Rainie said, struck yet again by the incredibly soulful expression in Loni's eyes, which was even more pronounced in person. She had a gaze that seemed to reach out and enfold you in warmth.

"Hi," the other woman said with a luminous smile. "I'm Loni, Parker's sister-in-law. I meant to come over to meet you sooner." She lightly thumped her temple with the heel of her hand. "Things have been crazy. A short time ago, I was a single professional woman who thought she'd never have kids. Now I'm newly married, have a ready-made little boy, and a baby girl born in March whose sole goal in life is to keep her mama running at high speed. I also think I may be pregnant again."

"Really? Congratulations."

"It's not for sure yet. I've just been feeling queasy the last few mornings, and my brain doesn't seem to be tracking half the time. If I'm not busy with family things, I'm working cases. My husband, Clint, says it best: The hurrier I go, the behinder I get."

Rainie wondered what kind of cases Loni handled. Though her creased taupe slacks and precision-pressed silk blouse would be suitable corporate attire with the addition of a blazer, she didn't have the look of a woman on the fast track. There was a quiet serenity and softness about her. She seemed more suited to artistic pursuits or possibly social services, although Rainie could also envision her as a lawyer who worked pro bono for little old ladies who couldn't afford her fees.

"Cases, huh?" Rainie raised her eyebrows. "Are you an attorney?"

Loni laughed and rolled her eyes in a delightfully girlish way that made Rainie like her even more. "Good grief, no. And trust me, that's probably a blessing. If I were an attorney, I'd aim for a judgeship so I could sentence serial killers, kidnappers, and child molesters. Not a good thing. I don't have a very forgiving heart."

Searching the woman's gaze, Rainie thought just the opposite was true, that Loni Harrigan had an extremely sensitive and loving heart. It was strange. Since marrying Peter, Rainie was usually suspicious of strangers, but something about this woman instantly breached the barriers that Rainie had erected around herself. Tucking Mojo under her left arm, she stepped forward, offering her hand.

"It's lovely to meet you. I'm Rainie, Parker's bookkeeper, but I assume you know that already." She grinned. "Otherwise, you wouldn't be here. Right?"

"Right."

Loni regarded Rainie's outstretched palm for so long that Rainie began to think she would refuse to shake hands with her. But then she smiled and finally clasped Rainie's fingers. The next instant, her pretty face drained of color, her eyes went oddly blank, and she swayed on her feet. Recalling that the woman might be pregnant, Rainie quickly put Mojo down and moved in to grab Loni's arm.

"Are you feeling faint? Come over here and sit down. I'll get you some water."

Loni sank gratefully onto Parker's desk chair. "I don't need water." She flapped a limp, trembling hand in front of her white face, attempting to smile but failing miserably. Then she bent forward to put her head between her knees. "Oh, sweet heaven," she whispered. "Oh, *God*, Rainie, I'm so sorry."

"Don't apologize. It's not your fault you feel faint." Rainie crouched by the chair. "Is it the baby, do you think? I can run get Parker."

"No, no." Loni breathed deeply, and then slowly lifted her head. "I'm fine. It's you who needs help." Her sky blue gaze clung to Rainie's. "He's searching for you," she whispered. "If he locates you, you'll be in terrible danger."

"What?" A chill crawled up Rainie's spine. "I'm sorry. I don't know what you're talking about."

Lips chalky, face shimmering with sweat, Loni replied, "You do know what I'm talking about, and you're in far too much danger to pretend otherwise. Peter Danning doesn't believe you're dead. He's hired a professional investigator. He's trying to find you. If he does, he'll kill you."

Rainie felt as if the floor had vanished from under her. She pushed erect so quickly that the blood drained from her head, making her dizzy. Grasping the edge of her desk for support, she circled to her chair and sank weakly onto the cushioned seat, only vaguely aware of Mojo tugging on her skirt again. Frozen and incredulous, she stared stupidly at Loni's pale face. Now, when it was too late, she remembered the story Parker had told her last night about his sister-in-law, that she sometimes invaded his privacy by revealing details about his past. At the time, Rainie hadn't focused on that information, but now, as she searched Loni's dazed, frightened eyes, she realized that there was something extraordinary about this woman. It was crazy and totally bizarre—but with a mere touch of their hands, Loni had somehow learned things that Rainie never would have revealed to her by choice.

As that realization sank in, Rainie's first thought was that her goose was cooked. All it would take was for Loni to make one phone call, and Rainie's new life would be destroyed. *Peter Danning doesn't believe you're dead,* she'd said. That meant she somehow knew almost everything, including the fact that Rainie had staged her own demise.

Mouth dry, throat burning, Rainie managed to ask, "Are you going to turn me in?"

"For heaven's sake, no." Loni attempted another smile, only with more success this time. "I would never do that. I know what he did to you, Rainie. I know why you ran. And thank God you did."

This isn't happening. The thought swirled through Rainie's mind like a leaf eddying on the surface of a whirlpool.

"Peter Danning meant to kill you during that cruise," Loni continued. "You never would have made it back to Seattle. But, of course, you knew that. It's why you vanished."

Are we really having this conversation? Rainie heard Loni's words, ascertained their meaning, but all of it seemed like a bad dream. She made a fist in her hair. "I'm sorry, but this . . . this is freaking me out."

Still pale, but visibly regaining her composure, Loni replied, "I'm the one who's sorry. I'm clairvoyant, and I often see things when I make physical contact with strangers. I shouldn't have shaken hands with you. I normally don't touch people when I meet them. It's always chancy. I never know when it'll give me a nasty jolt." She lifted her slender shoulders in a shrug. "I'm sorry for getting inside your head that way. I know it must be horribly unsettling. I just . . ." She shrugged again, looking as upset as Rainie felt. "You held out your hand, and I didn't want to offend you by refusing to take it. How rude would that be?"

Rainie would have preferred rudeness to this.

"It mostly happens only when I touch someone who has been through something terrible," Loni went on to explain. "I used to hate it, and deny it, and even tried to run from it at one point, but now I've come to accept that it's a gift, something I'm supposed to use to help others." Her larynx bobbed as she struggled to swallow. Her eyes went misty with heartfelt appeal. "Not everyone accepts; not everyone believes. I hope you aren't going to be one of those people, Rainie, because you are in desperate need of help."

Rainie shook her head. "I've never believed in clairvoyants. But you know things about me—things you couldn't have found out any other way. You're obviously very gifted."

Loni looked away, a distant expression entering her eyes as she gazed out the window. "Oh, I'm gifted, all right. My gift is so powerful that it nearly ruined my life. Until I met Clint, I thought of it as a curse." She took a deep breath and slowly released it. "When I touched you, I linked in with Peter."

Still struggling to accept that this woman was a genuine psychic, Rainie said, "With Peter, did you say? I'm afraid I don't understand."

"I got inside his head," Loni expounded. "I'm sure I don't need to tell you how evil the man is." Shivering as though she were chilled, she turned her gaze back to Rainie. "Tapping into his thought processes made me feel as if I were immersed in ice water. I've felt that kind of evil only once before, when I looked into the eyes of a serial killer."

Rainie lowered her gaze to her lap, remembering the madness in Peter's eyes when he grew violent.

"He's a heartless and very cunning predator," Loni said shakily. "He seeks out young women who've inherited money and lures them in like hapless little fish."

Rainie winced. The similitude of that description rankled, and yet she couldn't deny its truth. Peter had thrown out the bait, and she'd stupidly allowed him to lure her in.

"You mustn't blame yourself for being duped by him. He's a master of deception."

Rainie glanced up, feeling as if her every thought and emotion had been laid bare. "How can you possibly know that I blame myself?"

Loni looked quickly away, her expression chagrined. "I know everything. I'm sorry. It's an unforgivable invasion of your privacy. Just please believe I didn't do it on purpose." She turned up her palms, the gesture one of abject apology. "Have you ever downloaded software onto a really fast computer?"

"Yes."

"Well, that's what happens, sort of, little files of information transferring into my brain in the space of a nanosecond. That's why it shakes me up so badly. Too much, too fast—feelings, thoughts, memories, pummeling me from all directions. It takes a few seconds for all of it to settle in."

Rainie couldn't imagine such a thing. "So what exactly do you know about me?" she couldn't resist asking. "You say 'everything,' but that covers a lot of ground. Surely some of my memory folders remained inviolate."

Loni laughed softly. "Sorry. For a hacker like me, your firewall has a hole in it the size of a semi truck. I know that Peter has made you doubt yourself, and you're terrified of getting involved in another relationship. You really aren't a rotten judge of character, you know. You've got good instincts about people, and you need to learn to trust in them again."

Rainie passed a trembling hand over her brow.

"Peter is very handsome," Loni went on, "almost princely with that golden hair and aristocratic face. He's also extremely charming and adept at assuming whatever mask he must in order to make a young woman fall in love with him. You weren't his first victim." Her eyes got that blank look again, and her face lost color. "There were two others, smart, beautiful, and wealthy. He lured them in, got control of their money, and then murdered them in cold blood, the first with small amounts of poison administered over a period of weeks, the second in a car accident, which he orchestrated by hiring a thug to tamper with her brakes."

The room seemed to tilt. Rainie gripped the arms of her chair, afraid she might topple from her seat. "Oh, God, it's really true that he killed them, then?"

Loni searched Rainie's gaze. "You know he did. For you, that's one of the hardest things for you to accept, that you can never resurface and bring him to justice for what he did to them."

"I hoped . . ." Rainie shook her head. Her throat felt vapor locked. When she could finally speak again, her voice came out as little more than a whisper. "Even knowing firsthand what he's capable of, I still hoped he might have told me the story about killing them only to frighten me, an attempt to make me stay with him. I did Internet searches and verified that his first two wives did indeed die mysteriously, but a part of me couldn't accept that he'd actually murdered them. They were so young. How could he do that to them?"

"He did it for their money," Loni answered. "He ended their lives and walked away with every cent. No remorse, no trace of conscience. Some people are born with no compassion, and the evil in their natures takes over. Peter Danning is a very sophisticated, highly intelligent serial killer. You weren't his first victim, and unless he's stopped, you won't be his last. He feeds on the thrill of it. Pulling it off without getting caught makes him feel smugly superior. He honestly believes he's a cut above ordinary people, and everyone, in his opinion, is ordinary except him."

In that same resigned tone, Loni continued. "He searches long and hard for his victims, you know. When he finds a likely candidate, he digs up every tidbit of information he can about her past to compile a profile on her. He wants no unexpected surprises. His favored targets are young, lonely women without any immediate family. Your profile suited his purposes perfectly, and he set out to become your dream man."

Rainie had suspected for a long while that Peter had scammed her from the start.

"You interviewed on campus career day with a scout from Barrestol International," Loni droned on. "But you never in a million years thought you might get an offer from such a huge, sought-after company. You couldn't believe it when you answered your cell phone one afternoon a couple of weeks later and Peter Danning introduced himself. When he offered you an internship as his personal assistant, you thought it was the opportunity of a lifetime." Loni pressed her fingertips to her temple, her gaze growing unfocused again, as if she were eavesdropping on a distant conversation. "When you got off the phone, you grabbed your friend Maggie and danced around the room, so happy and excited that you could barely talk."

Rainie remembered that moment. It had seemed like a dream come true, only it had been the beginning of a nightmare instead.

Loni still had that distant look in her eyes. "You went for the interview. Peter charmed you. He was so handsome and polished. You were already falling a little in love with him before you even accepted the job." Loni sat back on the chair. "Now, when wonderful things happen to you, your motto is, 'If it seems too good to be true, run like hell.'"

Rainie's chin trembled. Since meeting Parker, that motto had been a singsong in her mind numerous times. He was too good to be true on all counts.

"What are you going to do with this information?" Rainie forced herself to ask again. "No offense or anything, but I can't help but feel terrified, not only for myself, but also for my friends."

"The ones who helped you escape?"

"You know about that, too, then?"

Loni nodded.

"They put their necks on the chopping block for me," Rainie pushed out. "I won't plead for myself, but I will for them. If you turn me in, please don't mention their involvement. *Please.*"

Loni held up a hand. "Rainie, I told you that I won't turn you in, and I meant it."

"If you don't, and Peter finds me, you could be charged with a crime yourself. Have you thought of that? You'd be protecting a criminal."

"You're a victim, not a criminal, and getting in trouble for protecting you isn't a huge worry for me. I work with several law enforcement agencies, including the FBI."

"What?" Another wave of dizziness washed over Rainie. "Oh, *God.*"

"Don't panic. I'm not a cop. They utilize my gift to help them solve crimes, mostly child abduction cases. Trust me when I say that they've come to believe in my abilities. If I were to give them the dirt on Peter Danning, they wouldn't hesitate to take it as gospel, and they definitely wouldn't come after me for trying to help you."

Rainie was shaking now. How could she trust this woman to keep her word? She was in contact with the authorities, possibly on an everyday basis. With one slip of the tongue, she could destroy Rainie's life.

"I know it's difficult for you to let your guard down again," Loni said, "but if ever I've known anyone who needs friends, Rainie, it has to be you. What if Peter finds you?"

"You're a psychic, and you don't know for sure if he will or not?"

"I can't always see into the future. Sometimes I see things that are happening right now, sometimes things that are going to happen, and sometimes things that occurred in the past. I've gotten better lately at controlling the visions, but they can still come to me willy-nilly. So, no, I'm not yet sure if Peter will find you. Having said that, though, I will warn you that he's obsessed and trying his damnedest." She paused, smoothing her palms over her knees. "You can't run again, Rainie. Please promise me you won't. You're safer here with Parker and, by extension, with the rest of us. The Harrigans are wonderful people. If you come clean, they won't hang you out to dry. Go to Parker. Tell him everything. Trust him to come through for you."

Rainie pushed to her feet so suddenly that Mojo's teeth caught in her skirt, making him yelp. "Oh, sweetie." With shaking hands, she picked up the puppy. "I'm sorry. I didn't mean to hurt you."

Mojo gave her an injured look and then buried his nose in the hollow of her neck. Stroking his soft fur, Rainie went to stand at the window. The very thought of coming clean made her quake with fright. *Parker.* She knew that he was developing feelings for her. He'd be furious when he found out that she'd told him so many lies, either flat-out or by omission. She also needed to think about the consequences for him if she told him the whole story and he tried to protect her. Knowingly harboring a criminal was a serious offense.

"I need some time to think," she told Loni. "What seems simple to you isn't so simple for me."

"It might be easier if you could turn loose of all that self-doubt. Just because you trusted the wrong person once doesn't mean that you're doomed to misjudge people again and again. Parker is one of the most loyal, kind, and honest men I've ever known. You haven't made a mistake by letting yourself fall in love with him."

Rainie turned and held up a hand. "Hold on. I care about Parker as a friend, but that's as far as it goes."

"Love is the most powerful emotion on earth," Loni replied with a smile as she stood up. "You can't fight it, so don't try. He loves you, too, you know."

"He may think that right now, but how is he going to feel when he finds out I'm married? That isn't to mention that I've broken the law and will go to prison if I ever resurface. What have I got to offer him but trouble and complications?" Rainie drew Mojo closer and rested her cheek against his softness. "Parker detests liars. When he finds out the truth about me, he'll be absolutely furious."

"Wrong. He'll do everything in his power to help you. I know he will."

"At what cost to himself?" Still clinging to the puppy, Rainie began to pace. "Where I come from, it isn't okay to hurt your friends. Peter is my problem, not Parker's."

Loni's eyes went soft with understanding. "Caring for him that much, how you can tell yourself that you're not in love with him?"

Rainie wanted to argue the point, but she was too exhausted and drained. Besides, Loni was right. Rainie was coming to care very deeply for Parker Harrigan. She just wasn't quite ready to bring the feeling out into the sunlight and examine it. "Caring for him only strengthens my resolve to leave. If I stay here, I might ruin his life."

"Parker's a big boy. Let him decide if he wants to take that chance."

"He won't understand how ruthless Peter is."

"Do you mistakenly believe that Parker can't be just as ruthless if a situation calls for it? Don't let that laid-back, country-boy manner of his fool you. He's as tough as a pine knot and sharp as a tack. Peter is wealthy and very influential. I'll give him that. And I can understand your fear of him. Just remember one thing: This isn't Seattle. It's Harrigan territory. Don't underestimate Parker—or this family. If Peter shows his face around here, his ass will be grass, and Parker will be a lawn mower." At Rainie's startled look, Loni smiled and shrugged. "Sorry. After a time, the Harrigan figures of speech have a way of rubbing off on you. Maybe I should say that Peter will be a mud hole, and Parker will stomp him dry."

Rainie could almost hear Parker saying that. She rubbed her cheek against the top of Mojo's head. The puppy had fallen asleep, a warm, limp bundle tucked under her chin. "As I said, I need to think about it."

"Just don't think about it too long." Loni turned for the door. "I won't say anything to anyone about this, not even to Clint. You have my word. It's your life, after all. But in my opinion, going to Parker is the only smart choice you can make." After placing her hand on the doorknob, Loni turned her dark head to look back. "Trust him. I know you're scared. I know it's hard. But I'd bet my last dollar that he won't let you down. Peter Danning's high-priced investigator could locate you at any time, and the next thing you know, Peter will be setting you up to have a fatal accident or to become the victim of a random act of violence. If you don't believe me—if you refuse to listen—you could die. Don't do that to me. Okay? I can't take that again."

The pain in Loni's expression told Rainie that someone, at some point, hadn't listened and had died as a result. The thought filled her with cold terror. She remembered the night that Peter had almost thrown her over the balcony railing, how frantically she'd fought to survive. To this day, she didn't know what had stopped him. It certainly hadn't been her superior strength. Now this woman was telling her that Peter might be only one step behind her.

"I'm scared," Rainie blurted out. "I'm so *scared*. You just can't know."

"Oh, but I *do* know, Rainie. I *saw*. Peter Danning is a monster, and he will never let you go. He has to make certain that you're dead. That's why he hired the private investigator, because he suspects that you aren't, and if he allows you to remain alive, you might decide to take your chances with the law and file for divorce someday. You'd be able to take half of his assets. He killed two women to attain that wealth. He'll never let you get your hands on a penny of it."

"A good amount of that money is *mine*—my inheritance from my father."

"Do you think he cares? It's his money now. You've inconvenienced him with your little disappearing act. That's how he sees it, you know, as an irritating inconvenience that he now has to rectify."

Every word Loni said rang true. Peter was just that cold and ruthless. "I don't know what to do."

"Ask Parker. Peter's investigator is going over passenger logs as we speak. Even if it takes him a while to find you, how long do you think it will take before he discovers that your best friend, Janet, works for that cruise line and frequently works aboard the *Ocean Jewel*?"

Rainie stared at the closed door for a very long time after Loni exited the office.

Parker was in Montana's stall wrapping the stallion's injured hind leg when Rainie entered the enclosure. He'd seen her feed Montana treats from the opposite side of the gate, but she was still a little too nervous with equines to give up the safety barrier. Or so he'd thought. Now, here she was, standing behind him in an occupied stall, bold as brass.

He straightened from his task and turned. The moment he settled his gaze on her, his heart jerked. She looked as if someone had just punched her in the solar plexus and almost collapsed her lungs. Her chest heaved with every jagged breath she took. Her face was stark white, her eyes huge puddles of hazel against her pale skin. But what really grabbed hold of him was her mouth. It quivered convulsively, which told him she was clinging to her composure by sheer force of will.

"What?" he asked with an edge in his voice.

He immediately regretted the sharpness of his tone. It just frightened him to see her like this. She had solid ground under her feet, but she stood with her boots set wide apart, as if she were bracing herself for a magnitude-six earthquake.

"I'm in trouble," she said thinly. "Why didn't you warn me not to shake her hand? Now she knows everything."

Parker went over that like a drunk presented with an algebraic equation. What the hell? "I'm sorry, honey. I'm not followin'."

Her thin shoulders lifted in a helpless shrug. "Loni. I let her touch me, and now she knows all of it. *All* of it, Parker."

Parker had been treated to Loni's unsettling ability to divine personal details about his past by merely touching his hand. He'd just never stopped to think that the same thing might happen to Rainie. "Oh, *no*."

"Oh, *yes*!" she cried. "She came over this morning to meet me." She pressed trembling fingertips to the base of her throat. "I shook hands with her, and now she knows everything about me, Parker! Why on earth didn't you *warn* me?"

"I should have. I'm sorry. I just didn't think."

"You didn't *think*? My whole life could be destroyed, and you didn't *think*? You've known from the start that my real name isn't Anna Pritchard. Did it never occur to you that maybe I have secrets I don't want other people to know?" She cupped a hand over her eyes. "Oh, God. I'm sorry. It's not your fault. I shouldn't be yelling at you. It's just . . . I'm just so scared. I can barely think straight."

"She won't tell anyone what she saw," Parker assured her.

"Her telling someone isn't my only worry," she informed him shrilly. "She says he's about to find me."

Parker's stomach dropped. "Peter, you mean?"

Her eyes welled with tears, and he felt as if he were drowning in the pain he saw there. "I'm scared, Parker. I am so scared. If he finds me, he'll kill me." Her mouth finally lost the battle and began to quiver so violently that her chin got into the act. "He killed his first two wives. And now he'll kill me."

Parker dropped the roll of bandages on the stall floor. Rainie wasn't keeping her voice down, and he was afraid someone in the stable might hear her. "Toby!" he shouted. "I need you over here."

When his stout, aging foreman appeared at the stall gate, Parker clasped Rainie's elbow and steered her from the enclosure. To his foreman, he said, "I've got business. Take over for me, would ya?"

"Sure, boss," Toby said.

Parker barely heard him. He was too focused on the violent trembling of Rainie's body as he guided her across the arena to the personnel door. When they spilled outside, she flicked a tear-filled glance at him. "Where are we going?"

Damned if he knew. "To the house, I guess. No one can overhear us there."

She stumbled, and he barely managed to catch her from falling. As upset as she was, Parker wasn't surprised that she lost her footing on the uneven ground, but when she bumped against him and didn't jerk away like an offended virgin, he found it alarming. It told him just how shaken up she actually was. She leaned in as if he were her only anchor in a storm. Afraid she might trip again, he curled his arm around her shoulders, pulling her even closer.

"Talk to me, darlin'. Why does Loni think Peter's about to find you?"

"He's hired a private investigator," she said shakily. "They've checked the passenger logs, and now the investigator is trying to locate me. It won't be long before he discovers that my friend Janet works for the cruise line. Once that comes to light, he'll quickly figure out that she boarded the ship with a fake ID, pretending to be the new me."

None of this was clicking for Parker. Cruise line? Janet? Pretending to be the new Rainie? Maybe he was just dense, but he felt as if he'd opened a book at the middle and couldn't make sense of the convoluted plot. He quickened his footsteps, wanting to get Rainie to the house as fast as possible. She needed a double jigger of bourbon to calm her down. Maybe then she would start making sense.

Once in the kitchen, Parker led her to a chair. The moment she sank onto the seat, she covered her face with trembling hands. "I'm married," she said, her voice squeaky and thin. "No divorce. I need to get that said. I'm so sorry, Parker. I should have told you, but I just couldn't."

He stepped to his kitchen liquor cabinet and jerked out a jug of Jameson. "I'm not stupid, Rainie. I figured as much." After grabbing a tumbler, he poured her two fingers of whiskey, which, with his thick digits, was a hefty jot. Walking to the table, he added, "And excuse me for pointin' it out, but that mess wasn't a marriage. A sentence in hell, more like. Do you think God blesses a union like that? You let me put bars on your bedroom windows and reinforce the door. You're terrified of the bastard. Do you think any promise you ever made to him could be sacred in any way? He ended the sanctity the first time he hit you. You're contractually bound to him, yes, but that's it."

He slapped the tumbler down in front of her, making her jump. He felt instantly sorry. Sometimes he forgot how timid she was—and all the many reasons she undoubtedly had for being timid. That was especially true when he was mad, and right now, he was flat pissed, not because of anything she'd done, but because she was so scared. Parker itched for the chance to knock What's-his-name's teeth down his throat.

He sat down across from her. "Bottoms up, sweetheart." He inclined his head at the whiskey. "Every sensible Irishman's cure for rattled nerves. Works like a charm. I guarantee it'll calm you down."

She looked at the glass as if it had magically appeared in front of her. Then she blinked and returned her gaze to his. "You knew? That I'm still married?"

"I suspected." He rocked back on the chair, studying the sweet contours of her face and wondering when, precisely, every precious line had become engraved on his heart. "Your bein' married doesn't matter. Not a whit. I love you, anyway." He hadn't meant to say that. He was definitely the old man's progeny. His mouth always engaged before his brain did. "And just for the record, there's absolutely no reason for that to alarm you. I meant what I said about us bein' nothin' more than friends, and I'll be content with that for however long I have to be." He paused to let that sink in. "I'll also point out that there's no reason for you to feel afraid of Peter. If he ever touches a hair on your head again, I'll kill him."

Her already wet eyes welled with sparkling tears. "You don't know it all. I've done a terrible thing."

"What?" Parker almost smiled, because he couldn't picture Rainie ever doing anything truly horrible. She didn't have it in her. "Let me guess. You tried to stab the son of a bitch with the scissors."

"No." Her throat worked as she struggled to swallow. "I killed myself."

Parker mentally circled that one for a long moment. "Come again?"

"I killed myself. A huge, elaborate hoax. He wanted to take me on a cruise, and I knew he meant to murder me during the trip and throw me overboard. I couldn't just go along with that like a lamb being led to slaughter. So, instead, I pretended to be oblivious, went on the cruise, and beat him to the punch." She reached for the tumbler and gulped down some of the whiskey, which brought even more tears to her eyes. "He'd figured out that I wanted to leave him. That was what started the whole cruise thing. That was my fault, I guess. Him finding out that I meant to leave him, I mean. Looking back on it, I don't know what I was thinking. I was just so upset when I couldn't liquidate the investments that I had to confront him."

"Whoa." Parker held up a hand. "Back up, honey. You're losin' me. What investments?"

"The ones he made for me with my inheritance money from my father's estate. When things got really bad, and I realized I had no choice but to run, I needed to sell the stocks so I'd have some money to get away. Only I couldn't touch the investments because he had them all under only his name. My own money, and I couldn't get my hands on a single cent!"

Her story still seemed a bit muddled to Parker, but he decided to sit back, hear her out, and hope that the picture finally came clear for him.

"After I confronted him about the investments, he demanded to know why I had been looking at his portfolio. I couldn't give him a reason without telling him that I needed my money to get away from him. He put two and two together, though, and figured it out. He flew into a horrible rage, dragged me out to the balcony, and almost threw me over the railing. To this day, I don't know what stopped him. Maybe he realized at the last second that killing me that way wouldn't look like an accident. After changing his mind, he wrapped his hands around my throat and swore that he'd see me dead before he would ever let me go. In order to convince me that he meant it, he informed me that his first two wives had made the mistake of trying to leave him, too, and he had killed them before they could file for divorce."

"Oh, honey." Parker couldn't think of anything else to say. She truly had served time in hell.

She wiped her cheeks with quivering fingertips. "Later that same evening, it came on the news that this guy had vanished from a cruise ship during his honeymoon. Peter suddenly started talking about us taking a cruise." She fixed him with bruised, aching eyes. "He was like that. It . . . it amused him to play cat and mouse with me. I knew if I went aboard a ship with him, I'd never live to see dry land again. I was so terrified, Parker. I had no money to get away from him, and I knew if I stayed, he was going to kill me.

"Until then, I'd never told my friends, Maggie and Janet, the truth about my marriage. I was—" She broke off and lifted her hands in a gesture of helpless bewilderment. "Ashamed, I guess. My fairy-tale romance had turned into a nightmare. Whenever they e-mailed me and asked how things were going, I gave them vague responses. I felt like an idiot for getting myself into such a mess. But after the balcony incident, I no longer had a choice but to turn to them. I called Maggie the next morning. She and Janet came up with the idea of my faking my own death. Did you ever watch the movie *Sleeping with the Enemy*?"

"The Julia Roberts film?" It hit Parker then. There'd always been something oddly familiar about Rainie, and now he saw it. Except for little differences in her features and eyes, she was almost an exact duplicate of the leading female character in that movie, right down to the flowing skirts, dainty tops, and quaint summer dresses. The wildly curly, sun-streaked hair. The funky white shoes she'd worn to that first interview. She'd mimicked that look. "I'll be damned," he whispered.

"That's where we got the idea, from that movie," she went on, her voice wobbling like an out-of-balance tire. She gulped down more whiskey. "Janet thought of it. She's my friend. Did I tell you that? I can't keep my thoughts straight. She and Maggie, they're both my friends. We met at university."

"Pepperdine?"

"Yes. I didn't lie about that. I actually went there, only under my real name, Lorraina Hall."

Parker rocked farther back on the chair to rest a boot on his knee. "I know I've been a little slow on the uptake here, but let me be sure I've got this straight. The three of you watched *Sleepin' with the Enemy* and decided to fake your death so you could get away from Peter?"

"Yes. It had been a long time since we'd watched the movie. But Janet remembered the plot, and we all watched it several more times." Her chin started quivering again. "If I faked my own death, we hoped Peter wouldn't look for me. Stan, this computer nerd we knew from school, got me a fake passport and other identification. I sent it to Janet, and she used it to board the ship, wearing a disguise. She went to the cabin that she'd reserved for me, and left the luggage, the ID, and some money. Then she went shopping in the boutiques, posing as the new me, Anna Pritchard, so my existence would be established on the cameras."

"Cameras. On the ship?"

"Yes. They're all over the place. Janet's a ship operations manager for the cruise line, so she knows the camera layout." She swallowed more liquor. "In college, people often mistook us for sisters, so she looked enough like the passport picture of me to pull it off. She wore the same wig and a lot of makeup, just like I did when the photo was taken. She got through security, no problem."

It was all starting to come together for Parker now. "And you boarded with Peter as yourself?"

"Yes." She pushed at her hair, her hand still quivering with nerves. "He never suspected a thing. During dinner that night, I excused myself from the table to go to the ladies' room, which wasn't far from the dining room. Janet met me there, and we switched clothing. Once I looked like Anna Pritchard and she looked like Lorraina Danning, we left the ladies' lounge with the outside camera documenting our departure. From there, I went to the cabin that Janet had booked for me, and she went to a camera-free area to change back into her own clothes. That's how Lorraina Danning vanished.

"Once in my cabin, I showered, layered on sunless tanning lotion and makeup, put on the wig again, and then waited for all hell to break loose, which it did as soon as Peter realized I was missing. For the remainder of the trip, I stayed in the cabin, pretending to be seasick. Everyone thought Lorraina Danning, the real me, had fallen overboard."

"So you hid out while everyone on the ship searched for you?" It wasn't really a question. The picture was growing clearer in Parker's mind with every word she said.

"Yes."

Parker remembered hearing about Lorraina Danning's disappearance on the radio now. "Peter Danning. He's under suspicion for murderin' you."

"Yes."

Parker pushed up from the chair and stepped to the cupboard for another glass. She wasn't the only one who needed a drink. When he returned to the table, he saw that Rainie had clasped her hands in her lap, her fingers so tightly clenched that her knuckles were white. He poured her more whiskey and then slopped some in a tumbler for himself. To hell with ice. He would have taken the stuff intravenously if he'd had a hypodermic needle handy.

"Damn it, Rainie. Why didn't you tell me sooner? I took you into town. We had lunch in the Romanos' kitchen. What if Pete or Rosa had recognized you? Or someone in one of the stores? You should have trusted me."

"I don't blame you for being mad at me."

Parker felt a lot of things, but anger at her wasn't one of them. "I'm not mad at you, sweetheart. I just wish you'd come to me sooner."

"You truly aren't mad?"

"About what? You doin' what you had to do in order to survive? Besides, I could never hate you." He studied her pale, tear-streaked face. "You look like her, you know."

"Like who?"

"Julia Roberts in that movie. The clothes, the hair. You did a great job of copyin' the look."

A strange expression flitted across her face, and then she burst into laughter that had an edge of hysteria. Splaying a slender hand at the base of her throat, she grimaced, squeezed her eyes closed, and said, "You're right. I guess I did copy her style. I needed to look totally different. And the character in that movie was my heroine—a woman who had the guts to plan an escape and then carry it out. I kept looking at myself in the mirror, wondering where I'd come up with this style. I guess I did it subconsciously." Her laughter vanished as quickly as it had come, and she fixed a frightened gaze on his. "And now the end of the movie is about to happen, Parker. He's coming for me." Another blip of hysterical laughter erupted. "Only I won't have a gun."

Parker's chest felt as if someone had stabbed him with an ice pick. How must she feel? She wasn't a large woman, and she had the musculature of a desk jockey who mainly exercised only her brain. Not that he was finding fault. She was the most beautiful woman he'd ever clapped eyes on. But that didn't mean she was equipped to do battle with a man.

"What if you'd gotten caught aboard ship?" The thought scared Parker half to death. "Did you think about the risk you were taking, that you might get arrested and thrown in jail? I think it's a federal offense to travel with falsified documents nowadays."

"Staying with Peter was riskier." She reached for the glass of whiskey again. "It's ironic, really. He intended to murder me, I got away from him before he got the chance, and now he's on the hot seat."

"When he started beatin' you, why didn't you call the cops?" Parker couldn't resist asking. "There are laws against spousal abuse."

She took another big gulp of whiskey. Parker could tell that the liquor was doing its job. She seemed calmer now. "You don't know Peter." She waved her hand. "He's smart, handsome, rich, and one of the most influential men in Seattle. Some men like that beat their wives, but no one wants to believe that they do. I did call the police once. But what police officer in his right mind wants to buck someone like Peter? He told them I was emotionally distraught and making it all up. He was so calm and collected and *believable*, and I was everything but. The moment the police left the penthouse, he made me pay. I learned my lesson and never made that mistake again."

It bothered Parker to think about how she might have been punished for the infraction. Rainie was such a sweet-natured, harmless soul. What kind of man would brutalize her? But looking into her haunted eyes, Parker had no doubt that it had happened. Even worse, he felt fairly certain that his imaginings were only the tip of the iceberg. He reached for his glass and emptied it with one gulp.

She gave him a searching look. "Do you think I'm horrible for letting Peter take the heat for something he didn't do?"

Parker wanted to plop the bastard's ass on a griddle and turn the flame up on high. "Horrible? He deserves that and more. I think you're smart and gutsy, but not horrible. You must have been scared to death when you left that dining room, and then on pins and needles for the rest of the cruise. That whole ship must have been crawlin' with cops who were flown in. Didn't they come to your cabin at some point?"

"Yes, but I was wearing the disguise and had proper identification. They asked if I'd seen Lorraina Danning, and I told them no." Her eyes filled with tears again. "I was so afraid you'd hate me. Everything I've told you about myself has been a lie. You detest liars, and I'm the biggest liar you've ever met."

Parker studied her for a long, searching moment. "That's not true. You were honest about all the things that matter, Rainie." He offered her a slight smile. "I know you love animals—all kinds, large and small. After seein' you with Mojo, I know that you have incredible patience. I know you're kind, because you started bringin' Montana little treats when his limp returned. You couldn't go past his stall without stoppin' to comfort him with a scratch behind the ears, even though he sort of scares you. I know that you're terrified of your feelin's for me, that you find it difficult to trust your instincts. I know that you miss your dad horribly and wonder sometimes if that isn't why you married an older man in the first place, and if that isn't why you're startin' to love me, because I remind you of him. I know you like sausage pizza, Italian food, and sweet wine. I know you'll ignore the ants and watch the clouds drift by with me, and also that you've got a great eye for images. I know a lot of things—the true things, the things that make you the person you are. Do you really think I give a damn about the rest?"

Her eyes swam with tears again. "You really don't?"

Parker poured himself more whiskey and took a belt. "From the first instant I clapped eyes on you, I thought you were the most beautiful thing I'd ever seen, and except for that one little glitch when I got pissed at you for lyin' to me, you've never done one damned thing to change my mind. Remember that conversation we had in your car? You said, 'In my other life, my name was Rainie.' I knew then that everything about you—everything you'd told me—was a lie. So in a way, none of what you told me was a lie because you let me know, right up front, not to believe any of it."

She laughed wetly. "I guess I did, didn't I?"

"You did. And here's another thing. I've dated a lot of good-lookin' women, and once I started to get to know 'em, I didn't think they were pretty anymore. As I got to know you, you just seemed more and more beautiful to me."

"Oh, Parker."

"It's true. I know you're not ready to grab my hand and jump off a cliff with me yet."

"A cliff?"

"Fallin' in love is like that. You have to hang on to each other and just go for it. No guarantees, no safety net. You have to believe in the other person enough to take the leap."

She nodded. "I did it once, remember. I'm terrified to do it again."

"I understand, and I'm okay with that. After all you've been through, I don't blame you, and I'm willin' to wait. We'll get there."

"Will we?" she asked tremulously. "I'm not sure I even want to try."

"I know," he said softly. "That's why I promised you I'll never push you to do anything you're not ready for. Just understand my side. You're the only woman I've ever cared about. I can't believe that God would bring you into my life and then not let it happen for us. We'll get there. You just need to take each moment as it comes, Rainie, and stop tryin' to analyze every damned thing. Way deep inside where nobody can see, you've been badly wounded, and you need time to heal."

Her mouth started to quiver again, and he wanted to move around the table to take her into his arms. But he knew she wasn't ready for that yet.

"I don't know if I'll ever heal," she whispered. "He did terrible things to me, Parker, things you can't even imagine. Even worse, I did things I don't want to remember, just so he wouldn't hit me."

Parker felt as if a large hand had clamped around his throat. He swallowed hard. A part of him shied away from hearing about the things Peter had done to her, but another part of him understood that Rainie probably needed to talk about them. "Well, darlin', when you're ready to get it off your chest, I'll be here."

She shook her head, her eyes still bruised and aching with memories. "I'll never be able to talk about it."

She already was talking about it. Talking around it, anyway. But he didn't think it was a smart idea to point that out to her just now. "If you never want to talk about it, that'll be okay, too," he told her, even though he knew she might never heal until she mustered the courage to share her memories. "Like I said, I'll never push for you to do or say anything that makes you feel uncomfortable."

She tightened her slender fingers around the tumbler with such force that her knuckles went white again. "Peter did."

Parker released a pent-up breath, not entirely sure he was ready for this, but the stricken look in her eyes told him that she'd been holding everything in for far too long. "Made you do things you weren't comfortable with, you mean?"

"I never knew when it might happen. No matter how good I was, or how hard I tried to do everything right, he'd still get mad." She fixed him with a shimmering stare, and he knew in that moment that she no longer really saw him. "Remember I told you that he bought expensive wine?"

"Yes."

"I hated some of it. It tasted like alum to me, this awful, dry, nasty stuff that I could barely swallow. I always pretended to like it because Peter insisted that I become sophisticated in my tastes. But this one night, the wine was so awful that I made a face. He drew back his arm and slapped me. From clear across the table, bang, and the next thing I knew, I was on the floor, my goblet broken, the wine pooled all around me."

Parker sat frozen on the tipped-back chair, not wanting to hear this, yet hanging on her every word.

"He grabbed me by the hair, smashed my face against the tile, and told me to lick up the mess, that he'd teach me to appreciate fine wine or kill me trying."

Parker closed his eyes. The picture taking shape in his mind made him feel physically sick. *Damn Peter Danning straight to hell.* Parker no longer wanted only ten minutes alone with the son of a bitch. He needed at least an hour so he could make the bastard suffer as badly as he'd made Rainie suffer.

"So I did," she whispered.

He jerked back to the moment. "What?"

Her small face contorted, her skin so white and drawn that she looked skeletal, her eyes huge spheres of haunted darkness above her jutting cheekbones. "I licked it up," she said in a choked voice. "Only I got some glass on my tongue, and he got mad when I gagged. So he shoved my face in it—and I thought—" She broke off, closed her eyes, and gulped for air like a hooked fish. "I thought I was going to drown. I couldn't turn my head. My nose was in the wine. I tried not to breathe it in, but I did anyway, and then I choked. I choked so bad that I vomited. He thought I did it on purpose, to show him how awful the wine was. He said I was an unsophisticated hick who would embarrass him in front of his colleagues, that I had no taste in wine, furnishings, clothes, makeup, *nothing*. So he started kicking me. In the ribs so the bruises wouldn't show." She grabbed for air again and then held her breath in a valiant attempt not to start sobbing. She went without breathing for so long that Parker could see the blood vessels in her forehead popping up, and he started to worry that she might pass out. Then she suddenly sputtered on an exhalation of breath. "It was always important for him to hit me where the bruises wouldn't show." She touched her cheek. "He only forgot once, when I accidentally dropped one of his crystal goblets."

"Oh, sweetheart." Parker's resolve not to go to her weakened, but still he held himself in check. "Come here," he said, patting his knee.

She held her breath again, so long that her beautiful, tear-filled eyes bulged a bit, and then on the release, she said, thinly and tautly, "I *can't*."

And in that moment, Parker knew she really couldn't come to him. He also knew he was a damned fool for just sitting there. One of them had to cross the chasm, and Rainie didn't have the courage to take the first step.

He pushed up. "If you can't come to me, honey, I'll come to you." In one fluid motion, he scooped her up off the chair and sat down, cradling her close against his chest. He wasn't surprised to discover how perfectly her body fit against his. They had been made for each other. He truly believed that. "No funny business, I promise. Just friends. Okay?"

She turned in to him and hooked an arm around his neck,

her face buried against his shoulder. "He broke my ribs that night. It hurt so bad I couldn't breathe, but I was afraid to go see a doctor. He would have beaten me up again if he had found out. So instead I wrapped a torn sheet around myself, fastened it tight with safety pins, and took aspirin for the pain."

Parker's feet felt as if they'd turned to water inside his boots. He pressed his face against her hair and clenched his teeth. He was definitely his father's son, he decided. He wanted to rant and rave and kick the walls. It wasn't easy for him just to sit there, holding her and doing nothing. She'd been hurt, hurt so badly, and he had a horrible feeling that this one incident she'd told him about was just that: only one moment during a hellish eternity. His heart hurt for her as it had never hurt for anyone. He wanted to soothe her with the brush of his hands and kisses on her cheeks. He wanted to tell her with his body what he couldn't say with words.

He settled for tightening his arms around her, trying to tell her with the urgency of his embrace that he was bleeding inside for her.

"He'll never touch you again," he whispered. "I swear it, Rainie. Never again."

Her wet lips parted, her breath hot and moist against his neck. "What if Loni's right, and he finds me?"

"He'll have to go through me to get to you, and I guarantee that won't happen."

"He's *big*."

Parker smiled sadly against her curls. To Rainie, the man probably seemed huge. "The bigger they are, the harder they fall," he whispered. "If I hit a man and he doesn't go down, I'll be circlin' behind him to see what the hell's proppin' him up."

"He shoved my head in the toilet once."

He closed his eyes. Clenched his teeth again.

"I said *shit*, and that was how he punished me for my filthy mouth, by shoving my head in the toilet bowl."

Parker didn't know when he started to rock. He registered the fact that he was swaying back and forth on the chair with a strange separateness, as if some man he didn't know had taken over—some guy who had better instincts than he did. Rocking was good. She was so young to have endured so much. A sweet, innocent, injured thing that needed to be rocked and comforted. So he rocked back and forth, back and forth, his chest feeling as if it might rupture from the pressure of his pent-up rage, which he wanted to spew out in a wall-rattling roar.

Instead, he rocked her, stroked her glorious hair, and tried to absorb her pain. She would fall quiet sometimes, and then suddenly she'd tell him something more, each story as horrible as the last. Parker didn't know how she had survived. He just thanked God that she had.

"He never once hit me until he got control of my inheritance. I was so gullible, Parker. He pretended to accidentally open one of my bank statements, and then he told me it was insane to let that much money sit in an account, drawing so little interest. He said he would invest it for me and triple the amount in a year."

Her voice had gone soft and drowsy, but she kept talking.

"I wanted us to get a house in the suburbs, maybe with a little land so we could have kids and a dog. He kept putting that off, saying the market was in a slump and it wasn't a good time to sell the penthouse. If he invested my money and tripled it, I hoped we could get a house sooner. I never dreamed he meant to invest all the funds under only his name so I couldn't get my hands on any of it."

Parker breathed deeply of her scent, which always made him think of warm apple pie. "I'm so sorry, Rainie."

"They say love is blind, and I definitely was. I look back on it now and wonder how I failed to see what he was up to, but by the time I figured it out, it was too late. The only money he gave me was a household allowance. I tried to cut corners so I could save to get away from him, but he figured out what I'd need right down to almost the exact cent. For a while, instead of sending his shirts to the cleaner's, I tried to do them at home, but eventually he found out."

She fell quiet, which told Parker that she'd gotten another beating for that transgression.

"He was jealous because he was older than me and thought I might be attracted to younger men. When I wanted to get another internship at a different company, he flew into a rage. When I volunteered at the hospital, he beat the hell out of me. When I joined the gym, he had a fit and turned one of the bedrooms into a workout center. He never wanted me to leave the house without him, and even when we went out together, he imagined that I was looking at other guys." She sighed shakily. "My chronology sucks. I'm telling everything out of order."

It didn't matter. Parker now had a clear picture of what she'd been through. He suspected that she'd neglected to tell him some of the more private things—the sexual things. It was difficult for him to imagine anything worse than what she'd already shared, but, like it or not, her unflagging dread of physical intimacy erected a red flag in his mind. She'd told him nothing about what had gone on in the bedroom. He suspected that her memories of those encounters were so horrible that she simply couldn't put them into words.

What she had chosen to reveal circled through his mind as he continued to rock her. Being beaten for allowing the building maintenance man into the apartment while her husband was gone. Being beaten for ogling a male ballet dancer. Being beaten for looking at a male movie star on television. Being beaten for serving the Tuesday special on the wrong night. The list went on and on, every instance so ugly that

Parker could barely wrap his mind around it. Only an animal did such things to a woman he'd sworn to love and cherish.

At last she fell asleep. He knew that by the change in her breathing and the limp way she rested against him. Moving slowly, he pushed up from the chair and carried her to the living room. The whiskey had done its job. After depositing her gently on the sofa and covering her with an afghan, Parker burst from the house, anger still roiling within him. His truck was parked out front. He strode directly toward it, drawing back one boot when he reached it to kick the front tire with all his strength. His toe connected solidly with the wheel rim.

Son of a bitch! Pain shot clear to his knee. He hopped around on one foot, calling himself a dozen kinds of fool and asking himself if he felt better now. *Not.* He wouldn't feel better until he'd kicked Peter Danning's ass good and proper.

"You mad at that truck, son?"

Parker stopped hopping and turned to see Toby standing a few feet away. "No, I'm pissed at the whole damned world."

Toby plucked a can of chewing tobacco from his hip pocket. With a flick of his wrist, he gave the lid an expert tap, then twisted it off to finger out a wad of chew. After tucking it inside his bottom lip, he spat, returned the can to his pocket, and said, "Breakin' your toe won't fix what's wrong in this old world."

"I didn't break my damned toe." Parker gingerly put weight on the foot. "I don't think so, anyway."

Toby chuckled and spat again. "That girl got your tail tied in a knot?"

Toe still throbbing, Parker shifted his weight to the opposite leg and planted his hands at his hips. "She's got trouble nippin' at her heels, Toby, bad trouble."

The foreman gazed thoughtfully at the house. "Anything you can't fix?"

"No, but I'm gonna need help. It's time for the Harrigans to circle the wagons. Can you call Clint and Quincy for me? Tell 'em to get their butts over here. I'll call Dad, Zach, and Sam."

Toby nodded. "You gonna be needin' me, too?"

"Not just yet, but I might soon, so thanks for the offer."

As Parker returned to the house, limping every step of the way, he went back over everything that Rainie had told him, the most alarming revelation being that Loni believed Peter Danning was hot on her trail. Parker didn't understand his sister-in-law's gift, but he no longer questioned its validity. If she said Danning was about to find Rainie, Parker believed it.

That meant there was no time to waste.

Chapter Eleven

Rainie awakened to the low thrum of deep voices interspersed with an occasional female intonation. For a moment, she couldn't think where she was, but then she recognized Parker's shade-drawn living room. Covered with a crocheted afghan in a colorful Native American design, she lay on the sofa. She pushed the coverlet away and swung her feet to the floor, feeling a little dizzy as she sat up. Unless her ears were deceiving her, her name was being spoken a lot in the kitchen.

She gained her feet and headed in that direction. When she reached the archway, she saw a bunch of people gathered around the oak table. Chairs had been brought in from the dining room to accommodate everyone, and extra leaves had been inserted to create more seating space. Two large bowls of popcorn flanked a platter of cookies. Aromatic steam wafted up from scattered coffee mugs. As Rainie took in the scene, she noticed a plump baby girl napping in a carrier beside one man's chair. Another man held an ebony-haired boy about eight or nine years old on his lap. Fast asleep, the child was curled against his chest, his lolling head cradled in the bend of the man's arm.

Most of the faces Rainie saw bore the unmistakable Harrigan stamp. One of those faces belonged to a woman, whom Rainie guessed to be about thirty years of age.

Samantha, she decided, the owner of the jeans she had borrowed. A tiny individual with large, dark eyes and a mop of wildly curly black hair, she was strikingly beautiful despite the slight irregularity of her features, a feminine version of her father's. Beside her sat a fellow who wasn't a Harrigan, judging by his build and coloring. Even slouched on a straight-backed chair, he seemed loftier of stature than the other men, and his hair was chocolate brown instead of jet. The burnished umber of his chiseled countenance showcased intelligent, arresting blue eyes outlined with thick brown lashes. Handsome, Rainie thought, just not, in her opinion, quite as handsome as Parker.

The moment Rainie was spotted in the doorway everybody stopped talking and turned to stare at her. Scanning faces, she spotted Loni, whom she now counted as a friend of sorts, but there was only one face she needed to see. When she located it in the throng, she was rewarded with one of those dazzling grins that had once unsettled her so.

Parker pushed up quickly from the table and strode toward her, the heels of his boots tapping sharply on the tile floor. After coming to stand beside her, he slipped an arm around her shoulders.

"Rainie, this is my family. They're loud, ornery, argumentative, and insufferable sometimes, but they're loyal to a fault. I asked all of 'em over to discuss the situation you're in." He rubbed beside his nose, a gesture she'd come to realize was a nervous habit of his when he grew flustered. "I know it's a highly personal thing, and I hope you aren't pissed at me. But the plain fact is, you're in a hell of a mess, and before this is over, we may need their help to get you out of it."

A hot tide of humiliation crashed over Rainie. How much had Parker told these people? Knowing Parker, everything. No one could ever accuse him of being the silent, circumspect type. She had met only two of the Harrigans. The others were complete strangers. How horrible to think that they now knew her deepest and darkest secrets.

The young woman with the Harrigan features smiled with understanding. "He didn't go into detail, Rainie, so please don't feel uncomfortable. I'm Sam, and when it comes to bad marriages, I've got you topped. One of these times, we need to get together over a drink and share war stories."

Rainie doubted that anyone could have experienced a marriage worse than hers.

"Could you clarify that statement?" the chocolate-haired man beside Samantha requested as he scooped up a handful of popcorn. "I don't want her to think your marriage to me is a disaster."

Samantha laughed and rolled her eyes. "Good point. My *first* marriage was the bad one, Rainie. The second one has turned out pretty good."

"Pretty good?" he echoed.

Samantha hugged his arm. "Excellent, perfect in every way, the stuff that dreams are made of. Is that better?"

"Marginally," he replied. To Rainie, he said, "I'm Tucker Coulter, Sam's husband, in case you haven't guessed. I'm glad to finally meet you."

"It's good to meet you, too," Rainie replied politely.

A jet-haired man sitting next to Loni and across the table from Samantha spoke up. "I'm Clint, Loni's better half." He winced when Loni playfully elbowed him in the ribs. "Okay, *okay*, your inferior half, then." He flashed Rainie a grin that reminded her strongly of Parker's. "I'm the oldest of all these yahoos."

"Yahoos?" the man holding the sleeping boy challenged. "Speak for yourself." Also a Parker look-alike, he directed a smile at Rainie. "I'm Quincy, the next-oldest, fondly referred to as the health nut of the family. They'll tell you all kinds of horror stories about my eating habits, but don't believe a word of it. If you come to my house for dinner, I won't make you eat seaweed or raw eggs."

"I'm pleased to meet both of you."

"Hi, Rainie," a young man who looked to be the youngest male of the brood called out. "I'm Zach. Good to finally meet you."

"It's nice to meet you, too, Zach."

His eyes dancing with mischief, Zach grabbed a cookie and popped it in his mouth. "With Dee Dee's chocolate-chip swirls within easy reach, I'm hoping you don't like cookies." He nudged the brim of his brown Stetson back to raise an eyebrow at her. "Sam's right, by the way. No need for you to feel uncomfortable. Parker has been the soul of discretion. That's so uncharacteristic of him that Dee Dee's about to shove a thermometer under his tongue to see if he's coming down sick."

"Under his tongue, hell," Quincy retorted. "She'd have to shove it up his butt. He can't keep his mouth closed long enough for an accurate oral reading."

Everyone laughed.

"What is so funny about that?" Parker demanded.

Sam rolled her eyes. "Don't be so sensitive, Parker. Zach and Quincy are paying you a compliment. We're all terribly impressed by your reticence."

"Hell, yes," Clint inserted. "Before you were out of diapers and could even speak clearly, you were talking nonstop. Mama nicknamed you Gabby. Remember that, Dad?"

Frank Harrigan's dark face creased into a reminiscent smile. "Em had nicknames for all you kids."

"What was mine?" Clint asked.

"You don't wanna know," Frank said with a huff of laughter. To Rainie, he added, "Ignore these knuckleheads, honey. They'd rather razz each other than eat. You get used to it after a while." Curling his arm around the shoulders of the well-rounded redhead who sat beside him, he said, "This is my wife, Dee Dee, the sweetheart who made the cookies. Belly up to the table and try one. They're the best this side of the Continental Divide."

Dee Dee blushed and flapped her wrist. "Oh, go on with you." Dimples flashed as she smiled. "It's lovely to meet you, Rainie. I kept meaning to come over, but I've been busy doing a little work on the house."

"Which means she's redoin' it from the floor up," Frank expounded. "Never give a woman your checkbook and tell her to go for it."

Dee Dee laughed good-naturedly. "That house hadn't been touched in over thirty years. A face-lift was long overdue."

"Amen," Sam seconded. "Quit complaining, Dad. That prehistoric linoleum in the kitchen was an embarrassment, and all the living room furniture had butt wallows. I couldn't sit on the sofa without slipping into a hole."

"The furniture wasn't *that* bad," Quincy protested.

"Neither was the linoleum," Zach chimed in. "I think it's just a woman thing."

"A *woman* thing?" Loni lifted her brows. "I think it's more a case of male blindness. The furniture and linoleum *were* awful, and it's high time for some changes."

"The interior designer speaks," Zach volleyed back. "Watch out, Dad. Next thing you know, you'll have flowery crap on all your bootjacks."

"Leave the bootjacks that Loni designed for me out of this," Clint warned.

"Why?" Zach asked. "No one else in the family is exempt from a little teasing. If none of us ever gives her a hard time, she'll feel left out."

Loni chortled with laughter. "Watch it, bucko. I touched your hand a few minutes ago. Go too hard on Clint's bootjacks, and I may feel inclined to talk about the latest buckle bunny in your life. Blond hair, blue eyes, an IQ smaller than her bra size. Ring any bells?"

"That's blackmail!" Zach cried.

Loni smiled smugly. "In this family, all's fair."

Zach groaned and held up his hands in surrender. "Okay, okay, I'll lay off your bootjacks." His dark brows drew together in a scowl. "And just for the record, her IQ isn't *that* low. What do you take me for, a low-down skunk?"

As Parker gently grasped Rainie's elbow and led her forward, the volley of good-natured teasing continued. Rainie didn't know if the Harrigans were always this way, or if they were attempting to keep the mood light to ease her embarrassment. She and Parker sat at the far side of the table, where late-afternoon sunlight slanted through the windows to bathe their shoulders. The tension that had gripped her spine minutes ago had eased somewhat, but it still wasn't entirely gone, making her sit unnaturally straight on the chair. As much as she appreciated this family's attempt to help her relax, she still felt exposed and a little resentful that Parker had told them about her marriage to Peter. It wasn't something she wanted strangers to know about.

Just then she felt a tug on the toe of her riding boot and realized that Mojo was under the table, enjoying a veritable buffet of shoes. The scrape of his sharp little teeth over the leather sent vibrations through her foot, and for some reason, the sensation helped to calm her down a bit. No matter how bad things might seem to her right now, life went on, and there were still wondrous things to smile about, namely a plump fur ball with puppy breath that stopped playing only when he slept.

"Would you like some coffee, Rainie?" Sam offered.

"Oh, no, thank you. My nerves are jangled enough."

"You want a little Jameson?" Zach suggested. "Parker usually keeps some on hand. It'll cure a case of jangled nerves quicker than a lamb can shake its tail."

Rainie's stomach rolled at the thought. She'd had quite enough whiskey for one day. "I'm good, Zach, but thanks for the thought."

"So, where were we?" Parker prompted.

The jocularity immediately ended, and all the smiles faded. Frank Harrigan had been sitting back with one arm curled around his wife's shoulders. At the question he straightened, settled his elbows on the table, and folded his work-roughened hands. "We were discussin' the legal ramifications for Rainie if she resurfaces."

Rainie shot a frantic look at Parker. She couldn't possibly resurface. These people didn't understand the danger that would put her in.

"We're not makin' any decisions for you, honey," Parker hurried to explain. "We're just discussin' possibilities. The best way to come up with a good plan of action is to toss around ideas and look at 'em from all angles."

"I can't resurface," she said tautly. "That's out of the question."

"Is it?" Three spaces down, Loni sat forward on her chair to look around Clint and Parker. "What if the authorities come to believe in your story and provide you with round-the-clock protection until Danning is incarcerated?"

"Peter may never go to jail," Rainie countered. "He's wealthy, influential, and very convincing. The one time I found the courage to call the police, they believed him instead of me. All that's changed since then is that I've gotten on the wrong side of the law, which will only weaken my credibility, not strengthen it."

"As I told you this morning, I have a few connections," Loni replied. "I don't think the authorities will take his word over yours this time around."

Clint chuckled, the sound deep and rumbling. "Loni is a master at understatement, Rainie. To say she has a *few* connections is like saying a dog has only a couple of hairs on its back." He took a sip of coffee. "She's in constant contact with law enforcement agencies clear across the nation. If she champions your cause, you'll have no worries."

Hands still on her lap, Rainie curled her fingers into tight fists. "I don't think my resurfacing is a good idea. None of you understands how dangerous Peter is."

Clint leaned forward to look Rainie directly in the eye. "He won't dare touch you if the law is on your side, and on the off chance that he tries, he'll have to go through all of us first. Parker has come to care for you. In our family, that means all the rest of us care about you, too. I know that may sound a little hokey, but that's how we Harrigans are. Right, Dad?"

Frank nodded. "The way I see it, if you can't count on your family, who can you count on?"

"But I'm not part of your family," Rainie protested.

"You are now," Zach inserted. "All of us just adopted you."

It was a lovely sentiment, but Rainie feared they hadn't considered the ramifications. "I can't, in good conscience, allow any of you to put yourself in a position where you may be faced with criminal charges. I'm not sure what laws I've broken, but I'm sure the list is long. By helping me or protecting me, you'd be making yourselves accessories after the fact."

"We're not worried about that," Frank informed her, apparently speaking for everyone. "For starters, you'll have Loni to vouch for you, so chances are good it'll be Danning in dutch, not you. Secondly, we don't mind a spot of trouble now and again. It keeps life interestin'."

"But—"

"No buts," Sam inserted. "Parker laid it all out on the table, explained the risks, and we took a family vote. We're in. I know you wouldn't guess it to look at him, but my dad has deep pockets and a lot of clout in this state. The rest of us aren't exactly small players. If Peter Danning comes here looking for trouble, he'll find more than he bargained for. He may be Mr. Big Stuff in Seattle, but this is Harrigan country."

"You don't understand." Rainie groped for the words to explain. "Peter won't come after me legally. That isn't the way he operates."

"No," Loni agreed. Panning the faces of everyone at the table, she continued. "On the surface, Peter Danning will appear to be on the up-and-up, doing everything by the book, but his true aim will be to take Rainie out." When several startled looks were cast in Loni's direction, she lifted her hands and shrugged. "It's true. He can't afford to let her live. Down the road, she could decide to turn herself in, tell her side of the story, and file for divorce. At that point, even if she went to jail, she'd be legally entitled to half of his assets, which are considerable. He'll never let that happen. The man's gotten away with murder twice, and he's just arrogant enough to believe he can pull it off again."

That pronouncement blanketed the kitchen in silence.

"In order to truly understand Peter Danning," Loni went on, "all of you need to start thinking completely outside the box. He's a criminally insane individual whose reasoning processes are incomprehensible to people like us. He investigates a young woman's background for months before deciding to move in on her. His chosen targets are young, wealthy heiresses with no immediate family or very many close friends. Once he marries her, he considers her to be a possession and a means to an end. That end, for him, is to kill her, making it look like an accident or a death by natural causes so he can pretend to be the bereaved husband and walk away with her money. Toss in a twisted sense of forever after—he honestly sees Rainie's defection as a personal betrayal—and you've got a very dangerous man with no conscience or any stops. Rainie has to die, period. He offers her no other way out."

Dee Dee shivered. "And I thought my first husband was a nutcase."

"Danning is a nutcase, all right." Loni pushed at her brown hair. "The problem is that he doesn't seem crazy until you really get to know him. He reveals that side of himself only in personal relationships *after* he has established a tyrannical balance of power. He lures young women in, pretending to be whatever they need him to be until he has them where he wants them. That's why Rainie fears him so deeply. She was totally taken in by him, and nine times out of ten, other people are as well."

"There's no need for you to be afraid, Rainie," Frank said gently. "If Parker can't handle him, and I'll be damned surprised if he can't, the rest of us will be standin' in line to take a turn at him."

Loni nodded. "That goes without saying, Dad. I think Rainie already knows that Parker will be there for her, and we've certainly done our best to assure her that the rest of us will be." She splayed her hands on the table, her usually gentle expression going taut and solemn. "But she also needs to know that she can count on the support of law enforcement. That's where I come in." She turned that luminous, insightful gaze on Rainie. "Will you at least give me the go-ahead to feel them out? I don't have to mention names. I can give them the bare-bones facts—that this man is a predator, that he murdered his first two wives, and that he would have killed you if you hadn't gotten away from him."

"What if they put two and two together and realize you're talking about me?" Rainie asked, her voice going shrill with anxiety. "My case is still under investigation, so it's fresh in their minds."

"What other option do you have but to take your chances with the cops?" Quincy asked. "According to Loni, the man's insane and won't give up until you're dead. You can't live the rest of your life looking over your shoulder. Sometimes you're forced into taking a stand. If you do it now, at least you'll have all of us behind you."

"I don't get why you're so worried about the police," Zach said. "Is there a law against faking your own death?"

Loni turned up her palms. "I don't think faking your own death is actually a crime, Zach, but there are often secondary criminal offenses that arise as a result."

"Insurance fraud is one," Tucker observed. He glanced at his wife. "All of us know about that firsthand. Not so long ago, Sam almost went to jail for equine mortality insurance fraud." He gave Rainie a questioning look. "Are there any policies out on you?"

Rainie's stomach clenched. "I, um . . . yes, Peter purchased a couple of life insurance policies on me shortly after we got married."

"For how much?" Tucker asked.

A cold sweat filmed Rainie's body, for she had never considered the insurance angle. "A couple of million, I think."

"Damn," Quincy said, and then whistled softly. "He covered all the bases, didn't he? With you out of the picture, he stands to get your inheritance plus two million in insurance benefits."

Zach shook his head. "He's a greedy bastard, isn't he?"

"His greed is beside the point," Tucker observed. "The problem is that life insurance policies make the legal ramifications all the more severe for Rainie. Insurance fraud is a felony."

"But Rainie doesn't stand to benefit," Zach pointed out.

"That may be difficult to prove if Danning tries to cash in on a policy." Tucker rubbed the back of his neck. "Rainie might have a hell of time proving that she wasn't in on the scheme."

"Which is why I'm encouraging her to step forward now,

before the situation grows any more complicated," Loni said.

A horrible sinking sensation filled Rainie's chest. Parker rested an arm over the back of her chair and curled a warm hand over her shoulder. The hardness of his palm and the gentle press of his fingertips soothed her somehow.

Loni pushed up from the table, her chair grating over the tiles as her legs nudged it backward. "If we contact the authorities now, it will be clear to any insurance companies involved that Rainie never had fraudulent intent. There's no question in my mind that law enforcement will go after Danning. The man has already killed two women, and Rainie would have been his third victim."

"That will be extremely difficult to prove," Rainie protested. "That he killed his first two wives, I mean. My friends and I already researched it on the Internet, and Peter was very careful to cover his tracks. The first one was cremated right after the coroner did an autopsy. I don't know what kind of poison he used, but it must not have shown up. And there's no telling what happened to the second wife's car after it plunged over that cliff. Without the car as evidence, it's only supposition that her brakes were tampered with."

"You won't need to prove anything to get law enforcement in your corner," Loni insisted. "I *saw* what he did. I *know* he's guilty."

Clint had been quiet for a while, but he spoke up again to say, "Loni isn't some crackpot psychic who uses smoke and mirrors for effect." He craned his neck to look down the table at Rainie again. "Since tying up with her, the FBI's success rate at recovering abducted children has risen substantially. So far, her visions have never been off base, not even *once.* If she goes to her law enforcement contacts with your story, her word won't be questioned. They know from experience that she's never wrong."

Rainie looked at Loni, who stood with her slender arms folded at her waist.

"It's true," she said softly. "My contacts listen up when I tell them something. I know it's scary for you to think about resurfacing, but once you do, you're going to discover that most of your fears are unfounded. These people are professionals. Their aim is to punish the criminal, not the victim, and you, Rainie, are clearly the victim. You've done nothing wrong." When Rainie started to speak, Loni lifted a staying hand. "I won't give them names or implicate you in any way until I'm certain, absolutely *certain*, that they will be on your side. How's that sound?"

Parker shifted his arm forward to encircle Rainie's shoulders. "I think Rainie needs to think about it. We've thrown a lot at her in a short time. I vote that we table this discussion until tomorrow so she can sleep on it."

"Parker's right," Frank said. "We don't want to push her into makin' a decision she doesn't feel comfortable with."

Rainie smiled shakily. "I appreciate all the support. Truly I do. But I would like to mull it over for a while."

"Just know this," Frank added. "However it shakes out at Loni's end, I can arrange for a top-notch defense attorney to negotiate all the details, makin' sure that you're protected legally."

"I can't really afford an attorney," Rainie confessed.

"I can," Parker inserted softly. When Rainie stiffened, he quickly added, "Just a loan. You can pay me back on a monthly schedule. I'll even tack on interest if that will make you feel better."

Frank scowled. "Have you considered the danger you could be in if you go home, Rainie? If this Danning character is lookin' for you, there's no tellin' what rock he may turn over next. We can't take a chance on him catchin' you alone."

Rainie hadn't thought that far ahead.

"I think you should stay here at the ranch," Frank suggested. "Ever since Samantha's horses were poisoned, we've been beefin' up security. When Clint married Loni, we updated the systems even more to keep reporters from houndin' her. The technologies are so advanced now that we no longer even need guards at the gates. The perimeters of all twelve hundred acres are guarded with electronic-eye gadgets and motion-activated cameras. If anything larger than a small dog crosses the fence lines, the folks monitorin' the cameras at the security company know about it immediately. If the interloper is human, they notify us and the police. In short, Danning can't come onto the property, day or night, without bein' seen."

"Rainie and I haven't had a chance to discuss where she should stay yet, Dad," Parker said.

"Well, she shouldn't go home," Frank stressed, pushing up from his chair. He circled the table to slip an arm around Rainie's shoulders, crowding Parker out in the process. "Stop lookin' like a rabbit caught in the crosshairs of a rifle, honey. No matter what you decide to do, you won't be facin' it alone. It's gonna be okay."

Tears sprang to Rainie's eyes. His hard, sturdy embrace reminded her painfully of her father. "Thank you, Mr. Harrigan. I appreciate that."

"Frank," he corrected, "or Dad, if you like. We don't stand on ceremony around here."

Now Rainie understood why Parker loved his family so much. They were behind him a hundred percent, and now, because he had asked it of them, they were behind her as well. For the first time in her life, she knew, up close and personal, how truly wonderful it would be to have a family like this.

* * *

When everyone had left, Parker sat across from Rainie at the table and gave her a searching look. "You still pissed at me for runnin' off at the mouth about your personal life?"

Rainie bit back a smile. It was so like Parker to get directly to the point. In the beginning, his directness had unnerved her. Over time, though, she'd come to appreciate that trait. She always knew where she stood with him, no guessing games.

"I was upset at first. Marrying Peter was the worst mistake of my life, and sharing the details is something I prefer to avoid. Your family was great about it, though."

"All of them understand," he said simply. "Sam didn't get into it earlier, but she went through almost exactly the same thing. Married a gold-diggin', vicious alcoholic. If something like that can happen to her, with all of us livin' a stone's throw away, then it can happen to anyone."

"Maybe so, but I'm still not proud of it."

His jaw muscle ticked as he studied her. "Sammy used to feel the same way. I never did understand that. It was Steve Fisher's sin, not hers."

"A person still feels ashamed," Rainie told him. "I allowed it to happen. I stayed when I should have left. I groveled to keep him from hitting me. I lost touch with who I was and became a pathetic, cowardly creature who obsessed about hanging the toilet paper in the wrong direction."

"The toilet paper?" His expression mirrored his bewilderment. "He hit you for hangin' it the wrong way? Holy hell. I grew up feelin' lucky if we had some, we went through it so fast." He sighed and raked sturdy fingers through his hair. "I'm sorry. Off subject. Just know that I don't think you should feel embarrassed about anything that happened durin' that marriage. I apologize for talkin' with my family about it and makin' you feel uncomfortable, but I couldn't see a way around it. We'll need Loni's intercession if you decide to contact the cops, and I'll feel better knowin' that everyone else is standin' in the wings, ready to provide backup." He held her gaze for a long moment. "I know you're reluctant to turn yourself in, and I totally understand why. But have you stopped to consider that the choice may soon be taken away from you?"

"If Peter finds me, you mean?"

He nodded. "You'll have to bring in the authorities at that point. Judgin' from what I've heard about the bastard, he has no stops."

"I could disappear again."

He considered that option with unshakable calm. "And what will stop him from findin' you again? Next time, you won't have me and my family, Rainie. You'll be a sittin' duck."

A shiver of dread coursed through her, for she knew he was right.

"That's why I called my family," he went on. "The more people you have to watch your back right now, the better. I'm also a firm believer that several heads are better than two, so I wanted to get their feedback. Your next move may predict the outcome of this situation. I didn't want to go off half-cocked and give you bad advice."

"I understand why you involved them," she conceded. "It's just . . ." She broke off, finding it difficult to put her feelings into words. "I feel funny about asking people I barely know for help."

"You're not askin'." His mouth tipped into a smile. "They're offerin'. Like Clint says, it's the Harrigan way. Our dad is big on family loyalty." He helped himself to one of the cookies that Dee Dee had left behind. "Speakin' of my dad, he made a good point. You really shouldn't go home and spend the night alone."

"But I have Thomas waiting. I can't abandon him again. It's not only about his getting food and water. He's my little friend, and he looks forward to being with me at night."

"He can stay here. He and Mojo got along all right when I was workin' on your house." His dark gaze drifted over her face. His larynx bobbed as he swallowed. "You don't have to bunk here with me, you know. The security is good on all six parcels. Dad and Dee Dee would love to have you. Same goes for Clint and Loni or Sam and Tucker. It's completely up to you. The cat will be welcome wherever you choose to stay."

Rainie didn't want to offend him by saying she wanted to sleep somewhere else. From the first, he'd worked hard to earn her trust, his efforts culminating today in a princely effort to protect her. He deserved to know that she appreciated all he'd done. It was just . . . difficult for her. He was a healthy, virile man, and if he truly was falling in love with her, which she believed he was, he might expect more from her physically than she was prepared to give. Rainie wasn't sure how she should handle that. She knew only that she'd taken the first step toward Parker that morning, and now it was time to take a second one, counting on him to be as patient and wonderful about the sexual aspects of their relationship as he'd been about everything else.

"I'd rather stay here with you," she told him. A part of her wanted to tack on, *Just, please, understand that I'm not ready for any kind of intimacy yet.* But another part of her knew the words weren't necessary, so she refused to say them aloud.

"Done, then." His firm mouth tipped into a crooked grin. "I'll love havin' you here."

An hour later, Parker forced himself to stand aside while Rainie tried to unlock the front door of her duplex. Her hand was shaking so badly that she kept missing the keyhole. When he could bear it no longer, he wrested the key from her quivering fingertips and disengaged the lock for her.

As the door swung inward, she clutched his wrist. "Parker, wait."

He angled a questioning look at her.

"He, um . . ." Her face lost color, and she moistened her lips with the tip of her tongue. "Seattle is only nine hours away. If he's found out where I am, he could be . . ." She cast a dread-filled glance at the door. "He could be in there waiting."

A surge of purely masculine pride almost made Parker bristle. Didn't she realize that he could whistle "Dixie" while he kicked Danning's ass? She had absolutely no reason to feel afraid. But when he searched her haunted gaze and recalled all the horrific events that she'd recounted to him earlier that day, he couldn't blame her for being terrified.

"No worries," he said. "You stay out here on the porch while I check the house."

"No!" Her grasp on his wrist grew more frantic. "I don't want anything to happen to you."

Parker wrested his arm from her grip and cupped her chin in his hand. Her skin felt as soft as duckling down beneath his fingertips, and her small oval face was, without question, one of the loveliest he'd ever seen. "Nothin' is goin' to happen to me, honey. Get that cemented in your mind. I know how to handle myself in a fight."

"He won't fight fair," she informed him shakily.

Parker chuckled. "And you think I will? I'm a country boy, darlin'. My dad taught me never to pick a fight, but if someone else starts it, I'll finish it, one way or another, even if I have to pick up an equalizer."

As he entered the small living room, she remained on the porch, wringing her hands. After returning from the kitchen, Parker saw her darting quick looks over her shoulder, as if she feared that Danning might sneak up behind her. His heart ached for her. How must it feel to be that frightened of another human being? As a child, Parker supposed he must have felt at a disadvantage physically, but it had been so many years ago that he could no longer remember it clearly. He'd also been blessed with a fabulous, caring father who had insisted that Parker learn to defend himself at a very young age. Even Samantha had been required to learn how to take care of herself. With his daughter, Frank had focused on different fighting strategies than he had with his boys, but the result had been the same. Despite her diminutive stature, Sam had learned how to protect herself. Those skills had saved her bacon in a fracas more than once as an adult.

After checking the bedroom, Parker called, "All clear."

At the summons, Rainie hurried into the house and closed the door. Resting a shoulder against the doorjamb, Parker watched as she engaged the dead bolt and a chain guard.

"What are you doin'?" he asked.

She whirled to face him. Circles underscored her large, hazel eyes, and her soft mouth was chalk white. "He could be out there." She clasped her hands at her slender waist. "I don't want him sneaking in on us."

In that moment, Parker wished he could take her in his arms and promise her that Danning would never hurt her again. But he'd already made that vow earlier. He had a hunch it would do no good to offer the same assurance twice. What she needed was a crash course in self-defense. As it was, she was completely dependent upon him to protect her. As certain as Parker was that he could do that, he also understood that it had to make her feel horribly insecure. She needed to believe in *herself.*

He beckoned her into the bedroom. "The sooner you pack, the sooner we can get out of here."

From her closet, she hauled a large suitcase that was almost as big as she was. As she began filling it with clothes and toiletries, she smiled faintly. "This reminds me of the day I packed to leave the ship. My hands were shaking then, too. I was so afraid I would bump into Peter as I disembarked and that he would recognize me." She plucked something black from a pocket of the suitcase. "My Elvira wig."

"Your what?"

She shook out the synthetic strands and tugged the net cap over her sun-streaked curls, instantly transforming herself into a vamp. The fake tresses were long, pitch-black, and as straight as a bullet on a windless day. "Voilà, I'm now a mistress of darkness."

Parker couldn't help but gape. "My God, the change is amazin'."

She shrugged. "It was even better with the full disguise. I looked like a totally different person. As it happened, I did see Peter as I left the ship. He walked right by me."

"You must have been scared half out of your wits."

She nodded as she doffed the wig and pushed at her tousled curls. "The whole week was a nightmare. I told housekeeping that I was seasick and took my meals in my cabin. Janet sneaked me extra food so I could leave most of the room-service meals untouched. People can't eat much when they're nauseated, and I didn't want to raise any red flags."

"Not everyone has friends who love them that much." Parker trailed his gaze over her sweet face. It didn't surprise him that she had inspired such loyalty in a girlfriend. Almost from the first, he'd felt drawn to her, and with that feeling had come a strong sense of protectiveness that no other woman had ever elicited within him. There was just something about her that had always tugged at his heart. "You're a very lucky lady."

She tucked the wig back into the suitcase. "Someday I hope to be there for Maggie and Janet like they were for me." She glanced up, fixing him with those expressive hazel eyes that revealed her every emotion. "I'll be there for you, too, if you ever need me."

"That's a promise I'll hold you to," he replied, his voice going thick. She was so incredibly dear, this woman, and with every passing day, as he came to know her better, he only loved her more. "It was very brave, you know."

She threw him a startled look.

"Findin' the courage to do what you did," he explained. "It took a lot of guts."

"I'm not brave, Parker. I did what I had to do to stay alive. That's desperation, not courage." She folded a cotton top and placed it in the suitcase. "My dad used to say I had a lot of gumption, but I lost it somewhere along the way."

She sounded so dejected that Parker couldn't let that comment pass. "You haven't lost it, honey. You've only tucked it away somewhere. Remember what I said about givin' yourself some time to heal? In a few months, you'll have as much spunk as you ever did."

She only smiled sadly and shrugged again, the gesture saying more clearly than words that she didn't believe him. In that moment, Parker vowed to find a way to restore her self-confidence.

While she finished packing, he stepped over to her bed and plucked a snoozing Thomas from her pillow. The tom immediately began purring. Parker cradled the battle-scarred feline in the crook of one arm to free a hand so he could give the cat scratches behind the ears.

As Rainie latched the suitcase, she suddenly got a concerned look on her face. "Oh, *no*."

"What?" he asked.

"I don't have a cat carrier."

"One of those cages, you mean?" Parker snuggled the cat closer. He hated to stuff the poor fellow into one of those tiny boxes. It seemed cruel to him.

"How can we transport Thomas without one? Most cats don't like cars."

"Why don't they like cars?"

"I don't know. I'm no expert. I only know that people usually put them in carriers to travel."

Parker cocked his head to study the tomcat's face. "We could run into town and buy one, I reckon."

"Mojo is locked in your bathroom," she reminded him. "Going to town will take an extra hour. If we're gone too long, he'll wake up and chew on your vanity cabinet and mopboards."

Parker considered the problem. "We could put Thomas in my toolbox," he suggested.

Her expression went from concerned to horrified. "We can't do that. It'd be mean."

He half expected her to wrest the cat from his arms. "Sweetheart, my toolbox is five feet long, two feet deep, and two feet high. I can remove most of the tools and toss in a saddle blanket for him to lie on. It'll be a lot nicer than one of those damned cat carriers. It's not airtight. He'll be safe and comfortable in there. It's only a thirty-minute ride."

She considered the suggestion. "Are you sure he'll be able to breathe in there?"

"Positive."

Nervous fingers toying with the tiny pearl buttons on her pink knit top, she finally nodded. "All right. That'll probably work."

The toolbox turned out to be every bit as big as Parker had claimed. "My goodness," Rainie exclaimed, "I think I could curl up for a nap in there."

"I told you it was roomy."

Parker removed most of the stuff from inside the box to make space for her pet, and then placed a folded saddle blanket over the remaining contents to create a soft surface. To get Thomas inside was a feat in itself and took both of them to pull it off. Rainie had to join Parker in the bed of the truck, hold the lid of the box open, and be ready to slam it closed the moment Parker slipped Thomas inside. To Rainie's surprise, the cat stopped squalling the moment she shut the lid. She imagined him sitting in there, terrified and unable to see in the darkness.

"Done," Parker pronounced. Placing a hand on the side of the truck bed, he vaulted over it to the ground in one fluid motion that made Rainie envy his strength and agility. "Let's roll so he doesn't have to be cooped up in there for very long."

Problem. Rainie had climbed up into the bed of the truck without any trouble, but climbing back down didn't look as simple. Like most ranch vehicles, Parker's truck was jacked up to keep it from high-centering in muddy fields. She walked to the lowered tailgate, looking for hand- and footholds. Just when she'd picked out a pathway of descent, Parker came around and held up his arms to swing her to the ground.

"You're kidding. Right?" She looked askance at his outstretched hands. She'd never been swung down from a high perch, and she wasn't particularly enthusiastic about trying it now. "I can manage by myself."

"Don't be a goose. Just jump. I'll catch you."

"What if you don't?"

"I will. I promise. Just jump."

Rainie remembered that cliff he'd been talking about earlier. *Trust.* She took a deep breath, inched forward until the balls of her feet rested on the edge of the tailgate, and then fell back, reluctant to take the leap. "I can't."

He gave her an exasperated look. "It's only four feet down, honey."

"It looks like a mile to me."

He started to laugh. And then, before she could guess what he meant to do, he caught her around the knees and bodily plucked her from the tailgate. Rainie shrieked and grabbed for handholds, her easiest target his head. His

Stetson went flying. Her hands knotted in his thick black hair.

"Don't drop me!" she cried.

He was laughing so hard now that he could barely talk. In a muffled voice, he said, "Drop you? And go bald before I'm forty? Turn loose of my hair, woman, so I can put you down."

Rainie saw that his face was pressed against the juncture of her thighs. She tried to unclench her fists, but her fingers refused to relax. The warm huff of his expelled breath sifted through her skirt, steamy against her skin. He suddenly went still. She guessed that he had just realized where his nose was buried. Rainie was mortified, but not so mortified that she could let go and risk toppling over backward.

He finally loosened his hold on her enough to let her body slide the length of his within the supportive circle of his arms. When her feet touched the ground, he didn't release her. His expression was devoid of laughter now. His eyes had gone serious and shiny. With a start, she registered that her fingers were still knotted in his hair. She quickly lowered her hands to his shoulders, but somehow that was even worse. Feeling all that warm, hard muscle and flesh under her palms made her heart skitter and her stomach flutter. She could also detect the steely ridge of his arousal pressing against her belly.

Smiling slightly, he loosened one arm from around her to smooth a flyaway strand of curly hair from her eyes. "Safe landing, just like I promised."

Except that Rainie didn't feel safe. She'd seen that look in a man's eyes before and knew what had put it there. "Parker, I—"

He angled a finger across her lips. "Shh," he whispered. "Don't say it."

"But I need to make it clear that—"

"It's already clear." He dropped his arms to his sides and

moved back a step to slam the tailgate closed and fetch his hat. Motioning at the truck, he said, "You ready to roll?"

Rainie turned away, her heart still slamming like a kettledrum. Once inside the truck, she could think of nothing to say. Fortunately Parker had never been at a loss for words.

"I should go into the cat-transport business. That toolbox is perfect."

Rainie shook her head. "Cat lovers might disagree."

"Why? You ever seen those tiny cages they stick cats in? And those cardboard carriers with the airholes are even worse. My toolbox is much nicer. At least Thomas can move around, and with that saddle blanket over the tools, he can even take a nap if he wants."

"That's true," she conceded.

"So stop lookin' so worried. The cat is fine."

Rainie nodded, but in truth, it wasn't the cat she was worried about now.

"Parker, about what just happened," she ventured.

He angled a look at her that was laden with meaning. "Nothin' just happened, Rainie, and nothin' is goin' to happen."

Once at the ranch, Rainie couldn't wait to get Thomas out of his temporary prison. Only when Parker opened the lid, the cat shot from the enclosure like a bullet from a gun. Before either of them could react, Thomas was streaking across the yard toward the arena and was soon nowhere to be seen.

"Damn it." Parker put his hands on his hips. "Here, Thomas!" he bellowed.

"That isn't how you call a cat," Rainie informed him.

He gave her a bewildered look. "How, then?"

Rainie showed him by example, calling, "Here, kitty, kitty," in a high-pitched voice.

Parker shook his head. "Darlin', my vocal cords weren't made to sing soprano."

"I'll do it then. You'll only scare him."

Parker carried her suitcase into the house while she criss-crossed the yard, calling shrilly to the cat. When Parker went back outside, Rainie was clear over by the arena building, trilling into the evening air, pleading with Thomas to come back. Parker sighed. He'd never been a cat person, but Rainie clearly was. If Thomas didn't return, she'd be heartbroken.

"Here, kitty, kitty!" he yelled. "Thomas!" Under his breath, Parker muttered, "Don't do this to me, you brainless fluff ball." Thinking the cat could have covered quite a bit of ground in the time since he'd escaped, Parker circled behind the house to search more area. "Here, kitty, kitty."

Nothing. Parker went back to join Rainie. She looked so forlorn standing there in the fading light, her skirt drifting around her slender legs like a flowery flag in the evening breeze. He walked up behind her and slipped his arms around her waist. She instantly stiffened and grasped his wrists, as if she feared that his hands might wander. *No way.* Parker knew they had a long way to go before she would be ready for anything remotely resembling intimacy. And oddly, he was okay with that. Now that he'd found Rainie, he finally understood what his dad had always meant when he said true love was about a whole lot more than just sex. Loving this lady was a multifaceted experience. As much as he desired her physically, he was willing to wait as long as she needed him to wait. Another of his dad's sayings sprang to his mind: *Anything worth havin' is worth waitin' for.* Rainie was definitely worth waiting for.

"He'll be all right, honey," he murmured near her ear, praying his reassurance wouldn't prove to be false. "There's nothin' out here to hurt him. We'll put food and water on the porch. Once he calms down, he'll come sniffin' for his supper."

Rainie reluctantly accompanied him to the house, but Parker didn't miss the worried glances she kept shooting behind her as they walked.

"He'll be fine," he said again. "Trust me on that. Okay? If there's anything I understand, it's critters. He'll be back before we go to bed, guaranteed."

Thomas didn't return. Parker listened for meows as he and Rainie shared an evening meal of canned chili and crackers, a repast that his houseguest barely touched. He kept an ear peeled as they cleaned up the kitchen and fed Mojo. After partaking of his meal, the puppy curled up under the table and went to sleep. No yowls had yet sounded from the porch. Rainie looked sad and worried. Parker could think of no way to comfort her.

"You said once that he loves tuna. How about if we open a can and go sit on the swing? Maybe he'll smell it and come to you."

"That might work," Rainie said.

After opening the tuna, Parker grabbed a couple of jackets from the wall pegs and draped one around Rainie's slender shoulders. As he pulled her hair out from under the denim collar, he knew he'd never loved anyone in quite the same way that he loved her. Just the scent of her—apples, vanilla, and cinnamon—made his senses spin and his arms ache to hold her close.

"What's the name of your perfume?" he couldn't resist asking. "I've never smelled the like."

She giggled. "It's my own concoction, a blend of extracts from my cupboard. Do you have any idea how much perfume costs nowadays? Even the copycat stuff is expensive. I decided to come up with my own scent."

He made a mental note to buy her some perfume, but then

just as quickly scratched the idea. He loved how she smelled.

The night had turned chilly. When they sat on the swing, Rainie huddled inside the jacket, shivering. Her summer skirt was made of thin, insubstantial stuff, offering little protection from the cold.

"That's central Oregon for you, hotter than hell durin' the day and colder than a well digger's ass when the sun goes down." Parker tucked her under his arm and drew her close. He felt her body brace against him, a telltale sign that she was more than a little worried about him making unwelcome advances. He guessed that was only natural. The dynamics of their relationship had taken a drastic turn that morning, and as young and innocent as Rainie was in many ways, she'd also seen the dark side of a man's nature. "Relax," he said softly. "If you're thinkin' I might put a move on you, get it out of your head right now. Nothin' like that is on my agenda."

"It's not?"

The surprise in her voice made him smile. "Absolutely not. We've got the rest of our lives, Rainie mine. I'm in no hurry." He ran his hand lightly over the jacket that covered her arm. "The way I see it, all really good marriages are built upon a solid foundation of friendship. I'm not denyin' the importance of a physical relationship. Don't get me wrong. But sex alone will never be the glue that holds us together. Our friendship will do that. Someday when we're old, we'll have the friendship to fall back on."

"You haven't asked me to marry you, and I haven't said I will, Parker. Aren't you getting a little ahead of yourself?"

"Nope."

"But I haven't said I love you, and I'm still married to another man."

Parker didn't need to hear her say that she loved him. He knew she did. He saw the truth of it in her eyes every time she looked at him. "You're contractually bound to Peter Danning, not married to him. There's a difference. Not even the Roman Catholic Church would hold you to the vows you made to him." He let that hang there for a moment. "Were you married to him in a church? I never thought to ask."

"No. We got married in Las Vegas the first time around."

"The first time around?"

"There's a policy at Barrestol against executives fraternizing with subordinates. Peter was so far up the ladder that he probably wouldn't have been fired for having a relationship with me, but it still would have reflected badly on him if anyone had found out. So I left the company. We were married in Vegas, I moved in with him, and he kept it a secret for almost six months. When he felt I'd been gone from the company long enough, he concocted a story about how we'd bumped into each other after I left and started dating. A few weeks later, he announced our engagement, and the second time, which was all for show, we were married in a vineyard by a justice of the peace."

"He's some piece of work, isn't he?"

"Appearances are everything to him." She shivered again. "That's one of the things I've always admired about you, Parker. You don't care what other people think."

"I care," he corrected. It occurred to him that he had encouraged Rainie to share her secrets with him but that he had shared very few of his own. Nothing deep, anyway. Nothing that hurt or made him feel ashamed when he thought about it. In order for her to truly know who he was as a person, he needed to correct that. "I just refuse to put on an act to impress anyone. For a while when I first went away to college, I tried to slick myself up."

"In what way?"

"Lots of ways. I stopped talkin' like my dad, for one, and tried to sound educated." Parker thought back to that time in his life and shook his head at the craziness that had overcome him. "I got it into my mind that my dad was a low-class, blue-collar worker from the marrow of his bones out, and I wanted to make somethin' better of myself. I went shoppin' for some fancy duds—khaki slacks, loafers, and dressy shirts with button-down collars." He jostled her closer with a quick hug, wanting to warm her so she'd stop shivering. "It took me about three years to mature and realize that the real challenge in my life was to become half the man my father is.

"It isn't about the clothes a man wears, or how he talks, or how sophisticated he is. It's about who he is on the inside. My dad is an honest, loyal, and hardworkin' man. There's nothin' fancy about him, but even with all my education, I'm surprised at how much he knows sometimes. He just went to a different school, learnin' everything the hard way. When I'm gettin' ready to breed a mare, I can quote genetic theory that sounds real impressive, but in the end, I'll make the same call my dad does almost every time. He can't tell me *why* he'd breed a black to a gray to get a certain color foal. He just knows that the mix will work. He can't say *how* he can tell a gray from a blue roan, but he can tell the difference with one close look. It blows my mind, but he's right every damned time. A man doesn't need to go to college to be well educated, bottom line, and when a university graduate with a master's degree gets to thinkin' he's better than everyone else just because he has some book learnin' under his belt, he's settin' himself up for a hard fall."

Rainie gazed off through the deepening twilight. "So you stopped wearing khaki slacks?"

"Yep. Went back to my faded old jeans and scuffed boots, and from that moment forward, instead of focusin' on how I looked, I focused on who I was. Samantha accuses me of takin' it too far. I'm the only one of my father's sons who talks exactly like he does, and with the passage of time, I've come to mimic him more and more. She swears up and down I didn't drop all of my Gs a year ago. What's up with me doin' it now? I don't have any answers. Maybe I've patterned myself after him so closely because I feel guilty."

"For what?" she asked.

Parker took a moment to answer, because confessing the truth made him feel like a worthless, ungrateful shithead. "For thinkin' he didn't measure up, that he was somehow less than my fancy-talkin' professors at university, and that I was gonna be better than him just because I was gettin' an education. An education that he paid for, by the way. I was an ungrateful brat. I know now it was just a stage I went through, and to my credit, it didn't last very long. But I'll always feel bad for thinkin' that way, even for a time. There isn't a finer man who's ever walked the earth, and if someone tells me I'm just like Frank Harrigan, I feel proud."

Rainie bent her head and dragged the toe of her shoe over a porch plank as the swing moved forward. "So that's why you downplay the fact that you attended college." She glanced up, her eyes shimmering in the gloaming, the tendrils of blondish hair at her temples trailing in the breeze. "I've wondered about that. Most of the time, no one would ever guess you have one degree, let alone that you studied equine genetics. That isn't like taking a course in basket weaving, Parker. It takes brains."

Parker stared off through the deepening twilight. "It takes brains to be the horseman my father is, too. What I learned after finishin' that coursework was that it's only a tool, not a measure of who I am." He deliberately sent her a questioning look, not wanting her to guess that he'd just bared his soul to her on purpose. "How did we get off on this?"

"I like being off on this. I'm finding out things about you that I never knew."

And he'd been remiss in making her wait so long. "You likin' what you see?"

Her sweet face softened in a thoughtful smile. "I'm liking it a lot. I've known for a long time that you're nothing like Peter. This just drives it home. If he had your education, he'd broadcast it everywhere he went. You act as if you never set foot on a university campus. In your position, he'd try to dazzle people with genetic theory. You seldom reveal that you know anything about genetics."

Parker couldn't help but laugh. "Darlin', if I got started in on equine genetics, your eyes would glaze over with boredom and you'd drop off to sleep."

She chuckled with him. "Probably so."

A long silence fell between them. When Parker finally spoke, his voice had gone thick and gravelly. "I'm sorry he hurt you so much, honey. Just for the record, if I'd met you under other circumstances, and I would have been fired for fraternizin' with you, I would have told my superiors to take the damned job and shove it."

She fixed him with those beautiful eyes that always made him feel as if he might get lost in them. "I know."

Those two words meant the world to Parker. *I know.* He glanced quickly away. She wasn't ready to make the scary confession *I love you*, but he could wait. She felt it. That was all he needed to know.

Just then he heard a faint meow. His gaze flicked to the front steps, where Thomas stood, looking forlornly up at them.

"Thomas!" Rainie cried, the gladness in her voice ringing like a bell in the descending darkness. She pushed up from the swing to hurry down the steps. "You poor baby! Where on earth have you been?" She cuddled the cat in her arms for a few seconds before returning to the porch. She set the feline gently on his feet in front of the can of tuna. "Are you hungry, big guy?"

The cat answered by tucking into the canned fish as if he hadn't eaten in days. Rainie hunkered down to stroke his back while he ate. When the tin was empty, Parker held open the screen and stood back while she carried her pet into the house. Thomas looked a little wild-eyed.

"The strange surroundings frighten him," she told Parker.

He closed the door. "He'll get used to it here. Maybe you should put him down so he can explore."

"I'll show him where the cat box is first," she said over her shoulder as she set off for the bathroom.

An instant later, the cat streaked back into the kitchen, his green eyes wide with fright. After taking one look at Parker, the feline dashed toward the living room. Rainie rushed into the kitchen, looking almost as upset as her pet.

"Where'd he go?"

Parker jabbed a thumb. "That way."

Rainie ran to the living room. "Oh, *no*!" he heard her cry.

"What?"

Parker adjourned to the other room to see what was wrong. He followed the direction of Rainie's gaze upward and saw Thomas huddled on the cornice board above the picture window. The feline looked like one of those cartoon cats, every hair on his body sticking straight out. Parker feared he might go into cardiac arrest.

"What's his problem?"

"He's terrified, poor baby." Rainie wrung her hands. Then she cast a worried look at Parker. "Maybe our coming here wasn't a good idea. He's probably lived his whole life in my side of the duplex. Being in a strange place is really scary for him."

No way was Parker taking Rainie back home. "He'll be fine, honey." He hoped. He made a mental note never to get her another cat after Thomas croaked. Horses and dogs were a lot more predictable. "He just needs some time to orient himself."

Famous last words. Thirty minutes later, when Parker had finished preparing the guest room for Rainie's use, the damned cat was still perched on the cornice board, and

Rainie was standing in the living room, gazing up at her pet with a heartsick look on her face. It took some convincing to get her to go to bed.

"He'll be settled in come mornin'," Parker promised.

"You think?"

She'd no sooner asked the question than Parker's clock chimed to mark the hour. With the first peal, Thomas yowled and Rainie jumped. The second peal sent the cat sailing from the wooden valance to Parker's recliner, and from there to the mantel. Rainie attempted to collect her pet, but Thomas wanted no part of it. With the third peal, he leaped down and streaked into the kitchen. By the time the tenth chime had sounded, God only knew where the cat had hidden.

"He's gonna be okay, honey," Parker assured her. "He can't get out. Once the house goes quiet, he'll be able to sniff around and get used to it here." He turned off the clock chime. "Maybe if you go to bed and leave your door open, he'll find you sometime durin' the night."

After taking Mojo out for a quick potty run, Parker returned to the house to find Rainie standing in front of the fireplace again. Thomas had returned to his safety perch on the mantel. Parker took it as a good sign that the cat had picked a slightly lower elevation as his first choice this time. Tucking Mojo under one arm, he dimmed all the lights and then went to grasp Rainie's elbow.

"It's been a long day, honey. You need to get some rest."

She nodded, her gaze still fixed on her cat. Parker wished she could talk with him about what was going through her head. The tom was upset, yes, but he was bound to acclimate to his new surroundings sooner or later. They just needed to wait him out. Rainie's distress over the cat's reaction seemed disproportionate to the situation, in Parker's opinion, and he suspected she was upset about something more that she didn't feel comfortable talking about with him. Off the top of his head, he could think of several issues that might be troubling her, but he'd never been good at guessing games. Was she afraid that he might get amorous once they went upstairs? Was she worried that Danning might break into the house during the night? Were her thoughts racing about the legal ramifications if the authorities learned that she was alive? He wished she'd just tell him. Instead she stood there, staring at her cat, looking like a forlorn waif.

"Come on," he urged softly. "It's time to get you tucked in for the night."

Her reluctance obvious, she accompanied him upstairs. Once on the second-floor landing, he escorted her to her bedroom door. Still wearing the jacket that he'd draped over her shoulders, she looked so young and upset when she turned to face him that he didn't follow through on his urge to kiss her good night, choosing instead to chuck her lightly under the chin.

"If you need anything, I'm right down the hall. I'll leave my door cracked open in case you holler for me."

She nodded and vanished into the bedroom. After the door clicked closed behind her, Parker stood there for a long moment, wishing that he could hold her close until she fell asleep. *Not.* She was coming to trust him, but she wasn't ready for that yet. *All in good time.* For now, he could only be there for her as a sounding board.

He sighed wearily as he went to his own room.

Chapter Twelve

Worrying about Rainie made it difficult for Parker to fall asleep, and it seemed to him that he'd dozed for only a few seconds when a creaking noise brought him wide awake again. He lay in the darkness, staring blindly at the ceiling, his ears pricked for the least little sound. Footsteps? Someone was on the stairs, and whoever it was didn't want to be heard. Taking care not to jostle Mojo awake, he slipped from bed, groped for his clothes, and hurriedly pulled them on. *Boots.* Parker trusted in the security system that monitored the property, but on the off chance that Danning had found a way to breach the perimeter and enter the house, Parker wanted to be wearing his shit-kickers. No self-respecting cowboy or horseman willingly engaged in a physical confrontation barefooted. Not bothering with socks, he jerked on his trusty Tony Lamas. Then he tiptoed out into the hall.

A rectangle of faint light spilled across the corridor ahead of him, the illumination coming from Rainie's room. Her door stood partly open. When Parker reached the opening, he flattened a hand against the wood to press the portal farther open. No Rainie. The bedclothes were rumpled, as if she'd tossed and turned in her sleep, but she wasn't there now. No light shone from under the closed door of the adjoining bathroom, either.

Concerned, Parker made his way downstairs. Thomas still perched on the mantel, sound asleep now, but Rainie was nowhere to be seen. Just as Parker turned to go back upstairs, he heard another creaking noise. Because he'd so recently sat on the swing with Rainie, he recognized the sound of the suspension chains grating on the eye hooks. *What the hell?* It was a strange hour for her to be sitting outside.

When Parker stepped out onto the porch, he saw Rainie hunched forward on the swing seat, elbows propped on her knees, head resting in her hands. All she wore over her cotton nightgown to protect her from the cold was the jacket that he'd lent her earlier. In central Oregon, the temperatures grew frigid during the wee hours. Making a U-turn, Parker went back into the house to grab an afghan. When he returned and draped it around her shoulders, she stirred to look up at him. Then she resumed the dejected posture.

Parker sat beside her. "Bad dream?"

Her voice was faint when she replied. "I have them pretty often, the same one, over and over."

He almost asked what her nightmare was about, but given all she'd told him yesterday, he figured he already knew. *Danning.* The thought made his muscles snap taut. The jerk had caused her enough pain.

"Want to talk about it?"

Without looking up, she shook her head no. But then she started talking anyway. "I feel so lost in the dreams, Parker."

"Lost in what way, honey?"

"It's hard to explain. Not physically lost and trying to find my way. It isn't like that. It's more an emotional kind of lost. Have you ever been in a maze of mirrors at the carnival?"

"Once, a long time ago."

"Well, I'm in a maze of mirrors in my dream. I wander from mirror to mirror, frantic to find my way out of there, and Peter is laughing because I can't." She shivered, the afghan a trembling drape over her shoulders. "But that's not the scary part."

That sounded pretty damned scary to him. "What is, then?"

"That it's not me in any of the mirrors," she said hollowly. "I run from panel to panel, but my reflection is always of a stranger, some woman I've never seen. I get so frightened, and Peter just laughs harder. I keep thinking, 'I'm here. I'm here somewhere.' Only I'm not." Her voice trailed away to a faint squeak that nearly broke his heart. "No matter how many mirrors I look into, I'm not there."

"Oh, honey."

She shivered again. "I think I keep having that same dream, over and over, because I know, deep down, that I'll never be truly okay again until I find my way back."

Bewildered, Parker studied the crown of her bent head. "Out of the maze, you mean?"

"No." She shifted the position of her cupped palms to cover her eyes. "To me," she said, her voice low and ragged. "I know it sounds loony, but somewhere along the way, I lost *me*."

His heart caught at the raw pain in her voice. "Ah, sweetheart."

"It's true," she cried. "I'm not the same person I used to be."

"None of us stays the same. Life has a way of changin' everyone."

"No, you don't understand." She finally lifted her head to give him a beseeching look with tear-drenched eyes shot through with silver in the moonlight. "I'm *completely* changed, no longer the person my father raised me to be. I've turned my back on everything he ever taught me."

Parker wanted to argue that point. Rainie had held true to countless fine qualities that her father had undoubtedly instilled in her. But he sensed that interrupting her right then might prevent her from saying anything more, so he held his tongue.

"The last promise I ever made to him was that I'd always come out swinging, that I'd never let anyone or anything beat me down." Her chin quivered as she made that admission, a telltale sign of how deeply it troubled her to say it aloud. "We were in the kitchen, and I was goofing around, shadowboxing, when he got all serious suddenly and started asking me to promise him this and promise him that. I think he knew he was going to die soon, and he was worried about leaving me all alone."

"Of course he was worried." Gazing down at her sweet face, Parker tried to imagine the gamut of emotions her father must have felt right before his death. "He loved you, and you weren't mature enough yet at only seventeen to fend for yourself. The thought of abandoning you, even though he didn't have a choice, must have broken his heart."

"Oh, but I was mature enough. It was how he raised me to be." She wiped under her eyes and swallowed convulsively. "When I was little and got discouraged, Daddy always said, 'There's no such word as can't.' He taught me to meet every challenge saying, 'I can,' and as I grew older, that became my mantra. When he died and left me all alone, I was terrified, but that mantra saved me from panic. I *could* go home from the hospital to that huge, empty house without him. I *could* attend the funeral without falling apart. I *could* live with the crotchety old housekeeper until I graduated. I *could* deal with the attorney. I *could* finish high school. I *could* attend college. I *could* survive the loneliness. I *could* handle my own finances. No matter how scary something seemed, I had that mantra to give me courage, and I'd keep saying it to myself, 'I can, I can, I can.'

"And I *did* it, Parker. I really and truly did, all by myself, without any support, I did all of it. I graduated from high school with honors. I graduated from college summa cum laude. I kept a tight rein on my spending and touched no more of my inheritance than was absolutely necessary. I was the daughter he raised me to be every step of the way until—" She broke off and squeezed her eyes closed. "I met Peter."

Parker wanted nothing more than to gather her close in his arms.

Spiked with wetness, her lashes fluttered back up. When he searched her beautiful eyes, he felt as if he might drown in her shimmery tears.

"During my marriage, my mantra changed to, 'I can't,'" she confessed tremulously. "Instead of believing in my strengths, I started focusing on my weaknesses, and pretty soon I became that person, a weak, spineless woman held prisoner in a penthouse behind unlocked doors. I'm still that person, even now. Don't you see? I think that's why I have the dreams about being lost—because I can't find the old me anymore. It's as if that part of me shriveled up and died."

There were a number of things Parker might have said to her right then, but when he ran them through his head, they all sounded canned and trite. *Time to share more secrets.* "I used to have horrible dreams about bein' lost."

"You did?"

"Yep. I was a lot younger than you are, so my dreams were probably simpler and more straightforward, at least on the surface, but when we're hurtin' and feelin' confused, I don't guess age is a factor in how lost we feel."

"What were your dreams about?" she asked, the faint note of hope in her voice unmistakable.

"Losin' my way and not bein' able to get back home. I had two different versions. In one, I'd search and search for our house, but I couldn't find it. In the other version, I'd think I found it, only to reach the front door to discover it locked. I know it sounds silly, but I was only a little tyke, and the dreams terrified me. I'd wake up pantin' for breath, my heart poundin' and my body drenched in sweat."

"It's like that for me, too." Her gaze still clung to his. "And the feeling won't go away. It stays with me long after I wake up."

He peered out from under the porch overhang. Like a curved shard of fine bone china, the moon hung surrounded by stars that twinkled like diamonds sprinkled willy-nilly on a drape of blue-black velvet. In the distance, ponderosa pines rose in silhouette against the sky, their conical tops swaying slightly in the breeze. Their scent, mingled with the faint perfume of alfalfa, grass hay, and clover, traveled to him on the chill night breeze.

With a push of his booted foot, he set the swing to moving again. The rhythmic creak of the chains above them soothed him somehow, and he hoped it would soothe her as well. "My dreams started right after my mother died. Lookin' back on it now, I think they stemmed from my real-life situation. My home was no longer the home I'd always known, and no matter how hard I wished for things to be the same again, they couldn't be, not with my mother gone. I was a very troubled, grief-stricken kid, tryin' to deal with a loss that a lot of adults couldn't have handled.

"One night, I got to missin' my mother so bad I left the house so nobody would catch me cryin'." He winked at her. "Bein' all grown-up is serious business to a five-year-old boy. I was afraid my brothers would see me blubberin' and call me a bawl baby. Anyway, my dad got scared when he realized I was missin'. After traipsin' all over the ranch in the dark, he finally found me in one of the horse pastures with my back to a fence post. Instead of scoldin' me for runnin' off, he just sat beside me and let me talk."

"He's a wonderful man, your dad."

"Yes, he is. As an adult I realize that he was probably in as much pain as I was, if not more, but when you're a little kid, you tend to be pretty self-centered. I didn't think anyone else missed my mother quite as much as I did. To me, it felt as if my whole world had been destroyed and could never be fixed. I yearned to feel her arms around me one more time, to hear her voice, to have her read me just one more bedtime story. My dad tried to fill her shoes, but he had a brand-new baby to care for, all us boys to mind, a house to run, and a ranch to keep afloat. He did his best, but he didn't know the songs she'd always sung to me, and he read the stories different, in a deep, growly voice that was nothin' like hers. Plus, he tried to skip passages so he could move on to the next kid and get all of us tucked in for the night. I missed my mother so much. It's difficult for me to describe the pain of it even now."

"I didn't realize you were so young when you lost her," she whispered.

"Young, old, and everywhere in between, we all suffer when we lose someone dear, and she was dear." After studying her pale, upturned face for a moment, Parker decided that she seemed calmer now. He didn't know if it was the rhythmic creak of the porch swing or the drone of his voice that was helping her to calm down, but he'd settle for either one. "She left a huge void in our lives that nothin' could fill."

"Did your dad manage to make you feel better?" she asked.

Parker sighed. "He taught me how to find the North Star so I would always be able to find my way home when I had bad dreams about gettin' lost. That helped a lot. The next time I had the nightmare, I had that star to guide me."

She followed his gaze to search the heavens. "How do you find it? There are so many satellites nowadays that I can't find Polaris anymore."

Parker helped her find the pointer stars in the Big Dipper, which led to Polaris, the last star in the handle of the Little Dipper. "If you can locate the Big or Little Dipper, you can always find the North Star. My dad didn't call it the North Star, though."

"He didn't? What did he call it?"

Parker smiled at the memory. "He told me that all of us have a bright light inside of us that can never be snuffed out, and that when we die, that light becomes a star. He convinced me that Polaris was my mother's light. Whenever I got lost, he said she would be up there to help me find my way home."

Rainie sniffed and rubbed under her nose. "How sweet. And you really believed him?"

Parker nodded. "Call me crazy if you want, but I still do to this day. In a symbolic way, of course. As a little boy, I saw the star with the trustin' eyes of a child, believin' with all my heart that it was my mother's light, always there to guide me. It was such a comfort to me. When I got to missin' her, all I had to do was look up, and there she was. Later, along about the time I got into middle school, I learned that my mother's star was called Polaris and had been in the heavens for centuries. But instead of bein' pissed at my dad for tellin' me a whopper, I found a deeper meanin' in the story he told me that night, one that comforted me even more. It still does even now."

"Which was?"

"That there truly is a light within all of us, a brightness way deep inside that can never be dimmed or snuffed out, not by anyone or anything, not even death." He paused a moment to let that settle in her mind. "We can be down and out. We can be on our knees, drownin' in the darkness without any hope, and suddenly there it is, that tiny glimmer of brightness inside of us to help us get back on our feet. Nothin' can take that away from us, Rainie mine. Some folks call it grit, others call it the soul, others an aura. I'm not well versed on all the New Age stuff, but I'm sure there are other names for it, too. In the end, what we call it isn't important. What matters is that practically everyone senses that there's more to each of us than mere flesh and bone. Even an aborigine in a remote place untouched by civilization knows that some indefinable part of his spirit is invincible." He turned to meet her uncertain gaze. "You feel it, too. That's why it's hauntin' you in your dreams. Way deep down, you know it's there inside of you, waiting to flare bright again. You only have to find it."

"I don't feel any light inside me at all right now," she whispered.

"Ah, but it's there, sweetheart." He looped an arm around her shoulders and drew her close to share his body heat. "When I look at you, it shines so bright it damn near blinds me."

She rested her head against his shoulder. "Thank you for being such a good friend, Parker. Somehow you always manage to make me feel better."

He bent to press a soft kiss to the curls at her crown. "Maybe that's because you can see your light reflected in my eyes when I look at you, a little reminder of who you really are."

A few minutes later, when Rainie returned to her room, she knelt before the window to stare up at the sky. It took her a moment to find the Little Dipper, but once she did, she focused on Polaris. Unlike Parker, who'd chosen to think of the star as his mother's light, she preferred to claim it as her own, a way to remind herself that there truly was a bright place within her that Peter's ugliness had never been able to touch.

"'Star light, star bright, the first star I see tonight,'" she whispered. "'I wish I may, I wish I might, have this wish I wish tonight.'"

She closed her eyes, wishing with all her heart that she could wake up in the morning feeling more in touch with who she really was, not the woman she had become during her marriage to Peter, but who she'd been before meeting him, a brave, confident, ambitious girl who had never felt truly afraid of anyone or anything.

When she lifted her lashes to gaze at Polaris again, she felt a little foolish for reciting a child's nursery rhyme and seeking comfort in a star. But at the same time, she felt more at peace than she had in years. There *was* a bright place within her that couldn't be snuffed out, that would *never* be snuffed out.

Peter had done his damnedest to destroy her, and he would try again if she gave him an opportunity. But that wasn't going to happen. *I can,* she thought with fierce resolve. *I can.* She was through hiding behind unlocked doors. She was finished with being a coward. Granted, she still felt a bone-chilling fear when she thought of her husband, but some of the greatest acts of bravery were committed by individuals who felt afraid.

Her feelings of fear didn't define her as a person. Only her actions could do that.

The following morning, the aroma of freshly brewed coffee, frying bacon, and other delicious but indefinable scents brought Rainie slowly awake. *Yum.* The air itself smelled good enough to eat. Next to her ear, a low humming droned irregularly. Reaching out, she found Thomas's warm, furry body curled up on the other pillow. Just as Parker had predicted, the cat had calmed down and come to find her sometime during the night. Rainie gathered him into her arms and stroked his back for a couple of minutes, relieved that he was no longer so terrified by the strange surroundings. *It's going to be okay,* she thought. *If Thomas can be brave, so can I.*

After the brief cuddle session, she sat up in bed, stretched her arms high above her head to enjoy a wake-up yawn, and then swung her feet to the floor. Judging by the smells wafting to her nose, Parker was cooking one of those gargantuan breakfasts he'd told her about. Rainie wasn't much for large repasts when she first awakened, but she did dearly enjoy her morning caffeine. Normally she stumbled out to the kitchen in her nightwear, with her hair going every which way, to grab a mug of wake-me-up before taking a shower, but here in Parker's house, she wanted to be fully clothed when she ventured downstairs.

After quickly performing her ablutions, she slipped into a pair of white capri pants and a blue knit top with cap sleeves. No makeup, she decided. She was still so groggy that she might impale her eye with the eyeliner pencil. Besides, it was high time that Parker saw her without cosmetic enhancements. He kept saying she was beautiful, but he might change his mind when he saw how pale and drab she looked without blush, mascara, and tinted lip gloss.

He was singing when she entered the kitchen, his deep baritone thrumming in the aromatic air. "She's got freckles on her cheeks, she's got dimples on her . . . but she's purty."

Rainie gulped back a startled laugh. *A cowboy's version of an off-color ditty?* At least he'd blanked out the word *ass*. "Good morning."

Standing at the stove with his broad back to her, he jumped as if she'd stuck him with a pin. Whirling with a spatula clutched in one big fist, he grinned sheepishly. "You caught me."

"I did. I've never heard that particular song. Where'd you learn it?"

"My dad, I think. Or maybe it was Clint who taught it to me." A flush colored his muscular neck. "How'd you sleep? No more bad dreams, I hope."

This morning he wore a cardinal red shirt, the collar opened to reveal a smattering of black chest hair, the sleeves rolled back over corded, sun-bronzed forearms. Rainie ran her gaze over him, thinking, not for the first time, that he was, hands down, the handsomest man she'd ever seen. How he managed to make such an impact in faded Wranglers and dusty boots, she'd never know, but she felt like a chocolate addict who'd just wandered into a fudge shop. *Not good.* She wasn't ready for any kind of physical intimacy yet, and he might think different if she started sending him mixed messages.

"No more bad dreams, thank heavens. I slept pretty well after I went back to bed."

He poured a measure of coffee into a mug and strode toward the table. "Cream, sugar?" he asked as he set down the cup. "I've even got some flavored syrups if you're into that kind of thing, amaretto, hazelnut, Irish cream. I keep them for Sam. When she drinks coffee over here, she wants a taste experience, maybe because I tend to brew it so strong."

"I'll stick with my usual black, thanks." Rainie sat at the table, eager for the first sip. "Yum," she said as she cupped the mug in her hands. "It smells divine."

He returned to the stove to turn something in a skillet. Rainie glimpsed round cakes. *Flapjacks?* When she splurged and fixed what she considered to be a full-fledged breakfast, she had flapjacks and eggs or bacon and eggs, always either/or, never everything at once. She found herself wondering how much of the food he planned to eat himself. Most of it, she hoped. She would feel terrible if he'd gone to all this trouble for her.

"About last night." He glanced over his shoulder at her. "I shouldn't have gotten off on all that stuff about bright lights. You were upset, and I went to bed feelin' bad about it."

Rainie remembered the peace she'd felt while kneeling before the window and flashed him a look of genuine surprise. "Why did you feel bad?"

The stove timer chimed, and he leaned sideways to turn it off. As he enveloped his hands in protective mitts, he said, "Because it wasn't about me and my experiences. I tend to run at the mouth, and I should have just listened to what you had to say." He drew a pan of what appeared to be homemade biscuits from the oven and set it on the granite countertop. Then, with a grin, he added, "Maybe I would have learned somethin'."

An ache of pure happiness spread through Rainie's chest. Never once had Peter expressed regret for dominating one of their conversations, let alone acknowledged that she might have had a thought worth hearing.

"I didn't mind." She set down the coffee mug and rested her chin on her folded hands. "In fact, what you said really helped me to sort things out."

"It did?" He flicked an incredulous look at her. "How's that?"

"I think you're right, that there's something within each of us that's inextinguishable, a part of me that Peter was never able to touch." Rainie's throat went tight and her eyes burned. "Last night after we talked, I thought about that, and I've decided that I'm ready to fight back. He tried to destroy me, and he'll try again if I give him half a chance. I'm not going to let that happen."

He straightened from the stove, slowly removing the baker's mitts and tossing them on the counter. "Good for you."

Taut with nerves, Rainie pushed out, "I've decided to contact the police."

He settled his hips against the counter and folded his arms. "You sure?"

She managed a stiff nod. "I'm positive. I'm terrified. Don't get me wrong. But it's time for me to face him down."

His dark eyes searched hers. "If that's your decision, I'm behind you a hundred percent. So is my family. You won't face him alone."

Rainie already knew that. "I think my wisest course of

action is to let Loni put out some feelers, like she suggested. When she thinks it's safe for me to step forward, we'll take it from there."

He rubbed his jaw. "Dad had a good point about getting you a top-notch lawyer. If the authorities believe Loni's story, it probably won't be necessary, but I'd rather be safe than sorry."

"Like I said yesterday, I don't have the money for legal representation."

"My offer of a loan still stands."

Peter would have tacked a price onto the offer, but Parker just reminded her that he would be there for her, no strings attached. No leverage, no emotional blackmail. That meant more to her than he would ever know. "I'll want to make monthly installments to pay you back."

He nodded and turned back to the stove. "Now for breakfast. Come grab a plate, honey, and load up."

"I don't usually eat much for breakfast."

"You'll need to be changin' your habits now that you're goin' into trainin'."

"Training?"

"Yep. I'm fixin' to teach you some Harrigan-style judo, and to excel at it, you need to build up your strength."

"What kind of judo did you say?"

"Harrigan-style." He grinned as he slid three eggs onto a plate and handed it to her. "Eat hearty. I've covered all the bases. Even made potato cakes. If you don't eat, you'll be starvin' come lunchtime."

"I can't eat *three* eggs, and I've never had any desire to learn judo, Harrigan-style or otherwise."

"Develop a desire." He plopped a biscuit slathered with butter on her plate and then added a potato cake and three slices of bacon. "If you're gonna contact the authorities, Peter will soon know where you are." He bent to kiss her forehead, his manner brotherly. "I don't intend to give the bastard an opportunity to catch you somewhere alone, but on the off chance that he somehow does, I need to know that you'll be able to kick his sorry, city-boy ass."

Just the thought gave Rainie a rush. "You can teach me how to do that?"

"Absolutely. Samantha trained with my dad when she was a teenager. She hated it at the time, but he insisted."

"Has she ever actually kicked anyone's butt? Without rendering him unconscious with a kitchen chair, I mean?"

"A couple of times, actually. And don't knock her for usin' a kitchen chair to take her first husband down. It doesn't matter how you kick a man's ass, only that you're standin' over him when the dust settles. Sam used a chair to even up the playin' field with her ex, but the next time around, all she had to fight with were her fists and feet. She still kicked ass."

"She's so tiny. It's hard to believe."

"Size isn't important." He winked at her. "Ask Sam yourself if you don't believe me. It's quite a story. It happened the afternoon she met her husband, Tucker. Some drunk out at the fairgrounds was mistreatin' a horse, and Sam intervened. The jerk smacked her, and Tucker jumped in to defend her. Unfortunately for Tucker, the drunk had a lunge whip in his hand and whopped Tucker in the face with the handle. Busted Tucker's nose and temporarily blinded him. The drunk took advantage, kickin' Tucker while he was down. Sam stepped in at that point and took the bastard to task. He was down for the count by the time Tucker recovered his senses. Unfortunately, he didn't stay down. In the end, Tucker backed the guy up against a horse trailer and finished him, but the fact remains that Tucker would have been badly hurt if Sam hadn't come to his rescue."

"That's amazing. How on earth did she do it?"

"Training, plain and simple. Don't ever tell her I said so,

but I'd hesitate to take her on. The girl is hell on greased runners when she gets her dander up."

"Really?" A thrill of excitement danced up Rainie's spine. "She's not exactly the Amazon type."

"Like I said, it's not about size. It's about knowin' a few moves and havin' the physical strength to execute 'em effectively."

"I've never been very strong."

"It's not about strength either, actually, only about bein' toned enough to do the dirty. Trust me, honey. I'll teach you how to take the bastard to his knees and keep him there."

Rainie stared dubiously at the mountain of food on her plate. "If I eat this, all I'll have to do is sit on him."

Two hours later, after consuming the largest breakfast of her life and speaking at length with Loni on the phone, Rainie found herself in the riding arena, wearing a pair of Parker's sweatpants that were huge on her, an oversize T-shirt, and a pair of old sneakers she'd brought from home. From a stall, Tina Stroud, one of the female stable hands, called hello.

"Change in dress code?" she asked, eyeing Rainie's attire.

"No, we're just going to work out for a while," Rainie replied.

Her short, frizzy brown hair ignited to gold by the sunlight pouring in through the open paddock doors behind her, the older woman held up a pitchfork. "Don't waste valuable sweat on calisthenics. I can put you to work in here and get you in shape, no problem."

"I'll second that," Jericho yelled from the rear of the building. "My gimp leg is hurting me today. I could use a helper."

"Ignore 'em," Parker told Rainie. He pointed at her and then thumped himself on the chest. "It's just you and me durin' these sessions. I want your total concentration."

He, too, was dressed in workout clothing, but his garments fit him a lot better, the T-shirt displaying a wealth of muscle that his regular work shirts didn't reveal. Since first meeting him, Rainie had consoled herself with the thought that maybe, just maybe, she harbored an unacknowledged weakness for cowboys in jeans and riding boots, which might explain her attraction to him. But, no, he just looked better than most men, no matter how he happened to be dressed. On a California beach in nothing but brief swimming apparel, he would still make her heart skip a beat.

With a start she realized he was studying her body as closely as she was studying his, not in a sexual way, but more as if he were looking for physical strengths and needed a magnifying glass to find any. Scowling, he grasped her upper arm and gave it a squeeze, much as he might have tested an avocado for ripeness.

"What?" she said.

He shook his head. "Nothin'," he assured her. "Nothin' that can't be fixed, anyhow. But it's gonna take some work."

Rainie's cheeks went hot. "What are you saying, that my body is a mess?"

"You've got a beautiful body," he replied. "But your muscle tone sucks."

"Maybe I should just take classes somewhere," she suggested. "They probably have gym equipment. Besides, if I'm going to learn judo, why not go for the real thing?"

"For starters, the minute you resurface, Danning will know where you are, and it's always better to have the element of surprise in your favor. If he starts tailin' you and finds out you're studyin' martial arts, he'll know you're gearin' up for a fight. Secondly, the real kind of judo can take years to master."

"And this won't?"

"Nope." He had her walk at a fast pace around the arena

to warm up, and then he began demonstrating how to do a stretch exercise. "Come on. Loosen up those hamstrings."

"Are you sure I have some?"

"Oh, you've got some, darlin'. They'll be screamin' hello at you tonight."

Rainie didn't like the sound of that. "I may not be a quick study, you know. I've never been very athletic."

"That's why I'm gettin' you started now, so you can build up your strength. Before you know it, you'll be a lean, mean killing machine."

Bent at the waist with one leg thrust out behind her, Rainie giggled. "A killing machine?"

He chuckled with her. "A slight exaggeration, but you get the picture. Every woman should know how to defend herself. Stretch it out, honey. I don't want you tearin' a tendon."

After doing stretches, they started off with jumping jacks. Rainie walked a lot, her idea of staying in shape, so her leg muscles and cardiovascular system were in pretty good condition. Jumping up and down and swinging her arms wasn't that difficult. She actually had fun. Next, Parker introduced her to lunges, and those were fun, too.

"I thought this would be hard!" she told him between quick breaths. "No problem. I can do this." She lunged her way across the arena and back, proud that she could cover such a distance without getting short of breath. "What's next?"

"Wall presses."

"Wall what?"

He escorted her to a planked wall and helped place her flattened palms against the boards, just so. "Feet lined up with your shoulders and well back from the wall," he told her.

Rainie scooted her feet back.

"Farther," he instructed. When she obliged him, he said, "Farther."

Pretty soon, Rainie's body was angled toward the wall

with only her arms to support her weight. *Uh-oh.* "This isn't very comfortable."

"It's not supposed to be. Now, keepin' your back straight and your head up, lean in and touch your nose to the board."

Rainie tried to do as he said.

"Elbows tucked in at your sides," he reminded her. "You've got your arms poked out like chicken wings. That's a surefire way to pull a muscle."

Rainie tucked in her elbows and touched her nose to the wall. "That wasn't so hard," she said as she straightened her arms. "Wall presses. Hmm. You learn something new every day."

"Again. Nice and fluid, no stoppin' in between presses. Keep touchin' that pretty little nose to the board. I'll count for you."

By the time Rainie had executed five repetitions, her arms had started to tremble.

"Again," Parker said. "Give me fifty. Not so fast. Do 'em nice and slow. The idea is to put a real strain on those arm muscles."

"Will you settle for twenty-five? My arms aren't used to this."

"Fifty," he insisted. "Go for the burn."

After thirty-two presses, Rainie's nose was flattened against the wall, and she couldn't for the life of her straighten her arms again. "I'm done."

"One more, sweetheart. Feel that burn?"

She felt it, all right. She strained to do one more repetition. Her arms quivered like blobs of jelly on a vibrating machine, but no matter how hard she strained, she couldn't straighten them again.

"Okay," Parker finally conceded. "Your arms are tired. Let's move on to somethin' else."

Something *else*? Rainie was ready for a break.

"Let's work on those thighs next," he said.

"I don't do squats," she informed him.

He gave her an odd look. "Why is that?"

"Some people don't do ovens or windows. I don't do squats. They make my legs ache."

"They're supposed to make your legs ache, and your butt, too, if you do enough of 'em."

"That's exactly why I don't do them. If it hurts, I avoid it."

He laughed. "It won't kill you to do squats. Strength in the thighs is extremely important. They're the powerhouse of the legs."

Rainie truly did want to learn how to kick Peter's butt, so she zipped her lip and did squats. After that torture ended, Parker introduced her to the joys of calf raises, which involved standing with the balls of her feet on a two-by-four and her heels touching the ground, and then pushing up onto her toes. The first ten repetitions weren't so bad, but by the time she reached fifty, her calf muscles were bunching into painful knots.

When she'd finally exercised what felt like every muscle in her body until it ached, Parker had her repeat the entire process, with no rest period in between. Doing circuits, he called it: jumping jacks, lunges, wall presses, squats, abdominal curls, leg lifts, kicks, and stretches. Rainie's body felt like a huge overcooked noodle by the time she was finished.

"Good job," Parker praised, making her feel proud of herself. But then he ruined it by adding, "Now that the warm-up's over, we can get down to some nuts and bolts."

"Warm-up?" She gaped at him, scarcely able to believe her ears. He'd been torturing her for almost an hour. "I need to rest, Parker. My muscles are quivering."

"You can't rest now. You'll cool down, and then we'll have to do the warm-up exercises all over again."

"We?" She knew she was glaring at him, but somehow

she couldn't stop herself. "It seems to me that you're using that word rather loosely. *You* didn't do any exercises."

He ran a hand over his chest, a curious glint entering his eyes as he studied her. "I'm the trainer. Normally a trainer only watches a person's form and makes sure the exercises are done properly. Would it make it easier if I did everything with you?"

"No. I'm only trying to point out that you did nothing but watch while I worked. Now I'm exhausted, and I can't do anything more right now."

"Sure you can." He chucked her under the chin. "The hard part's over for now. We're gettin' to the fun stuff."

Rainie reluctantly acquiesced, only to regret it a second later when he suddenly grabbed her from behind, one hard forearm at her throat, the other clamped like a vise at her waist.

"Okay, Peter just sneaked up on you from behind. What do you do to get away from him?"

Rainie angled her chin up. "You're choking me."

"Oh, sorry." He loosened his hold. "Better?"

Only marginally. Her backside was pressed against him, and that unnerved her. His body felt like a steel wall, with all of her soft, round places giving way to his hardness. How was she supposed to think clearly while he held her like this?

"Okay," he said again. Then, after a brief silence, "Where were we?"

The fact that he couldn't remember told her that he was as aware of her body as she was of his. "You're Peter, and I'm supposed to get away from you."

"Right." She heard him swallow—a hollow *plunk* near her right ear. "I've come up behind you, caught you by surprise. Reaction time is very important in situations like this. He's stronger than you are. He's taller. He outweighs you. If you give him time to maximize his hold on you or allow him to anticipate your countermove, your ass will be grass. So we're gonna work on automatic responses to attack, practicin' the moves over and over so you can do 'em without thinkin'. Understand?"

What Rainie understood was that *Parker* was stronger than she was, taller than she was, and outweighed her by a good margin. Did he really believe that he could teach her how to get away when he had such a huge physical advantage?

"What do you do to break his hold?" he asked again.

Rainie grabbed his wrist and tried to pull his arm from her throat. He braced against her, and all she accomplished was to tremble with the strain. His arm didn't budge.

"First lesson. Your strength is no match for his. You're not gonna outmuscle the guy. You have to think mean."

"I should stomp on his toes?" she tried.

"Nope."

"Elbow him in the ribs?"

"Nope."

"Kick him in the shin?"

"Shin kicks seldom work when you're backed up against your assailant. If you're wearin' hard-soled shoes, and you get lucky, you might get away by barkin' his shin with the heel, but chances are it'll only sting and piss him off."

"What, then?"

"Dip your head forward."

She did as instructed.

"Now snap it back as hard as you can."

Rainie flung her head back, but at the last second, she was afraid of hurting him and lost her momentum.

"Don't worry about me. I'm expectin' it. I'll turn my head. When I take the blow on my jaw and you can make me see stars, you'll be hittin' with enough force to make any man turn loose of you if he takes the blow on his mouth and nose."

Rainie repeated the motion. The back of her head thumped his jaw. "Ow!"

"You okay?"

"That *hurt.* Do you have a steel plate in there or something?"

He huffed with laughter. "When your adrenaline is up, you won't even feel it, honey. The skull is thick. You can knock his teeth loose with a good, solid head butt, and chances are, you won't be hurt at all. That's our aim, to get you to a point that you can do it that hard the instant he grabs you."

Rainie tried to picture Peter with bloody lips and loosened teeth, but the image wouldn't take shape in her mind. "That'd only make him mad. What'll I do then, run?"

"If the opportunity presents itself, hell, yes, run for all you're worth. But chances are, head-butting him in the mouth and nose will only make him turn loose of you for a couple of seconds. I'll teach you what to do next, but first we need to get this move down pat."

Rainie practiced butting his jaw until she had a slight headache. She was just starting to get the hang of it when Zach entered through the personnel door of the arena, distracting Parker with, "Hey, bro, have you seen Dad?"

Parker turned to reply to his brother just as Rainie snapped her head back. Instead of butting his jaw, she nailed him right in the face. He grunted and dropped his arms from around her. Horrified, she whirled around. He was bent over at the waist, hands cupped over his nose and mouth.

"Parker?" she cried. To her horror, she saw blood dripping through his clenched fingers. "Oh, my *God*, are you all right?"

His muffled response was unintelligible. Rainie grasped his wrist, hoping to draw his hands down so she might assess the damage. He braced against her.

"Well, well, well," Zach drawled as he strode across the

arena toward them. "It looks to me like Rainie is getting a crash course in how to kick ass and take names from a teacher with an attention deficit disorder."

Over the top of his bloody fingers, Parker sent his younger brother a smoldering glare. Tears ran from the corners of his eyes to trickle in silvery trails down his lean cheeks. "Nosebleed, no big deal."

"Oh, Parker, I'm sorry," Rainie cried. "I never meant to hurt you." She knew it was terrible of her, but despite her regret about causing him pain, she also felt a thrill of excitement. Head-butting actually *worked.* "You said you'd turn your head."

Zach snorted with laughter. "Be a little more careful with him next time, Rainie. He's delicate."

Chapter Thirteen

Over the next two weeks, communication between the Harrigans and law enforcement agencies began. Working in tandem with Frank Harrigan's high-priced attorney, Loni made all the initial contacts. According to her, the law enforcement officials she'd spoken with believed Rainie's story and were now delving into Peter Danning's background, hoping to corroborate Loni's claim that Danning's first two wives had died mysteriously and that Danning had benefited financially from their deaths.

Eventually Rainie knew she would have to be interrogated, perhaps more than once. The thought unnerved her. Even with Parker, she found it extremely difficult to talk about her life with Peter. How much worse would it be when she had to answer the questions of total strangers who might put her in jail if they didn't like her responses? Because she found that possibility so upsetting, she chose not to cross that bridge until she came to it. Parker maintained that worrying accomplished nothing, and she was inclined to agree with him. Better to take each day as it came.

And the days brought many events for Rainie to be glad about. Thomas settled in at the ranch and was soon roaming the property to hunt for mice and ground squirrels, as relaxed in his new surroundings as if he'd lived there all his life. Mojo grew like a weed, seeming to get taller, plumper, and ornerier on a daily basis. Teething, as all babies did, he developed an insatiable need to chew, which could no longer be controlled with toys. After calling Tucker's brother, Isaiah Coulter, who owned rottweilers and had raised a couple of litters, Parker went to a butcher shop for a supply of beef knucklebones, cut into quarters. Each morning when Rainie and the puppy got to the office, Mojo received a frozen bone to chew on. While working, Rainie grew accustomed to a vibrant grating sound that seldom ceased—Mojo, gnawing away on his bone.

During this lull before the storm, Parker endeavored to keep Rainie busy. Her days began with a huge breakfast, which she helped cook, and after kitchen cleanup, they went to the arena for a training session. Once Rainie was physically spent, she went back to the house for a shower and then to the office, where she attempted to keep up with her regular workload, even though she now had less time to devote to it.

"It doesn't matter," Parker insisted when she told him that she was falling behind. "The world didn't end before you came to work for me, and it won't end now just because you can't get everything done. It's far more important for you to train every mornin'. I never want you to be at a physical disadvantage with that bastard again."

In order to maximize Rainie's progress in the shortest time possible, Parker consulted with Quincy about her diet, his aim being to help her build muscle mass quickly. The second day of training, Rainie found herself drinking protein shakes in between the three sizable meals a day that Parker insisted she eat.

"I'm going to get fat!" she protested.

"No, you won't," he assured her. "Muscle burns calories, and you, sweet lady, are fixin' to build one hell of a lot of muscle."

That first week, Rainie was so stiff from the unaccustomed activity that she groaned as she got out of bed each morning, but by the second week, the aches and pains diminished, and she started to feel wonderful. There was a spring in her step, her energy level went up, and she could actually feel the muscles in her arms and legs growing strong.

"I'm becoming Iron Woman," she told Parker proudly, tightening her biceps for his perusal. "Just look!"

He felt her arms, smiled, and promptly increased the intensity of her training. Rainie complained loudly, but secretly she was excited about the progress she was making, a feeling that only increased when Parker suspended a huge training bag from a rafter in the tack room so she could learn how to kick and punch.

"Pretend it's Peter," he said. "Every time you connect with that bag, I want you to imagine that you're connecting with some part of his body."

At first, Rainie felt silly, but after a few sessions, the pretense became therapeutic in a weird way. Parker taught her different ways to throw punches and kicks. Her favorites were how to use the heel of her hand in an upward thrust to break Peter's nose, how to pivot on one foot, lean sideways, and deliver a power kick to one of his knees, and how to strike a blow to his testicles that would leave him curled in a fetal position on the floor for several minutes.

Rainie had never considered herself to be a violent person, and it bothered her at first that she liked the thought of hurting Peter. When she shared her concerns with Parker, he put her mind at ease.

"You're not violent, sweetheart. You're just finally feelin' the *rage.* All the time you were with him, fear consumed your thoughts. There wasn't much room for anger. Well, news flash: That isn't *normal.* He demeaned you. He toyed with you. He hurt you. In order to heal, you have to work up a good head of steam and release it. If you slug that damned bag, doin' your best to shove his nose gristle into his brain, where's the harm? Remember one of the worst times with him and imagine it happenin' different this time. Get good and mad, fight back, and kick the shit out of him. Even if you never get the chance to do it for real, pretendin' that you are may do you a world of good."

With each passing day, Rainie's enthusiasm mounted. She wasn't a killing machine yet, but the few tricks that Parker had taught her so far had bolstered her confidence immensely. When he continued to increase the intensity of her workouts, her resolve intensified in equal measure. *I can.* It became her mantra again, and sometimes when she trembled from exhaustion after a workout, sweat streaming down her body, she actually felt like her old self again, no longer Lorraina Danning, Peter's cowardly wife, but Rainie Hall, her father's daughter.

As much as Rainie came to enjoy her training sessions with Parker, her favorite time of every day was in the evening. They worked in tandem in his kitchen to fix supper, agreeing that each of them got to pick the main dish every other night. She learned that Parker truly did love high-fat foods and simple carbohydrates. When given a choice, he wanted red meat, potatoes, gravy, corn, and bread with plenty of butter. On her nights, he had to eat chicken, fish, squash, green vegetables, and salad, sans bread or gravy. At first he grumped about that, but then he began to appreciate the different tastes. Rainie just had to make sure there was enough food to satisfy his huge appetite.

After the meal, they cleaned up and then adjourned to the living room, the porch swing, or outdoors for a walk or horseback ride. True to his word, Parker never pressed her to take their relationship to a deeper level. He seemed content with friendship. Sometimes they just talked—about anything and everything. Other times, they made popcorn and watched a movie. She especially loved the times that they each settled down with a book, she with a romance or mystery, he with a police procedural or a private detective novel.

One night they decided to have a movie fest and watched the original Pink Panther series, featuring the incomparable Peter Sellers. Rainie laughed until she almost cried. Midway through one of the films, Parker suddenly froze the screen with the remote control and said, "That's *it*, the perfect way to teach you how to react if he catches you off guard."

"I'm sorry?" Rainie said, not following his train of thought.

"Surprise attacks. The houseboy keeps attacking Clouseau, tryin' to teach him martial arts. Why can't I attack you to teach you how to react automatically?"

"Oh, no." Rainie shivered and shook her head. "It's one thing when I'm halfway expecting it, Parker. I can handle that. But I'm not ready for you to jump me when I'm not. Peter used to do that." She shivered again. "It's all too fresh in my mind."

"I'd never hurt you," he assured her. "It'll be fun, and it's a great way to sharpen your reflexes."

Rainie wasn't so sure about that, but she'd come to trust this man as she'd never thought possible. "Okay, but if you get to attack me, I get to attack you."

"Deal."

A few minutes later in the kitchen, Parker hooked an arm around her neck and soon had her in a headlock. Doubled over at the waist and helpless to break his hold, Rainie nailed him in the groin with her elbow, taking care to aim off to the left so she hit his thigh and didn't actually hurt him.

"Excellent!" He released her and gave her a congratulatory thump on the shoulder. "If that had been for real, he'd be cryin' like a baby right now." He arched a dark eyebrow. "So what would you do next? Run, or finish him?"

"Finish him," she answered without hesitation. "That wouldn't keep him down. If I ran, he might come after me."

Parker nodded. "We'll work harder on all the finishin' techniques soon, but for now, we've still got some more getaway strategies to master."

That was the first surprise attack of many. Parker soon fell into the habit of grabbing Rainie several times a night. "Think fast," he always said. "Use whatever you can get your hands on as a weapon. Hair spray, get him in the eyes. Skillet, whop him on the head or in the face. Chair, whack him over the head. Always remember that every room contains objects that are potential weapons. Start thinkin' about that over the course of each day, trainin' your brain to notice the things that you can use to defend yourself. A file cabinet drawer, your computer monitor, a mixing bowl, a rolling pin, a cell phone. Even a bar of soap can deliver a stunning blow to the temple if you strike with enough force."

Doing as he instructed, Rainie slowly came to view her world and the ordinary things in it in a totally new way. One morning while doing her hair, she studied her hairbrush, thinking of the many ways she could use it to inflict injury on an assailant. Then her attention shifted to her hand mirror, yet another item she could use to defend herself. Parker was right: There were potential weapons all around her, and mental training was as important as, if not more important than, physically preparing herself for a confrontation. Being a female, she had anatomical limitations that would always give Peter an edge. In order to prevail in a confrontation, she would need to think fast and react even faster.

It bothered Rainie to think that she'd had just as many weapons within easy reach when she lived in the penthouse apartment with Peter. Why had she never thought to pick something up and clobber him? Instead, she'd felt helpless and terrified during his rages, her only thought being to appease him somehow. Never again, she vowed. The next time he came after her, she wouldn't cower like a mouse. She would fight back with anything she could get her hands on.

One evening Parker grabbed Rainie from behind when she was standing at the sink rinsing a pot with the nozzle sprayer, and Rainie let him have it in the face with the full force of the water. Instead of getting mad, he laughed, and before she knew quite how it happened, they were in a water fight that ended with both of them drenched to the skin.

As they cleaned up the mess, Parker praised her. "That was *awesome*! You used your head and whatever was handy. That's exactly what I've been tryin' to teach you. It's not about size and strength but about grabbin' an equalizer. The important thing is to go after him fast and hard. Water in the face won't really hurt him, but it'll shock him, possibly givin' you a second's reprieve to bash him in the head with somethin'."

"And if it doesn't, there's always dish soap in the eyes. That might blind him for a couple of seconds."

Parker flashed a broad grin and gave her a thumbs-up. "Dish soap. That's brilliant."

Before long, Rainie became as enthusiastic about the surprise attacks as Parker was. It was especially fun when she got to be the aggressor. One time, she jumped on his back, locking her arms and legs around his neck and waist, and held on fast, delivering pretend blows to his groin with her heels as he stumbled around the room. He finished that session by turning his back to a wall and bumping her gently against it.

"You're down for the count," he told her. "If he slammed you against a wall for real, you'd have the breath knocked out of you. So, now what do you do?"

Rainie quickly slid down the wall and into a roll, kicking at his knees with her heels as she went.

"Excellent!"

The practice attacks taught Rainie how to react in a variety of situations, but more important, they reminded her how to play. At some point, she discovered that Parker was ticklish, and after that, she had no mercy, often going for his armpits when he grabbed hold of her. Unfortunately, he soon learned that she was just as ticklish along her ribs and sought revenge.

One evening, a tickling episode ended with them sprawled breathlessly on the sofa, Rainie on her back, Parker draped atop her like a heavy, oversize blanket. When their laughter subsided and silence descended, they just lay there, gazes locked, hearts pounding, bodies joined. Staring up at him, Rainie got a hot, liquid, swirling sensation low in her belly. His face was so close to hers that she could see the tiny creases at the corners of his dark eyes, the individual lashes that outlined them, and the pores of his burnished skin. His breath smelled of coffee and spearmint, a combination that seemed intoxicatingly delightful to her in that moment. Her gaze dropped to his lips, which shimmered in the lamplight like polished satin.

And, just like that, she wanted him to kiss her. Always before, she had admired him but had nixed any physical urges. Now, lying heart-to-heart and body-to-body with him, the needs she had always smothered suddenly swamped her. With a quivering hand, she cupped his hard jaw. He searched her eyes for a long moment, and then, without a word, bent his dark head.

At the last second, Rainie lost her nerve. Memories of Peter's teeth grinding against her lips and of his brutal fingers digging into her breasts slammed into her brain. After getting a ring on her finger and his hands on her money, Peter had abandoned all pretense of being her lover. To him, foreplay had revolved around inflicting pain and causing humiliation. Being in control and exercising it with brutal force had been all that really aroused him.

Rainie was about to push Parker away when his lips grazed hers, the touch so light that it was like the flutter of a butterfly wing. Breath trapped at the base of her throat,

Rainie lay frozen beneath him, waiting for him to increase the pressure until it hurt, but instead he kept the contact whisper-light, teasing her mouth with the merest brush of his lips over hers. No bruising force, no discomfort, no use of strength. With a rush of expelled air, her lungs emptied.

"Oh, Parker."

She said his name with a note of surrender, but instead of taking that as an invitation to deepen the kiss, he rolled off onto the floor, taking her with him in the circle of his arm. When they landed, their positions were reversed, Parker on the bottom, Rainie on top. What disarmed her even more was that he then let his arms fall to his sides, allowing *her* to take the lead. She'd never initiated a kiss. In college, the guys had always been the assertive ones, and then after Peter came into her life, kissing and soft caresses had become a thing of the past.

Seeing the expectant look in Parker's eyes, she suddenly felt silly, embarrassed, and completely inept. She couldn't do this. But that thought no sooner entered her mind than another sneaked in to obliterate it. *There's no such word as can't.* So she lowered her head to kiss him. Nose bump. She giggled and backed away.

"I'm sorry," she told him. "Bad aim."

He smiled lazily. "My nose has been causin' me grief most of my life."

"I love your nose."

She angled her head before making her second approach, and that time, she found her target, a pair of slightly parted, warm, silken lips that responded sweetly to the slightest pressure of hers. Rainie indulged herself for a moment, savoring the taste of him, and then, somehow, her hands ended up in his hair, and she'd taken the kiss deeper, the tip of her tongue twining with his. *Parker.* In a flash of realization that stunned her, Rainie knew that she loved this man with her whole heart and soul.

He groaned and rolled with her again, burying his hands in her hair just as she had already buried hers in his. Angling his head, he took gentle control of the kiss, dipping deep into her mouth as if the mere taste of her were ambrosia, not something to be devoured quickly, but savored slowly. Her bones felt as if they were melting. Her heart felt as if it might slug its way out through her ribs. *Parker.*

Just as the swirling heat of desire drew her deep into its vortex, he broke the contact, lifted his head, and smiled down at her. "You are so sweet, Rainie mine."

And then he drew away. Rainie lay there, feeling bereft, which made no sense at all. She wasn't ready for sexual intercourse. That thought no sooner settled in her mind than a second one followed: Parker knew she wasn't ready, and that was why he had stopped. A burning wash of tears filled her eyes. He sat up beside her, and in the blur, he was a dark shimmer of black hair, burnished skin, blue chambray and denim.

"You okay?" he asked, his voice gone oddly husky.

She nodded, wanting to tell him that she was far better than just okay. She'd just waded off into depths way over her head, and he'd kept her from going under. "Thank you," she whispered.

"Thank *you.* That was, hands down, the best kiss of my lifetime."

"No, I mean—well, it *was* a great kiss—but I meant thank you for stopping."

He thrust out a hand to help her sit up. "Always, sweetheart. I gave you my word. I'll never press you to do anything you're not ready for."

A wonderful, warm rush of incredulity filled her. "Never?"

"Never."

"Never *ever*?"

He laughed. "Never ever."

"Does that mean I can kiss you whenever I want and nothing more will happen?"

His grin deepened, the warmth of it extending to his eyes. "That's right. You can play fast and loose with me any old time it suits your fancy."

Kissing, purely for the pleasure of it, was something Rainie had never indulged in very much with anyone. In fact, she honestly couldn't remember actually *enjoying* a kiss until just now. Always before, it had been a rubbery, oppressive, and wet sensation that had made her anxious to break away and catch her breath.

"I never did a whole lot of kissing," she confessed.

His grin faded, and a thoughtful, almost sad expression overtook his face. "I know."

Rainie almost asked how he knew that about her, but perhaps some questions were better left unasked. Maybe she'd been so inexpert at kissing that he could tell she hadn't had much practice.

"I, um, didn't date a whole lot at university," she felt compelled to explain, "and Peter didn't really like all the romantic stuff."

"Like kissin'?"

"Yes." She shrugged. Saying anything more would take her places she didn't want to go. "Maybe I'll get better at it over time."

He pushed up from the floor and extended a hand to help her stand. "You get much better at it, darlin', and I'll be spendin' most of my time under a cold shower."

Rainie giggled. Then she sobered. He was serious. She could tell that by the expression in his eyes and the slight, thoughtful upturn of his firm lips. "I thought maybe I wasn't very good at it or something."

His grin returned in full, devastating brilliance. "Sweetheart, kissin' isn't exactly rocket science. You have a fabulous mouth. I've wanted to taste it ever since I first clapped eyes on you. You could stand rock still and do absolutely nothin', and you'd still be a fantastic kisser. Trust me on that."

She'd come to trust him about everything else, so Rainie decided to take yet another leap of faith and believe him. It felt good to think that she might be fantastic at something besides bookkeeping.

Kissing was a lot more fun.

The next morning, Parker began teaching her more offensive maneuvers. By the end of their training session, he'd shown her how to gouge out a man's eyes with her thumbs, how to head-butt him in the nose and mouth with her forehead if he pressed a frontal attack, how to hit him in the throat with the heel of her hand to injure his larynx and possibly collapse his windpipe, and how to ram her fingers into his ears or up his nostrils if everything else failed.

"It's not your aim to disable him at this point," he reminded her again and again. "You just want to break his hold on you. The best way to do that is by inflictin' sudden, unexpected, and intense pain. Nine times out of ten, a male attacker will momentarily let go of his victim if she hurts him badly enough, and her first thought is usually to flee." At this point of the lecture, he bent his knees to get at her eye level. "That's what he'll be expectin', for you to run. Unless you're absolutely certain that you can outdistance him, that's the wrong thing to do. He's bigger, stronger, and faster. Once he recovers, he'll go after you. You'll be safest if you immediately press another attack while he's still reelin' from the first. That's when all the work we're doin' now on punchin' and kickin' will serve you well. You'll be strong, quick, and accurate with your aim. The son of a bitch won't know what hit him."

Rainie had come to love her time with the training bag. As if Parker sensed that, he often left her to practice her punching and kicking alone. For so long, she'd tried to block out all the horrible times with Peter, but now she deliberately made herself remember, bringing every detail of those abusive events center stage in her mind. That night when he'd gotten mad about the wine and knocked her off the chair, what should she have done? When the answer came to her, she re-created the scene in her head and kicked his ass. It felt so good. Correction—it felt *awesome*. Whether she could really do it in person didn't matter. Imagining that she could do it was almost as good. And it encouraged her to push herself to the limit, punching and kicking with such force that the rafter sometimes creaked from the pendulous swing of the bag.

"We've got time on our side," Parker continually reminded her. "I don't think he knows where you are yet, and by the time he does, you'll be well on your way to bein' ready for him. Chances are you'll never have to deal with him by yourself. I plan to do everything I can to make sure you don't. But on the off chance he somehow catches you alone, you're gonna clean his clock."

Rainie often had the recurring dream about being lost in the mirror maze, and it had become her habit to huddle somewhere after she woke up until the terror receded. But one night when she awakened with her heart slamming and her body drenched with sweat, huddling up no longer did the trick. Without thinking, she got out of bed, threw on her clothes, and left the house, her destination the tack room. She needed her punching bag with an urgency that rivaled an addict's need for heroin.

Once inside the arena, Rainie ran to the rear of the building. As she hurried down the hallway, bypassing the office, a voice inside her head whispered, *What are you thinking, Rainie? This is nuts.* But the need within her to face Peter still burned just as fiercely, and reasoning her way past it wasn't an option.

She flipped on the tack room light and advanced on the bag, not even bothering to close the door behind her. *Wham!* Using the heel of her hand, she punched the imaginary Peter right in his laughing face. In her mind, hundreds of mirror panels surrounded her, only now she saw herself reflected in them.

"I'm *not* lost," she cried as she kicked her make-believe tormentor in the groin and then in the knee. "Who's laughing now, Peter? Do you like that, you vicious bastard? Huh?" She delivered another blow, putting all of her strength into it. "How does that feel? News flash! From this point forward, no more free punches." Kick, kick, punch. "I'm fighting back. You're bigger than me! And you're stronger than me! Maybe I can't win! But you'll never walk away again without some wounds of your own. Got it, asshole? Never again."

Out in the corridor, Parker settled his back against the plank wall and squeezed his eyes closed against a rush of blinding tears. It wasn't often that he allowed himself to get emotional, but this was one of those moments when he had no say-so. *Rainie.* He'd known for several days that the punching-bag therapy was becoming one of her favorite exercises, and he'd hoped that reenacting the violent events of her marriage might help her to reclaim her pride. But hearing her say, "I'm *not* lost," drove home to him just how far she'd come in a very short time. He couldn't help but feel partly responsible, and that was one of the best feelings he'd ever had in his life.

He had followed her from the house out of concern for her safety. He'd heard her get up and rush outside. As much as he trusted in the security system that guarded the ranch perimeter, he still worried that Danning might find some way to breach the electronic fields. The thought of Rainie running around out in the dark with no one to protect her had unnerved him.

Now that he knew she was safe inside the arena, he needed to leave, but knowing that and doing it were two different things. *News flash! . . . Never again!* It was so good to hear that throbbing rage in her voice, with the force of her blows to the bag underscoring her fury. *Go, sweetheart,* he thought with a sad smile. *Beat him to a bloody pulp. Settle the score once and for all.*

Late one afternoon, sixteen days after Rainie called Loni and told her she wanted to contact the police, Parker came into the office with a solemn expression on his dark face. After closing the door, he leaned his back against the wood and nudged up the brim of his Stetson to meet Rainie's questioning gaze.

"The attorney just called Loni," he said. "Two FBI agents are flyin' in tonight. They'd like to meet with you tomorrow mornin' here at the ranch."

Rainie drew her hands from the computer keyboard and slumped back in her chair. She'd known from the first that this moment would come, but she still felt frightened. "What if they're coming to arrest me?"

"They aren't. The attorney would have warned Loni if that were the case." He hooked his thumbs over his hand-tooled leather belt. "He says they only want to hear your side of the story."

"So they can punch holes in it?"

"They can't punch holes in the truth." He sighed and passed a hand over his eyes. "If you wouldn't mind, I'd like to be with you and your lawyer when you talk to them."

Rainie didn't mind at all. In fact, she was relieved to have him offer. She pushed up from the desk and made her way toward him, wobbling just a little with each step. When she reached him, he seemed to know what she needed and enfolded her in his arms. "It's gonna be okay, Rainie mine. If it suddenly turns against you, we'll run."

"Where?"

"To the mountains."

"The *mountains*?"

"I can't promise you the Ritz in a wilderness area, but I can promise to take care of you. There's no way I'll let them put you in jail. It's not gonna happen, so don't even go there."

She curled her arms around his neck and clung to him. "Oh, Parker, where were you my last year of college, before I met Peter, when I most needed to meet you?"

"Waitin' for you," he whispered.

It was all that Rainie needed to hear, but as always, silence wasn't one of Parker's strong points.

"If I'd known you were out there," he whispered, "I would have come to find you, I swear. And I would have made all of it happen differently."

"How?" she asked with a dreamy smile, burying her nose against his shirt and making herself dizzy with the scent of him, a delightful blend of clean cotton, male musk, aftershave, leather, and horses.

"For starters, I would have headed you off at the pass, and you never would've taken that job at Barrestol."

She sighed and closed her eyes. "And then?"

He feathered his lips over her temple. "And then I would have dazzled you, makin' you fall head over heels in love with me. If Peter Danning had come sniffin' around, you wouldn't have known he was alive. He would've had to find himself another heiress."

Rainie tightened her arms around his neck. "And then?"

"Then I would have gathered you up in my arms, mounted my horse, and ridden off with you into the sunset."

She giggled. The fear had moved away from her. That

was part of Parker's magic, she supposed: his ability to push everything but thoughts of him from her mind.

"I'm scared."

"I know. Just remember that you aren't alone anymore, Rainie mine. You've got me, and my dad, and all my brothers, not to mention Dee Dee, Loni, and Sam. It'll be okay."

Chapter Fourteen

The meeting with the FBI agents took place in Parker's kitchen, with Rainie and her attorney, Raymond Quinn, facing the law enforcement officials across the oak table. While the two agents took Rainie's statement, Parker had been asked to leave the room, so instead of remaining beside her, as they'd both hoped, he had gone to his in-home office to place some orders for hay and grain. She missed having him with her. His solid strength and the hard press of his arm against hers had helped to calm her.

Hands clasped in her lap, Rainie was vaguely aware that she was clenching her fingers so hard that her nails lacerated her skin. But she couldn't stop herself. What transpired during this conversation would determine the outcome of her future, and in her mind's eye, she couldn't help but envision a jail cell.

It didn't ease her mind any that her male interrogator bore the title of Special Agent Slaughter. She wanted to ask if he had ever considered getting his surname changed to something less intimidating. A trim, middle-aged man with a thick head of gray hair and kindly blue eyes, he had a businesslike air, but despite his dark suit, pressed white shirt, and tasteful tie, Rainie could easily envision him in casual attire, grinning broadly as he bounced a grandchild on his knee.

His partner, Special Agent Simpson, a slender, brown-eyed blonde, met Rainie's gaze and smiled. "Before we get started, both Special Agent Slaughter and I want you to know that we believe your story, Mrs. Danning."

Rainie appreciated the comforting words and nodded, wishing she could relax. "I, um, don't go by Danning anymore. Would you mind using my maiden name, Hall?"

Simpson jotted a notation of that in her tablet. Then she took a sip of the coffee Parker had served and glanced at the older agent before looking back at Rainie. "If it's all right with you, I'll get the conversation started."

"That will be fine." Rainie just wanted this to be over.

"To begin," Simpson said softly, "let me ease your mind by saying that Loni Harrigan has proven herself to be a credible source of information time and again. From the start, we at the FBI were inclined to believe everything she told us about you and your extraordinary predicament. Since then, we've investigated your claims, and everything we've discovered tells us that you must be telling the truth. The story makes no sense otherwise.

"For one, why would anyone go to such incredible lengths to escape a marriage unless she was afraid for her life? Getting a divorce is a pretty simple process nowadays and isn't that expensive. Faking one's own death to get out of a marriage would be a lot of trouble, and quite melodramatic if a simple trip to a lawyer would accomplish the same thing."

"I couldn't go that route," Rainie inserted. "Peter would have come after me. My only safe choice was to vanish."

Simpson nodded. "We were also able to follow the money trail, and it's inarguable that Danning did take your inheritance money and invest it under his name. Third, we have reason to suspect that you may have had help to get away from him. Those involved put themselves at grave legal risk, which tells us that they must have believed your life was in danger. Otherwise they wouldn't have intervened as they did and broken the law in the process."

Rainie's heart caught. "Are my friends in trouble?"

Special Agent Slaughter leveled a solemn, thoughtful look at Rainie. "It is our aim at the FBI to go after felonious criminals, not Good Samaritans. Though your friends may or may not have committed felonies, our supervisors have decided that their actions were committed with good intent, so they're choosing not to investigate that angle of this particular case."

"So you're turning a blind eye?" Raymond Quinn asked.

Simpson's cheek dimpled in a suppressed smile. "Never that, Mr. Quinn. No self-respecting FBI agent would ever ignore the commission of a felony. We do, however, pick and choose our battles, our aim always being to make this country a safer place for U.S. citizens. We aren't into wasting our time or the taxpayers' dollars on frivolous investigations that may end up being tossed out of court. In this instance, we would anticipate judicial sympathy for Ms. Hall's friends. The three individuals in question didn't set out to harm society, only to save her life."

The lawyer flashed Rainie a quick smile. The tension that had gripped Rainie's body since the beginning of this interview suddenly eased from her muscles like water sluicing from a sieve. She bent her head and closed her eyes in silent gratitude.

"Moving on." Simpson leafed through the tablet. "Our first order of business will be to get your statement." She glanced up, her eyes softening with compassion. "I'll apologize in advance for the nature of some of our questions and also for the fact that this process will probably be very difficult for you. Unfortunately, even though we believe everything Loni Harrigan told us, we have to get the story straight from you as well."

"I understand." Rainie sat straighter on the chair. "I'll answer your questions as honestly as I can."

To start, Rainie had to tell the agents how she first met Peter Danning, and then she was asked to describe her relationship with Peter—their courtship, their marriage, and the events that led up to her disappearance. While Rainie talked, both agents took copious notes and often interrupted to ask questions. As Special Agent Simpson had predicted, the process was long and emotionally grueling for Rainie. By the time it was over, she felt drained and absolutely exhausted.

When Parker was invited back into the kitchen, he took a seat next to Rainie and reached under the table to clasp her hand. *I'm here,* he seemed to be saying. *I'll always be here.* She clung to his fingers, comforted by the contact.

Simpson said, "Now that we've gotten your statement, we need to update you on where we are with this case. Ever since Loni Harrigan contacted us, we've had Danning under a magnifying glass, trying to verify everything she told us." She glanced at Rainie. "In short, Ms. Hall, there isn't a question in our minds that he's the villain. We've done our homework and proven to our satisfaction that Danning's first two wives did indeed die mysteriously and that he walked away with huge sums of money after their deaths. We believe Peter Danning murdered them, and it is our hope that we'll be able to nail him. In order to do that, we need to build a bulletproof case against him."

"You don't have enough evidence to do that right now?" Quinn asked.

Slaughter shook his head as he returned his mug of coffee to the table. "Unfortunately, no. The man is clever, and he's cunning. When he murdered the first two women, he covered his ass nine ways to hell." He flicked a look at Rainie. "Pardon my language, Ms. Hall, but the last two weeks have been very frustrating for us, to say the least. We believe that your husband is a conscienceless killer who has struck more than once. He would have ended your life as well if you hadn't gotten away from him. But we have no solid evidence to file any charges against him."

Rainie released a taut breath. "I was afraid of that. He poisoned his first wife, but somehow no traces of poison showed up during the autopsy."

"And he had the remains cremated immediately," Simpson inserted. "As a result, we have no body to exhume, and because the coroner believed the young woman died of natural causes, he kept no autopsy samples. We've talked with him at length, and he noted nothing suspicious when he examined the body. Her medical records indicate that she died from a lingering illness that baffled several specialists. They couldn't determine what was wrong with her, but none of them suspected foul play."

"Poison that couldn't be detected unless they were looking for it," Rainie whispered. "Or something that left the system quickly, leaving no chemical trace."

Simpson nodded. "We believe so, yes. Some lethal substances are difficult if not impossible to detect, and we think Danning used one of them. But we can't prove it."

"The second murder was executed just as cleverly," Slaughter added. "The young woman was driving on a curvy road in rainy, slick-surface conditions and plunged the car off a steep embankment. The police didn't suspect foul play." He gestured limply with one hand. "Going on what Loni related to us about Danning's hiring a thug to tamper with the vehicle's brakes, we got a warrant to examine Danning's bank transactions, dating back well before the car accident. We found evidence of the payoff, a check for ten thousand made out to a man named Charles White. Mr. White had a record. He'd once been investigated in a murder-for-hire case but was never charged because there wasn't enough evidence to convict him. We feel certain that Danning hired White to tamper with Clarissa Danning's vehicle."

Hearing Peter's second wife mentioned by name made her seem more real to Rainie, not just some faceless woman who'd met with a tragic end, but a person who'd loved unwisely, just as Rainie had, and then found herself trapped in a deadly web.

"Have you talked to White?" Quinn asked.

"Mr. White died shortly after the car accident that killed Clarissa Danning," Simpson replied. "He fell down a flight of stairs and broke his neck."

"That's convenient." Parker's voice grated like a dull knife over the rough surface of a whetstone. "Danning saw him as a loose end and got rid of him."

"We believe so, yes," Slaughter agreed. "We just can't prove it. In order to put Peter Danning away and stop him from victimizing anyone else, we have to gather irrefutable evidence against him, and so far, we have none."

"So Rainie is sunk." Parker didn't phrase it as a question. "You haven't come right out and said it, but you can't help her."

"That isn't what we're saying at all," Simpson interjected. "But in order to help her, we must get proof to nail Danning."

"But he left no evidence," Rainie said, her voice shaky with nerves.

"Which only means that we have to create a situation that produces some," Simpson replied.

"I'm not following," Rainie said.

Abandoning all pretense of searching through her notes, the female agent met Rainie's bewildered gaze. Flattening her palms on the table, she said, "Let me cut to the chase. We've put out word to law enforcement agencies, making it possible for you to resurface without any legal ramifications, and now we would like you to file for dissolution of the marriage."

"*What?*" Rainie pressed her shoulder against Parker's solid arm. The sturdy, muscular brace of his body made her feel safe. "File for a divorce, you mean?"

"If Danning is the greedy killer we believe he is, he'll freak at the thought of your being awarded half of his ill-gotten gains in divorce court," Simpson replied. "We think he'll come after you, making an attempt on your life under the guise of an accident or a random act of violence."

"Exactly," Rainie cried. "He'll come after me and kill me!"

"He'll try," Simpson amended. "In order for us to catch him in the act, you will have to be under constant FBI surveillance."

Parker stiffened on his chair. "You want to use her as *bait*?"

"There is a certain level of risk. I won't lie to you about that." Simpson made direct eye contact with Parker. "But we will take every possible precaution to ensure Ms. Hall's safety. You have my personal guarantee on that."

Parker leveled a hard look at Slaughter. "Do you people have any idea what a ruthless son of a bitch Danning is?"

"We're well aware that the man is ruthless and probably psychotic," Slaughter retorted. "We're also aware that he'll strike again if we don't stop him. We need Ms. Hall's cooperation to do that."

"We've made arrangements with Mr. Quinn for you to sign the divorce papers this afternoon," Simpson went on, her gaze shifting to the lawyer. "If you agree to cooperate, he'll file them at your local courthouse first thing tomorrow morning. In the hope that we can end this as quickly as possible, strings will be pulled to get Danning served no later than tomorrow afternoon."

"But then he'll know where I am," Rainie protested.

"Exactly." Simpson pushed at her cropped blond hair. "We want him to know where you are, Ms. Hall, and we want him to make an attempt on your life. According to Mr. Quinn, you've been staying here at the ranch for safety reasons. We must request that you return to your residence as of tomorrow. You can come here to work during the day, of course. That's been your usual routine, but henceforth, you need to go home every night. Danning won't make a move unless he believes you're alone and unprotected."

Parker sat forward on his chair. "You want her to stay there alone? Are you out of your minds?" He sent a sharp look at the lawyer. "Why didn't you give us a heads-up about this so we could discuss it? I don't want Rainie's safety to be at risk."

"I wasn't informed until right before the meeting," Quinn replied.

"There's no other way," Simpson interjected softly. "And Ms. Hall won't really be alone, Mr. Harrigan. When she travels back and forth between here and home, she'll be tailed by two well-trained agents. They'll hang back, of course, so they won't be detected, but they'll be there in case she needs help. A transmitter will be placed on her car, enabling them to know when she's on the move and also to track her. That way, they can park well away from the ranch or her house and fall in behind her without being seen. We'll also have agents positioned all around her residence. If Danning shows up, his every move will be monitored, and they'll get on scene before Ms. Hall is harmed."

"You won't be able to prove deadly intent unless you allow him to make an actual attempt on her life!" Parker shot back. "What do you take me for, Ms. Simpson, a backwoods hick with no understandin' of the law? You can't arrest the man for enterin' his wife's residence. You can't arrest him for attemptin' to see her. You'll have to catch him red-handed, tryin' to take her life."

"When Ms. Hall signs the divorce papers this afternoon, Mr. Quinn will also file a restraining order. In that paperwork, Ms. Hall will detail her reasons for requesting the order, namely that she's afraid Danning will try to kill her. So we *will* be able to arrest Danning if he goes within a hundred and fifty yards of her. But we'll do so only in the event that we believe the situation has gotten out of hand."

"In other words, you plan to stand clear until he tries to take her life." Parker's jaw muscle started to tic. "I'm sorry, but that isn't okay with me."

"Her safety will be our number one priority."

Parker sank back on his chair.

"There's no other way," Slaughter interjected. "We want this man off the streets as much as you do. We're going to have to work together to nail him."

"A charge of attempted murder won't keep him off the streets for very long," Parker shot back.

"No, but once he's in custody," Simpson replied, "we can interrogate him and hopefully wring a confession out of him about one of the three slayings. Our people are well trained and know how to rattle a suspect. If he gets his facts mixed up, just once, then our chances of getting him to confess increase substantially."

The thought of going home to spend nights alone frightened Rainie, but she wasn't nearly as terrified by the prospect as she would have been a month ago. She squeezed Parker's hand. "I'm okay with it, Parker."

He sent her a smoldering look.

"It's something I have to do," Rainie hurried to explain. "If Peter isn't stopped, how many other young women may die? I can't live with that on my conscience."

"I'm not asking you to. But I absolutely *refuse* to let you stay alone at night, no how, no way."

"She has to stay there alone," Slaughter insisted. "Otherwise, Danning won't show his hand. As Special

Agent Simpson said, every precaution will be taken to ensure Ms. Hall's safety. The house will be wired so the surveillance agents will be able to hear what's going on. They'll move in the moment there's cause for alarm."

A sudden concern occurred to Rainie. "What about my friends, Maggie and Janet? Will you be protecting them, too?"

Slaughter shook his head. "It's not Danning's MO to go after them. Too obvious. He prides himself on being so slick he'll never be caught, and going after them would be a dead giveaway."

Rainie decided that was probably a correct assumption. Peter believed himself to be of superior intelligence. Going after Maggie or Janet would be rash and stupid, and Peter was far too cunning for that.

That afternoon Parker accompanied Rainie to the attorney's office to sign the divorce papers. He was uncharacteristically quiet en route, had little to say during the meeting with Raymond Quinn, and still seemed distant when they were once again in his truck, driving back to the ranch.

"Parker, please don't be mad at me," she finally said.

He gave her a brooding look and then checked his rearview mirror before changing lanes. "I'm not mad at you, honey. I'm scared half to death."

Rainie understood exactly how he felt. Her initial confidence about staying alone at night had given way to a bad case of nerves. Peter was smart. What if he managed to slip past the FBI agents and into her house? He might sabotage the microphones, making it impossible for them to hear what was going on. The very thought made her blood run cold. As hard as she had worked over the last two weeks to prepare herself for a physical confrontation with Peter, she still had a long way to go. Unlike the punching bag, he wouldn't just stand there and let her kick him.

* * *

After the supper dishes were done that evening, Rainie turned from putting something away in a cupboard to find Parker right behind her. With a shaky sigh, he drew her into his arms, the urgency in his embrace conveying without words just how worried he was.

"I love you so much," he whispered huskily. "I'm sorry for sulkin' all day. It's just difficult for me to put your safety into someone else's hands."

Her eyes swimming with tears, Rainie knew beyond any doubt that she had come to love him, too. No more reservations, no more excuses, no more holding her feelings in check. How could she not love this man? From the start, even when he'd had no proof to make him believe her story, he'd become her friend and supporter, and he'd been behind her ever since, never once threatening to expose her or trying to control her in any way. In the beginning, he could have done that so easily, using his knowledge of her wrongdoing as leverage against her. Deep in her heart, Rainie knew that was precisely what Peter would have done.

Curling her arms around his shoulders, she went up on her tiptoes, pressed close, and turned her face against his neck. "I love you, too, Parker. With all my heart. I love you, too."

He went absolutely still. Then his arms tightened around her. "Say that again?"

Rainie smiled, her lips curving against his skin. "I love you, Parker. I have for a long time. It's just really, *really* hard for me to say the words, even inside my head."

"Why?" he asked. "I've been waitin' for what seems like forever to hear them."

He'd been waiting for other things as well. Rainie felt the evidence of that, a hard ridge of masculine desire throbbing against her belly. "I was afraid of where they might take me, I guess. Loving you—admitting that I love you—is *huge* for me. Remember talking to me about leaping off a cliff with you? That's how it feels to me, as if I'm about to jump and do a free fall."

She swallowed hard, hating herself for being such a coward. If any man on earth had ever earned a woman's absolute trust, it was *this* man. Inside, she still cringed at the thought of having sex, though. Her memories of Peter's touch and the beatings that he'd meted out when her performance in the bedroom hadn't pleased him were still so fresh in her mind. She needed more time to distance herself from all of that. Problem: Parker needed her *now*, and he deserved to have his needs met. If she loved him, *really* loved him, she wouldn't think of herself. She'd think only of him.

"I'm ready to do that now," she whispered. "Take the leap, I mean."

He dipped his dark head to bury his face in her hair. "Are you, now?"

Rainie nodded and pressed her body more firmly against his. "I am, Parker. I truly am. Take me upstairs and make love to me."

Instead he just stood there like a tree that had put down roots, his arms locked around her, his body swaying slightly as if buffeted by a strong breeze. Finally he said, "Never, *ever* lie to me, Rainie. I know you *want* to be ready, and that you're willin' to pretend that you are in order to make me happy. But I'm not okay with that."

"But what if I'm never ready?" she asked, her voice taut with concern. "Sometimes you just have to force yourself."

She felt his mouth tip into a grin. "There are times when forcin' yourself to confront your fears is the only way to conquer 'em. I agree with you on that. But I'm not willin' to settle for that when it comes to sex. I want our first time together to be absolutely beautiful for you—so perfect in every way that you never even *think* about Peter Danning, from start to finish."

That was a tall order. Rainie squeezed her eyes closed, her chest aching with regret, because she wasn't sure she'd ever be able to deliver on that request. "What if that time never comes?"

"Never?" he echoed huskily. "Well, then, I guess we'll have to reassess the situation and come up with another plan of action. If you still aren't ready in six months or a year, I promise to consider the grin-and-bear-it method."

The grin-and-bear-it method? A giggle bubbled up her throat. She tried to swallow it back, but it escaped, sounding more like a wet snort than a laugh.

"What, exactly, is so funny?" he asked with a smile in his voice.

Rainie tightened her hold on his neck. "*You* are. A year, Parker? I can't believe you'd offer to wait that long."

"I'm not exactly happy about it," he admitted. "And to be honest, I don't think it'll take that long." He nibbled her earlobe, sending shocks of sensation spiraling into her belly. "But I'm willin' to wait if it does. When it happens, I don't want it to be a chore you're performin' to make me happy. I want it to be what makes *you* happy. When the time is right, you will be. You'll see."

His refusal to take what she had offered brought a fresh rush of tears to Rainie's eyes, and deep within her, a chink formed in the ice that Peter had put around her heart.

"Oh, Parker, no wonder I love you," she whispered shakily. "You're the most wonderful man I've ever known."

"Thank you, darlin'. That's one of the nicest compliments I've ever received." He loosened his arms from around her, took her hand, and led her upstairs. At her door, he took her face between his hands. "What would you say if I asked to sleep with you tonight?"

Rainie gazed up at him in bewildered confusion. "I thought you just said—"

He angled a thumb across her lips. "No funny business. I

only want to hold you and be with you. Tomorrow you leave. This is our last night together."

Unable to speak past the lump in her throat, Rainie only nodded. He followed her into the bedroom. When she went to the dresser for a nightgown, he stopped her with, "As a safety precaution, let's sleep in our clothes. I'm a man, not a saint."

She returned to the bed, he on one side, she on the other. As he toed off his boots, she kicked off hers. After pulling back the covers, they sank down onto their respective sides of the mattress and then rolled toward each other, jostling for a comfortable position, which ended with her head resting in the hollow of his shoulder. In the dim glow of the light spilling in from the hall, they were surrounded by shadows and the combined warmth of their bodies. Without speaking, he lightly stroked her hair, each pass of his hand telling her how deeply he loved her.

Rainie settled against him and closed her eyes, feeling utterly at peace for the first time in so long she couldn't remember when. Just then, a series of yips traveled up the staircase and into the room.

"Shit," he whispered.

Rainie giggled. "We forgot your sidekick."

He sat up and swung his feet off the bed. While jerking his boots back on, he said over his shoulder, "I'll need to take him out."

"I'll wait for you."

He pushed to his feet, a masculine silhouette in the dimness. "Be right back."

While he was gone, Thomas joined Rainie in bed and settled on the pillow that had so recently supported Parker's dark head. Sighing, Rainie petted her cat until Parker returned. Mojo stumbled across the rumpled bedcovers to curl up on the pillow with Thomas. When Parker had once again divested himself of his boots, he assessed the situation.

"Well, hell. Is that a bed or a kennel?"

Rainie patted her side of the mattress. "We can fit over here. It'll be cozier this way."

As he slipped in beside her and drew her back into his arms, he asked, "What'll we do when Mojo weighs close to two hundred pounds?"

Rainie smiled and snuggled close, loving the feel of his strong arms. "Get a bigger bed?"

They held each other long into the night, Parker controlling his physical urges because he knew that she was still haunted by terrible memories, Rainie feeling grateful just to have his warmth all around her. She was touched more deeply than he would ever know when he made no moves on her. He seemed content simply to hold her close. It was one of the most beautiful gifts he could have given her.

The following day, it was never far from Rainie's mind that she would have to go home alone that afternoon. She adhered to her usual routine, taking her breakfast with Parker, working out, and then going to the office to perform her job. When Parker joined her for lunch in the office, they dined on Chinese takeout in unaccustomed silence. Not even Parker seemed inclined to talk. Rainie had never known him to be quiet for so long. That told her he was as worried about the coming night as she was.

When her workday was over, he invited her to stay for dinner.

"I'm sorry," she said. "I need to stop by the store for some groceries, and once I get home, I'll have heaps to do. The whole place is probably covered in dust, and even though I emptied the fridge of perishables, it'll probably need a wipe-down with soda water to freshen it up."

His dark gaze held hers, and for a moment, she thought he might argue. But in the end, he only nodded and walked with her to the Mazda. Once she was settled behind the wheel, he rested his folded arms on the window opening and leaned close to say, "You've got my number on speed dial."

"Yes. I'll call if I need you."

"If you get nervous and can't sleep, don't hesitate, either."

She nodded and tried to avoid his gaze, afraid she might burst into tears if she looked directly into his eyes. *Alone.* For the next fifteen hours, she would be completely alone. "What if—" She broke off and swallowed to steady her voice. "What if they don't have any agents lined up to stand watch tonight?"

"I'm sure they have that covered," he assured her. "Try not to be scared, Rainie mine. The FBI is a pretty squared-away outfit. The agents are all very well trained. Nobody will get past 'em without bein' seen."

She turned the key in the ignition. The Mazda's engine purred to life, still running smoothly, thanks to the overhaul Parker's mechanic had given it. The memory made her heart pang. That long-ago morning, she'd been so afraid to give Parker her keys, thinking that he meant to keep her at the ranch until the police arrived. That seemed like a lifetime ago now.

"Well, good-bye," she said hollowly. "I'll see you in the morning."

He nodded and backed away from the vehicle. "Ten minutes," he called as she backed the car around to head down the driveway. "I can be there just that fast."

Rainie watched him in her rearview mirror as she drove along the rutted road that led to the highway. He was still standing there, gazing after her, when she executed the turn and lost sight of him. *Coward.* She glanced in the mirror, hoping to see a vehicle in the distance, but if two agents were tailing her, they were nowhere in sight.

With a shaky hand, she turned on the radio, but not even George Strait's honeyed voice could soothe her frazzled nerves. She wouldn't even have Thomas to keep her company, she thought forlornly. Because he had gotten so upset the last time she transported him, she'd decided to leave him at Parker's place, where he'd come to feel at home.

Her stop at the grocery store took over thirty minutes, so it was a little over an hour before she reached her place. After parking in the short driveway, she sat in the car for a long while, staring at the house. She didn't want to go in there. Peter hadn't been served the papers until sometime that afternoon. Odds were good that he was still in Seattle, and he was far too smart to do anything impulsive. Instead, he'd probably circle the situation, wondering why she hadn't been arrested. The FBI agents seemed to think that he would accept at face value the story he would be told by Seattle law enforcement officers, namely that she hadn't broken any law by faking her own death.

Rainie worried that Peter wasn't quite that gullible. He'd smell something fishy. She just knew he would. Besides, it had never been far from her mind that he might already know where she was. She'd been safe on the ranch over the last two weeks. For all she knew, he could have cased her house during her absence and be hiding in there right now, waiting to pounce on her. Would she have been notified if he wasn't available when they tried to serve him with the divorce papers? What if he wasn't in Seattle, but right here in Crystal Falls?

Stop it, Rainie. Just stop it! She forced herself to get out of the car and collect the grocery bags. As she walked toward the front porch, she whispered under her breath, "I can, I can, I *can*." But somehow the words gave her little comfort. Though she knew agents were watching her, she couldn't see them. What if they weren't out there?

Once in the house, she locked the door behind her, then walked straight into the kitchen. Her skin felt as if it had been turned inside out, and her heart was pounding like a piston. She set the bags on the counter and grabbed the rolling pin from a drawer. Then she took a tour of the house, ready to clobber anything that moved. *All clear.* She checked every conceivable hiding place, even looking under the beds.

Satisfied that her husband wasn't inside the house, she set herself to the task of bringing in her suitcase, unpacking, and tidying the rooms. That kept her busy until almost dark. Then she fixed herself a ham sandwich and some vegetable soup, sat at the table, and tried to eat. *Yeah, right*. Every time the floor creaked, she about had a heart attack. No amount of lecturing herself settled her nerves. Special Agents Slaughter and Simpson seemed positive that Peter would come after her. They just couldn't say when. And wasn't that just ducky? In the interim, all she could do was wait. Did either of them comprehend how frightening that was for her?

Chapter Fifteen

Before it grew fully dark, Rainie pulled all the curtains. Peter could be out there right now. She could imagine him peering through a crack in the drapes, smiling and planning his revenge. She envisioned him wearing gloves and a stocking cap to avoid leaving behind any trace of his DNA during a struggle. Her only comfort was in the knowledge that he wouldn't rape her. Peter was far too intelligent to leave any physical evidence that might implicate him, and semen was as damning as a fingerprint nowadays.

Unable to settle anywhere, Rainie started pacing from room to room. Within thirty minutes, she'd bitten her fingernails to the quick. *Oh, God.* She couldn't *do* this. She went to the phone, wanting to call Parker. She knew he would come if she asked. But then what? Peter wouldn't make a move unless he felt certain she was alone. By inviting Parker over, she would only be prolonging the torture. Eventually, she had to stay here alone and be okay with it. It was the only way to lure Peter into the FBI's trap.

Her feet almost parted company with the floor when a soft tap came at her back door. Scrambling to retrieve her rolling pin, Rainie faced the portal.

"It's me, Parker," came a hushed voice. "Shut off all the kitchen lights before you let me in, Rainie mine. I don't want to be spotted."

Parker? Rainie wanted to whoop with joy. Instead she dashed to the light switch and plunged the kitchen into darkness. Then she hurried over to disengage the dead bolt. The next instant, she was enveloped in his strong arms, a wonderful sense of safety radiating through her.

"Oh, *Parker*."

"It's okay now," he said in a gruff whisper. "I'm here. You don't have to be alone."

He moved away from her, his boots tapping softly as he made his way to the living room. The next instant, her television blared to life, the sound up so high that it made her jump. When he cut back through the gloom to her, he drew her into his arms. She shivered and pressed her nose against his shirt, immersing herself in the smell of him, a delightful blend of puppy slobber, horses, freshly washed cotton, and musk cologne.

"What on earth are you *doing* here?" she asked, keeping her voice low. "How did you get past the agents?"

"I didn't," he said with a laugh. "Bastards caught me at the edge of your yard."

"And they let you through?"

His arms tightened around her. "It took a little negotiatin' to bring 'em around to my way of thinkin'. I told 'em I could slip in without Danning seein' me, and that the only way they could stop me was to throw me in jail. They powwowed about it for a bit and then called the higher-ups. I reckon they decided my bein' here won't do any harm as long as Danning doesn't spot me." He buried his face in the lee of her neck. "God, Rainie, it seems like an eternity since you left the ranch."

She clung to him, never wanting to turn loose. "You can't stay, Parker. I know you tried to slip in without being seen, but the bottom line is, Peter will never make a move if he suspects you're here."

"He won't suspect. I parked my truck six blocks away

and worked my way through about three hundred backyards, all guarded by vicious dogs, to reach your back porch. Not even the agents saw me until I was right on top of 'em."

Rainie was smothering tearful laughter when he kissed her. *Silk on silk.* He tasted of coffee and mint, his breath soft and warm against her lips. She ran her palms over his shoulders, glorying in the strength she felt bunching beneath her fingertips. *Safe.* Now that he was with her, she wasn't afraid of anyone or anything.

As he lifted his head, she whispered, "I'm so glad you're here. Why didn't you tell me you were coming? I wouldn't have been so nervous if I'd known. I've chewed my nails to the quick. I couldn't eat. Why didn't you tell me?"

He pressed a light kiss to her forehead. "I wasn't sure I could get through. I didn't want to get your hopes up and then disappoint you." He straightened away from her to peer through the darkness. "You got all the curtains drawn? I don't want to be seen when we turn the light back on."

"All of them are drawn, but the kitchen ones are kind of thin."

"Got any tacks?"

A mere minute later, Rainie was stifling giggles in the darkness as she helped Parker tack towels and sheets over her kitchen windows. "They're going to hear us laughing," she whispered, "and think we're certifiably nuts."

"I don't think they can hear much with that television up so loud."

Only when the windows were safely covered would he allow her to turn on the kitchen light. In the sudden illumination, she stood and grinned at him, feeling so happy to have him there that she couldn't think what to say.

"You could have gotten in big trouble for this, you know. What if they'd taken you at your word and tossed you in the clink?"

He winked at her. "Like Dad said, a spot of trouble now and again keeps life interestin'."

Just then Rainie's phone rang. When she picked up, a strange male voice came over the line. "Ms. Hall, this is Special Agent Brandson. Are you okay in there? Our bugs are useless with that television up so loud."

Rainie glanced at Parker. "I'm sorry. We turned up the volume for a little privacy."

"Well, please turn it back down. We agreed to let Mr. Harrigan through because he convinced us that he wouldn't be seen. But we still need to monitor the house in case Danning makes a move."

"All right. We'll turn it back down."

After hanging up the phone, Rainie went to the living room and lowered the sound. When she returned to the kitchen, she shrugged and said, "I guess I'll count my blessings and just be glad that you're here. No private conversation allowed."

Bending close, he whispered, "I'll find the damned bugs. If we want to have privacy, I can temporarily move one of them and put it back later."

He grabbed her bowl of soup from the table and stuck it in the microwave. When it was hot, he insisted that she sit down and eat. "You won't be able to kick Danning's ass if you let yourself get puny again."

As he sat across from her, she paused with the soup spoon halfway to her mouth. "Was I *that* puny?"

His firm mouth tipped into a smile. Voice pitched low so he wouldn't be heard, he said, "Beautiful, too, of course, and definitely not puny in all the places that matter."

"What's that mean?"

"It means you have a knockout figure that keeps me awake at night, tryin' to picture you naked." He inclined his head at the bowl. "Now, eat, lady. I want you to keep your strength up."

Between mouthfuls, she asked, "How long can you stay?"

"Until right before dawn. Toby's at the house with Mojo and Thomas." He sat back on the chair, the outline of his shoulders evident under the wash-worn cloth of his shirt. "Hopefully the agents will let me slip through again tomorrow night. They may powwow again and decide Danning might see me, you know."

Rainie didn't want to think about facing the night without him. "I'm just glad they let you through tonight."

"I'll do my best to be here tomorrow night, too," he assured her. "If they give me any guff, I'll tell them to throw me in jail. If that happens, Dad will raise so much sand they'll rethink their decision right quick."

When Rainie had finished her meal, Parker grinned broadly and handed her his cell phone. "I'm thinkin' that there are a couple of people you've been wantin' to call." He arched a dark eyebrow. "It's safe for you to contact them now."

Rainie stared at him incredulously. "Maggie and Janet, you mean?"

"Why not? He knows where you are now. It can't hurt."

Rainie dialed Margaret first. When her friend answered on the third ring, tears filled Rainie's throat and she could barely speak. "Maggie," she pushed out. "It's me."

"Oh, *shit.* Hang up! Have you lost your mind, Rainie Ann? What if my line is tapped?"

Rainie laughed wetly and quickly filled Margaret in on the events of the last two days. "You're in the clear. The FBI says any charges they filed against you would be tossed out of court."

"I never cared about getting racked for helping you. There wasn't a choice. How are you, Rainie Ann? Are you happy? More important, *where* are you?"

"A place called Crystal Falls. It's wonderful here. I'm great!"

After the initial catching up was over, Rainie suddenly turned serious. "Maggie, listen to me. When Janet and I pulled the switch aboard ship, she walked away wearing a forty-thousand-dollar diamond necklace and my engagement ring, which set Peter back almost twenty grand. I want you guys to hock them."

"Hock them?"

"Yes, he gave them to me. They're mine. I want you to sell them and split the money. You won't be able to get what they're worth, but it should cover the loan you gave me, plus some. I want you and Janet to keep all of it."

"Ah, Rainie. We never cared about the money."

"I know, but I did. I want us to be square. Will you do that for me?"

"Do I get to spend my share however I want?"

Rainie laughed again. "Of *course.*"

"Good. I'm flying to Crystal Falls."

"Oh, I'd *love* that. But not until this mess is over." Rainie smiled at Parker, who sat watching her with a gentle expression on his face. "I can't have any company yet. But when I can, you'll be first on my list to call."

Moments later, Rainie was on the phone with her irreverent friend Janet, who shrieked with delight when she heard Rainie's voice. "Where are you, girlfriend? Is it safe for you to call me?"

"Absolutely safe." Rainie went through the spiel again, updating Janet on the situation. "Remember when I dropped the goblet and Peter beat the hell out of me?"

"Bastard. Yes, I remember."

"Well, I saw a town on the Oregon map called Crystal Falls, and that's where I am. It's wonderful here. I have a great job." She looked at Parker again. "And I've met a really nice man."

"Oh, shit. Rainie Ann, you don't have a very good track record. Are you *sure* he's nice?"

Rainie grinned and put Janet on speakerphone. "I'm sure. He's helped me out from the very start and been my friend through thick and thin."

"Give him a message from me. Tell him if he lays one hand on you, he's a dead man."

Parker suppressed a laugh, afraid to make a sound for fear she'd realize he was listening.

"I'll tell him," Rainie promised, "but I think hitting women is against the cowboy code."

"Cowboy code? Rainie, what'd you do, lasso yourself a cowboy?"

"Something like that. He doesn't have cows, though. He raises quarter horses."

"Horses, cows, it's all the same to me. Does he wear cowboy boots and a hat and all that stuff?"

"Yes. Do you have something against a Stetson and riding boots?"

"No." Janet chortled in delight. "Does he have any cute friends?"

Rainie rolled her eyes. "Janet, you're impossible. Cowboys aren't your thing."

"How can I know until I try one?"

Parker winked at Rainie.

"He's got a couple of cute brothers you might try on for size," Rainie informed her. "When it's safe for you to visit, I'll introduce you to both of them, and you can take your pick."

"How long before the coast will be clear?"

Rainie laughed. It felt so good to be talking with her friends again. "Soon, I hope. I just want this to be over. You know?"

"I just pray those FBI agents know what they're doing, and you don't get hurt."

A few moments later, when Rainie ended the call, she gave Parker his phone along with a fierce hug. "That felt so awesome," she whispered. "I love them so much."

He curled a hard arm around her. "I love 'em, too," he murmured huskily. "They stood by you and took huge risks to help you. I'll always feel indebted to both of 'em."

True to his word, Parker stayed until just before dawn and returned the following night, waiting for the cloak of darkness before walking the six blocks to her house. Over the next week, it became their ritual—his tapping on the back door and Rainie dousing the lights to let him in. With the bugs to contend with, they quickly determined their locations in the house, and when they wanted to engage in private conversations, Parker grew adept at moving them from room to room. One night he brought movies to watch. Another night he showed up with a board game. But mostly they just clung to each other like two partially uprooted trees that were trying to weather a fierce storm. When they slept, they lay wrapped in each other's arms.

On the eighth night, Special Agent Brandson called Rainie again, this time to request that she turn off the kitchen lights long before Parker's arrival so it wouldn't appear that she was flipping them on and off too quickly, which might be interpreted by Danning to be a signal of some kind. They wanted nothing peculiar going on that might alert him to the fact that she was being watched.

Only Peter still didn't make a move. As the divorce proceedings progressed, he hired a top-notch lawyer to defend his assets, claiming that Rainie was a gold digger who had married him only for his money. When the news media learned that his missing wife had resurfaced, Peter was also vindicated in the public eye, his sterling reputation as an upstanding Seattle businessman restored. Rainie was the one who took hard hits in the newscasts, portrayed as a young and beautiful woman on the take who'd used her feminine wiles to marry a wealthy older man. She was dubbed the "Runaway Bride." On the surface, it all looked normal in a celebrity sort of way. Even Rainie, who'd once looked into Peter's murderous eyes, began to wonder if he might allow the divorce to happen and let her lay claim to half of his money.

"Maybe he senses the trap," she said to Parker over lunch one afternoon. "Could be he's decided that it isn't worth it to risk his freedom to protect his assets. Even after splitting everything with me, he'll still be a rich man."

Parker tossed a half-eaten piece of pizza to Mojo, who'd nearly doubled in height and weight. As he wiped his fingers with a napkin, he replied, "Maybe he's content to play the hoodwinked rich man and wait for all the hoopla to die down so he can start searchin' for another victim." He rocked back on the chair and crossed his arms, the posture showcasing the breadth of his muscular shoulders and chest. "A man like him has to play the odds. Maybe the next gal won't have the guts to run."

"This is driving me *crazy*," she cried. "What if he's just biding his time until the FBI stops guarding me? Surveillance is costly. Eventually, if nothing happens, won't they consider reassigning the agents here to another case?"

"They might," he acknowledged.

"Then what? I'm left hung out to dry?"

He sat forward and reached across the desk to grasp her hands. "Sweetheart, calm down. The FBI won't call off their dogs unless they're confident that Danning no longer poses a threat to you."

Rainie gulped down a shrill protest and struggled to regain her composure. "I *know* him, Parker. He'll never rest, not as long as I'm alive. I belong to him. Don't you see? He's a twisted, sick man, and in his mind, I have to be punished for leaving him."

"You don't belong to him, not anymore," he assured her huskily. "You're mine now, and trust me when I say, I guard what's mine. If the FBI loses interest in the case and leaves you unprotected, my family and I will take over from there. Stop worryin'. Okay? You're gonna make yourself sick."

The truth was that Parker was every bit as worried as Rainie was. Why wasn't Danning making a move? One week soon became two, two became three, and Peter Danning was still maintaining high visibility in Seattle and playing the press for all it was worth. No matter how Parker looked at it, that made no sense to him. By all accounts, Danning was a maniacal killer. If he stayed true to form, he had to come after Rainie sooner or later. What if the man was actually cunning enough to bide his time until Rainie had no protection?

The suspicion intensified Parker's determination to keep Rainie in training until he felt confident that she'd be able to protect herself from any kind of physical attack. When she came to work each morning, safely hidden from prying eyes in the arena, Parker's first order of business each day was to work with her. He became a merciless taskmaster, putting her through a grueling exercise regimen, and then pushing her harder and harder as she trained with the punching bag and weights that he'd borrowed from Quincy's home gym.

"Strength, speed, and automatic reflexes!" he drilled, day after day. "Make him *your* victim and show no mercy."

The office work suffered as Parker lengthened Rainie's training periods, but as the days passed, his reward was to see the woman he loved become a toned, ruthless fighter. Early on, Parker could push his face at her, tell her to hit him, and then easily dance away, but as time wore on, Rainie became faster and faster, until one day when she managed to belt him with all her strength, squarely in his eye socket.

"Oh, my *God*!" she cried.

One hand clamped over his eye, Parker waved her away.

"I'm all right," he assured her. Then, as the pain radiated through his skull, he said, "Damn, girl, you're startin' to pack a wallop."

"I'm sorry. You always duck! I never meant to hit you for real."

It suddenly struck Parker as being funny, and he started to laugh. When he saw the indignant look that crossed Rainie's sweet face, he caught her around the waist with one arm and hauled her up against him. "Kiss it and make it better," he requested with a chuckle. "I'm *proud* of you, Rainie mine. This is *exactly* what we've been workin' toward, and now it's official. My lady can kick ass and take names."

She lightly touched his cheekbone, her hazel eyes shadowed with regret. "It was never my aim to kick yours."

Parker often felt that he might drown in the depths of those eyes, and the feeling came over him then, stronger than ever before. He bent his head toward hers, wanting, needing to kiss her. With each passing night that he held her in his arms, his physical yearnings became more and more urgent. He'd promised her that he would wait as long as she needed him to, but, *damn*, it was reaching a critical point for him.

Her eyes went soft with love for him, and to his surprise, her lips met his in soft surrender, issuing what he could only interpret as an invitation. A rushing sound pounded against his eardrums as he claimed her mouth. His heart started to beat so hard that he felt sure it might fracture one of his ribs. *Rainie.* He'd never wanted any woman as intensely as he wanted her. Her mouth. She tasted so damn sweet, like mulled wine with a touch of cinnamon. Always before, Parker had been cautious while kissing her, not wanting to do anything that might remind her of Danning. But this time he lost it, delving deep into the recesses of her mouth with his tongue, tracing the shape of her small teeth, teasing the sensitive skin between her lips and her gums. *Rainie.* God, how he loved her. The emotion roiled through him with volcanic force, and he no longer felt certain he had the strength of will to hold himself back.

"Showtime!" Jericho yelled from the opposite end of the arena. "I got tickets, ten bucks a head."

Parker jerked back to reality, realizing with a shock that he'd run his hands under Rainie's T-shirt and had been about to touch her breasts right there in front of God and everybody. Fiery heat rushed up his neck to pool in his face. He straightened quickly away from her and dropped his arms. She teetered toward him before catching her balance. Parker half expected her to blush with embarrassment and run for cover. Instead her beautiful eyes filled with a mischievous twinkle, and her soft mouth curved into a sultry, flirtatious smile.

"Later, cowboy."

He could scarcely believe his ears. *Later?* Could that possibly mean what he hoped it meant? He took careful measure of her expression, but before he could get a good reading on her, she danced away on the balls of her feet and resumed a fighting stance. With no little effort, Parker forced his mind back onto the training session.

They'd been practicing her takedown kicks and punches for days, and until this morning, Parker had always managed to dodge the blows. Now that he'd been treated to a fist in his eye socket, he no longer felt quite so confident in his ability to parry her thrusts. At the same time, he still didn't feel she was ready for him to curtail the one-on-one sparring. The more she practiced with him, the better prepared she would be for Danning.

"Okay, you obviously have your punching technique mastered," he said as they circled each other. "So let's work on your kicks for a while."

"I'm afraid I'll hurt you."

"Because you got in one lucky hit?" Parker circled her,

ready to dodge whatever came his way. "Don't wimp out on me. You're gettin' good, darlin', but you're not yet *that* good. Come at me with everything you've got."

It had become her habit to call out a warning before she took aim at a part of his body. "Knees!" she cried, and then came at him like a little whirlwind.

Parker bounced to one side so her foot met with empty air. "Excellent form," he told her. "More force, though. Put everything you've got into it. You won't hurt me, I promise."

After recovering her balance, she came at him again. "Groin!"

Parker angled his body to take the force of the blow on his thigh. "Good job!"

"Stomach!" she cried next.

He folded at the waist to minimize the impact as her foot connected with his belly. "Awesome, Rainie. You're so quick now that he'll never see it comin'."

"Groin!" she yelled again.

Parker turned at the waist to take the blow on his thigh again, but her foot came at him with such speed that he didn't react quickly enough. *Pain.* It exploded in his scrotum and shot up into his lower abdomen. A red haze blinded him. Dimly he was aware that he dropped like a fallen tree, his knees hitting the dirt with such force that the dust mushroomed in a cloud around him. *Oh, God.* Crossing his wrists, he thrust his hands between his thighs, hunched forward, and then rolled onto his side. Nausea crawled up his throat. The pain was so intense that he couldn't even breathe.

As if from a great distance, he heard Rainie saying, "Parker? Oh, God, Parker, are you all right? Talk to me. *Please.* Are you okay?"

Hell, no, he wasn't okay. He'd be singing soprano for the rest of his natural life. He curled into a fetal position, still struggling to inflate his lungs. *Sweet Christ.* He felt Rainie's arms come around his shoulders. A hot, wet tear struck his jaw.

"I'm so sorry! Oh, Parker, I'm so sorry!" She struggled to turn him over, but didn't have the strength. "Why didn't you dodge the kick? I called out the warning. You always give me such a hard time if I hold anything back that I just . . ." She tightened her arms around him. "Please be all right. I never meant to actually hurt you."

Parker blinked the world back into focus, and his lungs finally started to work again. The pain was starting to ease up. "I think we're done practicin' one-on-one. From now on, you'll just have to work with the bag."

"I'm *sorry.*"

"No need to be sorry, honey." Parker still felt as if he might puke. What if she'd turned him into a eunuch, and he could never make love to her? Just the thought of having sex made his abused testicles start throbbing again. He concentrated on his breathing, not wanting to humiliate himself by vomiting. "I'll be all right. Just give me a minute."

Jericho came limping over. Shifting his weight onto his good leg, he folded his arms and grinned. "I think you've created a monster, boss. She flat nailed you where it hurts."

Parker could not see the humor. He made a mental note to wipe that smirk off Jericho's face when he finally got back on his feet.

"Would you like me to help you to the house?" Rainie asked. "Maybe some ice will help."

Ice? Not on his balls, no how, no way. Parker groaned and closed his eyes. He wasn't sure how long he lay there, whether it was for only a couple of minutes or an hour, but finally the pain receded enough that he was able to sit up. Rainie still knelt beside him, her small, delicately carved face pale with concern.

"I'm all right," he assured her. "No permanent damage done." He hoped. He'd taken blows to the crotch several times, but never a dead-on kick. He sat there until he felt certain he could stand up without assistance. "My own damned fault, I guess. You don't tell a woman to come at you with everything she's got unless you expect her to do it."

"I really am sorry."

He thought he heard just a hint of a smile in her voice and sent her a wondering look. Sure enough, the corners of her mouth were trying to tip up, and her eyes danced with unmistakable delight. She shrugged, and her gaze went chasing off to the opposite end of the stable.

"I'm just—" She broke off and swallowed. "*Amazed*, I guess is the word. You're so much bigger than me, and stronger, too. I never *dreamed* you could actually teach me how to take someone like you to his knees."

Parker hooked an arm around her shoulders. "Help me to the office, Killer."

She giggled and hugged his waist. En route to the corridor, Parker decided no permanent damage had been done to his balls. The bump of her hip against his thigh felt too damned good.

Once inside the office, she turned to him and said, "I feel so *liberated*."

"Liberated?"

She hugged herself and spun in a circle, her beautiful hair flowing out around her. "Yes, liberated!" She whirled to a stop, her eyes large and luminous as they sought his. "I'm not afraid of him anymore. I know I can protect myself. Unless he's got a gun, of course, but Peter is too into up close and personal for that. If he comes at me with a knife, no problem. I think I can disarm him."

"Do you now?" A warm, light feeling moved through Parker's chest. From the start of her training, this had been his goal, to see that marvelous glow of self-assurance on her face. "That's great, sweetheart."

* * *

The feeling of accomplishment still hadn't left Rainie when she got home that evening. For the first time since her return, she didn't quake with fear when she entered. If Peter was hiding somewhere, he'd better be ready for one hell of a fight. After locking up, she marched straight into the kitchen. She sat at the table with a tall glass of iced tea and an apple as a snack. As she munched on crisp bites of fruit, her thoughts turned to Parker, and wondrous warmth filled her. True to his promise, he'd remained content with friendship, but now Rainie finally felt ready for more. Correction: She *wanted* more. That kiss today. Her eyes swept closed on a rush of sweet yearning. *Parker.* As a child, she'd listened to her mother read fairy tales, and deep in her heart, she'd always believed that someday her very own prince would come into her life. And now, at long last, he actually had. He even had a dashing steed.

The thought made her grin. Pushing up from the table, she went to her bedroom to go through her drawers, hoping to find something sexy to wear. Peter Danning wasn't the only man she now felt prepared to disarm. She just needed slightly different weapons. Problem: While she was shopping for clothing at Goodwill, seductive lingerie hadn't been on her must-have list. She had nothing but modest nightgowns and goofy-looking nightshirts in her drawers. Her underwear was equally boring.

Turning to the closet, she saw one of Parker's shirts on a hanger. He'd gotten into the habit of sometimes bringing a fresh change of clothes when he spent the night, and he'd left the shirt behind one morning. She had washed it and meant to give it back to him the next time he came, but she'd forgotten. *Hmm.* She pulled the shirt from the hanger and held it up in front of her. After she had a long soak in the tub, gave some special attention to her hair, dabbed her homemade perfume in strategic places, and added a little makeup, the shirt just might do the trick, especially with nothing on underneath it.

Her gaze drifted to the door casing where the bug was located. That definitely had to be moved. She had plans for this bedroom, and she didn't want any FBI agents listening in.

That night Parker arrived at Rainie's late, and he was worried about leaving her alone for so long. No help for it. One of his horses had gone down, and he'd had to call Tucker over to diagnose the problem, which turned out to be colic. After treating the mare, Parker had felt it necessary to wait for his foreman, Toby, to get back from town before he left the stable. He trusted no one else with an ailing equine, and colic could be deadly. Only Toby had an experienced enough eye to know if the animal was taking a turn for the worse. The foreman also knew what to do if that happened.

When Parker reached Rainie's back porch, he was out of breath from running the entire six blocks from his truck to her backyard. Since the second call from Agent Brandson, she'd fallen into the habit of keeping the kitchen lights off until he arrived to avoid arousing suspicion in case Danning was watching. Pressing close against the house to stay concealed by the dark shadows cast by the eave, he heard the television on inside the house. It sounded like a satellite music channel. Normally Rainie kept the television off until after he was inside, and even then, as per the FBI's request, she kept the volume low. It was up a notch louder than usual.

Parker's guts clenched. What if Danning was in there and had cranked up the volume a little because he knew the house was bugged? Every muscle in Parker's body snapped taut.

Stay calm. He couldn't go off half-cocked and kick the door in. He reached sideways to tap lightly four times on the wood, spacing the knocks in a special tattoo so Rainie would know it was him. He sent up a silent prayer that she would answer right away. If anything happened to her . . . Parker couldn't even go there in his mind. He'd come to love that girl so damned much. How he would live without her, he didn't know, and he never wanted to find out.

An instant later, he heard the dead bolt slide free. *Thank you, God.* Then the portal cracked open.

"Hi," she said in a stage whisper. "You're *late*."

He leaped up onto the porch and ducked inside. In the shadows, he saw Rainie move past him to refasten the lock. Then, before he could ask why she had the music turned on, she was in his arms, as delicious, warm, and sweet-smelling as fresh-baked apple pie. He gathered her close and felt only feminine softness under soft cotton. *No bra?* He ran a hand up her spine, his fingertips doing a quick search for a telltale band of elastic. *Definitely no bra.*

While he was pondering that discovery, she cupped his face in her slender hands and kissed him, her lips parted, her tongue darting between his teeth. Parker didn't know what to think. Was this *Rainie*? She was definitely issuing him an invitation—the kind that red-blooded, virile males had been eagerly accepting since the beginning of time. He ran his hand down the curve of her back, exploring with his fingers to find where the cloth of her top ended. Down, down, down. Not a top, he decided, but a shirt of some kind. Finally he came to bare, silken thigh. With a flick of his wrist, he dipped his hand under the material, and his palm met with soft, naked buttock.

Parker felt as if an M-80 detonated inside of his brain. Red flares of light flashed behind his closed eyes, and if he'd had a rational thought in his head a moment earlier, he didn't now. She locked her arms around his neck and jumped to loop her legs around his waist. *Holy hell.* His arms were filled with warm, soft, willing woman. And then she was kissing him again, robbing him of the ability to think clearly, let alone muster any self-control.

She was all over him, her sweet mouth devouring his, her

teeth nipping lightly at his tongue and lips, her unfettered breasts pressing softly against his upper chest. Parker still had a handful of soft, silken buttock, and he wanted to feel a whole lot more. Pivoting on one heel, he sandwiched her between him and the wall to help support her weight with the press of his body. Hands freed to explore, he skimmed his palms over her soft rump to find the dip of silken skin where the fullness tapered into firm, satiny thighs. *Oh, yeah.* With searching fingertips, he homed in on the feminine crevice between her legs until he found the tufts of damp, passion-slicked curls that guarded honeyed folds of hot, wet flesh.

Whoa, boy. Only his hands didn't seem to be receiving the messages from his befuddled brain. *It can't happen this way.* But somehow it was. He'd fishtailed into a downhill skid, and none of his brakes seemed to be working.

"Not like this," he managed to murmur against her lips between hard, jagged breaths. "Not like this."

She made fists in his hair, covered his lips with hers, and invaded his mouth with a tongue so sweet and tantalizing that every rational thought in his head leaked out through his ears. *Rainie.*

"Exactly like this," she whispered urgently, her breath as ragged as his. "I *want* you."

Parker had been imagining this moment for weeks and had his game plan all mapped out. He'd mentally choreographed every gentle kiss and careful touch, determined to make their first time together romantic and perfect for her. *Not.* The next thing he knew, he had her sprawled over the table like an array of smorgasbord delights, and he was devouring her like a starving man.

He moved his hips between her parted knees and jerked her shirt open. Buttons flew, hitting the wall and floor like high-velocity pellets, going *ping . . . plunk . . . ping.* In the dim light coming from the living room, he glimpsed her white, pink-tipped breasts, and before he could even register how perfectly shaped they were, he was pushing them upward with the cup of his hands so he could suckle her nipples. Not gently, no tantalizing buildup to make her want. He latched on and drew hard on the sensitive tips of flesh until they spiked into hard nubbins to be grazed with his teeth.

She jerked as if a 220-volt charge had just arced through her body, grabbed handfuls of his hair, and arched her spine in a convulsive spurt of pleasure. "Parker!" she cried out. "Oh, *yes*, oh, yes, oh, *ye-e-s-ss*!"

Her cries momentarily jerked him back to reality, and he almost clamped a hand over her mouth. *The bugs.* Providing a bunch of bored FBI agents with X-rated audio entertainment wasn't high on Parker's list of aspirations. But somewhere between thinking about muffling her cries and actually doing it, he lost the thought entirely, and all his common sense went with it. Her nipples throbbed against his tongue, so hard and distended that he could gauge every beat of her wildly racing heart. His body responded to the urgency in hers, sending his own needs into an upward spiral that made him tremble.

"Oh, *yes*!" she cried again.

Working her nipples with his mouth, he lightly trailed his fingertips down her sternum to her belly and then lower, bent on finding the sweetness at the apex of her thighs. She jerked again when he found his mark, and for a moment, he feared she might recoil. Instead, she lifted her hips and offered herself to him.

Parker's daddy hadn't raised no fool. One invitation was all the encouragement he needed. He dipped a finger inside of her and drew the slickness over the sensitive flange of flesh at her opening. At the first touch, she shrieked again, but he was beyond caring if someone heard her now. When her body started to jerk, the damned table started to rock with every spasm, the short leg thumping loudly on the floor. He stroked her faster and with more pressure until he brought her to climax. While she lay there limp and still quivering with the aftershocks, he peeled off his shirt, opened his fly, and moved back between her thighs to enter her. The instant her hot, wet slickness encased his throbbing shaft, he lost it. *Wham, bam, thank you, ma'am.* Only with a few table thumps for emphasis.

Approximately one minute later, give or take a few seconds, he collapsed on the tabletop, barely managing to catch his weight on one bent arm to keep from crushing her. His heart was chugging like an undersized locomotive trying to pull fifty loaded cars up a steep grade. *Damn.* He'd been waiting for this moment for weeks, and now it was over. He couldn't believe it. Over the course of his adulthood, he'd come to pride himself on being a man with a slow hand. Pleasing the ladies had always been his number one priority. But now, with the most important woman of his life, he'd humped her like a rabbit.

"I'm sorry," he managed to push out.

She looped limp arms around his neck. "Don't be sorry. It was *wonderful.*"

Wonderful?

"It happened for me," she whispered near his ear. "It actually *happened* for me, Parker. That's the very first time, ever."

He gave in to the pull of her arms to nestle his face in the sweet curve of her neck. Oh, man, how he loved her. It was so like Rainie to pretend that he'd made it good for her. He'd never known anyone with a kinder heart. "I'll make it better the next time, I swear."

She giggled and turned to kiss his temple. "You can't possibly make it better. Didn't you hear me? It happened for me."

Slowly, Parker's thoughts were starting to clear, and he could finally focus on what she was saying. It had happened for her? He tried to think what she meant, and then it hit him like a fist between the eyes that this was the first time she'd ever had an orgasm.

"You're serious?" Parker could barely wrap his mind around that. No wonder the girl was a bundle of raw nerves. "Your first time *ever*?"

"My very first." She touched the tip of her tongue to his skin, licking away the salt. "It was incredible. *You* are incredible."

Incredible. He liked the sound of that, and it definitely went a long way toward soothing his bruised ego. He drew back to gaze down at her beautiful face. In the soft glow of light, she looked drowsy, a slight, satisfied smile curving her lips. Parker wanted to sweep her up off the table into his arms, carry her to bed, and make love to her again, the way she deserved this time, but, God help him, he didn't have the strength.

He settled for straightening away from her before his arms folded under his weight, fastened his jeans, donned his shirt, and then sank to the floor, bracing his back against the wall. He needed a minute. Hell, maybe more than a minute. More like an hour. The lady had drained him dry. His brain still feeling like congealed mush, he went back over what had happened between them. Talk about a guy getting blind-sided. He'd never seen that coming.

She swung her gorgeous legs over the edge of the table to sit up. Pointy knees slightly parted, she unintentionally gave him a glimpse of sable curls. *Damn.* She was so beautiful, perfect in every way. As she wrapped the destroyed shirt around herself, he glimpsed small, flawlessly shaped breasts and a waist so slender that a man could encircle it with his hands. He wanted to thump himself on the head. A woman like Rainie should be savored like fine wine.

She slid off the table and came to sit beside him. He curled an arm around her shoulders and drew her close against his side, wishing he had it all to do over again. She rested her head on his chest and sighed, sounding blissfully content.

"Will it always be like that?" she asked softly.

"Better. It's been a while for me, and I wanted you so bad that I lost control."

"I like when you lose control." She snuggled closer. "We did it on my *table.* It was just like in the movies. I've always watched those love scenes and wondered what could possess people to act so crazy, tearing at each other's clothes and never even making it to a bed. Now it's happened to *me*."

Parker couldn't help but smile. Maybe he hadn't made such a poor showing, after all. She certainly seemed to think the sex had been phenomenal. His smile deepened. As much as Rainie might have experienced during her time with What's-his-name, she'd clearly never been treated to all the joyous mysteries of real lovemaking.

He looked forward to introducing her to more of those pleasures. *Later.*

Chapter Sixteen

Rainie wanted to make love again right away. She felt like a child who had just gotten her first taste of candy, and one small bite had only whetted her appetite for more. When she remembered how it felt when Parker kissed her breasts, a zing of anticipatory excitement went through her. Unfortunately for her, Parker looked completely spent, his dark head tipped back against the wall, the arm that he'd draped around her shoulders limp and heavy. She decided to let him rest for a few minutes before she suggested they do it again.

To entertain herself while she waited, she drank in visuals—the sheen of his black hair in the dim light, the shadows that delineated his chiseled facial features, the sweep of thick eyelashes that feathered his lean cheeks, and the shimmer of his firm lips. Though she knew he would detest the adjective, *beautiful* was the word that sprang to her mind. She loved everything about him. The tendons that corded each side of his arched neck were purely masculine. She yearned to trace the bump of his larynx and feel it bob when he swallowed. A tuft of jet-black chest hair peeked out at her through his open collar, also tempting her fingertips. He made her think of a priceless painting, crafted by one of the masters. The longer she stared at him, the more in awe she felt. She would never grow tired of looking at him.

His lashes fluttered up, and his strong white teeth flashed in a lazy grin. "What?"

Emotion welled at the base of Rainie's throat. She wanted so badly to tell him how much she loved him, but somehow mere words couldn't express her feelings. "I was just wondering if you ate dinner."

He stirred as if he were coming out of a stupor. "No, actually. Monte Carlo went down with the colic. Once I felt sure she'd be all right, I came straight here."

Rainie scrambled to her feet and flipped on the overhead light. "I'll fix you a couple of sandwiches and some soup. I had my favorite combo tonight, grilled cheese and tomato. My comfort foods. I eat them until they're coming out my ears. Does that sound good?"

"It sounds awesome."

As she opened the fridge and bent to get cheese out of the dairy compartment, she felt the tail of her shirt lift in back and reached to splay her hand over the cloth. When she glanced over her shoulder, Parker was watching her with a dazed look on his burnished face. She smiled to herself and went up on her tiptoes to get the bread from a cupboard shelf, well aware that she was displaying a lot of leg in the process. For weeks during her training, Parker's mantra to her had been, *Have no mercy.* Now he was her victim, and she intended to take those words to heart, giving him no quarter.

Parker was a gentleman to the marrow of his bones, and he would probably never consider pushing her for sex twice in one evening, especially not when she'd so recently shuddered at the thought. Not that she was finding fault with him in any way. She would always be grateful for his patience with her and his willingness to wait to make love until she felt ready. But that time in her life was behind her now.

She wasn't precisely sure what had changed within her, or why it had occurred so suddenly. She knew only that something wonderful had happened. Maybe she'd been moving toward this for weeks, inch by slow inch, and her astounding progress in self-defense training, culminating that morning in a takedown kick, had been the catalyst that took her the rest of the way. She felt free, absolutely and gloriously *free*. Peter no longer had a hold on her.

With giddy relief, she turned the chrome toaster wide side out so she could see herself in the reflective surface. The distorted image no longer made her break out into a cold sweat or called to mind her nightmare about being lost in the mirror maze.

"Rainie, are you all right?"

Parker's deep voice jerked Rainie back to reality. For a very long moment, she stared down at her reflection without really seeing it, but then she focused on her elongated, distorted image and smiled at herself. Fear of Peter Danning no longer ruled her life, and it never would again. She felt as light and buoyant as a falcon with the wind under its wings.

"I'm wonderful," she said over her shoulder, meaning it with all her heart as she resumed the task of making his meal.

A few minutes later, the kitchen was redolent with the smell of grilled cheese, melted butter, and hot tomato soup. When Rainie set the food on the table, Parker pushed up from where he sat with his back to the wall and approached the chair she'd pulled out for him. Concern filled his eyes as he sank onto the seat. "Are you *sure* you're okay? I'm sorry I went after you that way. I should've—"

"I'm *fine*, Parker."

Searching his worried gaze, Rainie felt her heart give a painful little twist. From the first, he'd been so careful of her feelings. Now she'd totally changed the rules on him. No wonder he was confused. As recently as last night, she would have recoiled at the thought of making love with him. Now she was parading around in a shirt without buttons or a stitch of underwear on underneath. She owed him an explanation. He clearly thought that her rapid turnaround might be the result of emotional yo-yoing and was afraid she might bottom out at any moment.

She sat down across from him. "Remember how you kept telling me that I only needed time to heal?"

He took a bite of sandwich and nodded as he flicked a bit of melted cheese from the corner of his mouth with the tip of his tongue. "Of course I remember."

"Well, you were wrong. It wasn't time that I needed, Parker. It was you."

His throat convulsed as he swallowed without chewing. "Me?"

"Yes, you."

He tossed down the sandwich. "You spaced out over there while you were workin'. That worries me."

"I only spaced out because I'd turned the toaster so I could see my reflection in the side of it, and I was thinking how good it was not to feel panicky."

His bewilderment obvious in his expression, he said, "Panicky?"

"I haven't been able to look at myself in the side of the toaster since I moved in here," she explained. "I kept it turned with the end out so I'd never accidentally see my reflection in the chrome. My image was always distorted and reminded me of my recurring dream about the mirrors."

"So why'd you turn it around and look at yourself a few minutes ago?"

A bubble of happiness formed in Rainie's chest. "Because I finally can." She tried to think how to explain. "I don't feel lost anymore, Parker. When I have the dream about the maze of mirrors, it's me that I see in the glass, and Peter isn't laughing anymore."

His eyes went suspiciously bright. "Ah, honey, that's awesome."

It touched Rainie that he had come close to getting tears in his eyes. Parker Harrigan was, hands down, the strongest man she'd ever known, both physically and mentally, but his emotions ran deep, especially when it came to her. Knowing how much he loved her was the most precious gift that he'd given her, and she doubted he even realized it.

Rainie lowered her gaze. What she needed to say wouldn't be easy, but she had to explain the sudden changes that she was undergoing. In order to do that, she had to journey back in time to her marriage. The only good part about that was her knowledge that nothing she ever told Parker would diminish his feelings for her. Through thick and thin, this man would always stand beside her, as solid and dependable as an immovable boulder.

"I've told you about a lot of stuff that went on while I was with Peter," she managed to say, "but never anything about the sexual aspects of it."

"You don't have to now," he assured her.

"Yes." She met his gaze dead-on. "I do need to tell you. It's the final step for me, Parker. The memories are like bits of rotten garbage inside my head, and now, thanks to you, I have all of them shoved into a plastic bag, ready to be tossed."

He touched a finger to his lips, stood, and stepped over to remove the kitchen microphone from its hiding place atop a door casing. It struck Rainie then that they'd just had wild sex about three feet from the bug. *Oops*. While preparing to seduce him, she'd thought to move the bedroom receiver into the guest room. Somehow she hadn't anticipated the explosiveness of their first joining—or that it would occur on her table. Heat inched up her neck. Then she shook her embarrassment off. What had happened between them had been so beautiful. Nothing, not even the knowledge that they'd been overheard, was going to make her regret a single second.

After the bug was relocated to the living room, Parker returned to the kitchen and resumed his seat. He straightened a leg under the table to hook the toe of his boot around her ankle. The contact helped to center her, and she knew that was his intention. He was sending her that message again: *I'm here, Rainie mine, and I always will be.*

"You can talk now," he said softly. "They won't be able to hear you clearly."

She took a long, bracing breath. There was no way to describe the darkest side of her marriage in polite terms, no way to pretty it up. She decided the easiest path was simply to tell him about it in a bald, straightforward manner. "Peter didn't enjoy ordinary sex. Early on, before he got control of my money, he pretended to, but our times together always seemed . . . I don't know . . . flat, somehow, sort of like taking a sip of a soft drink that's gone warm and lost its carbonation. It wasn't horrible, but it fell far short of what I had expected prior to our marriage."

"I'm sorry it was that way for you," he said huskily.

Rainie let her head fall back and closed her eyes. It was easier to go on if she didn't look at him. "Yes, well, in the end, flat soda pop would have been delightful compared to the way it became later, when he no longer felt it necessary to put up a front. I'm just going to say it, Parker. He had an insatiable sexual appetite, but he couldn't achieve gratification in a normal way. He was into perverted stuff, and simply engaging in those acts wasn't enough. He needed the double whammy of watching in a mirror while we—" She broke off and swallowed hard. Her throat was so dry she felt as if she were gulping down a wad of sandpaper. "I won't call it 'making love.' Even the term 'having sex' is too bland to describe what went on." She opened her eyes and lowered her chin to look across the table at him. "I think those incidents are what caused my recurring nightmare about being lost in the maze of mirrors. He used to make a fist in my hair, pulling so hard that it brought tears to my eyes, and make me watch in the mirror, too. I wasn't allowed to close my eyes. If I dared, he punished me in creative ways that somehow aroused him. Inflicting pain was a form of foreplay for him. Afterward, he would drag me back to the mirror and make me perform for him again, watching the entire while."

"Oh, sweetheart."

Rainie fiddled with the wicker napkin holder at the center of the table. She noticed that her fingers were quivering. "During those encounters, the person I saw in the mirror wasn't me. I can remember staring at my reflection and thinking that the woman I saw in the glass couldn't possibly be Rainie Hall, Marcus Hall's willful and intelligent daughter who'd once had the world at her fingertips. That girl would never have allowed a man to demean her that way. That girl would have fought back and possibly even died before she stooped that low. So inside my head, while I watched in the mirror, I separated myself from that person and told myself it wasn't really me.

"When I got away from Peter, the dream about the mirror maze started. In the dream, I'd race frantically from mirror to mirror, and my reflection was always of someone I didn't know. I think my mind was trying to make me face what had happened to me and come to grips with the fact that it really had been me who did those things. Only it was too horrible for me to accept, even in a dream, so I kept seeing strangers instead of myself.

"Then you found me on the swing that night and told me the story about your mother's star—and how you believed we all had a bright place within us that could never be touched, not by anything, not even death. That struck such a chord within me, Parker. When I went upstairs to my room, I knelt at the window and stared at the North Star, only for me it wasn't your mother's light, but my own. Does that make any sense?"

"It makes perfect sense," he said, his voice gone gravelly and thick.

Rainie pressed a knotted fist to the center of her chest. "I *do* have a bright place inside of me—a part of me that Peter and all the ugliness could never touch. It was that part of me that remained separate, that part of me that looked into the mirror and didn't recognize the person I had become. And that part of me is what finally gave me the courage and strength to get away from him."

"We're more than just flesh and bone," he said softly. "And that separate part of us is what defines who we really are. It doesn't matter what happens to our bodies. If I were in a terrible accident and lost all my limbs, that separate part of me would still be the same."

"Exactly." She looked deeply into his eyes, and in them she saw the love that had helped her to reclaim her sense of identity. "I was trapped in an impossible situation, a very dangerous situation, and my survival instinct kicked in. I did what I had to do. Staying alive became my whole focus. But those actions never defined me as a person. You helped me to see that, first of all by loving me when I could no longer love myself, then by teaching me to trust again, and finally by helping me rebuild my self-esteem. When I first started training, I didn't believe you could actually teach me how to defend myself against someone like Peter. Now I not only believe I can defend myself against him, I *know* I can. And in some weird way I don't understand and can't begin to explain, that knowledge has set me free. Peter Danning no longer has a hold on me."

This time when Parker's eyes went bright, Rainie actually saw tears gathering on his lower lashes. "I didn't do much, darlin'. You did it for yourself."

Rainie felt tears burning in her own eyes and smiled tremulously. "Maybe so, but you showed me the way. And

I'm okay now. You can stop worrying about me. I really am okay now."

He studied her for a long moment and then returned her smile. "I think you actually are."

She lowered her gaze to his sandwich and soup. "So, eat. I'm anxious to give you dessert."

"You've got dessert?"

She nodded.

"What, chocolate cake?"

She shook her head. "Something much better than that."

"What then?" he asked.

"Me."

He paused with the sandwich halfway to his mouth, his gaze sharpening on hers. "You?"

She grinned and lifted her eyebrows at him. "Nothing else, only me."

He laid the sandwich back on the plate, and then relaxed on the chair and crossed his arms. "In that case, I'd rather have dessert now and eat later."

"Are you sure you're recovered enough?"

His lean cheek creased in a grin. That was all the answer she needed.

For Rainie, their second time together was even better than the first. He began by scooping her up into his arms and carrying her to the bedroom, which was the most romantic thing she'd ever experienced. She looped her arms around his neck, acutely conscious of the hard strength in his shoulders and the play of muscle under his shirt. Once through the doorway, he strode to the bed, tossed her onto the mattress, and then turned to reach above the door frame for the bedroom receiver.

"I already moved it," she whispered throatily. "I thought we'd make love in here the first time, so I put it in the guest room."

He closed the door for additional privacy and then followed her down onto the bed, catching his weight on his bent arms and knees, his body forming a canopy of blue chambray and denim above her. His dark face hovering only inches from hers, his eyes glittering with desire, he didn't waste time on words but bent his head to kiss her. Eyes locked with his, she pressed a hand to his jaw, marveling at the contrast of his smooth skin and the slight rasp of his five-o'clock shadow. Then she touched his hair, fascinated by how the thick, silky strands felt cool as they slipped through her fingers.

As lightly as a butterfly wing, he brushed his lips over hers. His breath smelled of coffee, mint, and faintly of cheese, one of her favorite sinful pleasures. *Parker.* The taste of him was as intoxicating to her as mulled wine. She parted her lips, yearning for him to deepen the kiss, but he kept the contact whisper-soft, teasing her, making her heart catch and her body quicken. Her eyes drifted halfway closed, so she saw his chiseled countenance through the veil of her lashes, a blur of bronze capped by jet-black hair. Her heart began to slog in her chest, the hard, vibrant beats thrumming through her veins to make her secret, most feminine places throb with every surge of her blood.

Wanting him, wanting *more*, she made tight fists in his hair, seeking to deepen the kiss herself. He braced against her. "Oh, no, not this time," he informed her in a husky whisper. "I want to take it slow and savor every sweet inch of you."

He turned his head and nibbled seductively at her bottom lip, nipping gently at the soft, sensitive inner tissue and then soothing it with a rub of his tongue. Her breathing became fast and uneven. Her lungs grabbed frantically for more oxygen. She ran her hands over his shoulders, testing the thick, virile pads of muscle over bone. The power she felt under the cloth made her pulse stutter and skip a beat.

"Ah, Rainie mine, you are so sweet, so impossibly, incredibly sweet." As though trying to commit her face to memory, he began tracing each line and plane with feathery brushes of his lips: the slope of her forehead, the arch of her brows, the tip of her nose, the hollow of her cheek, the shape of her chin. With every touch, her skin felt more tingly and sensitive. When he moved lower to torment the tender place just under her ear, she made fists in his shirt, her body motionless, her lungs barely inflating, anticipation mounting within her until she wanted to scream.

Her shirt had fallen open, baring her breasts, and his every slight movement abraded her nipples. She longed to feel the warm, moist draw of his mouth there again. Her bones felt as if they were melting when he finally trailed his lips to the V of her collarbone, where he followed its shape with the tip of his tongue and pressed his parted lips over the pulse beat there as if he wanted to absorb the very essence of her. Next he treated her arms to a similar torture, kissing his way down to the bend of her elbow and lingering there to tickle her skin with light, almost nonexistent flicks of his tongue.

Her limbs became heavy. The erratic beat of her heart thrummed in her temples, and she floated in a mindless, resonant haze of desire, helpless to move, spellbound by the feelings he evoked within her.

"Parker, *please*."

He pressed his hot mouth to that place under her ear again, and then he drove her closer to the edge by trailing his tongue down her neck. She jerked and cried out when he finally gave her what she wanted and closed his mouth over one of her nipples. She arched up, her hands anchored to his shoulders. Spurts of pleasure zinged to the very center of her, turning the ache low in her belly into hot, molten need.

After abandoning her breasts, he lapped at her quivering belly like a kitten licking cream. Lower, then lower still, he cut a torturously slow path to the apex of her thighs. In some far corner of her mind, Rainie was shocked when she felt his mouth close over her moist flesh, but he obliterated every thought in her head with one light flick of his tongue. Spiraling. She felt like a bit of dandelion fluff caught in a whirlwind. *Parker.* He drew her into the spinning vortex, playing her body as if it were a stringed instrument, each masterful stroke of his tongue taking her higher and higher, closer and closer to the final crescendo. At the peak, she spun into oblivion, lost to sensation and glorious release.

Afterward, while her body still quivered and jerked from the throes of orgasm, he rose over her to strip off his shirt. In the dim illumination coming from the living room, his dark torso was limned in gold, the dips and hollows of his muscular chest delineated by shadow and shimmers of light. In all Rainie's life, she'd never seen anyone so beautiful. She watched as he swung off the bed to kick off his boots and shed his jeans. The coppery darkness of his upper body extended to his legs, not a result of exposure to the sun, but his natural skin tone, the deep, rich color of caramel.

"Lose the shirt," he whispered.

With any other man on earth, Rainie might have felt self-conscious, but she didn't with Parker. She sat up and peeled the sleeves down her arms. Then she lay back, naked in the shadows, her skin burning as his gaze moved over her.

"Damn, you are so beautiful," he said huskily.

"You're the one who's beautiful."

When he returned to her, he knelt between her thighs, the head of his shaft pushing at her opening. As he came into her, Rainie gasped at the feeling of fullness and heat. Then he plunged deep, setting off explosions of sensation deep inside of her. As he withdrew slightly, she looped her legs around his waist and lifted her hips to meet his next thrust. In all her life, she'd never felt anything so glorious. With every push, he took her with him, higher and higher, faster and faster, until they peaked together in an explosion of pleasure.

Afterward Rainie lay limp in his arms, so content and exhausted that she had no desire to move or even speak. Over the course of their relationship, Parker had introduced her to so many new sights—gorgeous sunsets, fabulous woodlands, undulating fields of pink clover, skies as blue as deep lagoons.

Now he'd given her the most wondrous experience of all—a taste of heaven on earth.

In a tangle of arms and legs, they dozed together as only lovers do, breathing in tandem, hearts beating as one. When Rainie awakened some time later, she couldn't quite tell where Parker's body started and hers ended. The tips of their noses were touching, which made her smile. Even in slumber, they'd sought the comfort of closeness.

As if he sensed her gaze on him, he fluttered his lashes open and grinned sleepily at her. "I was havin' the nicest dream," he whispered.

"What about?"

"We were cloud watchin' again, only in my dream I got to make love to you like I wanted to the first time."

She smiled drowsily. "Did you really? Want to make love to me, I mean?"

He chuckled and rubbed his nose against hers. "Of course." He tucked in his chin to focus on her face. "My dream didn't go well, though. Right in the middle of lovin' you, a horrible thought occurred to me."

"What was that?"

"That I wasn't wearin' any protection and needed to stop."

His gaze held hers with relentless solemnity, his expression devoid of humor. Rainie released a soft breath as her second oversight of the evening registered in her mind. "Oops."

"Yeah, a big oops. I can't believe I did somethin' so stupid. I *always* wear protection." He winced. "Not that I've needed to all that often. I don't want you to think I've bounced in and out of intimate relationships like a tennis ball. But on occasion, when I needed to scratch my itch, I always practiced safe sex. Now, with the one woman I love more than anything else on earth, I forgot all about it and put you at risk of pregnancy."

Rainie pushed up onto an elbow. His regret sounded in his voice, tugging at her heart. "It was my responsibility to think of it. I set out to seduce you, not the other way around. You didn't come here expecting to have sex with me."

"Nope," he agreed. "If I had, I would have stopped by a drugstore for some condoms." He sighed and reached up to toy with her hair. "Ah, Rainie mine, what if you're pregnant?"

Still facing him, Rainie snuggled back down and considered the possibility. "I'd love to have your baby, Parker. Call me crazy, but I won't gnash my teeth and pull out my hair if the test strip reads positive."

"There is one problem. Maybe I'm old-fashioned, but when the woman I love gives birth to my baby, I want her to be married to *me*, not contractually bound to some other man. Your divorce still isn't final."

Rainie caught the inside of her cheek in her teeth. One of the things she loved most about Parker was his old-fashioned values. "Even if I am pregnant, the divorce will be final long before the baby's born. Can't we just get married really fast?"

"I'm Catholic. Nothin' about marriage in the Church happens fast." His black brows snapped together in a scowl. "I guess I'm gettin' ahead of myself. You haven't even said you'll marry me straight out, let alone marry me in the Church."

Rainie finger-combed his glistening black hair, loving the

way it fell away from her fingers in glossy black waves over his forehead. "Of course I'll marry you, Parker. I love you. And it goes without saying that I'll marry you in your church. Your faith is important to you. Therefore it's important to me."

"Will it bother you to raise our kids Catholic?"

Rainie considered the question for a moment. Her first thought was that she knew very little about Roman Catholic doctrine. But then she focused on Parker and realized that wasn't true. He was a result of his upbringing, and his faith had played a huge role in making him into the man he was. She didn't really care what faith her kids were encouraged to embrace, just as long as they grew up with a strong spiritual framework, an unshakable belief in God, and good moral values. She felt confident that Parker would raise children in an environment that would foster all three traits.

"If our children grow up to be half as wonderful as you, I don't care what church we raise them in."

He chuckled. "What church did you grow up in? I never thought to ask."

"All the Christian denominations we could find. Daddy was eclectic in his religious affiliations." Rainie smiled at the memories. "He was an intellectual, remember, and he wanted to be a well-informed Christian who never allowed himself or me to become closed-minded. To that end, he had a rule that we could worship at a church for only six months before we moved on. He wanted to hear all the different interpretations of Scripture."

"That must have been interestin'."

Rainie grinned. "Yes, well, sometimes we moved on after only a week, and sometimes we stayed in a faith community a little longer than six months. It all depended on the spiritual tone of the church. I remember one time when the preacher started pounding the pulpit, renouncing all women who wore red as jezebels and handmaidens of Satan. I was wearing a red jumper. Daddy left that church in less than fifteen minutes, and we never went back."

"I'm glad. I like red."

Rainie tugged lightly on a tuft of his chest hair. "Really? I like it, too, especially lacy red underwear."

He dipped his head to nibble on her ear. "You *are* a jezebel."

She turned her face to meet his mouth with hers. "Right now, all I can tempt you with is me. When I went shopping for a new wardrobe, looking sexy wasn't one of my priorities."

"You'd look sexy in a gunnysack."

She felt his hardness against her thigh. "No protection, remember? If Peter finds another way to stall the divorce, I could end up at the altar eight months pregnant."

He deepened the kiss. When he momentarily came up for air, he said, "My only concern about that has already been addressed, that you'll marry me as fast as we can manage it. If you get pregnant, I'll be the happiest man alive."

"Really? Even if we can't get married right away?"

"Even if. All that matters to me is knowin' that we'll eventually be a family."

It was all that mattered to Rainie, too. In fact, it would be her dream come true. She could think of nothing that she would love more than holding his child in her arms. She gave herself up to his kisses and slipped away with him into pleasure's oblivion.

Over the course of that night, Rainie lost track of how many times they made love. She knew only that they were both still awake when the night sky began to lighten, marking the time when Parker had to leave her.

"I don't want you to go," she whispered, hugging his neck.

"I don't want to go," he whispered back.

The only sound in the house, aside from their breathing, was the drone of the music channel on her television.

Evidently the volume level wasn't so high that the agents outside felt it interfered with their surveillance, because Brandson hadn't called to ask her to turn it down. When Parker drew away from her and started to get dressed, Rainie lay back against the pillows, staring solemnly at the ceiling.

"I hope he makes his move soon," she said hollowly. "That's the only control he has left over my life now, making me wait."

Parker paused in buttoning his shirt to look over his shoulder at her. "Reverse that. He isn't controlling you. You're controlling him. He just doesn't know it yet."

She thought about that for a moment and then grinned. "You're right. He used to love to play cat and mouse with me. Now our roles are reversed. I'm the chunk of cheese, but when he comes for it this time, snap!" She brought her palms together to mimic the mechanism of a mousetrap. "That'll be the end of Peter."

Parker chuckled and bent to kiss her good-bye. "I love you, Rainie mine. Come to work early this morning."

"Why come early?"

His mouth tipped into a slow, devilish grin. "You think I'm finished with you, lady? Think again. I want to make up for all the lost time."

"But where? The arena is filled with people."

"The office isn't, and neither is my house. Maybe we'll compare tables and see which is best, yours or mine."

Rainie giggled and flapped her hand at him, convinced he was teasing. But an hour later when she arrived at the ranch, she quickly found out otherwise.

The weeks wore on, and still Peter Danning didn't show his face in Crystal Falls. Concerned, Rainie went to Loni for a reading several different times, but Parker's clairvoyant sister-in-law could pick up nothing about Peter by touching Rainie's hand.

"I'm sorry," she said. "It happens this way sometimes. I just can't *see*."

During the hours after dark and before dawn, Rainie and Parker made love as much as possible, but despite their insatiable desire for each other, there were physical limitations that sometimes dictated. When they were too tired to explore each other's bodies, they fell into the habit of exploring each other's minds. Parker shared his saddest and happiest memories with her, and soon Rainie found herself doing the same. For so long, she'd felt distanced from her past, but being with Parker had enabled her to recall moments that had once meant so much to her.

He held her especially close when she told him about all her failed attempts to find her grandparents after her father's death and tried to explain how sad it made her feel to know that their children would never know her side of the family. "My mom was an orphan, and my father severed all ties with his relatives. If we ever do a family tree, my side will have no branches, and if our kids have physical or character traits that aren't obviously Harrigan in origin, I won't be able to tell them what individual in my lineage passed those traits down to them."

"Ah, Rainie, if I could find your grandparents for you, I would."

A tight sensation came into her chest. "Yes, well, finding them would be no guarantee that they'd be interested in meeting me, so maybe it's better this way. I can pretend that they would have wanted to meet me if only they'd known I existed."

Parker talked with her about his sadness over his mother's death. "It wasn't just losin' my mother that devastated our family. My dad was never quite the same after she died, so in a way, we lost part of him, too. We Harrigan men only love that way once, and Mom was it for him. He cares very deeply for Dee Dee, don't get me wrong, but it's more a strong friendship and affection that he feels for her than a romantic, once-in-a-lifetime kind of love."

"Does that bother her?"

He smiled slightly. "Nah. They got together when they were older. Neither of them expected fireworks. They get along well and enjoy each other's company. After workin' for him for so many years, she's like a mother to us kids. What they have is special in its way. I'm so glad Dad has her in his life now. He spent enough years alone."

"What was your mother like? Can you remember her?"

"Some of my memories are dim, others as clear as if they happened yesterday. She was tiny like Samantha, and pretty as a picture. I can still remember the sound of her voice, which was soft and almost musical, but what I remember most clearly is her laugh. You know how some people just let go and when you hear them laugh, you can't help but chuckle, too? That was what her laugh was like, and she laughed a lot, one of those people who could always find humor in almost any situation. Dad says she was the light of his life, and I truly believe she was."

Rainie cupped her hand to his lean cheek. "There you go, talking about inner light again."

He smiled and caught her thumb in his teeth. "Maybe that's because yours shines so bright."

Several weeks after Rainie filed for divorce, special agents Slaughter and Simpson returned to Crystal Falls and requested another meeting. As before, the gathering took place in Parker's kitchen. This time, the meeting was much more relaxed. Rainie's attorney wasn't present, and Parker served some of Dee Dee's peanut-butter cookies to go with the coffee.

Special Agent Simpson opened the dialogue with, "I'm sure you've probably guessed our reason for wanting to meet with you today."

Beneath the table, Rainie threaded her fingers through Parker's. "I'm assuming it's because Peter has yet to make a move, and you're coming to think that he may not."

The blonde nodded. "Exactly. When we went into this, we fully expected the situation to pop right away, but evidently Danning is smarter than we thought." She smiled and shrugged. "We're not happy about that. It was our hope to nail him, drag a confession out of him, and put him behind bars for the rest of his natural life, but it doesn't appear that it's going to play out that way."

"You surely aren't plannin' to leave Rainie high and dry." Parker's body stiffened. "You gave her your word that she would have 'round-the-clock protection. You gave *me* your word on it, too."

"We have no intention of leaving Ms. Hall high and dry, Mr. Harrigan. But we can't ignore the fact that final dissolution of the marriage is a mere two weeks away. Once that occurs, it is our belief that the danger to her will be over."

"So you'll continue to protect her until the divorce is final, and then you're out of here?"

"At that point, she'll no longer need us."

"Bullshit," Parker said. "Are you forgettin' that Danning is certifiably nuts and totally unpredictable? How can you think he'll just let her go?"

Special Agent Slaughter cleared his throat and said, "Danning is inarguably crazy. We agree with you about that. But it isn't entirely accurate to say that he's unpredictable. Serial killers are infamous for establishing a murder pattern."

"He's not your run-of-the-mill serial killer," Parker shot back.

"True, but when you trim away the expensive suit, all the polish, and the meticulous planning, he isn't really so different from all the others," Slaughter replied. "We brought in an FBI profiler to do a case study on him, and the first thing he picked up on is that Danning, like most serial killers, follows the same pattern, time after time. Danning may *think* he's brilliant and absolutely unique because of the way he goes about killing his victims, but in truth, he is fundamentally similar to every other serial killer we've profiled."

"I'm still not clear on how that makes Rainie safe once the divorce is final."

Slaughter took a sip of his coffee. "I completely understand your alarm, Mr. Harrigan. But, please, just hear us out." When Parker sat back to listen, the agent continued. "If you look at every infamous serial killer on record, they all follow basically the same pattern. First there's the hunt for a victim. Some killers are opportunists who hang around in public places, waiting for a woman who fits their criteria to happen along. If she seems vulnerable, he strikes. In Danning's case, the hunt is more a matter of research."

"He has very specific victim criteria," Parker inserted.

"Yes," Slaughter agreed. "He looks for young, lovely, gullible, and wealthy young women with no family and few friends. But other serial killers have specific criteria as well. Bundy, for instance, targeted young women who bore a striking resemblance to one another. Many psychologists believe that he was exacting revenge against some female figure in his past and chose victims who looked like her."

"I'm still not gettin' how that relates to Danning."

"Hear me out, and perhaps you will." Slaughter chose a cookie from the platter but then set it aside on a napkin, forgetting to eat it as he warmed to his subject. "After the hunt is successfully executed, the killer captures his prey. Bundy usually lured his victims into his car, charmed them into trusting him, and then disabled them. Danning lures his victims into marriage, charms them out of their money, and also renders them helpless. At this stage, there usually follows a period of torture, sometimes brief in duration, sometimes long, depending upon the killer's pattern. Bundy's attacks were brief but brutal. Danning prefers to toy with his victims over a long period of time."

Rainie shivered and closed her eyes.

"I'm sorry," Slaughter said softly. "I know this is an unpleasant conversation for you, Ms. Hall, but I think both you and Mr. Harrigan need to see the similarities between Danning and someone like Bundy in order for me to put your minds at ease."

Rainie lifted her lashes, steeled her spine, and nodded.

"The period of brutality," Slaughter went on, "is normally sexually arousing for the serial killer, and it's common for him to be almost ritualistic in its execution, sometimes to a point that he leaves what we call his trademark at every crime scene. Bundy often viciously bit his victims, for instance, and that became one of his trademarks. After the torture period, be it brief or prolonged, the killer finally murders his victim. At this point, he is high on adrenaline and the thrill of the kill. Outwitting law enforcement and getting away with the murder is his finale, what turns his crank the most, because it makes him feel superior to the poor cops who are chasing their tails, trying to nail him. Most serial killers are very charming and intelligent individuals. They're often high achievers in school and later in their professional lives." He leveled a look at Rainie. "Is any of this striking a chord with you?"

Rainie nodded. "You're describing Peter, almost to a tee."

"Exactly. His pattern is different on the surface but fundamentally the same, and that pattern is extremely important to him. It's a game to him, and the only way he'll play is by his rules."

"Where are you goin' with this?" Parker asked.

"Things haven't gone according to Danning's plan, and now we believe he's decided not to play." He raised a finger to forestall Parker from interrupting again. "First off, Ms. Hall vanished without a trace right before he intended to kill her." He raised another finger. "Then he came under suspicion for killing her. *Not* his usual pattern. Part of the thrill for him is murdering his victims without the cops ever suspecting foul play. After Ms. Hall thwarted him and he came under suspicion, things began to fall apart for him. Unwilling to give up, he hired a pricey investigator to locate Ms. Hall, but she was so clever that finding her wasn't easy. Before the investigator could track her down, she threw yet another wrench in the fan blades by filing for divorce."

"But—"

"Just hear me out," Slaughter requested of Parker again. "Danning has undoubtedly considered this situation from all angles and knows that he will fall under suspicion again if anything happens to Ms. Hall prior to dissolution of the marriage. If he waits until after dissolution, he can't walk away with her money. Two important aspects of the game have been ruined for him. In short, the gratification he usually feels won't occur, so the fun is gone."

"The fun?" Parker echoed.

"I know it's sick," Simpson inserted, "but he's obviously a very sick man. The profiler feels that the danger to Ms. Hall is nearly over. Once the divorce is final, Danning's usual pattern is blown to smithereens, and the pattern is everything to him, a ritual of sorts. He will eventually strike again, but he'll choose a different victim—someone who fits his criteria in every way. Ms. Hall no longer does. He could never woo her again, or lure her into the trap. That being the case, he'll move on and find a young woman who will play the game according to his rules."

Rainie sank back in her chair, utterly exhausted. "So if I can make it through the next two weeks until the divorce is final, I'll be safe from him."

"Absolutely safe." Simpson smiled. "You can put Peter Danning and the past behind you forever, moving forward with your life."

That sounded so wonderful to Rainie. She squeezed Parker's hand and smiled at him. "Two weeks, only two weeks, and I'll be free."

Parker didn't return her smile. Instead he turned a burning gaze on Slaughter. "What if your profiler is wrong? Don't they ever make mistakes?"

Slaughter chuckled. "Rarely. As difficult as it is for people like us to understand the workings of the criminal mind, that's a profiler's job, and he lives, breathes, eats, and sleeps inside their heads. This particular profiler specializes in serial killers. Danning fascinated him from the first because he's so different from most serial killers on the surface, yet so much the same when the layers are peeled away. This man is very good at what he does. If he says Danning will back off and regroup once the divorce is final, I'm willing to go to the bank on it."

"Rainie's life hangs in the balance," Parker reminded him. "You gave me your word that her safety would be your top priority."

"And it *is* our top priority. We aren't in the habit of asking people to cooperate with us and then leaving them to suffer the consequences, Mr. Harrigan. According to the profiler, Ms. Hall will be in more danger over the next two weeks than she's ever been. The clock is ticking. Danning knows that time is running out. If he doesn't strike soon, the game is over. To ensure Ms. Hall's safety, we're bringing in more agents to protect her until the clock strikes midnight."

Parker at last relaxed on the chair. "So you think he may still make a move?"

Slaughter frowned thoughtfully. "My gut tells me it's unlikely. It's very risky business for him at this point, and he's not in the habit of putting himself at risk in any way. But on the off chance that I'm wrong, it only makes sense to beef up security until the gavel drops. Once that occurs, the danger to Ms. Hall will be over."

Simpson cradled her mug in her hands. "We aren't the only ones who need to be extra cautious over the next two weeks," she said, looking directly at Rainie. "You'll be safe here on Mr. Harrigan's ranch and safe while at your home. But when you're driving to and fro, you're more vulnerable. We'll continue to have you tailed by two agents whenever you're commuting, but to avoid detection, the car will continue to hang back. If you see someone thumbing for a ride, don't stop. If someone is broken down along the road, call nine-one-one to get them help but don't pull over. It's important for you to realize that Danning may be getting desperate at this point and might make a move when you least expect it. Don't forget that even for a second."

"I could drive her back and forth," Parker offered.

Simpson shook her head. "If you do that, Danning will know something's up. She has to go it alone. If he decides to make a move, he'll watch her for a while, learn her habits. An escort would send up a red flag."

Parker sighed, then glanced at Rainie, his expression somber. "Don't stop for anyone or anything. All right? I don't care if you hit a deer. Call the cops and keep driving."

"What if I get a flat tire or my car breaks down?"

"Roll up all the windows, lock the doors, and wait. Your tail won't be far behind you." Simpson set aside her coffee, pushed to her feet, and offered Rainie her hand. "We're going to get through this, Ms. Hall, and in two weeks, it'll be nothing more than a bad memory."

Rainie stood to shake the woman's hand. "I so appreciate all that you've done for me. I'll never forget you." She turned to Slaughter and expressed the same sentiments. "You've both been absolutely awesome."

Slaughter took his cup over to the sink. Retracing his steps to the table, he said, "As we understand it, you've opted not to appear at the divorce hearing?"

Rainie hugged her waist. "I prefer not to see Peter again

if I can avoid it. If the judge rules in his favor because I don't appear, I honestly don't care. My attorney says I will at least be awarded my inheritance money. That's all that really matters to me."

"I don't blame you for not wanting to see him," Simpson sympathized. "Let your attorney handle it. Seeing Danning won't make him lose any sleep at night."

Rainie laughed humorlessly. "So . . . this is it, then?"

Slaughter rested a hand on her shoulder. "You won't see us, but we'll be there. Trust me on that. When the divorce is final, we'll be in touch, probably to tell you we're pulling the plug on the case. The only reason we might change our minds about that is if Danning does something suspicious."

"Such as?" Parker asked as he came to slip an arm around Rainie's waist.

"We've been monitoring his financial transactions. So far, we've noted nothing fishy. But if he should withdraw a large sum of cash from the bank or write a check to a suspicious individual, we'll go on red alert. As I told you at our first meeting, we believe he hired White to kill one of his wives. He may try the same tactic again."

After that meeting, Rainie was far less upset than she had anticipated. She now felt confident in her abilities to defend herself in a physical confrontation with Peter, and with the finality of the divorce fast approaching, she had to agree with the FBI that Peter had decided to cut his losses. She knew him. If he was going to come after her, he would do it before a judge could grant her a portion of their marital assets.

As the days passed, her complacency grew in some ways, and her anxiety mounted in others. Strings had been pulled to hasten the divorce proceedings, Peter had done very little to impede the progress, and she would soon be a free woman. During those final days, it was never far from her mind that the clock was ticking and that Peter might be gearing up for a last-minute onslaught. Even with Parker there at night to hold her in his arms, she began having trouble falling asleep, and once she did drift into slumber, she slept so fitfully that she got little rest.

One morning after yet another night of her tossing and turning, Parker suggested that she see a doctor for some tranquilizers. At first, Rainie protested, insisting that she didn't want to become dependent on drugs in order to sleep.

"Sweetheart, this is a stressful time in your life. You don't have to take the pills if you don't need them. I just think it might be helpful to have somethin' on hand when you have trouble restin'."

Rainie finally acquiesced and made an appointment with a physician who wrote her a script for Ambien, a fast-acting sleep aid. Most nights, she didn't need to take it, but as Parker had predicted, the medication did come in handy when she felt nervy and got a bad case of the wide-awakes.

As the court date for the divorce drew near, Rainie conferred with Raymond Quinn and once again opted out of being at the hearing. Though she did hope to get the original amount of her inheritance money returned to her and had asked her lawyer to get her personal effects from Peter as part of the divorce settlement, she didn't care a whit about how the judge ruled on the rest of Peter's assets.

"I feel as if it's blood money," she confided to Parker. "If I appeared in court and fought for it, I'm certain the judge would award me my fair half of everything he has, but I just—" She broke off and searched Parker's gaze. "Will it bother you if I simply let it go, Parker? I won't come into our marriage with nearly as much, bottom line, but I'll feel better about it."

He hooked an arm around her neck and drew her firmly against him. "Sweetheart, you can come into our marriage in the buff and without a penny to your name. All I want is you, all I care about is you, and I'll be a happy man whether you're wealthy or as poor as a church mouse. As for Peter's money? I honestly don't want any part of him, and that includes his assets. Trust me when I say we'll be well set financially without a dime from him."

Rainie pressed her face against the hollow of his neck and breathed deeply of his scent, which always worked on her senses like an intoxicant. "Oh, Parker, I love you so much."

"I love you, too, Rainie mine, I love you, too."

When the day finally arrived that Raymond Quinn called to tell Rainie that the dissolution of her marriage was a fait accompli, she and Parker celebrated with a bottle of champagne and soft, romantic music via a satellite station on her television. As they danced slowly to the lazy lilt of a song, they whispered dreamily of their future together. The first decision they needed to make was in regard to the money Rainie had been awarded by the judge, an even half of everything Peter had. On the one hand, imagining her ex-husband's rage, Rainie felt a long overdue satisfaction, but the flip side was receiving a great deal of money she didn't really want.

"Whoever once said that revenge isn't sweet was never married to a monster like Peter," she murmured to Parker.

"What're you gonna do with all the cash?" he asked softly.

Rainie thought about it for a moment. "Would you care if I donated it to a foundation for abused women?"

Parker snorted and then barked with laughter. "That's *perfect*. I love it! Hell, I'll make a donation myself. Talk about sweet irony."

Rainie hugged his neck. "You know one of the things I love most about you?"

He bent his dark head to nibble on her ear. "No, what's that?"

"You not only respect my right to make my own choices,

but you also support me in whatever I decide, even when it's a little crazy. It's no small amount of money that I'm thinking about giving away, you know. Will I ever make a decision that you buck me on?"

She felt his mouth tip into a grin. "If you decide to leave me, I'll chain you to my bedpost. Other than that, probably not. You've got a good head on your shoulders. Why wouldn't I trust you to make your own choices?"

It was a question that required no answer, so Rainie seduced him instead.

That night a phone call from Special Agent Slaughter marked the end of Rainie's 'round-the-clock protection. When she and Parker retired, she felt the tension in his body as he gathered her close in his arms.

"Penny for them," she murmured.

He sighed and rubbed his cheek against her hair. "Promise not to get mad?"

She couldn't imagine growing angry with him for expressing his thoughts. "Of course I won't."

"I'm scared to death for you," he confessed. "I'm afraid he'll come after you now, and I know that no matter how diligent I am or how hard I try, I can't be with you twenty-four hours a day. I think you should come live with me at the ranch. I don't give a shit how it looks. I want you there, where I know you're safe."

Rainie had circled the same thought many times. "It's over, Parker. I have to move on with my life. I can't allow Peter to control me anymore or influence my decisions." She rolled over onto her stomach, propped herself up on her elbows, and searched his dark eyes. "I want to be *me* now. I *need* to be me now. The real Rainie Hall would never live with a man prior to marriage. Call me hopelessly archaic, but that's a part of who I am. If I allow fear of Peter to change that about me, where does it stop? When I look in a mirror, I have to know who's looking back at me."

He reached up to smooth her hair. "What's so different about you stayin' nights there from me stayin' nights here?"

"Appearances. Here, we're sneaking. There, we'd be shoving everyone's nose in it. It matters to me what your family thinks of me. Can you tell me that your father approves of people living together prior to marriage?"

"No," he said stiffly. "But he'd make an exception in this instance because of Peter."

"And then Peter is still controlling my life!" Rainie rolled away and stood up. Scooping her hands through her hair, she stared down at him with burning eyes. "Try to understand, Parker. I can't let him control me anymore. I just *can't*." She pressed the center of her chest. "He took *everything* from me, *everything*. And I let him. I *crawled* for him. I performed for him like a . . . like a circus poodle. I can't go back to that. I *won't* go back to that. I'm finished with dancing to his tune. I'd rather die."

"Don't talk that way."

"It's *true*. I'd rather let him kill me than allow him to control me."

"Rainie, honey, calm down."

"I can't calm down until I'm convinced you understand," she pushed out around a sob. "I have to know who I am when I look in the mirror, Parker."

"I know. I know, sweetheart." He sat up and stretched out a hand to her. "I'm sorry. Okay? I'm not thinkin' straight. Of course you need to stay here."

When she took his hand, he drew her back to lie beside him and wrapped her firmly in his arms. "Just understand this. Okay? I can't let you stay here alone. If that bugs you, think of it as Peter controllin' me. I have no problem with knowin' who's in the mirror when I look at myself. My nose is unmistakable."

Rainie burst into tearful giggles and punched him playfully in the ribs. "Idiot. I love your nose."

He nuzzled her with the appendage under discussion. "I'm considerin' a nose job."

"Touch that nose, and I'll make you pay."

They fell silent for a moment, and then Rainie steered them back to the original topic. "I'm still working out every day. I'm as ready as I'll ever be to take him on, if it comes down to that."

"I know. It's just—" He broke off and said nothing for several seconds. "I don't want to shake your confidence. You'll be able to put up one hell of a fight, and chances are, you'll kick his sorry ass. I just worry about him catchin' you off guard or bein' armed with a deadly weapon. All the self-defense trainin' in the world doesn't make a person impervious to a bullet."

Loving him as she'd never loved anyone, Rainie threaded her fingers through his hair. Though she was as frightened as he was, she pretended otherwise for his sake. "I'm going to be fine. Peter isn't the type to use a gun. It'll be okay. You'll see."

"Maybe so, but if you don't mind, I'd like to call in my family for backup."

"How so?"

"I can be here with you at night, and you're safe at the ranch durin' the day, but what about when you're drivin' back and forth? You won't have a tail anymore. I'll feel better if one of us is always behind you. If everyone in the family helps out, it'll be a different vehicle every day, so he doesn't get suspicious, and we can all hang back, like the agents did." When he felt her stiffen, he said, "Please, Rainie, at least consider it. We won't have to do it forever, just a couple of months or so. I need to know for sure in my own mind that the crazy bastard has decided to back off."

Rainie felt a suffocating sensation center itself in her chest, but she pushed it away. Parker had given way to her about allowing her to stay at her house until they could be married. She needed to make a concession, too. "All right," she agreed. "If your family doesn't mind doing it, I'm fine with it, too."

Over the days that followed, Rainie relaxed more and more. Peter didn't show up. The chilly October temperatures heralded the beginning of her life with Parker. Halloween decorations began to appear in store windows and on her neighbors' porches. She began to think less and less about Peter and focused instead on the coming holidays and her future with the man she loved.

During that time, the Harrigans joined ranks to tail Rainie back and forth when she traveled to and from work. One day it was Sam and Tucker who acted as her watchdogs. The next, it was Frank and Dee Dee, then Hank, and then Clint and Loni. They weren't quite as adept at staying completely out of sight as the agents had been, but Rainie felt that they did an awesome job for amateurs. Their dedication was also a reminder of the wonderful family she would soon call her own. Through her marriage to Parker, she was inheriting a devoted mother and father, brothers and sisters, plus a niece and nephew. It was a fabulous feeling to know that all of them would love her and stand behind her as if she were related to them by blood.

Immediately after the dissolution of her marriage, Rainie and Parker started meeting with Father Mike, the parish pastor at Parker's church, for marriage preparation classes, which Parker insisted had to be rushed in case Rainie was pregnant and also because of the danger to her while living alone. Because both of Rainie's unions with Peter had been officiated by a JP and not a man of the cloth, getting the marriages dissolved in the eyes of the Church was a simple and fairly quick process. Once that procedure was under way, Parker made their engagement official by taking Rainie to shop for rings. She picked a small but gorgeous diamond solitaire.

Father Mike disapproved of cohabiting and encouraged Rainie and Parker to maintain separate households until their nuptials. Parker didn't protest, but he was up front with Father Mike about staying every night with Rainie at her residence. The priest listened thoughtfully to the story about Peter, considered the problem, and then finally conceded that it would be best if Parker continued his nightly sojourns to Rainie's house.

"No more hanky-panky, though," the priest said, wagging a finger at them. "The two of you can abstain until the marriage takes place. Holy matrimony is a serious undertaking, and you need to do it right."

After that discussion, Rainie concurred with the priest. "We do need to do this right, Parker. Father Mike is hurrying us through the prep work because of the extenuating circumstances. It'll only be for a few weeks. We can survive almost anything short-term."

Rainie was glad of Parker's company at night, but she was also determined to honor their agreement with Father Mike to abstain from sex until their marriage. Her willpower lasted for almost a week, and then Parker kissed her. Big mistake. She finally learned, firsthand, how physical desire could make two levelheaded, mature individuals temporarily insane. Their encounter began in the kitchen, and the trail of their discarded clothing marked their path to her bedroom door, where Parker lifted her against the wall and made love to her standing up.

It was the best sex Rainie had ever had, made all the sweeter because it wasn't merely a physical joining, but also a melding of their hearts.

Afterward they collapsed on the bed, wrapped in each other's arms. Parker laughed weakly. "Well, there went abstinence out the window. On a bright note, if I'm gonna burn in hell for it, I can't think of anybody I'd rather sizzle with."

Rainie twisted away, flipped up onto her knees, and

straddled him, her blond-streaked curls forming a curtain around their faces as she leaned down to kiss him. "If I'm going to hell, I want to enjoy you as much as I can before I get there."

He chuckled and rolled with her in his arms to be on top. "I like the way you're thinkin', lady," he whispered huskily. "I'll also add that I can't believe anything so beautiful can possibly be wrong."

What they felt for each other *was* beautiful, and Rainie didn't believe anything that happened between them could be wrong, either. She decided that it was a matter of conscience and returned Parker's sultry kisses without a trace of guilt.

Chapter Seventeen

Halloween fell on a Friday, and Rainie was excited about celebrating the occasion with Parker. For several days in advance, she spent her alone time decorating her house before he arrived in the evening. She carved three pumpkins: one for her front porch, one for the table, and one for the bedroom. She draped orange and black streamers adorned with dangling witches and goblins from the ceiling. Her windows were covered with ghoulish cutouts and silhouettes.

Right after lunch on Halloween day, she went to find Parker in the stables. She located him in Montana's stall and slipped inside to hug his waist. After giving him a long, languorous kiss, she leaned back to smile up at him. "I'm leaving early. I want tonight to be special. It *is* our first Halloween together, you know."

Parker tugged his cell phone from his belt, punched a button, and waited a moment before saying, "Hey, Clint. Rainie's leavin' here in a couple. Can you tail her early today, or would you rather opt out and let me do it?" He listened for a moment and then smiled. "Thanks, bro. I really appreciate it. I'm still babyin' Montana's leg and need to apply salve and a wrap. I could have Toby take care of it, though."

After listening for a moment and then saying good-bye,

he snapped the phone closed. "Clint has nothin' goin' on, so he'll follow you into town."

Rainie wanted this day to be carefree and special, and she wished with all her heart that Peter no longer cast a shadow over her life. Unfortunately, that wasn't a reasonable expectation and probably wouldn't be for a few more months. "I hate that I'm putting you and everyone in your family to so much trouble."

"It's no trouble, honey. Clint needed to go into town to run some errands anyway, so your leavin' early will save him the extra trip. Once he sees you home, it'll still be early enough for him to take care of his own stuff."

"He'll be on duty a little longer than usual today. I have to stop by the store for the ingredients for mulled wine and cookies."

He narrowed an eye at her. "What all are you plannin' for tonight, anyway?"

"Lots of fun stuff. I need to mull our wine, and I want to bake and decorate cookies, and I have to get the candy set out so we'll be ready for all the trick-or-treaters when they start coming around five. After all that's done, I need to get into my costume. I'm going to wear a black caftan, my Elvira wig, and a witch's hat."

"How old did you say you are?" he asked as he released her from his embrace.

"Old enough to know better, but still young enough not to care," she replied flippantly. Grabbing the front of his shirt and hauling him toward her, she added in a sultry voice, "And don't pretend you don't like me this way. I'll know you're lying."

He laughed and adjusted his Stetson. Without fail, she always knocked it askew when she kissed him. "Don't get so wrapped up in Halloween that you forget to lock up tight as soon as you get in the house, and be sure to keep the phone close at hand until I get there."

Over the last few days, Rainie had so seldom thought about Peter that this second reminder made her frown. "Don't spoil the fun of Halloween. I want to pretend, just for today, that Peter doesn't exist. I don't want to think about him. I don't want to talk about him."

"Fine by me. Just be careful. Okay?"

"I'm always careful. It's becoming second nature for me." She touched a fingertip to the dimple that slashed his cheek. "I want tonight to be perfect," she whispered. "Absolutely perfect."

"Sweetheart, if I'm with you, it can't be anything but perfect. Make plenty of mulled wine, okay? And don't drink it all before I get there. We'll get tipsy together, and when the kids stop coming, I'll show you the cowboy version of bobbin' for apples."

The husky timbre of his voice told Rainie that Parker's version of apple bobbing would probably make her shiver with delight. She went up on her tiptoes to graze his lips with hers. "One more for the road?" she whispered.

Angling his head to possess her mouth, he delivered on the request. She laughed when she saw that his hat had been bumped off center again. Reaching up to straighten it, she said, "Try to come early. You can help me frost cookies."

One hard arm still locked around her waist, he said, "I'd rather frost you."

Just at the thought, Rainie's skin tingled. "Hmm. Which parts of me would you frost?"

"Use your imagination."

Rainie did just that all during the drive into town.

Clint was executing a curve in the country road when his truck engine suddenly sputtered, hiccoughed loudly, and then died. The vehicle shuddered to a slow stop. The Dodge had been running perfectly yesterday when he went into town, so what the hell was wrong with it now? Sometimes diesel rigs burped and coughed when the fuel filters got dirty, but Clint's mechanic changed them regularly.

He glanced through the dusty windshield at the back of Rainie's Mazda, which was quickly getting so far ahead of him that he could barely see it. He keyed the ignition, hoping the vehicle might roar back to life. Instead, it only hacked, shuddered, and died again. Fuel injector pump? It was the only thing Clint could think of besides a clogged filter that might cause the vehicle to behave this way.

"Well, *shit*!" What he really, *really* wanted to say was the F-word, but Loni had a strict rule against that because of the kids, so Clint never allowed himself to transgress, not even while alone, afraid that habit might lead him to slip up when little pitchers with big ears were present. He tried the ignition switch again, got the same result, and settled for yelling, "Son of a frigging *bitch*!"

He jerked his cell phone from his belt, started to dial Parker, and saw only one bar in his signal window. He tried to call out and couldn't. "*Damn* it!"

He was in a dead zone. Mountainous sections of Oregon were famous for expanses of highway where no signal came through. He glanced up to determine precisely where he was. *Double damn.* He was at the bottom of Haymaker Hill. Normally when he was on this section of road and lost his signal while talking with someone, he just called back when he got out of the dead zone. Not possible this time. In order to call Parker and let him know that no one was tailing Rainie, he would have to hoof it nearly three miles to the summit.

Clint piled out of the pickup and broke into a run up the incline, which would grow much steeper as he neared the top. Ranch work kept him in peak physical condition, and he didn't mind jogging up a hill. He just wished he were wearing some decent shoes. Riding boots had never been intended for long-distance running. *Stupid truck.* Parker was counting on him to look out for Rainie this afternoon, and now he'd let him down.

As Rainie made her way up and down the aisles of the supermarket, she was still focused on Parker and the kinky delights of frosting. Just imagining them made her feel a little weak at the knees. Unfortunately, it also distracted her, and she had to double back in the aisles several times because she'd overlooked something on her list.

She was glancing at her wristwatch by the time she opened the trunk of the Mazda to stash her groceries. It was only a little after one o'clock, but even so, time was running short. Thank goodness she'd thought to get premade icing. All she'd have to do was add dabs of food coloring to create the colors she needed. If she put the wine on the stove to simmer first, it could mull while she mixed the cookie dough and did other stuff. Then maybe she could carve out an extra few minutes for a nice, hot bath in scented water before she put on her costume. If Parker wanted to decorate her like a Halloween cookie and slowly devour her, she wanted all parts of her to be pristine. And that wasn't to mention the cowboy version of bobbing for apples. What, exactly, had he meant by *that*?

Rainie was still considering the possibilities as she unlocked the driver door and slipped behind the steering wheel. She dumped her purse on the seat beside her. Humming the theme song of *Legends of the Fall*, she drew the door closed, fastened her seat belt, shoved the key in the ignition, and sparked the engine to life. As she backed from the parking space and shifted into drive, she smiled dreamily. If someone had told her a year ago that she would meet a cowboy, fall wildly in love, and feel this happy, she never would have believed it. It just went to prove that miracles could happen, heroes actually did exist, and fairy-tale endings weren't only for storybooks.

Just as the car began to roll forward, something flat and cold angled across Rainie's larynx, the pressure so abrupt and forceful that it snapped her head back against the rest. For a moment, her brain went into a free fall of confusion, and her only thought was, *What?*

"You unfaithful, spoiled, stupid little *bitch*."

The voice near Rainie's ear was one straight out of her nightmares. *Peter.* Oh, God, he was right there in the back-seat of her car. Terrifying thoughts ping-ponged inside her brain. *A knife.* He had the flat side of the blade pressed against her jugular. With only a turn of his wrist, he could kill her. She could imagine it all too clearly. The warmth of her blood streaming down her neck to pool in the cleavage of her breasts. The wet gurgle of crimson as she fought to breathe. She remembered telling Parker that she could defend herself even if Peter came at her with a weapon. *Not.* Somehow she'd never envisioned this scenario, with her hands on the steering wheel, the car rolling forward, and the knife already in position at her throat.

She'd locked the car. How had he gotten in? And why, oh, why hadn't she checked the back floorboard before getting in herself? Just because she knew that Clint was somewhere in the parking lot and watching her vehicle was no reason for her to be careless. *Stupid, so stupid.* Any idiot knew to look through the back windows. It was a simple safety rule that all women with half a brain followed nowadays. Where had her head been? *Parker.* She'd been daydreaming about Parker.

Oh, God, oh, God. Where was Clint? Had Peter harmed him? The thought no sooner entered her mind than she discarded it. Like Parker, Clint was in superb physical condition and could handle himself in a scuffle. Besides, it wasn't Peter's style to face off with a man who could fight back. Clint was fine. He *had* to be fine. Peter had probably just delayed him somehow.

Rainie could almost hear Parker's voice whispering in her mind. *Be smarter than he is. Use your head. He may be bigger and stronger, but you've got the element of surprise on your side.* Only nothing he'd taught her covered a situation like this. A random act of violence. This was so classically Peter. He was probably already tensing to slit her throat, his plan being to leave her slumped over the steering wheel. He would take her purse to make it look like a robbery.

Rainie forced her mind back to what she needed to be thinking about, not Peter's plans, but how she might come up with one of her own. How could she catch Peter by surprise and take control of the situation? Butting him in the face with the back of her skull wasn't possible. The seat's headrest was in her way. She thought about slamming down hard on the brakes, but the car wasn't moving fast enough to throw him violently forward. She also worried about the backlash of reverse momentum. With a lethal weapon at her throat, she'd have to be nuts to bring the car to an abrupt stop. Not a smart move. Same went for tromping on the gas and driving into a light post.

Bracing herself, she forced her gaze to the rearview mirror. Shock spilled through her like ice water. Peter wasn't wearing a stocking cap, as she'd once imagined he might. Instead he had no hair, absolutely *none*. His head was as bald as an onion. His thick, golden eyebrows had vanished. Even his eyelashes were gone.

He smiled at her—the same thousand-watt, charming smile that had fooled so many people into believing any lie he told them. "DNA precaution. I watch forensic shows a lot, and the percentage of murderers who are caught because they leave a trace of DNA at the scene is incredibly high. I don't plan to make the same mistake."

Rainie gaped at his reflection, totally forgetting to steer.

"Watch out, you stupid bitch! Pay attention to where you're going!"

She jerked her gaze back to the windshield and cranked the wheel sharply left to avoid a collision with the rear bumper of a Cadillac.

With his free hand, Peter grabbed her hair. His fingers seemed to stick in the strands. The cruel clench of his fist brought tears to her eyes. *Gloves.* He was wearing latex gloves. In the rearview mirror, she glimpsed the maniacal leer that had haunted her dreams for so many months. She was right back where she'd started, she thought dizzily, seeing his reflection, only now he had no interest in playing sadistic sex games. Oh, no. He'd come here to kill her. She saw it in his eyes.

So why didn't he just slit her throat and get it over with? The thought made her whole body quiver, and for a horrible moment, she almost lost control of her bladder. She didn't want to die. She wanted none of this to be real so she could go back to Parker. Her divorce was final, damn it. She was *free.* They were taking marriage preparation classes and planning a future together. She yearned to have his babies, see them grow up, and then sit on the porch swing with him someday as an old woman. It couldn't end like this. It simply *couldn't.*

Only it was. If wishing Peter away had worked, she would have been rid of him a long time ago. Terror. That was Peter's specialty, evoking terror. *Calm, stay calm.* She had to *think.* With the knife blade at her throat, staying calm was a tall order. *Parker.* Rainie envisioned his dark face, so different in every way from that of the man behind her. She remembered the kisses they'd shared a short while ago. Now she might never get to experience a Halloween with him. No getting tipsy on mulled wine. No opening the door to pass out candy to cute little kids in goblin costumes. No ending the evening in each other's arms and finding out what cowboy apple bobbing was all about.

A wave of intense sadness washed through Rainie. And then anger took its place. She hated Peter Danning. No, *hate* was too mild a word. She *despised* him. He might kill her. Correction, he would kill her if he had his way. But she'd be damned if she would go out sniveling and begging for her life. He had reduced her to that once. *Never again.* If she had to die, she would go out as Rainie Hall, Marcus Hall's gutsy daughter and the love of Parker Harrigan's life. This vile, twisted, vicious excuse for a man could destroy her physically, but she would never again allow him to obliterate her sense of self.

Rainie drove the Mazda to the end of the parking corridor and pressed on the brake. Peter jerked hard on her hair. "Did I tell you to stop? Willful as always, I see."

Rainie stiffened against the pain. "Which direction should I go?" She met his glittering gaze in the mirror. "Going straight is out, unless you want to collide with those parked cars."

He pulled harder on her hair and pressed the flat of the blade more firmly against her larynx.

"Go ahead," Rainie pushed out, her voice twanging from the pressure. She would *not* give him the satisfaction of knowing how frightened she was. "Get it over with. Kill me, Peter. I'd rather die than breathe the same air you are."

"Shut up and drive."

"Where to? I'm not a mind reader."

"That pesthole you live in." He laughed softly. "I gave you *everything*, a palatial home, beautiful clothing, and expensive jewelry. You had it *all*, and you threw it away for a low-rent shack and an uneducated farmer."

Rainie thought of Parker—the gentle brush of his knuckles over her cheek, the love in his eyes every time he looked at her. To think that she might never see him again made her heart hurt.

"What has he given you?" Peter demanded. "Name me one damned thing. Look at this junk heap you're driving. Look at your clothes. A homeless person dresses better than you do."

Rainie remained silent, refusing to engage in a stupid debate about the finest man she'd ever known. It would be a waste of breath. A slimeball like Peter was incapable of appreciating all the many gifts she'd received from Parker. Restoring her pride and self-confidence. Loving her with no strings attached. Filling her life with laughter and joy and contentment and peace. As the thoughts ran through Rainie's mind, she felt a sob welling in her throat, because she should have said all those things to Parker and couldn't remember if she had.

"Drive," Peter ordered. "We'll have plenty of time to talk about the folly of your choices when we reach your house."

Rainie hung a right to take the bypass. The traffic flowed faster on the motorway. She concentrated for a moment on breathing—slow and deep. When her head cleared a little, she was better able to focus. *Take control of the situation*, Parker had told her at least a thousand times. Only how? With the seat between her and Peter, all the self-defense moves that Parker had taught her were useless. Maybe, if she could accelerate to a high enough speed on the bypass, there would come a moment when Peter drew the knife from her throat. All she needed was a millisecond. If the opportunity came, she'd slam on the brakes and put his sorry ass through the windshield. He wore no safety belt, and the old Mazda had no air bags. As a plan of action, it wasn't much, but for the moment, it was all she had.

As she merged with the bypass traffic and gained speed, Rainie decided to do her best to piss him off, her hope being that he would react true to form by ranting and waving his hands. If he got mad and lowered the knife for just an instant, she might have a fighting chance.

"You know, it's funny," she said with a forced laugh. "No, actually, it's *hysterical*. You really believe that the life you gave me was first-rate."

"It was better than what you've got now, that's for damned sure."

"Wrong!" Rainie wasn't worried about his slitting her throat now. They were doing fifty-five, and Peter would never put his own safety at risk. "I'm with a *real* man. Unlike you, he knows how to love a woman, and he never has any trouble getting it up."

He leaned forward to breathe heavily in her ear without actually touching her. "I'm stiff as a rod right now."

"Only because you think I'm afraid. Inflicting fear and pain are the only things that turn you on. Well, news flash, Peter: I'm not scared of you anymore."

His only response was to laugh. "Just drive, Lorraina. We'll see how brave you are when we're alone in that hovel you call a home."

Anxious to join Rainie at her place for an evening of Halloween festivities, Parker had decided to leave early. He was smiling as he closed up the office. Helping her to make cookies would be fun, especially if he could talk her into wearing the black caftan with nothing on underneath. *Oh, yeah.* Rainie and mulled wine. What a combination. He needed to stop by the house for a quick shower and to grab his camera. Their first Halloween together. Rainie would get a kick out of taking pictures of the little kids who came to the door.

Parker had just left the arena when his cell phone started playing a rumba, Clint's special ring tone. He jerked the apparatus from his belt and snapped it open. "Is Rainie all right?"

"I don't know." Clint sounded out of breath. "My damn truck broke down at the bottom of Haymaker Hill; then I couldn't pick up a signal. I just ran all the way to the summit."

"So no one's tailin' her?" Parker's heart jerked with fear. "Damn it, Clint. What the hell's wrong with your truck?"

"I don't know. It started sputtering and then died on me. I couldn't get it going again."

Parker had a very bad feeling about this. Clint's ranch mechanic kept all of the Circle H vehicles in perfect running condition. It made no sense that the truck would suddenly die. *Oh, God.* Rainie was unprotected. He needed to call her and tell her to stay inside the supermarket until he could get there.

Rainie prayed with everything she had all the way to her house, but Peter never once drew the knife from her throat. As she parked in the driveway and cut the engine, her cell phone suddenly began to play "The Way We Were," a ring tone that she had assigned exclusively to Parker.

"That'll either be lover boy or his brother, calling to tell you that your watchdog of the day had car trouble and couldn't follow you into town." Peter leered at her in the mirror. "Everything is going exactly as planned except that I expected him to call sooner. Answer, put him on speaker, and then tell him you're already home and everything's fine. Be convincing, or I'll slit your throat."

Unable to turn her head because of the knife, Rainie groped in her purse for her cell, flipped it open with one hand, pressed the speaker icon, and put the phone to her ear. "Hi."

Parker's voice came over the line, taut with concern. "Sweetheart, Clint's truck crapped out on him at the bottom of Haymaker Hill. He didn't follow you into town. I'm fixin' to leave right now. Just stay inside the store until I get there. All right?"

"I've already finished my shopping and left the market." She met Peter's glittering gaze in the mirror. "No worries, though. Everything's fine. I just got home and I'll lock up tight as soon as I get inside."

"Promise? I'm a little worried. Clint's mechanic is top-notch. It seems odd that the truck suddenly broke down that way."

Peter clenched his fist in her hair again. Some things never changed. He still delighted in inflicting pain.

"I'm fine, Parker. Really."

"You're sure? Did you watch in your rearview mirror to make sure no one was followin' you?"

Rainie yearned to cry out, *No, because he's right here in the car with me!* But she knew Peter would kill her if she dared. So instead she put a smile in her voice and said, "I'm perfectly fine, Parker. I can't wait to go inside, put on the cider, and start making the fudge."

"Fudge? Yum. That's my favorite, a lot better than sugar cookies."

Please, Parker, pick up on that, Rainie thought frantically. *I'm supposed to make mulled wine, not cider, and Halloween cookies, not fudge. Who makes fudge for Halloween?*

"Well," he said, "if you're sure you're fine, I'll stop by my place to grab my camera and a quick shower before I leave then. I smell like horses and wintergreen liniment."

No, no, no. You're not getting it, Parker. Think. I've been planning to decorate cookies for days. "All right," she forced out. "I'm going to freshen up, too. I'm all sticky from racing around the store. I'd like a nice bath before I put on my leotard and tutu."

"You're dressin' up as a ballerina instead of a witch?"

In the rearview mirror, Peter's face contorted with rage,

and he pressed the knife harder against Rainie's throat. His message was clear: He was onto her.

Thinking quickly, Rainie said, "I have both costumes and changed my mind. A ballerina is a lot sexier than a witch."

"You've got that right." Parker whistled under his breath. "I can't wait to see you in a tutu. Forget the fudge. I'll have you instead."

Tears burned in Rainie's eyes. "Sounds like a plan."

"Have a good look-see around the neighborhood before you get out of the car. All right? If you notice anything suspicious, just lock the car doors, call me back, and sit tight until I get there."

"All right," Rainie agreed.

"I love you."

The tears spilled out onto Rainie's cheeks. "I love you, too, Parker. You'll never know just how much."

"Call me once you're safely inside the house. Don't forget, or I'll get a speedin' ticket tryin' to get there."

"All right," Rainie agreed.

After Parker broke the connection, Peter jerked hard on Rainie's hair again. "Home, sweet home."

She stared through the sun-streaked windshield at her front door. Home, Peter called it, but he was so very wrong about that. The word no longer conjured images of a place in her mind. Her true home, her only home now, was in the circle of Parker's arms. She loved him so much. They had their whole lives left to live. She couldn't allow Peter to rob her of that.

Grabbing frantically for composure, she said, "If you keep that knife at my throat as we walk to the porch, one of my neighbors may notice and call the cops."

"I'll take my chances." He threw open the rear door. "One wrong move, and I'll slit your jugular and leave you to drown in your own blood. Got it?"

Chin lifted to an awkward angle to accommodate the

knife blade, Rainie collected her purse, the phone, and her keys, and then opened her own door to carefully exit the car, her body poised for action the moment he lowered the weapon. Only instead he reached over the rear door to shift the knife into his left hand before she fully gained her feet. Pushing her ahead of him, he kicked both doors closed. Rainie felt like a bit of flotsam carried forth on a wave as they crossed the yard to her front steps.

When they reached the door, he produced a key. Rainie stared stupidly at his gloved hand as he disengaged the lock and then toed the portal open. As they moved inside, he kept the knife at her throat as he reached back to close the door and refasten the dead bolt.

"Where did you get that key?"

He laughed softly. "I jimmied open a window yesterday and found your extra keys hanging by the kitchen door. Car key, house key." He clicked his tongue. "Not smart, Lorraina. It's always a good idea to hide your spare keys so intruders aren't likely to find them."

Rainie's back was pressed against his chest. His closeness made her skin crawl.

"But, then, all of you are dumber than ropes. Did lover boy and his family honestly think I wouldn't watch you for several days before making a move? Dumb fucks, all of them, taking turns and tailing you in their respective vehicles, hoping I wouldn't catch on. News flash: I not only caught on but figured out their schedule."

"You disabled Clint's truck somehow, didn't you?" It wasn't really a question. Rainie had always known that Peter was as intelligent as he was cruel. "How'd you pull that off? The perimeter of Clint's ranch is under electronic surveillance."

"True, but he drives into town almost every day. That's why I chose to make my move when I knew he'd be the one following you. He went to a ranch supply store yesterday.

While he was inside, I picked the lock on his diesel tank and shoved a satchel of dirt inside. A special satchel, of course, made of material that takes a while to dissolve in diesel. After sitting in the fuel for so many hours, it was badly compromised. Then he jiggled it up good on that rough road leading from his ranch to the highway, which finished the job. The dirt got loose in the tank and started clogging up the fuel filter. Bingo. His truck broke down after he drove only a few miles." He bent his head to breathe heavily in her ear. "Time to call lover boy back and tell him you're safe and sound inside the house with all the doors locked."

Rainie had hoped Peter might forget Parker's request for a return call. She flipped open the cell phone. Parker answered on the second ring. "Inside and locked up tight?" he asked.

"Yes."

"Good. I'll be there in about forty minutes. Quick shower, and I'm out of here. I can't wait to see you in that tutu."

"See you." Rainie ended the call without telling him that she loved him, something she never did. She could only hope that struck him as strange. "So now what's the plan?" she asked Peter. "Am I going to be murdered by a burglar? Fall and break my neck? The suspense is killing me."

"Nothing so predictable as that," he whispered. "Poor Lorraina, so stressed out over the divorce that you saw a doctor and got something to help you sleep."

He'd been in her medicine cabinet? "I'm not following."

"Of course you're not, darling. You have a brain the size of a pea. So to satisfy your curiosity, I'll summarize my plan for you. As I'm sure you'll agree, it is sheer genius."

He shoved her ahead of him into the kitchen. "You've come home from a trying day at work. You're depressed. You're exhausted from not sleeping well. Having a nice soak in the tub and going to bed early sounds good, so you take a couple of sleeping pills, light some candles, and slip into a bubble bath to enjoy a couple of glasses of wine."

"Wrong. The prescription is for Ambien. It says right on the bottle not to take it with alcohol, and I have a romantic evening planned with my fiancé."

"I know, I know," he crooned. "But you must not have read the warning label. Lots of people don't. So you *are* going to mix the sleeping pills with alcohol, darling. Then you'll get in the tub, drink a bunch of wine, and get ever so sleepy. Sadly, the combination of the drug and the wine will make you lose consciousness, and you'll slip under the water."

"What about the romantic evening?"

"Quarrel, perhaps, or simple emotional instability. You were going to make fudge and changed your mind. You were going to be a witch and changed your mind. Flighty Lorraina, always changing her mind."

Rainie saw a bottle of cheap pink wine on the counter by the sink, already opened to breathe. She still drank boxed wine because it was less expensive. Parker knew that. *Bad mistake, Peter.* Only even as the thought sank into her brain, she wondered if Parker would remember her wine preferences. A single goblet and the container of Ambien had been placed beside the bottle.

"It'll be a lovely way to go," Peter whispered. "In a nice, warm bath—growing drowsy. We'll chat while you fall asleep, do a little catching up. When you're out, I'll help you slip under the water. Chances are you'll never even wake up, sweetness. Your farm-boy lover will be the one to discover your body. So romantic and heart-wrenching, don't you think? Candles, wine, and tragedy."

"You'll never get away with it. Parker will know. I hate taking pills, and I'd never mix them with wine. Besides, we have plans for this evening. He'll know I would never have doped myself up on sleeping pills."

"Maybe, maybe," he said in a singsong voice. "But there'll be no evidence of foul play, no sign of an intruder. Even if he yells to high heaven that something's not right, the cops won't listen. You don't really believe that I haven't planned every detail of this, do you?" He clucked his tongue again. "There'll be no trace of my DNA in your car or house, and as I'm sure you've noticed, I'm wearing gloves to avoid leaving fingerprints. They'll do an autopsy, of course, but all they'll learn is that you mixed sleeping pills with alcohol. They'll assume that you accidentally drowned in the tub. There will be nothing to tie me to your death. *Nothing.* Another perfect murder. It's my specialty."

Anger roiled within her. "Wrong. You won't walk away with any money this time."

"Won't I?" He laughed softly. "Your parents are dead. You have no siblings, no children, no extended family, and no will. After your tragic death, I'll have my attorney petition for a reversal of the divorce-court ruling. You don't even have any of my assets in your possession yet. Possession is nine-tenths of the law. It may take a few months to iron out all the unfortunate wrinkles, but eventually your half of everything will revert back to me. There's no one else to inherit. I'll buy roses for your grave, darling, and toast your memory with a bottle of obscenely expensive wine."

Rainie barely heard him. She was staring at the bottle of pills. The Ambien was fast-acting, effective in about fifteen minutes. With the added effect of wine, the pills might kick in even faster. Her limbs went cold with dread. Parker was grabbing a shower before he left. He'd never get here in time to save her. She was on her own.

"You can't force me to swallow pills."

Peter pressed the knife more firmly against her throat. "In that case, I'll move on to plan B and just kill you the grisly way. Afterward, I'll kick in the back door, tear up the house, steal anything that's worth stealing, and take your purse as I leave. It won't be as neat, but I'll still manage to pull it off." He leaned down to smile at her. When Rainie looked into his eyes, all she saw was pure evil. "Have you ever seen someone get their throat cut, darling? It's not a fun way to die. You spew red bubbles out the hole like a whale and choke to death on your own blood. It takes several very *long* seconds before your oxygen-starved brain blinks out. Do you know how long a second seems when you can't breathe? It's a slow, horrible way to die. Wouldn't you rather just go to sleep?"

Rainie preferred to buy herself some time by taking the damned pills and drinking the wine. Fifteen minutes. If God was up there, pulling for her, maybe she would get an opening to hit Peter or kick him.

He laughed near her ear. "I knew you'd see reason. Pour yourself some wine, my sweet, and wash down three pills. I'd make you take the whole damned bottle, but that might arouse suspicion. Then we'll mosey our way to the bathroom. Your bath is already drawn, waiting for you. You can have a couple more goblets of wine while you're soaking. I hate to rush you, but I do have places to go and people to see."

With shaking hands, Rainie filled the goblet and then picked up the prescription bottle, twisted off the cap, and tapped out three small tablets onto her palm. After tossing them into her mouth, she tongued them over her lower molars to rest inside her cheek. She knew they would start to dissolve soon, especially when she drank the wine. But she might delay the efficacy of the pills by a few minutes if she didn't swallow them immediately. Anything to buy herself extra seconds. Sooner or later, he would relax his guard and lower the knife. He *had* to. Otherwise, she was going to die.

He kept the knife at her throat as she lifted the goblet. The taste of the dissolving tablets was so horrible that she almost gagged.

"Drink, drink, drink," he urged kindly. "Be my good girl."

Be my good girl. Revulsion made her stomach turn. During their marriage, that had been one of his favorite phrases—as if it had somehow prettied up the reality of what he forced her to do. During those interludes, she'd wanted to die more times than she could count. Now she was about to get her wish.

Thinking of Rainie and the coming evening, Parker soaped up and stepped under the spray of water to rinse. He was scrubbing his neck when he suddenly remembered something Rainie had recently said to him. *Halloween just isn't Halloween without cookies decorated like pumpkins.* He froze with the washcloth at his nape. If she felt that way, why the hell had she suddenly decided to make fudge instead? A cold sensation moved up Parker's spine. Cider instead of mulled wine. A tutu instead of a witch costume. No saying she loved him before ending the call. *Shit.*

Parker slapped off the water faucet without bothering to rinse. Dripping wet, he ran to the phone beside his bed and speed-dialed Rainie. *Shit, oh, shit.* Something was wrong. She'd tried to tell him. *Jesus, sweet Jesus. Let her be okay. She has to be okay.*

Rainie had just gulped down the first glass of wine when her cell phone went off in her purse. "The Way We Were." It was Parker calling her again. She met Peter's gaze.

"Answer, darling. Put lover boy on speaker, and mind every word you say."

Rainie reached for her purse and dragged it across the counter toward her. She fished inside for her phone. "Hello?"

Parker sounded out of breath. "Hi, sweetheart. Sorry for

buggin' you, but I can barely wait to get there and just wanted to hear your voice."

"It's good to hear yours, too," Rainie replied.

"I've been thinkin' about tonight. Once the kids stop comin', are you up for some stargazin'? We'll snuggle up in a blanket and get tipsy. I'll bore you with the story about my mother's star again and see if you can find it without me helpin' you."

Rainie's throat tightened. This was her opening to let Parker know something was wrong. But what if Peter caught on again? "That's a challenge I'll gladly accept. You want to make it more interesting by putting some money on it? Venus is pretty easy to spot."

Much to Rainie's relief, Parker never missed a beat and didn't reveal, even by an inflection of his voice, that she'd named the wrong star. "I've got ten that says you won't be able to find it."

"You're on."

"I've still got to shower. I'll see you in about forty minutes. Okay?"

"Can't wait."

"See you," he said softly, and then broke the connection.

Rainie's hands shook as she closed her phone. *He knew.* Parker never ended a conversation without saying he loved her.

Still dripping wet and buck naked, Parker immediately called the cops. The dispatcher who answered was female. Parker quickly related his suspicions to her, namely that Peter Danning had finally made his move and Rainie was in terrible danger.

"What makes you think that, Mr. Harrigan?" the dispatcher asked.

Parker felt like an idiot as he stated his reasons—that his brother's truck had broken down, that Rainie was making fudge instead of Halloween cookies, cider instead of mulled wine, and that she'd suddenly changed her mind about dressing as a witch. "And just now when I talked to her, she referred to Venus as bein' my mother's star when she knows damned well it's Polaris."

Apparently the dispatcher thought his reasons sounded idiotic, too, because she said, "People change their minds and forget things sometimes. Did she specifically *say* that something is wrong?"

Parker's temper snapped. "Listen, lady. I'm not gonna waste precious time discussin' this with you. Get a car over to her place, *now*, or I swear to God, I'll have your job. You readin' me loud and clear?" He gave the woman Rainie's address. "The bastard will kill her. She needs help. See that she gets it!"

Parker hung up and grabbed his soiled clothes, which he'd dropped on the floor only minutes ago. *Soap.* He'd never gotten rinsed off completely. His jeans snagged on his wet legs. He hurriedly dragged on the shirt and stuffed his bare feet into his boots. Then he bolted from the house and ran to his truck.

Peter poured Rainie a second glass of wine and made her drink that as well. Then, still holding the knife at her throat, he made her grab the bottle and forced her ahead of him to the bathroom. True to his word, the bath was already drawn, the top layer of bubbles mostly evaporated. Along the edge of the tub, three lit candles sat like miniature sentinels.

"Strip," he ordered. "Everything off. I promise not to look." His voice rang with sarcasm.

Rainie bent her knees to set the bottle of wine and empty goblet on the tile surface that enclosed the tub. Then, feeling oddly numb, she kicked off her boots and began unbuttoning her blouse. If only she'd worn a pullover top, she might have gotten the knife away from her throat for an instant.

But no. Her blouse and bra came off easily while he held the weapon firmly beneath her chin. She toed off her boots and socks. Her filmy skirt and panties fell to the floor without a hitch once she'd worked them down past her hips.

Naked. Her skin burned with humiliation. She'd thought never to let this man look at her body again. She stepped into the water. It had grown cool, and she shivered as it licked around her lower calves. He stayed with her, the blade ever at her throat as she sank to her knees and twisted to sit down.

She wasn't feeling the effects of the drug yet. As he sloshed more wine into the goblet, she sank as deeply into the water as she could to conceal her body from his gaze. He smiled that horrible smile she remembered so well.

"Feeling shy, Lorraina?"

"Sleepy. The pills work fast." In truth, half of them were still in her cheek, gooey and dissolved to paste, but they weren't all down the hatch yet. *Be smarter than he is. Outwit him.* She let her eyelashes droop, then pretended to struggle back to alertness. "How will you explain being bald?" she asked with a fake yawn. "Surely people at work will notice that and ask questions. You don't even have any eyebrows."

"Emotional breakdown." Hunkered down and bent forward to keep the knife under her chin, he pulled a sad face. "My wife left me. I was suspected of killing her aboard a cruise ship. The police and reporters gave me no peace. I've been seeing a psychiatrist, taking medication for depression. Suddenly my hair started to fall out. Terrible thing." He shrugged and winked at her. "The hair-removal products that are on the market now are fabulous. I dabbed it on in little spots at first so my hair appeared to be falling out in patches. My doctor assured me that emotional trauma can do strange things and that my hair will grow back once my life settles down." He glanced at his watch. "I have a feeling it's going to smooth out drastically in only a few more minutes. How are you feeling, darling?"

Rainie fluttered her eyelashes again and let her head nod. Then she jerked it erect. "I'm fine. I told you this wouldn't work." She slurred her words slightly. Her heart was pounding. If she pretended to fall asleep too fast, he would get suspicious. But if she waited too long, she might fall asleep for real. Parker was on his way. He'd probably called the police as well. Unfortunately it took only a few seconds to drown. "I still feel wide awake."

He shoved the full wineglass under her nose. "Drink it straight down."

"I can't hold another one."

"You'll find a way. The alternative is so ugly. Cutting your throat in the bathtub would be tidier, though. No blood and gore all over the floor. It's your choice."

She downed the wine as ordered. This time, the remainder of the dissolved pills went down with it. She wondered how long it had been since she'd first put them in her mouth. She truly was beginning to feel drowsy. Time was running out. She sank a little lower in the tub and pretended to struggle to keep her eyes open.

"Back to my emotional breakdown," he droned on. "The confidentiality laws that protect a psychiatric patient's privacy are very strict nowadays. Unfortunately, they aren't bulletproof. So I took the added precaution of lying through my teeth to my doctor and letting him see my hair fall out, more and more, week after week. If my records are subpoenaed and he is called to testify, my emotional upheaval and hair loss will be verified by an expert witness. I went to Snohomish to buy the hair-removal cream, wore sunglasses and a hat so I wouldn't be recognized, and paid cash, leaving no paper trail. They'll never be able to prove that I denuded my body on purpose. Losing every hair on one's body is rather extreme, of course, but it's not medically impossible."

While Peter boasted about his cleverness, Rainie scanned the area around her from under droopy eyelids. *Almost any-*

thing is a potential weapon. She stared for a moment at the bar of soap. Then her gaze shifted to the wine bottle. Last, she studied the goblet in her hand. Definitely a potential weapon, almost as lethal as a knife. She let her head nod forward. Then she blinked and jerked erect.

"I'm fine," she told Peter, speaking sluggishly. What frightened her most was that not all of her slurred speech was an act now. The combination of the wine and drug was hitting her hard. "You're screwed, Peter. Before I go under, Parker is going to show up and kick your sorry ass into next week."

"In that case, I'll just shove you under."

Rainie let the wineglass loll sideways in her hand and leaned her head back. She closed her eyes, then fluttered them back open again. It was important that she appeared to be fighting sleep. Finally she closed her eyes and let her head roll sideways, watching him through the veil of her lashes.

A train. Parker slugged the steering wheel with the heel of his hand. *Holy Mary, mother of God.* He counted the cars ahead of him. Then he took measure of the damned train. *Five minutes, shot.* Frustration and terror for Rainie made his skin feel electrified. He clenched his hands. Relaxed them. Clenched them. *Sweet Jesus.* Needing to do something, he dialed the police again. Different dispatcher this time.

"Has a car been sent over to Lorraina Hall's home?" Parker was so upset he shouted the question.

The male dispatcher said, "We had no officer in the immediate area, sir, but we do have a car on the way."

"I'm stalled at the railroad tracks. Train passin'. I can't get through. How far out is the car?"

"The officer will get there as quickly as he can, sir. ETA is fifteen minutes."

"She may not have fifteen minutes!" Parker cried. "Call for another car. Get somebody over there *now*!" Parker could not believe it took the cops so long to respond to an emergency. "The bastard is gonna kill her. Are you readin' me loud and clear?"

"This isn't our only emergency," the dispatcher replied. "We're doing the best we can, sir."

Their best wasn't good enough. Rainie was alone in the house with a homicidal maniac.

Fooled by Rainie's pretense of being asleep, Peter whispered, "Farewell, Lorraina," and at last he took the knife from her throat.

Rainie tightened her grip on the stem of the goblet, and then with all her strength, she belted him in the face with the bowl. He cried out. The thin crystal broke on impact and shards went flying. *Don't hesitate. You may have only one opportunity. Speed, strength, agility. Go after him with everything you've got, Rainie mine. No mercy.* Before Peter could react, she smacked him a second time, driving the spikes of sharp glass deep into his face.

"Ah-hh-h!" he cried, grabbing for the glass that had attached itself over his nose. "God *damn* you!"

Rainie grabbed the bar of soap, twisted up onto her knees, and swung, clocking him on the temple with all her strength. He toppled sideways, hitting the wall with his shoulder. Before he could recover his wits, she grabbed the wine bottle, leaped from the tub, and brought it down on his head. The sound of the thick glass striking flesh and bone almost made her vomit. *Don't run. Finish him. He's bigger, stronger, and faster. He may give chase, and you won't be able to outrun him.* She raised the wine bottle over her head and struck him again. And again.

Dizziness made her vision spin. Her legs buckled. She crashed to her knees near his feet. The wine bottle rolled away from her over the floor, going *ka-thunk, ka-thunk, ka-thunk.* She felt blackness closing in. *No, no, no!* If she lost consciousness now, he might regain his senses and kill her. With rubbery fingers, she grabbed the edge of the tub, hauled herself erect, and ran, her wet feet slipping and sliding. *Phone.* She had to get help. Careening like a drunk, she made it into the kitchen. Her purse sat on the counter. She staggered over, fished inside for her cell phone, and speed-dialed Parker. He answered on the second ring.

"I'm almost there, honey."

Rainie's lips had turned to rubber. She could no longer feel her arms or legs. The room twisted and lurched around her. Black spots swam before her eyes. When she tried to talk, her tongue felt like a dry sponge and would barely work.

"Peter," she managed to push out. "Thleeping pillths and wine. Need ambulanth. Hurry."

It was all she could get out before a blanket of blackness came over her.

Parker already had the accelerator tromped clear to the floor. He dialed 911 again. The same female dispatcher who'd taken his first call answered. Parker cut her off and said, "Ms. Hall just called me. Danning drugged her up on sleepin' pills and wine. She lost consciousness while she was talkin' to me on the phone. Get every car you can over there, and an ambulance as well. She's gonna need immediate medical attention."

She put him on hold for a moment. When she came back on the line, she said, "Three cars are on the way, and so is an ambulance. It's going to take a few minutes for them to get there, though, Mr. Harrigan."

Parker was shaking with fear. "I'm three minutes away. I'll get there before they do."

"Before you hang up, can you give me more information about Ms. Hall?"

Parker clenched his teeth in frustration. She was unconscious and in the house alone with a killer. What the hell else did they need to know?

"Sure," he bit out as he took a corner with a squeal of tires.

"Do you know any of Ms. Hall's medical history? It may be helpful to the EMTs. Is she allergic to any medications?"

Parker had never been so scared in his life. It was difficult for him to think clearly. Fudge instead of cookies. Cider instead of mulled wine. A ballerina instead of a witch. *Damn it to hell.* She'd tried to signal him, bless her heart, and he'd totally missed the hints. An old lady in a Ford Crown Vic pulled out from the curb directly in front of him. Parker hit the brakes. His truck went into a sideways skid. The moment he regained control of the vehicle, he passed the car, praying as he did that a child wouldn't dart out into the street. He was in a residential area now.

"Sir," the dispatcher said, "can you answer the question? Is Ms. Hall allergic to any medications?"

Parker jerked himself back to the moment. He remembered when Rainie had filled out a form at the doctor's office to get a sleep aid and glanced up at him to ask, *How do you spell 'penicillin'? I can never get it right.*

"She may be allergic to penicillin. That's all I know."

Parker took the corner onto Walnut on two wheels. Up ahead, he saw Rainie's Mazda parked in front of her one-story duplex. He aborted the call, tossed aside the phone, and pressed even harder on the gas pedal even though it was already clear to the floor. In front of her house, he stopped dead center in the street, shoved the gearshift into park, and left the truck running. *Rainie.* As he raced toward her porch, he felt as if he were in one of those dreams where everything happened in slow motion. Running, running, and never getting anywhere. It was like pushing against a headwind. After scaling the steps, he found the door locked. He drew back and rammed it with his shoulder, once, twice, three times. Finally he heard the framework break. With one more hit, the door gave way.

Parker burst into the living room at a run. Where was she? *Sweet Jesus.* Where was she? He glanced in the bedroom. Nothing. Raced for the kitchen. He was well into the room before he saw her, crumpled on the floor.

"Rainie?" He dropped to his knees beside her naked body. His hand shook as he felt for a pulse. At first, he could detect nothing. Then he found it, a faint and slow beat. She was alive, maybe just barely, but still alive. In the distance, he heard sirens. *Please, God, let it be the paramedics.*

Pushing to his feet, Parker left her to search the house, his fists knotted, his body trembling with rage. The second bedroom was empty. He veered away from the doorway to advance on the bathroom. He took only two steps into the enclosure before he saw him, slumped in a sprawl against the wall. *Holy mother.* What looked like a wine goblet protruded from the bastard's face, and two long gashes on one side of his bald head were streaming blood. *Down for the count.* Parker didn't bother to feel for a pulse. He hoped the son of a bitch was dead. He turned on his heel and ran back to Rainie.

Dropping to his knees, he peeled off his shirt to cover her nakedness and had just gathered her limp body into his arms when three policemen burst into the house. Cupping a hand over the side of Rainie's skull so her head wouldn't loll, Parker gave them his take on what he thought had happened and directed them to the bathroom. A moment later, one of the cops returned.

"He's alive. He'll have one hell of a headache when he wakes up, though."

Parker fixed anguished eyes on the officer's face. "She's

fadin' out on me. I can barely feel her pulse. The bastard gave her a bunch of sleeping pills and made her drink wine."

The man pressed his fingertips to Rainie's throat. His brown eyebrows drew together in a concerned frown. "It's faint, but there. The ambulance will be here shortly."

Parker didn't know if Rainie would last that long. He hunched his shoulders around her. The pain in his chest was so sharp he could barely breathe. "I can't lose her," he said raggedly. "I just can't. You know? How will I live without her?"

The cop picked up the bottle of sleeping pills from the counter, pulled his radio from his belt, and left the kitchen. Parker heard him talking in the living room, but most of it was police jargon he couldn't understand. A moment later, the officer returned and said, "I gave the EMTs a heads-up. They're on the line with the hospital right now so they can start treatment immediately. She'll make it, son. Those boys are very well trained."

Parker could only pray the man was right. Her body felt as cold as death.

Moments later, the ambulance arrived, and four EMTs raced into the house with a gurney. Parker was forced to relinquish his hold on Rainie as the medics went to work, one taking her blood pressure and pulse while another inserted an IV catheter in her arm. Before Parker could inquire about her condition, they had pumped her stomach and had her on a gurney to remove her from the house. Heart in his throat, he followed them out.

"Is she gonna be okay?" he asked as they pushed the gurney into the back of the ambulance. Two men jumped in with her. The remaining two closed the doors.

"We'll do all we can!" one of them called as they circled the vehicle.

The next thing Parker knew, the ambulance was leaving,

siren blasting and lights swirling. He ran to his truck to follow it to the hospital.

Rainie awakened slowly, first becoming aware of light sifting through her lashes to hurt her eyes and then registering sounds around her. Footsteps, a clank of metal, distant voices. She blinked and opened her eyes.

"Hello, beautiful. It's about time you woke up."

Parker's dark face came into focus. Smiling sleepily, Rainie determined that he was sitting on a chair beside her bed—only it wasn't her bed or her room. Bewildered, she glanced around. "A hospital?"

He stood and stepped over to gather her into his arms. Deep lines of exhaustion scored his cheeks and fanned out from his eyes. His lips looked pale, and his hair lay in furrows over his crown, as if he'd repeatedly raked his fingers through the thick strands.

"Parker, are you okay?"

He laughed and buried his face in her hair. "Am *I* okay? Ah, Rainie, I've never been so scared for anyone in my whole life. Don't ever put me through this again. My heart can't take it."

It all came back to Rainie then in a horrifying rush. She hooked an arm around Parker's neck. "Oh, God, Parker. Peter was in my car when I came out of the supermarket. He put a knife to my throat."

"I know," he whispered. "It's okay, sweetheart. You kicked his ass good and proper."

Rainie shivered at the memory. And then she laughed shakily. "I *did*, didn't I? I pretended to fall asleep so he'd lower the knife. The instant he did, I smashed the wineglass in his face."

He tightened his arms around her. "I almost lost you. Thank God they pumped your stomach before all the wine and Ambien got into your bloodstream."

Rainie stiffened. "Peter. Is he . . . dead?"

Parker chuckled. "No, but he probably wishes he was. You worked him over pretty good. He's here in the hospital, too, only he's under armed guard. Once he can be transported, he'll be taken into FBI custody and will stand trial. Special Agent Slaughter called. He says the bastard went into a rant when he woke up, furious because you'd bested him. How the hell could a stupid little pea brain like you outwit him? He's the great Peter Danning, who's committed two perfect murders. He was so fit to be tied that he confessed to killing his first two wives in front of two doctors, three nurses, and a handful of cops."

Rainie smiled blearily. "That is *so* like Peter. His temper always gets the better of him."

"His highfalutin attorney will try to say he was on pain medication and didn't know what he was sayin', but Slaughter says he divulged too many details about how he committed the murders. The poison he used to kill his first wife, for one, some weird chemical that leaves no trace. How would he know about it if he didn't actually use it? He also admitted to hirin' White to mess with Clarissa Danning's brakes and then killin' the bastard to keep him quiet. He knew too many details about exactly how White died not to have been there. Slaughter says Danning will be behind bars for the rest of his natural life."

Rainie hooked both arms around his neck. "Oh, Parker, I love you. When Peter put the knife to my throat, I kept thinking that it couldn't end for us that way. And I couldn't remember if I'd ever told you how very grateful I am for all the wonderful gifts you've given me. The list is as long as my arm."

"The feelin's mutual, sweetheart. That's what love is, you know, a fabulous, wondrous gift." He ran a hand into her hair. "I just have one bitch."

She stiffened. "What's that?"

"I wanted to kick his sorry ass myself, and you kicked it so good, there was nothin' left for me to obliterate."

She smiled drowsily. "Yes, well. It was an ass I needed to kick."

"I know," he whispered. "And you did a fine job of it. No more lookin' into mirrors and feelin' lost, Rainie mine. You put an end to his control over you forever. I'm so proud of you."

Rainie was proud of herself. Even as sleepy as she still was, remembering that moment when she'd shoved the broken goblet into Peter's face gave her a sense of liberation.

"They told me that you can be released as soon as you wake up. If you're feelin' up to it, darlin', I'll take you home."

Rainie smiled dreamily and breathed deeply of his scent, that fabulous, intoxicating blend of smells that was exclusively his own. Oh, how she loved him. "I'm already there," she whispered.

"You're already where?" he asked.

"Home," she whispered. "Already home."

As Rainie said those words, she knew they were absolutely true. She was finally, at long last, right where she belonged.

In Parker Harrigan's arms.

Epilogue

On a crisp, snowy Saturday a few months later, Parker and Rainie's wedding took place in the Catholic church that Parker had attended all his life. Because it was a small, rural parish, it had been fairly easy to book the church, and Father Mike had bent over backward to get the marriage scheduled as quickly as possible. Clint was Parker's best man. Quincy, Zach, and Samantha's husband, Tucker Coulter, were his groomsmen. Along with all the Harrigans, the entire Coulter clan was inside the church proper. Tucker's sister, Bethany; her husband, Ryan; and her in-laws, the Kendricks, were present as well. Rainie loved the thought that her new family had so many members, in-laws, and friends. There would be frequent social gatherings for her and Parker to attend.

Out in the vestibule, Rainie trembled with a bad case of nerves, not because she had a single doubt about marrying Parker, but because there were so many people in the pews, filling both sides of the church. As she walked down the aisle, every eye would be upon her. Janet straightened her veil and winked at her.

"That Parker is so gorgeous. I'm thinking that Quincy needs a sweetie. What do you think?"

Rainie could only laugh.

Maggie handed her the bouquet. "I've got dibs on Zach.

He is *so* sexy. Still eclectic in his tastes, unfortunately, but I'm thinking I might addict him to one flavor."

Samantha, Rainie's matron of honor, shook her head. "My poor brothers don't stand a chance."

Rainie just giggled again. She was too nervous to think clearly. As her matron of honor and bridesmaids fell into formation and proceeded into the church, she clutched the wool sleeve of her escort's black tux. "Oh, Grandpa, what if I trip and fall on my face?"

Marcus Hall Sr. chuckled and patted her hand. "Don't worry, honey. I'll catch you from falling."

Tears filled Rainie's eyes as she gazed up at his face, an older version of her dad's, a visage she'd thought never to see again. Silly of her. She was about to marry a man who'd presented her with her very own star to serve as her guiding light and had filled her life with love and joy. She really shouldn't have been surprised when he worked another miracle by locating her paternal grandparents. Marcus and Sybil Hall, Ohioans of long standing who'd mourned the loss of their eldest son for many years, had never received any of Rainie's query letters. Unfortunately, she hadn't had Parker's investigative resources to find them. They'd been delighted to learn that they had a granddaughter.

"I'm so glad you're here to give me away," she whispered tremulously. "It's almost as good as having Daddy with me."

Marcus's eyes went bright with tears. He blinked them away, smiled, and bent his silver head to kiss her cheek. "My only regret is that I haven't been with you all your life."

Rainie shared the same regret. From her grandparents, she'd finally learned why her father had severed all contact with his family. Rainie had guessed it mostly right. Her mother had met with her grandparents' disapproval, not because they were snobs who looked down on an orphaned young woman, but because Rainie's mother had spent her teens in a reformatory for female juvenile delinquents and had a rap sheet. In addition to drug-related offenses, she'd been convicted of prostitution and armed robbery before she turned sixteen.

The mother Rainie remembered had been a wonderful, sweet, understanding woman with a gentle smile and soulful eyes. It boggled her mind to think that her mom had once sold her flesh to get money for a fix and had held a gun to a man's head, ordering him to empty a till. But facts were facts. After hearing the story, Rainie had researched her mother's past, and sure enough, Susan Hall had been found guilty on both counts. That didn't alter Rainie's love for her mother. Instead it had driven home to her an important life lesson: Some people were capable of changing, and when they did, it was wrong to hold their past mistakes against them.

Sadly, her grandparents had learned that same lesson the hard way, destroying their relationship with their eldest son in the process. Now, at around seventy, they were helpless to correct their own mistakes. They could only move forward, trying to forge a strong and loving relationship with their long-lost granddaughter. Rainie was more than happy to give them that opportunity.

After their honeymoon in Hawaii, Parker and Rainie planned to fly to Ohio to meet the rest of her paternal relatives. According to her grandparents, she had three aunts, four uncles, a passel of first cousins, and too many second cousins to count. Rainie looked forward to seeing all of them, and wished they could have attended her wedding. Airfare for so many would have been a huge expense, though. It made more sense for Rainie and Parker to make the trip.

The vibrant strains of the organ filled the church. Her grandfather smiled down at her. "You ready to walk down the aisle and let me give you away to that young whippersnapper?"

Rainie nodded. As she and her grandfather began the halting journey up the center aisle, her gaze drifted to the left side of the church, which was filled with people who'd chosen to sit on the bride's side to keep the numbers in the pews fairly equal.

Through her veil, Rainie watched Tucker Coulter's niece, Chastity, who was Bethany and Ryan Kendrick's four-year-old daughter, walk before them down the aisle, scattering rose petals over the burgundy carpet to blaze a trail for the bride. She was darling in a lacy pink dress, with her sable curls bouncing over her shoulders. Ahead of her, Clint and Loni's son, Trevor, was the ring bearer. He looked so cute, a miniature of his father and uncles, and took his role very seriously.

Parker's side of the church was packed with his family, shirttail relatives, and friends. All her life, Rainie had yearned for a sense of belonging, and now she had finally found that. Someday when she and Parker charted their family tree in the Harrigan Bible, her side would have plenty of limbs and branches after all. That was a glorious thing to know as she moved toward the rest of her life.

He stood to the right of the altar, so handsome in his black, Western-cut tuxedo and dress Stetson that Rainie's heart felt as if it might burst with happiness. She had taken instruction to become a Catholic, and today, in addition to entering into holy matrimony, she would receive her first Holy Communion.

Parker's heart was in his eyes as he watched her come toward him. When at last Rainie reached him and her grandfather stepped aside, she took Parker's hand with a joyous sense of rightness. He smiled at her through the folds of her veil, telling her without words that he felt the same emotions.

As they stepped forward as a couple to kneel before the altar for Father Mike's blessing and their nuptial Mass, a shimmer of multicolored light from the stained-glass windows fell over them. That felt right to Rainie, too, symbolic of the inextinguishable light within her that Parker had helped her to rediscover.

His big, warm hand tightened around hers. *Home.* In that moment, Rainie knew with absolute certainty that she would never again question who she was.

This man had shown her a star in the heavens that would always guide her, and if she ever lost her way, that shimmer of brightness would be there to lead her back to him.

This was where she belonged, with Parker Harrigan.